Rite of Spring

Rite of Spring

Andrew M. Greeley

WARNER BOOKS

A Warner Communications Company

A
BERNARD GEIS ASSOCIATES
BOOK

For the Kenskis

Henry
Margaret
Kate
Carolyn
Erin Noele

Warner Books, Inc., 666 Fifth Avenue, New York, NY 10103

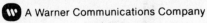 A Warner Communications Company

Printed in the United States of America

First Printing: November 1987

10 9 8 7 6 5 4 3 2 1

Library of Congress Cataloging-in-Publication Data

Greeley, Andrew M., 1928–
　　Rite of spring.
　　I. Title.
PS3557.R358R5 1987　　　813′.54　　　87-40168
ISBN 0-446-51295-8

Book design: H. Roberts Design
Maps by Heidi Hornaday

NOTE

Like all the men and women who live in the Time Between the Stars, Brendan Ryan is a creature of my imagination. The City and the Neighborhood and the Beach might be better places if the Ryan clan were God's creatures rather than mine. But, for weal or woe, they correspond to no one in what is loosely called the real world. Msgr. John Blackwood Ryan is like no known rector of Holy Name Cathedral.

Cindasoo, who will return later, God willing, speaks authentic AE (Appalachian English, a variant of American English) and is not intended to be a stereotype. In fact, she "talks funny" partly because it's fun, partly to protect herself, and partly because she is a covert Appalachian militant.

—AG

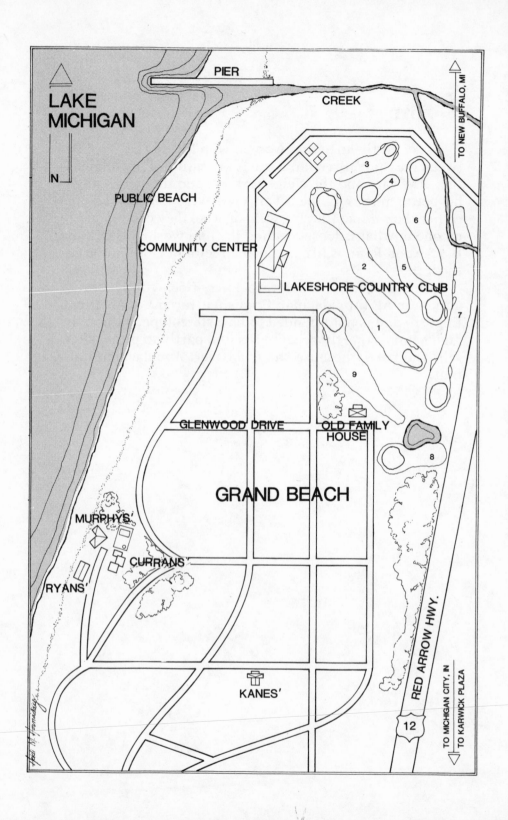

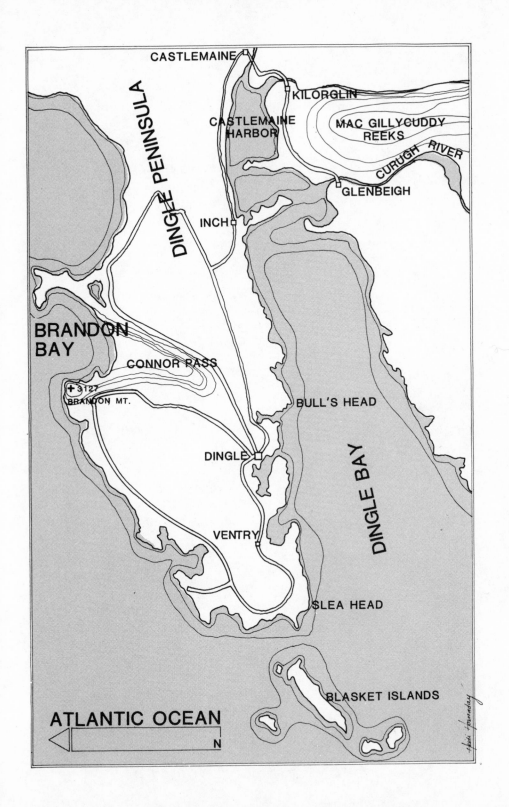

All things rising, all things sizing
Mary sees, sympathizing
With that world of good,
Nature's motherhood.
Their magnifying of each its kind
With delight calls to mind
How did she in her stored
Magnify the Lord.

—*Gerard Manley Hopkins*
"May Magnificat"

You have seen, Thomas, and have believed. Blessed are those who have not seen and yet believe.

—Gospel of the Second Sunday of Easter, Cycle A

Passion is but one manifestation of hope, the trickiest of God's games.

—Msgr. John Blackwood Ryan

one

A MORNING IN SPRING

1

I wanted the woman, body and soul, as badly as I had ever wanted anything in all my life.

I had entered Dufficy's Irish Store on Michigan Avenue to buy a present for my daughter, Jean, a student at Stanford, who was going to Ireland for the summer.

The woman and I had exchanged a few words, a couple of quickly averted glances. I could hardly remember what she looked like when I stumbled out of the store.

Yet she was my destiny. I knew it. So, it seemed, did she.

The image of her body, pliant and happy under mine, hit me as I was leaving the store. I must have her. I, Brendan Ryan, the quietest of quiet men, had made up his mind.

I must have her. I would have her.

Soon.

Thus spring came violently to Michigan Avenue the last week in April, and with it the beginning of my fall from grace.

4 · *ANDREW M. GREELEY*

I leaned against the window of Stuart Brent's book-store as exhausted as though I had run four miles. The gentle touch of a morning breeze against my face hinted at the caress of a woman's hand. The delicious lethargy that pervaded my body suggested that I had been enfolded in her embrace, her breasts pressed soothingly against my chest. My lightweight gray suit, prudently withdrawn from mothballs after I had heard the morning weather forecast on WFMT, was already wilted. My tailor-made broadcloth shirt was soaked with sweat.

What did she look like? I must remember. A smile, a soft voice with a touch of the brogue, a white dress, a delicate and tasteful scent . . . nothing more: the beginning, perhaps, of Brendan Ryan's foolish pursuit of the Holy Grail.

Should I return to Dufficy's Irish Store and look again? No, that would be a mistake. I must not be late for the discussion of my tangled financial and legal affairs with Nick and Eileen. Already they thought I was not serious enough about the litigation.

As other pedestrians brushed by, barely aware of my existence, and autos crowded noisily toward the Ohio Street access to the Outer Drive, I looked down at the neatly wrapped package in my hand—the elegant green and white paper emphasizing Dufficy's image as Irish indeed, but Michigan Avenue Irish. *Ruins of Medieval Ireland*, a present for my daughter Jean who hoped to go to Ireland in pursuit of her new career as a photographer—a career discovered a few months before in a first-quarter sophomore class at Stanford. The wrapping was wet from my perspiring fingers.

I tried to dry my hand on the sleeve of my jacket; it would go to the cleaners that night anyway. Jean hated me. Her suggestion that we have dinner before she returned to Palo Alto for exams was doubtless designed merely to extract money from me for the Irish trip, money that her mother wouldn't give her. Yet her interest in Ireland matched my own. She would not notice the sweat-smudged paper. Compulsively fastidious as always, I wanted the present to be perfect.

It was not that hot yet. High in the low eighties, said

the announcer, as usual with the educated solemnity of a distinguished professor's inaugural address. It was no more than seventy at ten o'clock in the morning. I was sweating not from the heat, but from a sudden and furious outburst of sexual passion, totally unexpected and barely resisted.

I should be ashamed, I told myself resolutely. I should summon the energy to detach myself from the window of Stuart Brent's—filled with colorful books about African art, I noted absently—and proceed with all deliberate speed to the prestigious offices of Minor Gray and Blatt, the firm to which Nick and Eileen and I all owed our legal allegiance.

I felt no shame or guilt. Rather, I was as exultant as a teenage boy with a crush on a new girl in the neighborhood. I stepped toward the door of Dufficy's, proudly marked with a quote from Yeats, as though to establish that it did indeed belong on the Magnificent Mile, cheek by jowl with Stuart Brent's, at least as snobbish as the supercilious bookstore if not more so.

I had to know what she really looked like.

As I write these words, the face and figure are already fading from my memory. I try to recapture those first paralyzingly vivid impressions with the melancholy realization that I may well have created them myself, that Ciara had no existence other than in my imagination.

I do not think of myself as a passionate man. I am sure my friends and associates would agree with this judgment. There was relatively little sex in my marriage. Madonna, my former wife (if, in these days of lunch-counter ecclesiastical annulments, that is the proper term for her), claimed not to enjoy sex. After Jean's birth and several unsuccessful attempts to establish a pattern of normal sexual relations (whatever that term may mean), I found that I did not enjoy it much either. Our moments of passion were occasional, the occasion usually being when Madonna had had a few more drinks than she could manage and turned, if I may use the word, lewd. While these brief incidents were exceedingly pleasurable, I did not look forward to them with much eagerness. I assumed, since I felt no need to seek a lover or have recourse to prostitutes, that I was at the low end of the curve of sexual need.

In forty-two years of life I had made love to only one

woman, both rarely and poorly. Therefore I was utterly unprepared on a warm day in April to step off Michigan Avenue and, surrounded by Aran Island sweaters and Waterford crystal, into a sexual encounter so peremptory that I would walk out a few moments later as soaking wet as though I had been jogging in a steam bath.

The interlude was brief, a minute or two at the most. A book chosen, a few words exchanged, a package wrapped, a bill paid, a receipt neatly folded into my wallet. Yet I knew after my first glance at her shy smile behind the cash register that here was the woman for whom I had waited all my life.

My temptation, as violent as a spring morning with tornado warnings posted, was hardly to rape. Already I adored the woman. I would make her mine forever with only the most tender seductions.

As I said, a teenage crush.

Perhaps, I thought, as I paused in front of the words of Willy Yeats, I had already possessed her and been possessed by her. I could not positively say that we had not made love. I was aware that not even our hands had touched in the exchange of book and money, receipt and package. Yet something had passed between us that had never occurred in twenty years of marriage to Madonna.

The woman in the store, the woman in the white dress with the shy smile, felt the same temptation I did. She was as frightened of it as I was. And as vehemently attracted to me as I to her.

I turned away from Dufficy's and hurried down Michigan Avenue. I must not keep my patient law partners waiting.

Now I tease the roots of my memory, searching like a dentist for a tender nerve. Fertility was much on my mind that morning, not, as it were, in the front pages of my own internal daily newspaper, but on the back pages, in the feature section, in the part of my brain over which I glance very hastily when trying to order my agenda each morning. President Reagan was embarking for China. Chris Wallace had spoken on the *Today* program from Peking as I was eating breakfast (coffee and toast). Hart and Mondale were clubbing each other into the ground. The Cubs were, unaccountably and doubtless accidentally and transiently, in first place. I had to see Nick and Eileen about possible litigation to recover some of the money taken from me by John King Sullivan, my longtime friend and commodities broker. I had scheduled a luncheon appointment and a meeting after lunch with clients nervous about their tax shelters. Then I had to talk to two overzealous IRS agents who had doubts about a tax shelter for yet another client.

Only the last gave me much promise of pleasure. Although I avoid competitive situations as often as I can, some kind of atavistic Celtic battle lust emerges when I protect my clients from the depredations of the Service—an enemy which, in my more candid moods, I admit is faced with a difficult if not impossible task and constrained by limitations and legislation which, if I were on their side, I would despise. Yet in battle with them, Brendan Herbert George Ryan becomes, however superficially, Finn MacCool, mythological Irish warrior hero.

Invulnerable and always victorious.

Then I would revert to Brendan Ryan, ineffectual father, for supper with Jean, an uncertain encounter with a young woman who seemed a total stranger.

The fertility subtext, however, was present on my agenda for that day in spring—to change back my metaphor. Eileen Kane was pregnant, as was Catherine Curran, Nick's wife—elderly pregnancies both. Eileen had quoted her shocked obstetrician with an aloof and disdainful smile. After some preliminary grumbling, which did not appear very sincere, the two women seemed exceptionally happy and swore that the current pregnancy, elderly or not, was the easiest yet.

My daughter, whom I would meet in a few hours, was marvelously nubile, herself a lure for male reproductive urges. I rejoiced and yet felt sad. Madonna had known I wanted more children desperately. But she had insisted that the demands of raising one child were more than enough and that, anyway, she would not endure the discomforts of pregnancy again merely because I was an only child and had a kinky need for a large family.

"Large families," she had said, "are dumb. Believe me, I know."

She was the second of seven, a quarreling, contentious clan whose factional boundaries seemed to change with the seasons.

I never discussed the matter with Jean—I never discussed anything with her—but I hoped that, an only child, too, she would want several children. Grandchildren might compensate for the family I had never had. I knew that these hopes were ridiculous. Jean would protect her children from me with contempt, just as Madonna had protected Jean from me.

All these reflections are noticed only in retrospect, as I try to sort out the puzzle of the woman who apparently never existed, a masturbatory fantasy, as the psychiatrist I consulted (once) insisted.

All I was aware of that morning was that with the abrupt coming of spring warmth to Chicago and the appearance of light spring dresses, the Magnificent Mile becomes a distracting showcase of breasts and thighs, bellies and buttocks, throats and ankles, emerging instantly and dramatically at about the same time and with the same life-renewing effect as crocuses and tulips.

This was a mostly academic observation in, to switch the metaphor again, the feature pages of my brain. I dabble in scholarship, perhaps because I should have been a professor instead of a lawyer. Madonna often called me a dilettante, and I suppose the charge is valid. "Jack of all trades and master of none," she would say with her usual fine touch for an original phrase. Evolutionary biology, in any event, is one of my fields of interest. The human body, I told myself that morning, is designed to produce reactions in the body of the opposite sex that lead to reproductive and quasi pair-bonding behavior. It is interesting, I observed, superciliously, I fear, that despite our sophistication these days about sex and fertility, the same processes are going on when spring appears that did millions of years ago.

I trust I establish sufficiently my pedantry. I was engaged, or so I thought at any rate, in an abstract consideration of academic theory. None of these womanly bodies, in a wide variety of appealing shapes and ages, were to be mine. They were data rather than prizes to be pursued. Although I was technically free to remarry, I could not imagine myself ever risking that relationship again. As a Catholic, old-fashioned about sexual morality if little else, it would be unthinkable for me to take a lover.

I was not, I would have said, a tumescent adolescent ogling every neat pair of legs on Michigan Avenue.

And so, in a discreet and expensive Irish export shop, I would be seized by the same kind of primal lust that doubtless beset my male ancestors hundreds of thousands of years ago. For a woman whose physical appearance I could barely remember five minutes later, when, spent and shaken, I turned away from Dufficy's and strode down Michigan Avenue with what I hoped was brisk common sense.

There is no fool, I told myself, citing another one of Madonna's insightful dicta, like an old fool.

Later, Blackie Ryan, Eileen's brother and my cousin, would bluntly correct the dictum: "There's no fool like the fool who thinks he has withdrawn from the human condition."

I imagine myself striding towards the Chicago River, a comic figure trying to escape from the human condition into which he has been unceremoniously deposited. Perhaps that absurd vaudeville character, a ridiculous little man with silver hair and a dimpled chin, is indeed me. Yet I knew him in another century and on the other side of the mountain.

Foolish adolescent horniness, I assured myself. You'd make a complete jackass of yourself if you went back to that store and drooled over her. Put the whole absurd incident out of your mind.

Even then, however, a part of me knew better. I would return and I would pursue, just as my imaginary ancestor had pursued a female who had attracted his attention at the entrance of his cave—or, perhaps more accurately, at the edge of a communal waterhole (presumably smaller than Lake Michigan)—long before we became human.

I confess that I had no doubt she wanted to be pursued,

evidence enough to the psychiatrist of my masturbatory fantasies.

I insisted as I crossed the river on the Michigan Avenue Bridge, under a lacy blue sky and a gentle sun which turned the buildings along the river pastel, that I would not return to Dufficy's that afternoon. I would certainly not ask her if they carried any books by serious contemporary Irish photographers.

The first thing I did in my office, with Nick and Eileen listening, was to phone the IRS agents and postpone the appointment till the next morning.

I had toppled from the pedestal of grace.

2

Something happened between the bridge and Minor Gray and Blatt's corporate aerie on the LaSalle Street canyon that disconcerted me as it always does, but which at the time seemed to have no relationship to the as yet undefined woman in Dufficy's. Now that I must ponder the possibility that Ciara never existed save as a creature of my fantasy— and all the implications of that for my own sanity—the incident at Michigan and Wacker Drive takes on special importance.

You must understand that in addition to being the quietest of quiet men, I am strange in another way.

I see things and people that others don't see. I recognized this phenomenon early in childhood, when I would tell my parents or my playmates about people I had seen. Their shocked reaction quickly taught me to distinguish sharply between my "special" events and "ordinary" events.

The phenomena that happened long ago or will happen sometime in the future or are happening at some great distance now are easily recognizable as distinct from the phenomena that others can see. The best way I can describe them is to say that they are played on a videotape that seems to be either in front of or behind the tape of ordinary consciousness. I suspect that it was more difficult as a child to make the distinction, but I learned, under the pressure of circumstances, to recognize the difference quickly enough.

I don't ask you to believe that such events happen. I will be content for the purposes of this story if you accept as a given that I experience them as happening. Or think I do.

I normally turn left on Wacker and walk to Dearborn. Michigan Avenue is more aesthetically pleasing because of the lake and the park on the left. But one saves a few minutes of time, particularly if one makes the lights, by cutting across the Loop on the diagonal street. Ordinarily I keep to the river side of Wacker, both because I like the river and because I am wary of the southwest corner of Michigan and Wacker.

However, on that warm April morning, in another century and on the other side of the mountain, I had no time for foolish fantasies. The green light was an opportunity to be seized. So I grabbed it, perhaps to make up for the opportunity I had definitively ruled out a few blocks back.

As best I can remember my state of mind at the time, enough to testify to it in a court of law but hardly enough to convince a psychiatrist, I was not reflecting at all on the southwest corner as the site of Fort Dearborn, the massacre of whose garrison is marked by the first of the four stars in the Chicago flag (presumably to become five stars if Mayor Washington and Alderman Vrdolyak permit the 1992 World's Fair to occur).

As soon as I crossed the line of the fort's wall, marked by metal studs in the sidewalk, I walked into another century. I saw the garrison leave the fort and begin its fateful trek through the dunes toward the Vincennes Trail (on which I had walked many times as a boy). They would never reach the trail, and only a handful would escape from the ambush that waited at what we now unromantically call 18th Street.

As usual the half-breed scout "Captain" Billy Wells led the way, his face painted black in anticipation of the death that he knew waited for him.

How can I describe for someone who has not had such

an experience (technically known as retrocognition) what it is like? The settlers and troops are not ethereal and ecto-plasmic creatures. They are as real to me as are the summer-suited pedestrians purposefully rushing along Michigan Avenue with their important and expensive briefcases. I see their worried faces, hear the crying children, sense their fear. Yet the traffic on modern Michigan Avenue does not completely vanish; it fades into the background perhaps, yet it remains. For a few moments I feel that I have a choice between the two worlds, that if I warn them, the garrison and the settlers will not die.

I try to warn them. I choose with futile heroism to abandon 1984 for 1814. It doesn't work. The first Chicagoans fade away slowly, leaving me embarrassed and awkward, wondering if anyone else has seen them and then whether I have made a fool of myself.

So far, at any rate, no one seems to have noticed my hesitancy on the brink of another world. This interlude was rather brief. Only a few minutes, unlike the hour and a half in a previous experience.

On Michigan Avenue, who notices a man standing near the wall of a building, peering quizzically into the distance?

And into the past.

Need I say that, good lawyer and amateur scholar that I am, I have checked every detail—the clothes, the uniforms, the construction of the fort, the physical appearances of the people, even the weather? In most instances, I have all the details right. An occasional disagreement with the history books can be explained by the fact that the books are wrong.

Or that I have deliberately projected details into my vision to persuade myself that it's authentic and not a product of a vivid imagination in a man who had a taste for Chicago history as a child. In some sense it does not matter. Most people don't have such experiences, whether they be projection or retrocognition. I've had them all my life.

I am, you see—and I'd never admitted this to anyone before that morning in April—a psychic. Not before then, nor for some time afterward, in point of fact. Not the kind of freak who performs on the stage, mind you, or who finds criminals for the police. Rather, I am part of that five to ten percent of the population which has frequent and varied psychic experiences—extrasensory perception, clairvoyance, déjà vu, retrocognition, antecognition, communication from great distances. Even an occasional contact with the dead. Everything but out-of-body experiences.

When I was a kid, I thought everyone could see the people and the events I saw. My parents lovingly explained that it was all right to see make-believe people when you were very young, but grown-ups didn't talk about such things. Since then I've learned that maybe sixty percent of us have such experiences once in a while. And a few of us have them often. I did a considerable amount of reading about psychic phenomena in college and occasionally dig into the literature today. But, for the last twenty years, until I met—or perhaps created—Ciara, I did not pursue the subject seriously.

It was not, you see, all that important. It didn't cause any special problems in life and wasn't much of a help either. At best it was of minor interest. At worst it was a nuisance—which was most of the time. I have no idea what causes it, although I'm amused when I run into an article by some scientific dogmatist explaining that the phenomenon can't possibly exist.

Do I pick up psychic energies that are lurking at what was in 1814 the mouth of the Chicago River? Or do I recreate the scene for myself out of my own forgotten memories of books I read when I was a little boy? Or both?

I don't think anyone knows, and I personally find Irish history and evolutionary biology and medieval common law (on which I've published a few articles and about which I contemplate a book) much more interesting fields and also more useful.

Most of the time what my psychic kink (call it that, if you want, for the lack of a better name) picks up makes no sense at all. I feel sorry for the performers who must fake a good deal of the time because the signals they receive from their audiences are so confusing. Sometimes it is dead wrong: my vivid images of a Sox World Series victory celebration turning into a race riot last autumn, for example. Other times it misses the point completely: long ago I learned that it was an unreliable guide for commodities investment. Occasionally it is both scary and accurate—a pleasant evening visit from an aunt of my mother's who had died in England that very day (a woman whom I'd never met and for whom I had no close feelings). Sometimes it is helpful—call my parents, who now live in Tucson, because they're worried about how I'm surviving the divorce trauma.

I would, however, have called them anyway.

All in all, until Ciara, being a psychic was of less importance in my life than being five feet eight inches tall and having silver-blue eyes which women from four to eighty-four find "cute."

My colleagues arrived in my office promptly at ten-thirty, Eileen a specialist in criminal litigation and Nick an expert in civil trials. We had been classmates though not close friends at St. Praxides grammar school. Eileen, who is married to Red Kane the columnist, is my cousin. Nick is married to her cousin on her mother's side, Catherine Collins, the artist who escaped from a prison camp in South America. When divorce and embezzlement threatened to wipe out much of my life, they came riding to the rescue, as the Ryan clan always does, whether I want to be rescued or not.

"We can probably recapture a quarter of a million for you." Nick tossed a sheaf of papers on my unadorned and uncluttered desk. "Net of expenses. King Sullivan has accounts all over the place."

Nick is a tall, broad-shouldered athlete who has never been close to being out of condition. His thin brown hair is always short and neatly combed, and behind thick black-rimmed glasses, his pale blue eyes watch with the patient mildness of an Indian hunter. Nick's carefully disciplined charismatic energies make him a natural leader; he's a member of the executive committee of the firm and will be managing partner someday unless he finally accepts a seat on the federal bench.

"But we won't pick up anything," Eileen's arresting green eyes considered me coolly, "unless we get a criminal conviction against King."

They both despised King Sullivan from our school days, but because I still considered him my friend, they carefully refrained from attacking him in my presence. He was an adversary to be studied clinically and objectively, not a son of a bitch to be denounced.

"How're you doing?" I asked, smiling at her.

"Great." Eileen relaxed and beamed happily. "Little Redmond here," she patted her stomach, "is kicking up more of a storm than all the others put together. And you're changing the subject."

Pregnancy mellowed Eileen Ryan Kane, but only a few minutes at a time.

"First things first," I said lightly, causing her to beam again. "And Catherine?"

"Great," Nick replied proudly. "Says she wants at least three more."

"Crazy woman," Eileen snorted, not in complete disagreement. Her voice suggests bells sweetly ringing in the distance, across fields of wheat or perhaps flower-strewn meadows—a recollection of her youthful flirtation with a musical comedy career.

I picked up the sheaf of notes Nick had given me. Impregnation was part of my fantasy in Dufficy's, an intensely pleasurable part. I would fill this woman's appealingly flat belly with my child. Is it normal for potency to enhance the pleasure of sex? I wondered. When a couple has determined to have a child, are their unions more rewarding? It had never been so with Madonna, not even at the beginning of marriage, when we both wanted her to conceive.

"The government will not go to trial unless they're sure of your cooperation." Nick removed his glasses and began to polish them. "That's final."

"Patsy and the kids," I began tentatively, knowing we were going down the same path again. King and Patsy, priding themselves on their Catholic traditionalism, had produced seven kids, the eldest of whom was a high school dropout and part of the Chicago punk rock scene. King was an alcoholic, probably incurable, and Patsy—dear, gloriously lovely Patsy—had been in private mental institutions twice, at least.

Had fertilization, in the name of publicly proclaimed religious principles, made their sex life any more rewarding? I doubted it.

"It's up to you," Eileen sighed, an Irishwoman's immemorial protest against the obstinate childishness of men. "He won't go to jail in any case. They'll plea-bargain for a *nolo contendere*. The trial will last five minutes. There's lots of money on both sides of the family."

She was wearing a royal blue maternity jumper and a print blouse with a bow. There were gray streaks in her dark hair, but her round, wholesome face was youthful and vital, and her figure, carefully disciplined like everything else in Eileen's life, seemed even more desirable in its blooming pregnancy, a defiant reassertion of the powers of life. I envied Red Kane and felt a brief, vivid stab of desire for her.

When we were certain that Madonna was pregnant, we suspended our meager sex life. That morning I pondered the ecstasy of making love to a pregnant woman. Indeed, the ecstasy of making forbidden love to my pregnant partner and friend.

I drove off the mind-bursting images of Eileen's full and naked body next to me in bed and tried to concentrate on my financial problems. The images did not leave easily. I was already caught up in my dangerous rite of spring.

While I make more than enough money as a tax lawyer, since my law school days, I have invested in the commodities market, mostly for the fun of it. Economics is another one of my dilettante interests. A small investment in a futures contract was at first merely a way of testing my instincts that the experts were wrong about the business cycle and I was right.

"Gambling, pure and simple," Madonna had dismissed my little hobby. "Horse players die broke."

She did not object to spending my Board of Trade income, however; and while I'm broke, or nearly broke, at the moment, the reason is not that I've made bad guesses about the market.

I take long-term positions, rather than trading the daily swing of the market, and these days mostly in government bond contracts at the Board of Trade and T-bill contracts at the Merc. Basically, if you think the economy is going up, you buy contracts (go long), expecting that the interest rates will rise and your bonds will be worth more money. If on the other hand you think that the economy is going to slacken, you sell (short) and profit from the fact that you can meet your obligations with contracts that cost less than your sale price.

Taking a position, they tell me, requires the steel nerves of an experienced poker player. I don't have steel nerves and I don't play poker, but I am able to resist panic when the short-run trends go against my position and I have to use some of my capital to cover my margins. I make it a practice not to pay any attention to *Wall Street Journal* forecasts because I feel that by the time their reporters have information, it's already dated.

I've lost a fair amount of money because of confidence in my own economic judgment against that of the experts. But I've made a lot more than I've lost, which is all a commodities investor can expect.

I don't trade myself. I am totally unsuited by temperament and personality for the frantic rumble of the trading pit. I take my positions early in the year, September or October, call my brokers (until recent years at one of the big firms), tell them what to do, and sit back and wait for six months.

When King Sullivan's string of travel agencies folded, I transferred my accounts to his new commodities firm, set up by his father, who was a retired trader. While commodities trading is the last refuge of Chicago Irish with more money than sense, King was my friend, and I felt that it really didn't matter who called in my orders.

It turned out that it did matter. For several years King had been using my money to trade both ends. He would, for example, go short on my account and with the same funds buy on his own account. In a large firm with effective controls a broker couldn't do this without someone blowing the whistle on him. There was no one in John King Sullivan's office who could blow the whistle on him.

Last autumn I felt that the economy would soften in the spring, despite the election campaign, and that the smart long-term position was short. I also saw an opportunity to regain some of my capital, three-quarters of which had been consumed in the divorce settlement—a flat payment of two million dollars to Madonna and another million in a trust fund to guarantee to myself that I would not lack money for the alimony payments.

Nick and Eileen gritted their teeth over the settlement but did not argue.

King, desperate to cover his own losses, did not fill my orders. He simply used my money for his own short-term margins and lost it all—nearly a million dollars. I was the biggest of his victims but not the only one. The Feds finally caught up with him.

My friend Father Ron Crowley, who is a radical liberation theologian (although pastor of an affluent Lake Shore parish), tells me that I should practice the gospel injunction to forgive my debtors and that in any event commodities trading is a grievous sin of exploitation.

Nick Curran had different advice: "It's not just your money, Brendan; King has been taking people for years. You let him off this time and he'll be into a new scam next year."

Charitably, he did not say what he thought: John King Sullivan had always been a crook.

"I don't need the money," I said slowly, glancing out the window at the flowing tides of people on LaSalle Street. Ron was probably right: there was nothing of eternity in that frantic movement of humankind. "Rebuilding my capital was only a game. King and Patsy are friends."

King, Patsy, Ron, Madonna, and I had been friends since the first grade. Nick was a loner until the Ryans, the "other" Ryans, picked him up in his teens. Eileen was always on the opposite side because even in the first grade

Patsy and Madonna had detested the "other" Ryans. If this reaction bothered Eileen and her brothers and sisters, they managed to keep their dismay well hidden.

"Strange kind of friends," Nick began. "What have they—"

"Nick." Eileen's green eyes, normally ice cool, flashed a warning, mother superior admonishing a novice. "It's Brendan's choice."

All my life it had been my choice.

Yet, to finish Nick's question, what indeed had they ever done for me?

"I have precisely the capital I had in 1967, when I began to invest." I opened a drawer of my desk and pulled out a manila folder. "There are certain tax advantages to my situation . . ."

So it went, as always. I paid less attention to the conversation that morning because I was preoccupied by the woman in Dufficy's. Were her eyes green like Eileen's? I thought not, but I couldn't be sure.

And was she carrying my child, as Eileen was carrying Red Kane's? Of course not. That was imagination, like the Fort Dearborn garrison.

Do women enjoy being impregnated? If they want the child especially? It depends, I decided, reviewing the literature on evolutionary biology, on how many they already have and how a society values fertility.

What must sex have been like when men and women knew that if conception resulted, there was a one in six chance of a dead baby or a dead mother? Maybe they didn't comprehend the exact statistics, but they knew the reality well enough.

I shivered slightly.

"All right, Brendan?" Eileen asked anxiously. Once, briefly, we had been in love. It was still a tender memory between us.

"Sure, just shaken by how much can go wrong in human lives."

"If we could have seen the future in the first grade . . ." Nick said thoughtfully.

My mind drifted back to the woman in the store. Much

younger than Eileen, but something like her. Did she want to be pregnant? Was I picking up her psychic vibes?

I try to ignore other people's emotional emanations. I am not a voyeur, and in any event the vibes are usually confusing. This was a different relationship, however.

Different relationship? I did not even know the woman's name or what she looked like.

At lunch one day, while we were waiting for Nick and Red and Catherine (I had been delicately pulled into these weekly family sessions after Madonna left me), Eileen had been grousing, more or less in good humor, about the difficulties of "elderly" pregnancy. It was, she assured me in her crispest courtroom style, all Red's fault.

"Don't you want the baby, Eileen?" I asked innocently.

"Oh, Brendan, you poor darling." She touched my hand affectionately. "Don't pay any attention to my blather. Certainly I want him. Do you think someone my age becomes pregnant by accident? My doctor says it's irrational. Who cares? Law is fun. Babies are more fun."

It was an argument that would not stand up on appeal, yet I knew what she meant. Some of the younger women attorneys in our office had tried to give Eileen a hard time: pregnancy after forty was a violation of her obligations to other women.

"Mind your own goddamned business," Eileen had replied, picking up her reading glasses and returning to the brief on which she was working.

I abandoned my efforts to sort out sex and fertility. It was spring, and I had no woman and was alienated from my only child. Like my ancestors for millions of years, I wanted a woman to fondle and impregnate and a child to bounce on my knee. I would find both in the cool, stylish darkness of Dufficy's. I stirred uneasily. Even if I couldn't remember her physical appearance, I had to have her.

"You're too good, Brendan," Eileen sighed again, and stood up. "Thank God we never let you in a courtroom."

"Some people are fighters and some are not." I shrugged my shoulders in apology.

"I'm not sure you're not a fighter." Nick closed his folder. "You haven't fought yet, that's all. Anyway, we're agreed that we'll make a decision next week? The U.S. Attorney will have to decide shortly thereafter whether to go to a grand jury."

We were agreed.

I could see no connection that day between the woman in the store and King and Patsy Sullivan. Or Ron Crowley. As I say, a psychic "gift" is not all that much use.

If I had seen the link, I might not have gone back to Dufficy's.

No, that's not true. Nothing would have kept me away from her. I had to find out her name. I would have returned to Dufficy's before dinner with Jean no matter what I had known about the future. Even as Eileen was praising my goodness, I was picturing the woman's body submitting, willingly, to mine. The image of pleasure was so powerful, I had to dig my fingernails into the palms of my hands to control it.

Yet I was not sure I would remember her. If there were two young women in the store, would I know which one she was, this woman who was carrying/would someday carry/ wanted to carry my child?

3

"Not to say photographs." She frowned thoughtfully. "Not like your man Ansel Adams that died the other day, Lord have mercy on him. But we have picturebooks that are not just scenery, like this one." The frown changed to a shy smile as she hesitantly handed me the book. "All the pictures were taken before 1900...."

Admiration and tenderness had temporarily replaced lust. There had been no problem recognizing her. She was everything that my first impressions had suggested, the kind of woman I had dreamed about since I first comprehended that women and men spend their lives together and share their bodies with one another.

"I think my daughter will like that," I said, trying to

sound serious and self-controlled despite my pounding heart. "And if you have Jill Uris's books . . ."

She was a heroine from a nineteenth-century Irish novel, tall (at least five feet seven), graceful, so soft-spoken that I could barely hear her, with a classical figure, a pale complexion, which colored quickly, under long, jet black hair, a high, clear forehead, big gray eyes, which were alternately studious and impish, faint crow's-feet that suggested both laughter and wisdom, and an oval face with delicately sculpted features, suggesting sensitivity and intelligence. She was, I guessed, about thirty, perhaps a little older, and, incredibly, without a wedding ring.

"Has your daughter been a photographer for long?" she asked while scanning the shelves behind her.

"Only a few months." I realized how much I resented Jeannie. She was a spoiled little brat. I'd never been able to admit that to myself before. "She's just nineteen, searching for a career. This may not last the summer."

"Ah, but wouldn't it be wonderful if it did?" She found the books. "She might see more in Ireland than we do. Sure, wasn't Mrs. Uris a better photographer than himself a novelist?" she added, with what might have been a wink.

The best part of her was her smile; it started slowly, even hesitantly, like the sun debating whether to emerge at the end of a rainy day, and then exploded in merriment, almost always ending in an unself-conscious laugh, especially when the smile hinted at a slight reprimand for my lack of faith in my daughter. Unlike most Irish immigrants, even her teeth were unblemished.

"He had some of the history right, but he didn't understand the personality or character." I thumbed through Jill Uris's books without the faintest notion how Jeannie would react. "I'll take these two."

She knew, as women usually do, that I was carefully evaluating her. She was embarrassed, unwilling to look me in the eye save for a quick glance, but not at all offended.

"Have you been to Ireland often, Mr. Ryan?" she murmured with a sigh that would have put Eileen Ryan Kane to shame. Blushing again, as if her question were too bold, she laid the books on the counter and began to write up the bill with her left hand.

"I've never been there," I admitted. "My wife doesn't like to fly . . ." I wanted to kick myself for mentioning a wife, especially since by decision of the Metropolitan Matrimonial Tribunal of the Archdiocese of Chicago I did not and indeed had never had one. "How did you know my name?"

"Wasn't it yourself that was on television the other night, talking about the World's Fair?" She looked up at me, her face scarlet, and then quickly looked away, though not before that blinding smile had turned into another laugh. "And sounding so terribly learned about the wicked dances at the first two of them?"

"Little Egypt and Sally Rand." She watched Channel 11, our educational station and, unlike ninety-five percent of my fellow Chicagoans, knew I was on the executive committee for the 1992 fair. "I suppose you Irish wouldn't approve."

"And with our women going into battle stark naked in ancient times." She bent over her calculations.

"And your men with incurable breast fixations in the same days; didn't himself have to be soaked in water all night long after the women of Ulster challenged him naked to the waist at the gates of the city? And you have me at a disadvantage, Miss . . . ?"

She was flustered, as well she might be. Her own full breasts, pushing against the thin fabric of a simple white belted dress, were superb. I battled unsuccessfully with images of her among the women of Ulster and myself as Cuchulain.

"He heated enough bathwater for the whole of Ireland for two months. But those were the old days. And my name is Kelly. Ciara Kelly." She pronounced the name as "Keyra" with ever so slight an "a" sound between the "y" and the "r." "C-I-A-R-A. It comes to forty-two pounds . . ." She shook her black hair in dismay. "Forty-two dollars and twenty-five cents, Mr. Ryan."

"Wouldn't I be knowing how to spell Ciara?" I gave her my Visa card. "Is that a Dublin accent?"

Her voice sounded like the waves breaking against rocks, low, soft, and yet somehow powerful.

The gray eyes wandered back to my face as she made the imprint from my card and considered me speculatively. It was my turn to be embarrassed, to feel my face grow warm.

"A mixed-up accent, a bit of Dublin and a bit of the West."

She was not about to reveal too much to me. I noticed for the first time an ugly scar on the back of her right hand, curving up her forearm.

"Have you been in Chicago long?"

"Not to say long." She lowered her eyes modestly and slipped my purchase into a bag. No carefully wrapped package this time. "Thank you very much, Mr. Ryan. Do come again."

I was being dismissed, but without prejudice.

"That time you sounded almost English."

"Perish the thought." She laughed easily, the viola section of an orchestra. "More like Trinity College."

I walked to the door, I hoped with dignity and self-possession. Even in Ireland, how could someone so desirable have escaped marriage?

I turned in the doorway. "Do you like Chicago?" I asked, paying no attention to the disapproving stare of the older woman standing guard over the Waterford.

Ciara Kelly was grinning at me, not exactly wickedly, more in benign amusement, a gracious countess with a pet serf. "Wouldn't I have to be seeing a lot more of it to make an educated judgment?"

"And would you ever answer a question except by asking another?"

She shook her head, as though I were a silly little boy. "And wouldn't I be a bit daft if I told one of the lord mayor's commissioners for the World's Fair that I didn't love Chicago?"

I escaped quickly, knowing that I had lost the first encounter and not minding a bit.

Harold would be pleased to hear that someone thought he was a lord mayor.

Evaluate me, will you, silver-haired Yank? Take off my dress in your imagination, will you? Well, sure I don't mind all that much, so long as you're after knowing that when it comes to blarney I can talk rings around you.

Rain clouds had drifted in from the west, but Michigan Avenue was bathed for me in purest gold. She found me amusing if not attractive, interesting if not appealing. Pretty good for a start. I was acting like a fifteen-year-old with his first crush; so what?

4

The longer I waited for Jean, the more I resented her. She had always been her "mother's little girl." Even as a baby she would cry in my arms and Madonna would brusquely snatch her back, complaining that I didn't know anything about babies.

It was Madonna's unshakable conviction that I was incompetent at everything from circuit breakers to tennis. Indeed, when she told me that she wanted a divorce—the day Jean graduated from high school—one of the reasons she gave was my refusal to try to improve as a tennis doubles partner even though I knew how important tennis was to her.

Jean screamed at me that I had ruined her graduation day, a worse temper tantrum than those that had more or less constituted our relationship during her teen years. She was her mother's teenager; for me there was rage and silence.

Now, like her mother, she was keeping me waiting. She would sail into the quiet dignity of Les Nomades anywhere from half an hour to two hours late, insouciantly refusing to explain or apologize, and would sulk if I asked why she was late. I hoped that unlike the last time I took her to supper she would wear something more appropriate than jeans, Indian beads, and a cowboy shirt tied several inches above the belt.

Her tardiness gave me time to fantasize about the appealing mixture of shy modesty and leprechaun wit hinting at wickedness that was Ciara Kelly. I would have her, of that I was sure, but I was still too bemused to plan my campaign. Storybook romantic and principled feminist that I am, I forced myself to include in my flamboyantly bawdy fantasies the careful notation that she was a treasure, and must be treated as such. She would be seduced indeed, and with violent, consuming passion, but protected, reverenced, cherished.

There were also a few dark clouds of bafflement and potential disappointment lurking in the bright sky of my erotic imaginings. Why was she not married? I would have, needless to say, been terribly disappointed if she were, yet there was mystery here that could mean trouble. And why was an educated woman (had she not said Trinity College?) working in a shop, even one on Michigan Avenue? And whence the ugly white gash on her arm?

Those who are in love, I read somewhere, are only happy when they can torment themselves with doubts. I was certainly in love, for the first time in my life.

My reveries were ended by Jovan, hovering at my table. "Your very lovely daughter, Mr. Ryan."

I glanced at my watch. Only ten minutes late after all. Blackie Ryan would later insist, when I was driven to seek spiritual advice from him, that my problem is that I fit people into molds of my own making and cannot cope when they escape from the mold. At first glance I did not think that the chic young woman in the white suit and lavender blouse with a slender neck shawl and amethyst pendant and earrings was my daughter. Too neat, too well groomed, too effusive, brown hair too short, brown eyes too happy to see me.

"Daddy, Daddy, you look gorgeous." An enthusiastic hug and a whiff of inviting scent. "And so happy! Do you have a girlfriend? You should marry again, you know. You are too absolutely cute not to find yourself a woman. Presents for me?" Rapid tearing of paper. "How totally awesome! Those shots are really there!" She was more interested in the nineteenth century than in Jill Uris. "Those poor people. Not so long ago, either. Thank you soooo much!" A generous kiss. "Uhmm . . . Definitely you should have a gorgeous woman."

Jean was short and trim, in most ways a carbon copy of my mother, though Madonna rejected the comparison out of hand. (Indeed, Jean was kept away from my parents as much as possible. Their quiet reserve was not appropriate for their only granddaughter, who was trained from her birth for social success.) She was pretty rather than beautiful, neatly shaped rather than voluptuous, energetically sensuous rather than overtly sexy, yet with the hint that beneath the ever-shifting and often shallow enthusiasms lurked the tinder for intense sexual flames, waiting for the right man to ignite. Marc Chagall's Chloe.

That night she was a very lovely, if not quite fully formed young woman, even if I was too dumb to compliment her. Rather, I murmured somewhat pedantically that I doubted I was qualified for marriage, seated her at our table underneath the Art Deco poster of the Arc de Triomphe, and nodded slightly when she ordered a "tiny kir" and raised an eyebrow for my approval.

Now, I thought, comes the appeal for money. The change in persona from sullen teenager to fashionable and affectionate daughter is part of the strategy.

"Daddy." She leaned forward and whispered, as though telling me a state secret. "Caitlin Murphy broke a boy's arm!"

It was perhaps the last opening gambit I expected to hear from her. Caitlin was the doyenne of the third generation of Ryans, daughter of Eileen's older sister, Mary Kate, and Joe Murphy, both of them psychiatrists.

"How do you know Caitlin?"

"Oh, she saw some of my pictures in a student magazine." Jean waved her hand, dismissing the importance of the facts of the case. "And she's in the photography masters program at the Art Institute and she wrote me the nicest letter and isn't she the most beautiful woman and so we had lunch today and this boy made a pass at her and she broke his arm and isn't that too much?"

I would have to admit that Caitlin, a tall, ravishing

honey blonde with the lithe grace of a gymnast, was breath-taking. She had apparently also inherited the family pro-pensity for picking up strays. Jeannie had become a stray. Poor child, I could hear them say. I resented their patronization, though God knows I was more than depen-dent on Caitlin's Aunt Eileen and Cousin Nicholas.

"She broke his arm at lunch? Today?"

"No, silly, cute daddy." She grinned appreciatively at me. "In some bar on Rush Street or someplace. She told me about it at lunch. This boy made a pass and she said no, so he, like, pawed her, and she said if you do that again I'll break your arm. And so he did it again and so she, like, broke his arm. She's black belt in karate and isn't that too much?"

"Did she seem to enjoy it?" How proud her grand-mother, Kate Collins, Ed Ryan's first wife, would be, Lord have mercy on her, as Ciara would have said, of such a zany descendant.

"Certainly not." She sipped daintily at her drink. "She's not a sadist or something like that. The boys at the Zoo and places like that won't paw her again, will they?"

"Not unless she wants them to."

My daughter rolled her eyes, a gesture I was sure she'd picked up from Caitlin at lunch. "When she wants a boy to paw her, he'll know all right, and Daddy, why don't we know the other Ryans better? I mean, I know Mom couldn't stand them and all, but were you ever close to them? They *are* relatives, aren't they?"

So we ate our turbot in wine and lemon sauce and drank our Meursault and talked not of the money I still thought she wanted, but of Caitlin's family.

She and Caitlin were not close relatives, only fourth cousins. Her great-great-grandfather, Michael Ryan, and Caitlin's great-great-grandfather, James Ryan, had come to Chicago after the Civil War. The brothers fell out over Irish nationalist politics, which were fierce in Chicago in those days, and the two families drifted apart. By the time of my father, another Michael Ryan, and Caitlin's mother's fa-ther, Ed Ryan, there was no memory of the reason for the fight and no hostility. We were the South Side Ryans and they were the North Side Ryans, and in the days before everyone had an automobile, distance made us strangers—distance and social class: their family had much more money.

Then, after the Second World War, Ed Ryan and his wife moved to the South Side, to St. Praxides, where my father had been raised and where he returned when he and my mother came back from England. So the kids of both families grew up in the same neighborhood, distant relatives but strangers. We were friendly but not friends. Ed and Kate and their brood were extroverts, outgoing and gregarious, doubtless like Caitlin, while my mother and father kept to themselves, partly because they were quiet people and partly because they loved each other so much.

Jean nodded wisely. "So now we're the North Side Ryans and they're the South Side Ryans."

"I guess. Can I tell you more about my mother and father? Maybe it will explain me."

She patted my hand affectionately. "I understand you, Daddy. But tell me about them. I must see them on the way back to Stanford at the end of summer. I look so much like Grandmother Ryan in her wedding picture."

Her mother, I thought, would be profoundly offended.

There was never a time I can remember when my parents were not deeply in love with each other. Even now, when I visit them in Tucson, an ambience of affection—physical affection—fills their house, despite the fact that they are in their middle sixties. After they came home from the war, in which they saved each other's lives and a lot of other lives, too, they existed only for each other and for me. My father's insurance business was successful enough, but he could have made much more money if he did not come home most days on the 1:20 Rock Island to be with us. They were always friendly to others, and my mother, who was English and a convert, went to Mass at St. Prax's every morning, but they were content to let the world drift by. They had their books, their son, and each other. After I grew up, Mom went to work at the agency, and you could see both of them walking hand in hand down Longwood Drive after the 1:20 pulled into the station. I suppose their narrow, indeed miraculous, escape during the war explained most of it. But they were quiet, uncompetitive people, and they produced a quiet, uncompetitive son.

Who was, I didn't tell her, nearly as unlucky in love as his parents were lucky. Perhaps because he wasn't competitive enough.

"How totally neat! You mean they, like, actually sleep together?" Her eyes glowed in approbation.

"They love each other more than they did when they were your age," I said, thinking that such love may produce children who are not quite suited for the world in which they have to live. Perhaps the arm-breaking Caitlin had had a more appropriate family experience. "So maybe that's why I grew up with kids like Ron Crowley and Patsy Walsh and John Sullivan as friends instead of the other Ryans."

I did not mention her mother and did not say that, left to my own, I would probably have drifted towards my cousins.

"Ron Crowley." She wrinkled her nose. "Is he a bomb at St. Jarlath's!"

"Jean." I felt my anger rise, as it often did when Jean displayed adolescent omniscience. "He is one of the most admired priests in America."

"Not by the young people in the neighborhood, he isn't!" Her temper flared as it did every time I became pedantic in response to what I took to be childish ignorance.

I ordered my "parent" instincts to be silent.

"Father Ron?" I said in a tone that indicated astonishment but acceptance of her version of reality. By way of distraction I also signaled the waitress for our dessert order. "I thought he would be a wonderful pastor."

We both ordered white chocolate mousse. "Bad for my figure," she groaned.

"There never will be anything wrong with your figure," I said, patting her hand as she had done mine earlier and thinking of how leathery and emaciated Madonna looked since she had gone on her diet and exercise fad.

"Sweet daddy," she said, delight shining on her pixie face. "I know there won't be if I really do have Grand-

mother Ryan's genes. That's just something you're supposed to say."

Then we returned to Father Ron. Despite his record as
a crusading missionary in South America, his brilliant
work in the inner city of Chicago, and support for disarma-
ment and economic justice, the word on the young adult
circuit from St. Jarlath's—next to our home parish on the
North Shore—was that he was "like, totally authoritarian,
a real Nazi." He abolished the parish council, dismissed
most of the staff, had a popular curate transferred, fired a
seminary professor who said Mass on Sunday and had the
reputation of being a fine preacher ("Too many people were
calling to find out what Mass Father Cross was saying"),
banished teenagers from the parish gym, let the young
adult club fold, and insulted the congregation every Sunday because they spoiled their children.

I was appalled; big, handsome, gregarious Ron had become exactly what he hated most in pastors. One more of
our group who had reached passionately for happiness and
had found instead frustration and bitterness.

"It must be hard, Daddy," she made a face at the taste
of Jovan's complimentary Serbian liqueur but didn't put it
aside, "to see your friends fu . . . messing up their lives."

"You're a mind reader, Jeannie. I don't quite understand it. We were so happy when we were young."

She nodded solemnly, not understanding but sympathetic.

It had been a charming dinner with an interesting and
intelligent young woman, my lucky day for fascinating fe-
males. Unfortunately, I blew it.

"Now, about the money you'll need for the trip to
Ireland." I took out my checkbook.

Jean recoiled as though I had put a tarantula on
Jovan's spotless white tablecloth.

"I don't need . . ." Her eyes filled with tears. "That's not
why I wanted to have dinner. . . ."

My pen poised over the open book, I realized what a
fool I was.

Jean jumped to her feet, pain turning to rage. "I don't

want your money," she shouted. "You're a stupid asshole. Mom's right, you're a dried-up old bastard."

"Jean . . ." I tried to reason with her. Jovan had appeared from nowhere, horrified at the disturbance of the serene environment of his restaurant.

"And I don't want your presents either." She threw Jill Uris's book at me and, shaking with sobs, stormed out of the room. I noted dismally that her legs, moving rapidly under the slits in a tight skirt which hinted at nylon-sheathed young thighs and flanks, were trim and elegant. Anger and passion in my daughter, I thought abstractly, were closely linked.

Jovan's dismay turned to polite sympathy. He placed a hand on my shoulder, like a wise Trappist monk. "A mistake, eh, my friend? It is hard with beautiful daughters. It will not be forever, she loves you too much."

He had never met her before, but he saw what I had missed.

I went home to my apartment building, worked out with weights for twenty minutes, and then swam an hour in the pool. I was not thinking of a body that would be presentable for a young lover. I was thinking rather that without my daily exercise I would not sleep a wink.

I took a warm shower, wrapped myself in a clean terry-cloth robe, made a cup of apple cinnamon tea, and sat by the window looking at the mixture of stars and clouds hovering above the blackboard-smooth lake.

Ciara Kelly was, I warned myself, very likely my last chance. Without her I was indeed destined for the fate Jean predicted for me, a dried-up old bachelor who for all the example of his parents had never learned how to love.

5

The weather, the monsignor said as he began his fatally inaccurate prophecy about our class, was one more blessing on the most blessed class in the twenty-year history of the parish. Most of the thirty-five of us, he noted, had begun in the first grade together, only a few years after the war was over and before the parish had begun to expand.

"You are the last of the one-room classes, the high-water mark of the parish's early years. The beauty of this day and the beauty of the ceremony in our brand-new church are merely an overture for the great achievements that lie ahead of you."

Our grammar school graduation day in June of 1956 was as close to a perfect spring day as Chicago ever sees: shimmering sunlight, light breezes, crystal blue sky, temperature in the low eighties, little humidity.

The monsignor was guilty of a slightly mixed metaphor, but it suited the emotions of the day: proud parents, sniggering boys, crying girls. We pretended to be more interested in the round of parties after the sun went down and in King's plans for beer in the forest preserve. Yet in our hearts my group believed that the monsignor was right. We were indeed special, and we would in due course show the world how special.

How wrong we were.

It was a wonderful summer, not much rain and not too much heat. Or so it seems in my memory. The girls went wild about Elvis Presley, and we made fun of him, agreeing readily enough that he was indeed a "hound dog." We saw *Around the World in Eighty Days* and *The King and I* and tentatively kissed in the darkness of the theater (I confess that I didn't). We sang "Que Sera, Sera," though we didn't mean it, and "On the Street Where You Live" and "I Could Have Danced All Night" from *My Fair Lady*.

We played volleyball and basketball in the "courts" (the church parking lot); hung out in front of Lewis's drugstore until the owner or the police banished us; necked in the forest preserve (well, they did; I didn't) except on weekends when the blacks took it over for barbecue roasts; and drank beer in the schoolyard (well, I didn't) and threw the cans on the front lawn of the convent. We went on our class picnic to Potawatami Park and turned over the rowboats as soon as they were launched (despite the imprecations of the young priest). We bragged that we were not afraid of high school (though we were), pretended to know much more about sex than we did, passed around early copies of *Playboy* (to the girls' dismay—though they were not above peeking), promised that we would always be friends, and committed ourselves to filling the next year with fun, fun, and more fun.

Our biggest excitement that summer was breaking into people's homes, especially on weekends, when many of the parents were away at Long Beach or Grand Beach or other summer locales. I suspect that we were secretly envious, despite our protests that the Club (our local country club) was much more fun. (My parents didn't belong to the Club, needless to say; I cannot imagine a place that would have made them more uncomfortable. But I tagged along with the children of members.) Mostly we were content to rearrange furniture and kitchenware, enough to let the occupants know we'd been there.

King would select the victim, study the house, lay the plans. Ron would egg us on when our courage flagged. The girls would stand guard. I would climb up on Ron's shoulders and pry open the window. The reign of terror attracted considerable attention from the police, but we were never caught.

I vetoed an attack on the house of the "other" Ryans, contending that they were relatives and fearing that we might do more damage than break a few dishes or spill some cosmetics once we got inside—so great was the distaste of the others for the Ryan clan, especially for their mother, who, everyone said, was a Communist.

And I heeded my father's delicate warning one night over sherry (certainly we had a glass of sherry before dinner, doesn't everyone?).

"Well, I hope those young mischief-makers try Ned Ryan's old house while they're up at Grand Beach."

"Darling, what a terrible thing to say." My mother looked up from the decanter in utter dismay.

"It'll serve them right. The imps, I mean. Ned Ryan charged a Japanese battleship with a destroyer escort in the Philippine Sea and won. If he sets his mind to hunting down the punks, they'll end up in reform school."

"It would only serve them right," my mother agreed.

"Anyone else's house," my father put aside his copy of the *Chicago Daily News*, "and the parents will buy off the owners and the police. No one buys off Ned Ryan."

Mr. Ryan seemed such a mild man. I wasn't sure whether my father meant what he said. I'm still not sure. And I'm afraid even now to ask either him or Ned.

We didn't raid their house, despite my friends' protest that I was a creep. And we didn't stretch our luck with any more raids.

The golden days, we thought, would never end. Eighth grade graduation day, with its flashing light bulbs, maroon and white ribbons, diplomas in dark blue binders, girls tottering on unfamiliar high heels, sentimental mothers, and proud nuns, was a spectacular beginning to the song of our lives. Unfortunately the rest of the music did not live up to the overture. Our lives are like an unfinished symphony, a statue whose sculptor died after a promising beginning, an abandoned novel with a fascinating but flawed premise, a film which was never released despite exciting advance publicity.

We worked for tutoring programs in black and Hispanic parishes for two years before John Kennedy's Peace Corps and the volunteer enthusiasm of the early sixties. On two Sundays a month we went to the county infirmary at Oak Forest to visit the "old people" with the Vincent De Paul Society of the parish.

If you've ever been in wards filled with the indigent aged, you know how depressing they can be. The sights, sounds, smells—above all, smells—were as far from our comfortable upper crust of the middle-class life as were the lower circles of Dante's Inferno. The question was not whether you got sick at Oak Forest but how soon. Ron and I were ill in the first half hour.

"I don't ever want to be old," he said, as we vomited behind a tree on the grounds. "I want to die when I'm healthy and getting close to old age—forty or something like that."

In retrospect it was a strange prophecy. Psychic or not, I can't claim a premonition at the time.

The girls were much better at it. Patsy was a persistent missionary, plugging away at old men and women who had not gone to confession or received Communion for forty years. Madonna sang, danced, told stories, wrote letters, gossiped. You could see their eyes light up when she slipped into the world, a trim, self-confident blonde angel of lightness and cheer.

She organized, produced, and directed musical shows, with which we toured the wards at Christmastime. The old people wept when she left.

"I want to spend my life helping people like that, Brenny," she said to me in the T-bird as we drove home after one such musical review. "I'd be a nun, only I don't know that that would do much good. I mean, I want to make it so that people don't have to live that way."

"Hmm . . ." I said.

"No, that's not true." She frowned at a stoplight that dared to slow her progress. "I'd enter the order after high school if Daddy would let me."

We graduated from high school and forgot about Oak Forest.

"We peaked out when we were seventeen, Brenny," King groaned as he made himself another drink on the day he admitted that he had misappropriated my money.

"I know." I looked up at him, hardly able to believe that this fat, balding, battered man, a wounded oversized bull, was the same person as my handsome, mischievous teenage friend. "Why did it all end so soon?"

He hesitated, then poured another jolt of J&B into the tumbler. "I'll be damned if I can figure it out."

No more can I.

We reached for the stars, or thought we did, and fell on our faces. We were failures, most of us tragic failures. By the Memorial Day weekend of 1984 our fates were sealed. Alcoholism, theft, divorce, insanity, sudden death—our promise was cut short even before it had a chance to wither.

I don't yet understand why. No one would have guessed when we graduated from grammar school in June of 1956 that we were doomed. Our group was hailed as the most promising class St. Praxides had ever produced. Madonna was voted the outstanding girl, Ron the outstanding boy. King was the class president, Patsy crowned the Blessed Mother in May. I had the highest average in the class. Ron captained the football team, King the basketball team, Madonna the volleyball team. The "other" Ryans were, for once, left out, not that they seemed to notice it.

Madonna Clifford, slender and blonde, even at fourteen was said to be a great beauty. Patsy Walsh, short, cute, vivacious, was the driving energy behind every party. Ron Crowley, big, strong, genial, placated worried parents and teachers. King Sullivan, clever, witty, resourceful, devised the games, the tricks, the surprises.

I tagged along, not a hanger-on exactly, but because they wanted me. I could never understand why and still can't, except that I was the brightest kid in the class. I didn't belong with the stars and often would rather not have been there. I guess I was the mascot, the pet, the even-tempered go-between who could mediate the quarrels.

The girls both went to the brand-new Mother McAuley High School on 103d Street, where Madonna was the outstanding senior, and then on to St. Mary's of Notre Dame. Ron and King enrolled at St. Ignatius, where Ron won the senior prize and surprised everyone by rejecting his football scholarship at Notre Dame and signing up for the seminary. King went to Notre Dame but was expelled during his sophomore year, when he was caught for the second time with beer in his room. Neither of the girls graduated from college.

I went to St. Rita's High School, which was closer to home, and then to Loyola to which I could commute. The others in the group objected vigorously, not understanding the great attractiveness of a home steeped in love, as was our little house on the hill overlooking the park and the Rock Island station at 93d and Glenwood Drive.

I was the only one who went into the service, despite the protests of my wife and her family. My family history left me no choice. Military intelligence of course. A year in the Pentagon in a group that warned of the dangers of involvement in Vietnam that hesitated between minimum force and maximum force. Then nine months in that country, mostly in Saigon, as part of a team that sent warnings to Washington about the tenacity of the Viet Cong. No one listened. I came home in 1966, two years after the Tonkin Gulf resolution, with a medal, the bars of a captain, and grave fear for our country.

The months in Vietnam were not a complete waste. For others the memory of the war might be a lifelong burden. For me one particular incident, the cause of my medal, stands as ambiguous evidence that my life may not be totally worthless. Everything else I've done in my forty-two years is devoid of generosity and courage. For a few hours in Vietnam I proved to myself that I was capable of both, if the necessity arose.

That's not very much, I suppose, but it's all I have.

I paid a price for that one shining moment, as the song from *Camelot*, which we sang in the summer of 1960, put it. The year overseas ruined our marriage. Madonna, who did not mind the prospect of moving to McLean, Virginia, as an officer's wife, soon found that she would not be rubbing shoulders with senators and ambassadors at Washington cocktail parties. She quickly came to hate our tiny, furnished apartment. She took our new daughter home to mother with great relief. Comparing what her father could provide in the way of comfort with what I could provide—her family had moved to the North Shore to escape the "niggers," as her mother bluntly put it—she probably felt that it was a mistake to have ever married me. She was able to contain her enthusiasm for me on return. She was never an antiwar activist, but my bars and my medal did not impress her. It was always, "your goddamn war."

I had thought about an academic career, perhaps in economics or history, but I realized that, on a professor's salary, I could never support her in the style she would demand. So I went to work for my father and struggled through four years of night school at DePaul. I clerked at Minor Gray and Blatt, was hired as an associate the day I graduated, and then became a partner after two years (at the same time in 1972 that Eileen Ryan Kane also became a partner, when she left government work and the firm decided it needed competent women immediately). These were not inconsiderable achievements. But Madonna was unimpressed. Her father was a distinguished, outspoken, and thick-skulled surgeon. I could never be as good at anything as he was at everything.

Patsy and King already had two children and were expecting a third, King had been wiped out twice on the Board of Trade and had cracked up his Mercedes in a drunken accident on the Dan Ryan, Patsy had spent some time in the psychiatric ward at Little Company of Mary, Ron was leading the post–Vatican Council agitation against an old-fashioned seminary rector, and my wife, despite considerable literary and administrative talents, was content with attending women's charity luncheons (with her mother) up and down the North Shore.

We peaked out, in retrospect, shortly after our high school graduation, between the time Ron left for the seminary and the girls quit college—Patsy to marry King after he had been thrown out of Notre Dame and Madonna because she hated the nuns, the other students, and everything else about St. Mary's.

There were excuses. King's father was a successful trader all right, but he was drunk every afternoon and a heavy-handed authoritarian. His mother was so ineffectual as to be practically nonexistent. Mr. and Mrs. Walsh separated when Patsy was in college because he was not sufficiently successful at the practice of law to support her social ambitions. Mac Crowley was a jock who never grew up. Dr. Melvin Clifford was an insufferable boor (as my mother remarked in a rare moment of exasperated uncharitableness), and his wife one of the most mindless women I've ever known.

"It seems to me," my father began mildly as we dug into carne seca chimichangas at El Charro, Tucson's famous Sonoran restaurant (underneath a picture of someone who looked like Pancho Villa), "that the difference between my generation and yours is that we were perhaps too eager to assume responsibility for our behavior and you are perhaps too eager to reject such responsibility."

"Rather," my mother agreed with equal mildness.

"A good point," I agreed, realizing how often I justified my weakness in dealing with conflict in my marriage by arguing that I grew up in a family where there was almost no conflict.

"On the whole," he played with his wine margarita, "I think our fault was the less serious. It is better to exaggerate personal responsibility than to deny it."

"How does it seem with Jean's generation?" my mother asked, pining as always to know her granddaughter better.

"I'm not sure," I admitted. "Yet it does seem to me that with your greater responsibility there is less guilt. And with our lesser responsibility there is more guilt. Madonna, poor woman, has been running from guilt all her life. That's why she has to blame me."

"How sad," my mother murmured softly.

Yet we were not sad as children. At least we did not seem sad. As I remember my youth, it was very happy. If the rest of the group was unhappy, they were good at hiding it.

The five of us had good times together as far back into the early years of grammar school as I can remember—the two couples always together and Brendan Ryan as the unobtrusive fifth wheel. It was expected that Ron and Madonna, the most attractive and the best-looking of the class, would be paired. I loved Patsy, or so I thought, from the first day of the first grade, mostly, I suspect, because we were the shortest persons in the class and hence partners in every orderly "rank" the nuns established. Sadly for me, it seemed then, all her considerable affective energies were directed at King Sullivan. Their marriage, as he mumbled incoherently at the wedding banquet, fulfilled a romance that had begun at the Club even before they had entered St. Praxides.

That was right before he collapsed in a drunken stupor.

When it was necessary in the teen years for me to have a date, Patsy and Madonna (never, *never* Donna, by the way) chose one for me, normally a pleasant and presentable girl who offered them no competition and showed proper gratitude for being permitted into our group, even on a temporary basis.

Only once did I kick over the traces. I was never quite forgiven. It was one item on the agenda of my offenses when Madonna ordered me out of the house twenty-two years later.

It was senior prom time. Kate Ryan's death, though not a surprise, had shattered the whole family, especially Eileen, whom my mother had observed was the most fragile of all of them.

"Will Eileen Ryan be going to the senior prom?" she asked me at supper one night. For all her diligent efforts, she could never quite understand the arrangements of American secondary education. I explained that there were many senior proms, one for each high school, and that maybe Eileen would find a boy to take her to her own prom but that I doubted any boy would invite her to his prom.

"Most extraordinary," she murmured. "She's such a beautiful child."

"What the boy is saying, Jocelyn," my father wiped his mouth carefully with a napkin, "is that she is so self-possessed and so intelligent that she scares boys her own age. It is not unusual at that age in life in our country. Eileen will survive."

"You do think she is lovely, don't you, Brendan?" My mother filled my wineglass (civilized living in her house dictated one, possibly two glasses of "claret" with the evening meal).

"I hadn't noticed."

In retrospect my father was quite right. Eileen was more than most of us her age, male or female, could handle. So we reacted, as adolescents do, by pretending that we were unaware of her existence.

"Who are you going to take to your prom?" My mother did not give up easily.

"I don't know. Patsy and Madonna will find someone, then we'll triple at the McAuley prom."

"Can't you find someone by yourself?"

"I suppose."

That was the end of the conversation, save for a know-ing wink from my father.

I called the "other" Ryans' number later in the eve-ning. Eileen answered.

"Waiting on the phone, Cousin, for a cousin to call who needs a prom date?"

"Your prom or mine, Cousin?" One of the few un-guarded remarks that I have ever heard cross her lips.

I took a deep breath, fearing the rage of my friends. "Both, I hope."

Silence. Then, "Oh, Brendan . . ."

"Is it a deal?"

"It's a deal."

The group was furious. They would not have to tolerate her at the St. Rita's prom because none of them was going, or the St. Ignatius prom because I would not be going to that. The McAuley dance was the sticking point.

"I will not be seen in public with that creep!" Madonna stormed.

"She's so stuck up," Patsy protested.

"A wet blanket on any party," King agreed.

None of this was true, but my friends believed it, I daresay, at the moment more strongly than they believed in the existence of God.

"Guess you'll have to find someone else to double with," Ron said. "You really should have asked us, Brenny."

"No one in the whole school will double with such a drip." Madonna's thin, pretty face crinkled in derision.

I didn't defend my cousin or my decision. I merely stuck by it.

To my surprise, Eileen was the toast of the St. Rita's prom. Her long brown hair, flashing green eyes, and matching strapless green gown (for which little artificial boning was required) stopped traffic on the dance floor. There was much joking about our names being the same.

"She's my mother," I explained to one of the wide-eyed Augustinian priests.

"Actually, we're secretly married," she said in a stage whisper.

I brushed her lips when we arrived at the door of her house shortly before 5:00 A.M.

"I'll never forget this, Cousin," she said fiercely. "Never."

"I'm sure I won't either."

Somehow it had been arranged that my crowd from St. Rita's and their dates would journey the next day to the Ryan house at Grand Beach. Mary Kate, Eileen's older sister, was in charge. The rain poured down all day, so we spent our time singing. Eileen, who had "taken" voice for as long as I could remember, led us from the piano, tirelessly banishing the temptation to boredom. After a while, as we stuffed ourselves with an apparently limitless supply of food, no one noticed the rain.

"What a dame!" one of my classmates said to me. "She even knows the second stanzas of songs."

The McAuley prom was not so pleasant. Patsy and Madonna, with the cruelty at which adolescent women can be so skilled, did everything they could to make Eileen feel unwanted and unnoticed. I consoled myself with the copout that she seemed unaware of their rudeness. Now I suspect that she had too much class to acknowledge it.

The boys who had been constrained to come to the prom noticed her all right, especially since I had absolutely forbidden her to replace the green dress with another.

The drinking party at the Cellar (on the lower level of Wacker Drive) which followed the dance was organized by a committee of parents who, in flagrant disregard of the laws of the sovereign state of Illinois, as I would later realize, argued that kids would drink on prom night and that it was better that the drinking be supervised.

Eileen and I left the party and walked silently, hand in hand, to watch the sun come up over the lake. This time she kissed me, and, if the truth be told, with considerably more vigor than I had dared to attempt.

"You're wonderful, Brendan." The green eyes glistened. "I love you."

I didn't know quite what to say. So I took her hand and we walked back to the Cellar to collect my tipsy friends.

The other two girls attacked her bitterly to me the moment we came through the door—in tones just loud enough so Eileen could hear them as she departed for a visit to the women's room.

"Did she let you fool around with her?" Patsy, her face contorted to an ugly sneer, began the attack.

"There's a lot of her to fool around with," Madonna blew cigarette smoke at me, "if you like fat women."

"I can't believe she'd wear that gross dress."

"She must have put the makeup on with a shovel."

"How can you stand such a disgusting girl?"

"She's cheap, everyone knows that."

"You ought to be ashamed of yourself, Brenny, making us sit at the same table with her."

Eileen did not seem to hear them. Later, on the dance floor, she made only one comment. "There's only one reason why you should be friends with those people, Brendan." She crinkled her nose thoughtfully. "And I don't think it's a good reason."

"What's that?"

"They need you."

"Need me?" I looked into her deep, magic green eyes.

"Without you they'd fall apart. And they know it."

"I don't know what you mean."

"Poor Brendan." She tightened her grip on my hand. "You think they're doing you a favor. It's the other way around. They'll fall apart eventually anyway."

A prophecy?

Maybe not. She might merely have seen what was obvious to everyone but me. I'm still not sure.

There was no senior summer romance between us. The Ryans decamped for Grand Beach in mid-June. My friends still thought the lake shore was "boring" and that the Club was the only place to spend the summer. We cheered for the Kennedy nomination, shivered at *Psycho* (the boys whistled at Janet Leigh), danced the Twist, made fun of Chubby Checker, avoided *La Dolce Vita* because the Church "condemned" it (not that we would have understood Fellini anyway), sang "Never on Sunday" and "Tom Dooley," and watched *Maverick* reruns.

No one kept me away from Grand Beach, however. I could have gone there if I had wanted to. I could have dated Eileen at Loyola during our college years, since neither of us went away to school. But then, with Ron in the seminary, it was more or less understood that I would marry Madonna.

Years later, when Eileen joined our law firm and I was promoted to a partnership, we continued to keep our distance, friendly but not friends, understanding perhaps that there were energies between us that were not quite under full control.

"That trollop," Madonna stormed when she learned that Eileen was a full partner (information that reduced to zero the importance of my partnership). "Red Kane married her because he had to. Where there's smoke there's always fire. I won't have anything to do with her."

I sensed that some of the time her marriage with the columnist, one of the nicest men in Chicago for my money, was not happy. All the more reason to keep my distance. When she and Nick Curran took charge of me during the divorce, Nick was the leader and Eileen lagged behind uncertainly. Then, last fall, when she was trying the Hurricane Houston case, something changed between her and Red. "It was mostly my fault," she whispered to me one day after lunch in early January. "We wasted twenty years and made it only by the skin of our teeth. I'm not going to waste another twenty minutes."

Have I always been half in love with my cousin (distant enough so the relationship would not have been an "impediment"—as the Church called such things in the days when it worried about marriage and divorce)? I suppose. But I would have done less well than Red Kane in responding to her. Of that I am sure.

Or perhaps, after all, not so sure.

More to the point, was Ciara Kelly a psychic clone of Eileen? Different color hair and eyes, different personality, similar figures perhaps, but Ciara was taller. Same kind of woman?

No doubt about it.

On those warm prom nights in 1960, awkward, over-dressed, nervous, feeling slightly ridiculous, under an enor-mous obligation to have a "good time" that we'd never for-get, my friends dismissed Eileen Ryan as "out of it." I didn't agree, but I wasn't sure enough of my own tastes and judgments to disagree either.

Yet she made it and none of us did—professional suc-cess and personal happiness. The latter only recently and only by the skin of her teeth, as she insisted.

None of the rest of us even came close.

6

"Jesus and Mary be with this store," I said to Ciara Kelly as I closed the door quickly to keep out the wind gusts and the pounding rain.

The Cubs were still in first place, even if spring had de-parted.

"Jesus and Mary and Patrick be with those who shop in it," she replied, her brogue this morning more West of Ireland than Trinity College. "It's yourself who knows the customs and not ever visiting there, for which God forgive you. And did your daughter like your present?"

Her hair was swept back and done up in a knot on her head. Even in low heels she was as tall as I. She wore gray slacks and a white blouse and a gray sleeveless sweater, clean and neat but hardly chic. No makeup or jewelry, something I had not noticed the day before. Her neck, a lovely ivory arch, was as pale as the blouse. No sun for a long time. Had Ciara been a nun? That would explain a lot.

"She loved them at first." I was caught off guard by the question. I had not come to talk about Jean.

"At first?" Her gray eyes looked up from the package she was wrapping. "And then?"

You could not fool those gray eyes for long; in their depths was a shrewd horse trader at the county fair.

"We had a fight. My fault. She didn't take the books. I was stupid."

"Fathers are that way with nineteen-year-old daughters. You can give it to her tonight. Nineteen-year-old daughters forgive easily, especially when you say you're sorry." The storm-banishing smile again. "You do tell her you're sorry when it's your fault, don't you, Brendan Ryan?"

"I won't see her tonight. We don't live together." I was stumbling for an explanation. "My wife and I are separated. An annulment, actually."

"That's a shame." She finished the ribbon on one package and began folding an Aran skirt into a green and white box. "You could mail it to her then with a card—there's a nice selection of Georgian Dublin cards over there. Fill one out and we'll mail it for you. No extra charge. . . . Course, if you want a refund," she peeked at me, her face crimson, embarrassed because of her boldness with a customer, "we'll be happy to do that too. I shouldn't be blathering away with my big Irish mouth . . ."

"Not at all, that's an excellent idea. I really didn't come in about the books. I just happen to have them in my briefcase . . ."

"Or there's some color pictures of sailboats off the West of Ireland . . ."

"Lovely." I glanced at them. Dories in the rain and a stiff wind. Tricky and dangerous. "Better not. I don't think Jean approves of my passion for sailing." Her mother surely doesn't, I added to myself.

"Do you sail now?" Her shyness disappeared. "What kind of a boat do you use? I did some of it in a boat just like this one when I was a wee one."

For a second or two she was a reckless hoyden, a tomboy sailing in the teeth of a gale. Her face glowed in a happy memory.

"A little bigger, I'm afraid. A thirty-foot Peterson."

"Jesus, Mary, and Joseph! A battleship!"

"Not quite," I said, noting to myself that I had now one more trick to play in my seduction game. And one more reason to be fond of her.

I chose a picture of Trinity College and wrote, "Sorry. Give me another chance. I love you, Dad," on the card and wondered how to deal with Ciara Kelly's ability to steer me away from my plans for seduction. I was new to the game, and I had selected an elusive Irish woman as my target.

I desperately wanted to take her in my arms and cry on her shapely shoulders for the youth that my friends and I had lost so easily and for which I had mourned the whole sleepless night long.

Instead I gave her the card and the books.

"Shouldn't you put the card in the envelope?" She held it gingerly.

"I should indeed, but why don't you look at it, since you know so much about young women, and tell me whether it's right."

Tears formed in her wonderful eyes. A weeper, like any good Irishwoman.

"If it's not she doesn't deserve you." Ciara took the books shyly from me and began another package. "And I'm sure she does."

I probe at my memories of that rainy morning when tornadoes were sweeping the land. Was the painting on the wall that day, the painting from Keenan's keep that would become so important a few weeks later, when I was searching for the will o' the wisp that had been Ciara Kelly? I can't say whether it was or not. My eyes were too busy studying her face and admiring her body to notice anything else. There was, even then, an electric current of hot sexuality leaping back and forth between us, like lightning dancing on Lake Michigan during a storm.

"Solti's doing the *Rite of Spring* tomorrow night," I said, plunging into my real reason for returning a third time to Dufficy's Irish Store.

"By himself, is it? Would you write your daughter's address on this label, please."

I wrote out her Stanford address. "With a bit of assistance from the Chicago Symphony. It's easier that way."

"Heaven knows we'd need some kind of sacrifice to bring spring to Chicago." She noted with a faintly raised eyebrow the California address. "And the poor girl dancing herself to death."

"Probably only figuratively. She'd be revived later as part of the rebirth ceremony."

"Ah, in Celtic lands surely. Nobody makes an Irishwoman dance until she dies. But does your man Stravinsky know that?"

The label was pasted on the package, and she stood ready to dismiss me again.

"Our springs are very short in Chicago." I took a deep breath. Now it starts. "So I thought maybe you'd help me help Sir Georg put us on the right track again. Dinner beforehand?"

She froze. It was as if I had injected a serum into her veins that turned a vital and interesting woman into a stone statue. She bowed her head and wrapped her arms around herself as though to keep out the winter cold.

"I couldn't do that, Mr. Ryan, sir. I'm sorry. I just couldn't. It's nice of you to ask me. I'm sorry if my blather deceived you."

"I'm sorry if I've been offensive." I felt my face turn to fire. "I didn't mean—"

"You haven't been offensive at all, Mr. Ryan. Not at all." Her voice cracked as though she might sob. "I appreciate the invitation. I just can't accept it. Please."

"No problem." Dauntless lover that I am, I began to look for the quickest possible way out. "Thank you for the help with the books."

"You're welcome, sir." Chin on her chest, shoulders sagging, the ice statue melting away, the snow woman disappearing in the slush. "I'm sorry."

The odd thing, I thought to myself, as I hurried down Michigan Avenue, is that I'm sure she wants to go. She likes me. She feels the same attraction I do. It pleases her too. What the hell happened? How did I blow it this time?

When I reached the sanctuary of my office, there were two phone messages, one from Patsy Sullivan, the other from Father Ron Crowley. It could not be a coincidence, I thought. I'm going to be subjected to more pressure to let King Sullivan off the hook.

I felt guilty that I had not wrestled with the ethical and human complexities of the issue in the last twenty-four hours. I had wasted too much time fantasizing about a woman who was frightened by a perfectly proper and perfectly courteous invitation to dinner and a concert.

I returned the calls. They both wanted to talk to me. Wouldn't take long. No, Patsy didn't have time for lunch. She had to be back to their home on Glenwood Drive when the "kiddies" came home from school. With the neighborhood like it is now, she didn't want them coming into an empty house.

Her presence in the house had not stopped her eldest son from buying drugs from the black kids of whom she was afraid. That was unfair and unjust, I told myself.

Ten o'clock tomorrow morning? Fine.

No, Ron didn't have time for dinner and a concert. Too much work in the parish. No, I don't expect you to drive up to this madhouse. What about a drink? Sherlock's Home? Tearing down the building? Really? A pity. Someone should demonstrate. Top of the Hancock? Fine.

Sometime between now and then I'd have to work out my position. I was caught between two sets of friends. Old friends and new friends. I'd have to decide which twosome to hurt—Nick and Eileen or Patsy and Ron.

Then it dawned on me that Nick and Eileen would not be hurt at all. Or angry or disappointed. I wasn't quite sure what to make of that insight.

And I didn't think at all about Ciara Kelly.

Until I fell asleep. She took full possession of my dreams. Pushy Irish bitch.

The next morning there was an envelope on my desk. "Delivered by hand to our switchboard, first thing this morning," my secretary remarked. "By a young woman . . ."

Mrs. Magner has worked for me since I came to the firm. Having successfully married off her own children, she now found me a new and interesting challenge.

The handwriting on the card, a photo of the black marble bust of James Joyce that American Express had erected in St. Stephen's Green on his centenary, was astonishingly cramped, not what I would have expected from such a gracious woman as Ciara Kelly. I had no trouble reading it, however:

"Picture me as looking as sad as himself. And him with

the excuse of bad eyes and me only the excuse of cold feet. I'm sorry. Ciara."

I looked up Dufficy's number, wanting to protect my romance from Mrs. Magner's well-meaning interest. If I had asked her to call and she had spoken to Ciara, my present uncertainty would dissolve.

Maybe I designed matters so it wouldn't dissolve.

"Dufficy's," said the low, rich, raspberries and cream voice that I instantly recognized.

"Ciara Kelly? Brendan Ryan."

"Is it now?"

"Do you know where Orchestra Hall is?"

"Isn't that the place where the symphony orchestra plays?"

"Woman, if you keep answering questions with a question, you might get a good spanking."

I couldn't believe that in my anxiety I had said something so dumb.

Her response was immediate. "Ah, wouldn't that be an interesting erotic experience now. But, so's not to push my luck, Brendan Ryan, and not really deserving a second chance, yes, I know where it is."

"There's a club on the top floor . . ."

"The Cliff Dwellers, is it, the one that just admitted women members?" She was giggling at me.

"Would you be wanting to know whether it's the Cliff Dwellers? Well, it is, woman, and if you want to get anything to eat before the concert you'd better be there at six."

"Could I meet you downstairs in the lobby?" Shy and plaintive now. "I promise. No more questions."

"The food isn't spectacular, but I made an appointment for late in the afternoon . . ."

"Serves me right enough. I'll eat everything that's put before me, like me mother taught me."

"See you then . . ."

"You're a desperate man, Brendan Ryan."

"What does that mean?"

"It's a compliment." She hung up before I could ask for more of an explanation.

Thus did I fall from grace.

Or maybe, I don't know, fall into grace.

two
ADORATION
OF THE
EARTH

7

"**D**o you realize what your revenge will do?" Patsy leaned forward, her fingers twisted together in agonized prayer, perhaps to the Sorrowful Mother, for whom she had had a great devotion as a little girl. "Not to King or to me but to the kiddies? Do you want to get back at us so badly that you'd destroy their future?"

We were sitting across from one another, on two of the easy chairs I had arranged around the Sheraton table in my office—for relaxed conversations with clients worried about the IRS.

None of us had aged more dramatically than Patsy. All that remained of the cute little tyke, the child from a Walt Disney film, whom I began adoring the first day of the first grade, were the glowing brown eyes, and now the glow was from pain, not from enthusiasm. She wore jeans, a sweatshirt, and a Windbreaker, looking in our prestigious law offices like she might be a welfare mother or a battered wife. In a way she was both, I suppose. Her figure was as well-shaped as a sack of potatoes, her face puffy and spent, her hair disorderly, her shoes scuffed. Everything about her said, "I am a martyr for my kiddies. I devote so much of my life to them that I have no time to take care of myself."

Patsy always needed a cause. Now she had one that was inexhaustible. She needed to sacrifice herself for others, and the "kiddies" were the unchallengeable others.

"I don't want revenge, Patsy," I said wearily.

Women at forty, Catherine Curran—who was approaching that turning point—had insisted vigorously at lunch a couple of months back, don't have to fall apart, not unless they want to. Certainly not, Eileen had agreed, and they want to usually because of a need to deny their sexuality.

"Is a million dollars worth the lives of five children?" She rummaged through her old and littered purse, found a partially used tissue, and dabbed at her eyes. "Do you hate us that much?"

Almost as though I had committed the crime by permitting her husband to steal my money.

Why had she married King? In 1962 that's what a woman did when she left college, especially if your closest friend was "practically engaged" and there was a boy who wanted to marry you. If Jean were dating someone like King, I imagine it would occur to me that he was not a very good marital prospect. In those days, however, I agreed with my contemporaries that King was bright, lots of fun, with sleek, dark Tyrone Power good looks, and a surefire success. All he needed was to find a woman who would make him settle down and straighten out.

Marriage was just the thing for John King Sullivan. Surely his parents thought so. Patsy would finish the molding of the man that they had begun. Patsy's parents also were enthused about the marriage, even though both bride and groom were just twenty. They were, I think, more impressed by the wealth of King's father than they were by King's evident alcohol addiction. In any meaning the word may have, he was an alcoholic by his twentieth birthday, despite the implicit conspiracy in the neighborhood to pretend that he was not.

Madonna told me many years later that Patsy lost her

nerve a few weeks before the wedding and went over to the rectory to call it off. Incredibly, the priest she talked to (not the curate of our teens, who once remarked that a sign of a successful parish was the number of canceled weddings every year) persuaded her to give King the second chance for which he pleaded. That night King solemnly swore that he would stop drinking the day after their wedding. Poor Patsy believed him. Maybe King believed himself.

"I'm not going to try to regain any of the money, Patsy," I said, arriving at my decision as I talked to her. "I've told my attorney . . ."

"That hateful Nick Curran, he's always envied King. . . ." She twisted the tissue in her restless fingers.

I could not imagine anything further from the truth.

"I've told them that we will drop all civil action. The money doesn't make any difference to me."

"You'll still talk to the grand jury." The glow in her eyes was accusing and contemptuous.

I shifted uncomfortably in my chair and played with the sailboat model from the table. "I'm an officer of the court, Patsy. I don't want to talk to the grand jury. If the United States Attorney asks me to, however, I don't see how as a lawyer and a citizen I can refuse."

"You've always been one for high principles, haven't you?" she snapped bitterly. "Do you know what a trial will do to my kiddies?"

I thought to myself that it probably wouldn't make their lives much worse.

"There won't be a trial, Pat. There'll be a plea bargain and King will be placed on probation."

"With a courtroom scene and more headlines and it will be all your fault."

Patsy had acquired at least one skill in twenty-two years of marriage: now she knew how to hate.

Could she have "shaped up" King as everyone had confidently predicted she would at the wedding banquet at the Martinique on 95th Street—the best site her parents could afford?

A pretty, intelligent bride seems to have all the cards on her wedding day. If she'd said postpone the wedding for a year and prove to me you can stay sober, maybe he would have shaped up. Or if after marriage she had been willing to play her ace—stop drinking or I'll leave you—King might have changed.

Yet who is to say that King had the strength of character to respond to such demands? There was room for only one strong person in the family in which he was reared—his father. The difference between him and my wife, I tell myself now, is that Madonna might have been able to learn the self-discipline necessary for maturity if she had the motivation. King didn't even have the raw material from which character can be built.

I am in no position to be critical of Patsy. I did little to help Madonna—and she would have denied that any change was necessary in her character. Indeed, her version of our marriage was that after twenty years of trying to make a man out of me, she gave it up as a bad job.

What do you do to "shape up" a spouse? Neither Patsy nor I had learned the answer to that question. I knew I had failed Madonna, though I didn't know how. Did Patsy feel that she had failed King? Was her dedication to the kiddies a form of expiation?

"I'd walk out on the whole lot of them," Madonna told me contemptuously. "I wouldn't sacrifice myself for a drunken husband and a pack of brats."

Sure enough. Madonna decided not to sacrifice herself for me or for one child.

"It will be very quiet," I tried to reassure her. "Don Roscoe only wants publicity when he looks good."

When he goes after black basketball stars like Hurricane Houston or politicians, not when he goes after commodities brokers whose families have been major contributors to the Republican party for decades.

"Maddie is right about you." She leapt out of her chair and stormed towards the office door. "You have no balls. I hope you enjoy your yacht. Think of my kiddies while you're out there, and what you're doing to the man who was your best friend all your life."

I groaned softly to myself and walked down to Eileen's office. She was studying a law journal.

Eileen's office is sufficiently like the others in our for-

tress at Jackson and LaSalle so that you will know she is
indeed a member of the firm, and sufficiently different so
that you will know she is a woman member of the firm. The
carpet is beige, the desk walnut, the law journals somberly
imposing. But light blue and yellow sunbursts by Catherine
Curran decorate either wall, and the chairs and couch are
covered in the same color fabric—whether the sunbursts or
the chairs came first is a question she refuses to answer. In
addition to the sunbursts two miniature woodcuts of womanly nudes in dawn colors hang on the wall opposite her
desk; since you can't see the models' faces, you don't know
whether one might be Eileen—and she won't tell you. (I've
been afraid to study them too closely, but, knowing a little
of her sometimes unusual sense of humor, I wouldn't be
surprised if she were both models.) The prints are delicate
and far from obscene. But the model has a lovely body, and
it is hard not to turn around and stare at them.

She denies that it is psychological warfare.

"No reading glasses?" I asked her, ignoring the nudes
as I did habitually.

"Contacts. Part of the new deal with Red." She was
wearing a seersucker maternity dress and looking fresh and
self-contained, a woman for whom pregnancy was an
honor, not a burden.

"His idea?"

"Course not," she grinned. "Did I see Patsy Sullivan
rush by my door? Poor Brendan."

"I've made a decision, Eileen. No civil suits. I'll testify
before the grand jury under subpoena."

"Fine." Why had I expected her to be critical? "I hope
that satisfied her?"

"No, it didn't."

"Poor Brendan. I suppose you're being blamed for
harming the kiddies?"

"Yep."

"Poor kiddies. I worry about her. She's a manic-
depressive, you know. Probably in a manic state now."

"Can't they treat that with drugs these days?" I sank
into one of her chairs and poured myself a cup of her always
warm chamomile tea.

"My sister, Mary Kate the Shrink, says such people can

be treated if they will take their pills every day. But at the high and the low point of the cycle they often won't take the pills."

"Poor Patsy."

"Poor everyone."

Several hours later I was sitting in the sleek bar at the top of the John Hancock Center, brooding over the changing colors of the lake far below and listening to the well-bred late-afternoon hum of executives with well-padded expense accounts and well-padded expensive women. I was drinking soda water, and the pastor of St. Jarlath's, Father Ron Crowley, was already on his third vodka martini. I might have matched him with my usual serious drink, John Jameson's straight up, but I was having supper shortly with Ciara Kelly and I'd need to have my wits about me for that.

"How come you're not drinking?" Ron gestured expansively.

"I'm going to the concert this evening."

"You don't have a date, do you?" He laughed crudely. "Some nice, comfortable, matronly widow? No, certainly not. You always were a loser with women, weren't you, Bren? Like you are with everything else."

"Course not." I laughed with him. No, not a comfortable widow at all.

The sun was slipping behind the high-rises, turning Lake Michigan into a golden plate, sparkling as though someone had carelessly scattered several handfuls of gems on it.

Ron looked like a colonel in British India who had eaten too much mutton, drunk too much claret, and gambled too much money at late-night games in the officers' club. His face was permanently flushed, his long and unkempt blond hair was laced untidily with a dirty gray, his eyes were bloodshot, his fingers trembled when they were not wrapped around the martini glass, his black clerical shirt, stuffed with stomach, hung out over his belt. The dashing young clerical radical of a few years ago looked fifteen years older than he actually was.

I remembered very clearly the night he told us he was going to be a priest. He had left early for Notre Dame because his athletic scholarship required him to be there for freshman football practice.

It was at dusk in mid-August of 1960 that he drove up to the park at 100th Street in his VW convertible. The park was kind of an oversize drugstore corner, where you smoked and waited for your friends and checked out the girls and tried to find out where everyone was going and drank beer and made out after dark.

Ron climbed out of the car, the perfectly conditioned college linebacker, thigh muscles bulging against his white bermuda shorts, arm and chest muscles bulging against his green Notre Dame T-shirt.

"Back from football practice?" Madonna asked uneasily. "You didn't get cut?"

"I quit." He leaned over the side of her T-bird convertible (the new one with the automatic hardtop cover) and spoke with the same quiet self-confidence that had made him captain of the team and outstanding senior at St. Ignatius. "Madonna, guys, I'm going to the seminary. I've always known that I was meant to be a priest. I can't keep running from God. I hope you don't mind."

We embraced him, shook his hand, congratulated him. In those days in the Neighborhood, there was no greater calling than the priesthood. Even if it broke your heart, as it did break the hearts of both Madonna and King, you still celebrated when one of your friends announced that he had a "vocation."

Later that night, King admitted his skepticism to me over the beginnings of his second six-pack: "He won't last. He found out in the practices at N.D. that he'll never be the all-American his father was. So he chickened. He thinks he can surpass the old man by being the one thing the old man never was."

My unvoiced doubts pertained to women. Ron in those days was breathtakingly handsome. Despite Madonna's vigilant eye, young women threw themselves at him with dizzy recklessness. Ron was not immune to them either. He dressed at the leading edge of fashion, the first one of our generation to show up at Sunday Mass in a charcoal gray suit with a pink shirt (yellow the following week). Women of every age adored him. While he never exceeded the line that Madonna had drawn as the limit of their sexual playfulness, he confided often to King and me that there were others who were not nearly so strict.

Maybe, I said to myself, it's either celibacy or polygamy for Ron. Monogamy would be too difficult.

Perhaps King was right about Ron's motivation—it was a surprisingly sophisticated insight for him. But he was wrong in his prediction: Ron did stay in the seminary, sweated out the terrible turbulence of the Church in the sixties, and was ordained just after I came home from Vietnam. His charm and energy and zeal made him a marked man, and the era made him a radical. He volunteered for the inner city, fought with his pastor, whom he charged with racism even though the man had been in "black work" for twenty-five years, volunteered for Latin America, came back as an advocate of Hispanics and the "Third World," was assigned to the Peace and Justice Office of the diocese, labored mightily at the "Call to Action" conference in 1976 (an attempted coup of lower-level bureaucrats—claiming to be the "people"—against their bishops), and became a champion of "liberation." There was not a militant cause, not a protest meeting, not a crusade in which he was not prominent.

He wore himself out, running down his enormous physical energy, and took off six months for a sabbatical to "pray and reflect." In fact he used the time to learn the dynamics of "community organization" and returned, sounding like a Marxist, to take on the Cook County Regular Democratic organization. He endorsed Jane Byrne for mayor and helped her in the primary, which no one thought she was going to win until the snows came. She dumped him, as eventually she dumped everyone, before the general election. Then he went to work for the American Civil Liberties Union and gave that up when he found that he would never comprehend the dynamics of Jewish family infighting, which constitute the politics of that organization.

No one denied his sincerity, energy, or dedication, even when they disagreed with the goals of his most recent crusade. Many priests who would not think of walking on a picket line admired his integrity and courage. Cardinal Cronin, who must have found Ron's simple analyses maddening, nonetheless visited him when he was in the county jail. ("You're a goddamn fool, Ron," the cardinal was quoted as shouting at him, "but you're my goddamn fool.")

"I mean it, Brenny." He frowned heavily to indicate that it was him talking and not merely the vodka. "It's natural that men should dominate women. We always have. It's structured into the nature of things. They're weaker and we're stronger. Okay, the world is slightly civilized now and we have to pretend that everyone is equal, but deep down they want to be dominated. This feminism business is only a transient thing. You can't say that in public or there'd be hell to pay. But it's true. Anyway, they want to be dominated. It's in their nature. Find yourself a well-built widow and push her around a little. She'll love it."

Was this really the Catholic peace activist of a year ago? The militant civil rights and antiwar protester of the seventies? The "Third World" enthusiast so often celebrated in the pages of the *National Catholic Reporter*? Had the pastorate of a rich suburban parish completely transformed him, or was Ron a burned-out case?

"Doesn't that legitimate rape and sexual harassment?" I asked dubiously.

He quaffed half his martini at a single swallow. "No woman," he licked his lips, "is ever raped who doesn't want to be raped. You can't say that these days without offending the nutty nun feminists, but that's the way it is."

We had been discussing his problems in the parish, which, according to him, were the result of the necessity of tightening up after a "hyperpermissive" predecessor had let all authority collapse. "You can have only one boss, Brendan, you know that." The nuns who taught in his school, objecting to the "clear lines of responsibility" that he had laid down, were leaving. Good riddance to them. They would be replaced by nuns from Italy, who knew their place and would work for a lot less. Teach sound doctrine too. Would the well-educated and affluent parishioners of St. Jarlath's complain about grammar school teachers who could barely talk English and who had not attended American colleges? Too bad. Let them send their kids to the public schools.

"The trouble in your marriage, Brendan," he continued magisterially, "is that you were too soft on Madonna. If you had socked her in the chops a couple of times a year, everything would have been fine. She wanted that, you know, and you didn't have the guts to give it to her. Never treat a woman as an equal. They don't want it. They enjoy a good beating now and then. A belt on the mouth when she made one of her dumb comments would have been good for Madonna."

"She felt that candor was part of her appeal." Maybe he was right, but I was not the one to belt any woman on the mouth.

"Candor? Is that what you call it?" He reached for a handful of popcorn. "She'll be a crude loudmouth like her father until someone pounds it out of her."

I could still hardly believe what I was hearing. When Madonna walked out on me, Ron had rushed to console me, mostly by telling me how much Madonna had suffered through the years of the marriage. Her decision, he assured me, was much harder on her than it was on me, but it was a sign of maturity and self-possession. Now he was telling me that I should have belted her as often as necessary (which for the last several years might have been almost every day).

The 95th Bar darkened rapidly. A fast-moving line of clouds was racing in from the western suburbs, blotting out the sun. The lake turned amber, then purple, and then a threatening greenish black. I would have to hurry to Orchestra Hall if my carefully selected light gray suit and color-coordinated tie were not to be soaked before I had a chance to impress the woman.

"Now, about King ... No, I have to drive back.... Well, one more won't hurt.... What about you? ... No, you don't have a date tonight, do you. ... Sorry, only kidding. Anyway, about King. Do you understand how fragile he is now? The biopsies were negative, but the tests scared the daylights out of him. He knows it's time to settle down finally, if only for Patsy and the kids. He goes to AA every night and is really into it. He's pulling himself together, Brenny, and this time, with a little bit of luck, he's going to make it. Is your money so important that you want to endanger what might be his last chance?"

"I don't want the money back," I began.

"You do too." He dismissed my plea with a wave of his martini glass. "All you ever wanted was to be rich. And you've never forgiven him because Patsy loved him instead of you."

"I'm not bringing any civil actions." Perhaps, Ciara Kelly or not, I should order a Jameson's. "I will only testify before the grand jury if I am subpoenaed; there's no question of a trial; all Don Roscoe wants is a plea bargain to boost his conviction percentage. If you want to get King off the hook, talk to Roscoe."

"What will happen," he sat straight up in his chair like he was an appellate judge, "if you refuse to testify under subpoena?"

"I might be held in contempt of court and sent to jail."

"How likely is that?" he asked airily, as though it were unthinkable.

Did it finally come to that? Did friendship require that I run the risk of going to jail for a friend who had betrayed me? Was I willing to risk it? I suppose so, but I was no longer sure that King was my friend or ever had been.

Moreover, there was no danger of his being sent to prison.

"With Don Roscoe you can't tell. He has reason to want to get even with our firm."

"The American legal system is totally corrupt." He drained the martini glass. "It would not be sinful to disregard it."

So there was some radicalism still left—when the authority belonged to someone else.

"Far from perfect, but the best we have," I replied firmly.

"So you wouldn't go to jail to protect your friend? Wouldn't Jesus be willing to do that?"

"I'm not Jesus."

"You claim to be a follower of his, don't you?"

The group had decided that I was the criminal, not King, and that I should run the risk of jail in his place. It was a belief that approached lunacy. Yet all four of them now believed it absolutely. (I was sure that Madonna had cast her vote for conviction with the others.) The matter was so obvious to them that its self-evident truth was beyond discussion. I was to be the fall guy again.

No way. I had other things in my life now. Like Ciara Kelly. My Holy Grail.

"I've made my decision, Ron. It stands." The first time in my life since dating Eileen for the prom that I had stood up to them.

"God have mercy on you, Brendan." He shoved his empty glass out of the way, stood up heavily, and strode away from me with a briskness which was supposed to convey that I was not even worthy of contempt.

The effect was spoiled somewhat by the uncertainty of his weaving step and the trouble he had finding the elevators.

So I had at last broken with the group. It had taken long enough, heaven knows. I was astonished by the deterioration in Ron. I felt sorry for them. But I was not going down the same drain as they. Let the dead bury their dead; I bravely cited scripture to myself.

No one had told me about any biopsies for King. Friends indeed.

As I paid the bill, I glanced out at the now dark and somber lake and saw, or thought I saw, tombstones. Doom for me and my friends? Psychic nonsense. Maybe for them. But not for me.

I had a date, and my heart sang with joy.

A date with Ciara Kelly.

8

She was waiting for me in the lobby of Orchestra Hall. Ignoring the raindrops that were starting to fall, little wet mosquitoes stinging at my, I hoped, low-key sexy suit, I paused to admire her, to enjoy my desire for her, and to probe the quick but powerful sensation that she was carrying my son. . . . No, not my son, my child, gender unspecified.

She was wearing a tailored pinstripe white dress with a thick gray belt, emphasizing her slim waist, and gray buttons on the bodice, emphasizing her glorious torso. Her hair was still piled on top of her head, and her throat, framed in the V neck of the dress and adorned by a slender gold Celtic cross, was like the ivory in a Book of Kells print. There was a touch of makeup at her lips but no jewelry besides the cross. Elegance achieved at very modest cost.

I permitted myself to fantasize briefly about slowly removing her clothes. I had seen only two women naked in my life. She would be much more spectacular than either.

In none of these longings, images, and fantasies did issues of religion or morality arise. Having broken with my group, it seemed that I had almost abandoned the careful and precise sexual principles of my Catholic childhood. The only norm that mattered now was the command to make Ciara Kelly my woman.

I pushed open the door and entered the lobby. Her face lit up when she saw me. I had to strain to hear her soft words.

"Ah, Brendan Ryan, don't you look dapper now? Sure, a person would think you were dining with some grand lady. . . ."

"I am."

"You're not supposed to say things like that." She flushed and turned away. "And myself such a shy Irish biddy that I'm afraid to ride up to that Cliff Dwellers place by myself."

"I'll be proud to walk in with you. Every head will turn."

"Go 'long with you now." A gentle poke at my arm.

As we rode up the elevator in faintly embarrassed silence, I realized again that ours was a mutual attraction. She was as powerfully attracted to me as I was to her. Unaccountably, the woman liked me. She was as ill at ease with her agitated emotions as I was with mine. We were both reckless gamblers, throwing caution to the winds for perhaps the first time in our lives.

I tried to imagine practicing Ron Crowley's strategy on her. Maybe Ron was right. Maybe Madonna needed more pushing around. It wouldn't work for five seconds with Ciara Kelly. She did not wear an armor of solid muscle as did Eileen Kane. On the contrary, she was if anything soft as well as pale; in a few years she would need to worry about exercise should she want to keep her figure. Yet she was a big, strong woman. Belt her in the mouth and she'd belt you back. Hard.

I laughed at the absurdity without thinking that she would hear me.

"I amuse you, do I, Mr. Ryan?" She cocked a contentious eyebrow as we left the elevator.

"I spoke with a man this afternoon, who advocated keeping women in line by belting them in the mouth."

"And you considered the advisability of that policy in the present instance." She preceded me up the stairs to the top floor of the building, the "Attic" as the club was called in its early years, after it was founded by a group of Chicago architects, most of whose names are now legendary. She turned her head back to keep an eye on me. "And decided that it would not work at all."

"A man could get hurt." The rear view of her, which I had not previously considered in such elaborate detail, was in its own way as interesting as the front view, a set of complementary geometric curves that demanded careful study and exploration.

"He could indeed." She stopped at the door of the club, fascinated yet hesitant, a little girl entering a new school. "This is a grand place!"

"More like an English club, I am told, than are many of the English clubs."

"None of them have that grand lake out there, smiling at us like a mother with her child. And no watercolor paintings of sailboats either." She glanced around the paneled walls of the crowded room. " 'Tis a fine place to be taking a woman to dinner, and herself a coward when you asked her."

"Have you sailed recently?" I took her arm and guided her through the tables to our place in the corner near the book rack.

"Not in years. I'm terrible out of condition, to tell the truth."

"Would you like to sail on the *Brigid* with me on Sunday?" I pulled out the chair for her. It was a question that in my campaign strategy was not programmed until tomorrow.

She watched me very seriously as I sat down across from her, considering her answer carefully. "I'd like that, Brendan Ryan." She nodded solemnly. "I'd like that very much." A quick grin banished the seriousness. "Sure I'll be so dreadful clumsy for want of practice that you'll throw me over the side."

You're as much in love, woman, as I am. I agree. Hang the consequences.

"Against such a chilly possibility, would you like a drink now to warm you up?"

She glanced around the room with mock slyness. "I don't suppose that such a terrible grand place would have a wee drop of John Jameson's?"

"On the rocks?"

She looked at me in mock horror. "Do I seem altogether uncivilized?"

"Only altogether lovely." I felt my face grow warm. Hers turned crimson to match.

We toasted each other with the tiny shot glasses. "Slainte, Brendan Ryan."

"Slainte, Ciara Kelly."

I don't remember much of the dinner conversation. Her voice was so soft that I had to lean close to hear her words.

She had, it seemed, four different dialects—thick West of
Ireland, Dublin literate, British Isles educated, and plain
old American with softer consonants and richer "a" sounds
than you would hear from a Chicago native. She moved
among them unself-consciously, depending on how vulnerable she felt. The dense brogue, sometimes almost untrans-
latable, correlated with a flushed face and the deep Irish
sigh that suggests to those not familiar with it the advent of
a serious asthma attack.

I learned that she was thirty-four years old, a few more
years of life behind her than I had thought. She offered
nothing more about her background, and, despite my nervous curiosity, I resolved not to ask.

Yet I wondered again that night why a woman of
obvious intelligence and education would be working as
a sales clerk for a salary which, judging by her inexpensive
clothes, could not amount to much. A tiny cancer of suspicion gnawed at the back of my brain: she knows you're
wealthy.

We had a second drink, rather to my surprise. "Would
you be wanting another?"

"Well, to prepare for all the dancing, I suppose I
should." Much like I suppose I should really say the Stations of the Cross after the Rosary—a moral and religious
obligation.

Since it was Solti's last week before he returned to his
other jobs in Europe, the Cliff Dwellers was filled, but I recognized none of my friends. Moreover, when we were
shown to our seats in the hall, none of the regulars around
me seemed to be there. At the end of the season, tickets are
often exchanged or given away. Somehow I was relieved. I
didn't want to have to explain Ciara Kelly just yet. In days
to come I avoided restaurants where I was known or might
be recognized, telling myself that it was not yet time to display her.

And perhaps, from what I know now, because she was
not there to display.

We paused again at the door of the concert hall while
Ciara drank in the great ivory and red room.

"Like it?"

"It's too nice for someone such as me," she whispered, as if she were in church.

"Go along with you, woman. The best is none too good for you."

"Listen to him, will you?"

Safely in our place, halfway back on the main floor center, she studiously consumed the program notes.

"Do you come often to the concerts, Brendan Ryan?"

"Not too often the last couple of years. I have season tickets, but my wife lost interest in classical music and I didn't like coming alone."

Sir Georg appeared to the usual enthusiastic applause and was greeted with a whispered "Darlin' man" from my companion.

She sat straight upright as he raised his baton and leaned forward tensely to catch every note of music, every nuance of direction. The Beethoven overture caused her to clench her fists and smile. Stravinsky's masterpiece seemed to take possession of her soul.

After the first few bars, she clutched my hand frantically, as if I were to keep her from joining the priestess in her mad dance, which was to bring the fertility of spring alive again. Stravinsky's wild, frenzied rush of spring vitality appeared to be pouring into her body and flowing out of it.

Well, Brendan, you've found yourself an odd one.

When Solti finished, with a military snap of his baton and a polished imperial bow to the orchestra, then wheeled to face the cheering audience, she crumpled like a used tissue; her damp hand slipped out of mine; and she looked at me out of the corner of one watery gray eye.

"Haven't I been making a terrible fool out of myself now?" The West of Ireland brogue was so thick that at first I thought she was speaking in Gaelic.

"I think you reacted just the way Sir Georg and old Igor wanted you to react."

We stood with the rest of the crowd and yelled for half a dozen more bows from conductor and orchestra.

I suggested that we stretch our legs in the lobby, and Ciara, still pale and limp from the music, gratefully agreed.

Solid sheets of rain were pounding the pavement of Michigan Avenue, and the lions on the Art Institute across the street were intermittently illuminated by blue phosphorescent flashes of lightning. Thunder rumbled almost immediately after the lightning; the storm was above us and moving out over the lake.

"It'll be over before we leave; it's not one of your Irish all-day rains."

She nodded, still in the grip of Stravinsky's manic dance.

I glanced around the lobby, an Irish politician casing the house at a wake. No one I knew.

Except Madonna. And in tow a certain notorious Chicago gossip columnist, surely alcoholic and rumored homosexual, who specialized in mean and picky hatchet jobs. I turned away, hoping she would not notice me.

No such luck. In a few moments Madonna jabbed my arm. "I knew you'd find a girlfriend." In the same tone as if she'd said she knew I was going to take up cocaine. "Aren't you going to introduce us?"

Her diets, health food, and jogging had made her not thin, but emaciated. Once a lovely, slender woman with intense sex appeal, she had become a scrawny bird of prey with sharp, hawkish features caked in powdery beige makeup; brittle, strawlike hair, and the bent-forward-from-the-shoulders posture of a praying mantis.

I was embarrassed, angry, and yet heartbroken for her. In the name of looking younger than her age, she had made herself look older. As Ron had destroyed his physical attractiveness with neglect, Madonna had destroyed hers with excessive care.

I made the introductions with as much aplomb as I could muster under the circumstances. I presented Madonna as "Madonna Clifford," the name she used in her North Shore art gallery advertisements.

So there would be no mistake, she quickly added, "Although we were married for almost twenty years, he's ashamed to admit it."

"Oh." Ciara was ashen.

"Did you like the Stravinsky, Madonna?" I tried to sound pleasant.

"Stravinsky, havinsky." She dismissed my small talk as the kind of ineffectual dodge she had come to expect from me. "You're welcome to him, my dear. Maybe you can make a man out of him. I couldn't. You've got your work cut out for you." And then, turning to me, "Kind of young, isn't she, Brendan? I figured you'd go for someone fat all right, but much older. See you around, my dears."

She bounced away, trying unsuccessfully to create the ambience of the witty, frothy woman about town.

I was wishing that one of the thunderbolts would strike me and carry me off, perhaps to Alpha Centauri.

"I'm sorry, Brendan," Ciara said quietly. The first time she hadn't added my last name.

"Why should you be sorry?" I snapped irritably.

"Because you've been unfairly hurt."

"Thanks, Ciara," I relented. "Madonna has always prided herself on her candor."

"That's what it's called, is it now?"

"She hasn't always been that way." I rose to my presumed wife's defense. "She was once a sweet and lovely girl. Life has not been good to her."

"Poor woman." Followed by the prolonged asthmatic sigh. "Still, I can see why you sought the annulment." Her various brogues were replaced by plain American.

"It was her idea, not mine." We joined the crowds walking back into the auditorium for the rest of the concert.

"Really?" Ciara was startled. "Ah, but it's none of my business now, is it?"

I had no answer for her. During the Mozart concerto, however—early Mozart and light and happy—it was my turn to capture her hand and hold it. There was not the faintest hint of resistance.

Maybe if I had known what would happen to Madonna and had heard Ron's advice years earlier, I thought, I would have listened to him. No, there had to be a better way. She had failed me, surely. But I had failed her too. If Ciara Kelly was thinking I was a bad risk or doubting my masculinity because I didn't walk away from such witchery, she might very well be correct in her judgments.

The storm had indeed passed over, leaving in its wake the rich, earthy, fertile smell of spring. The last of my senses had been captured by my new woman.

"You're going sailing with me on Sunday." I ticked it off on my fingers.

" 'Tis true."

"And we're going back to Orchestra Hall on Saturday for a whole evening of Mozart." Another finger ticked.

"Ah, are we now?"

"Aren't we now?"

"Who's answering with questions this time? . . . All right, don't hit me. . . . We are."

"So what are we doing tomorrow night?"

"Well . . ." She seemed to be searching for an excuse.

"Well . . ." I persisted.

"I see in the papers that this place called The Body Politic is doing Brian Friel's *Volunteers*. You know, the *Freedom of the City* man."

"And *Philadelphia Here I Come* and *Translations*, which they did last year."

"Well . . ." Her face took on an expression of leprechaun craftiness.

"Well . . ."

"Well, would you ever think we might see that?"

"I think it might be arranged."

She clapped her hands with innocent enthusiasm. "I'd enjoy it ever so much. . . . And there I go, sounding English. Ever so much indeed!"

She lived at Chestnut Place, a modestly priced red brick rental skyscraper. There was no invitation up to her room. I would have been astonished if there had been.

"Thank you very much, Brendan Ryan." She extended her hand to me. " 'Twas a glorious evening." She smiled gentle approval of me and everything I stood for. "You're a desperate man altogether."

"Thank you, Ciara Kelly, for making it glorious." I held her hand and kissed her forehead. "I'll see you tomorrow."

She slipped away quickly so I wouldn't see her face. I was sure, however, she was crying.

As I finish writing these words, I briefly think to myself that Madonna met her. She can confirm that Ciara Kelly really existed.

Then I realize how foolish and futile such a thought is.

9

"I do not intend to waste the rest of my life," Madonna's face was warped in anger and hatred, a harpy swooping down on its prey, "enhancing your public image by pretending to be nothing more than a good wife and mother."

We were perhaps two hours into Madonna's announcement, after Jean's graduation party, that she wanted a divorce. There was not much discussion, only bombardment. Madonna was now a middle-aged Barbie doll, not unattractive certainly, but with a petulant frown permanently frozen into the lines of her face.

"I thought you were happy in the wife and mother role," I said wearily, now hoping that the nightmare would soon end and I could quietly leave. She had carved out the role for herself, or so it had seemed to me.

"How could any woman be happy," her lips twisted into a contemptuous sneer, "married to a man without balls? Do you realize how lousy a lover you are, Brendan? You're as useless in bed as you are on the tennis courts. I've taken lovers ever since you went away to your goddamn war. I have a right to sexual fulfillment. And, while I'm at it, I had my tubes tied after Jean. So there never was a chance for the stupid son you wanted."

I didn't altogether believe her. I'm still not sure whether she was telling the truth or merely tormenting me.

In the previous exchange I had been denounced as a "patriarchal chauvinist" because I wouldn't let her pursue her own career—despite the fact that I was the one who raised the career question in the early years of marriage until she finally told me she never wanted to hear the word again. A "patriarchal chauvinist without balls"? Perhaps somewhat contradictory, but anger, not logic, was Madonna's agenda.

I was overwhelmed by her attack. Yet I could not take it seriously because I suspected that it had all been carefully practiced in the Femtherapy group of which she was a member. The script was being acted out now, not with me as the relevant audience, but the group to which she would report triumphantly the next day. I was nothing more than a witness at the dress rehearsal. They would swarm around, hug and kiss her, and celebrate her freedom.

And they would congratulate her on forcing me to listen to "every last word."

I was sad because I had loved her deeply once, or thought I did, and because I had thought that someday, somehow, our marriage would "work out." I was resigned because I knew that there was now no saving the relationship; Madonna might have second thoughts later, when she came down off her emotional high and when she lost interest in the Femtherapy group, but she was much too proud ever to admit a mistake. And, finally, I was relieved; I would no longer have to bear her noisy contempt.

So I recited my lines in the script with little enthusiasm. Should we not try again? She was sick of trying with me; it was a waste of her precious time. Maybe we ought to go into family therapy? I was the one who needed the therapy, not her. Perhaps we might talk to a priest? She had talked to Father Ron, and he said it was about time that she drew the line. And so on.

Eventually it was over—at the end a screaming and crying session with Jean in which she sided with her mother—and I was out in the mild spring night. Alone and guilty because I did not feel more pain.

I ought not to be thinking that I was well rid of her. The tempting thought, however, would not go away.

As I look over these pages I am painfully aware that my initial intention to be fair and objective about Madonna has only been paid lip service. I must be at pains to explain that

she was not a ranting monster. She was a lonely, frightened, angry woman. I was a convenient target for her loneliness, fear, and anger; and a fair target, too, because I did
nothing to protect her from those devastating emotions. Indeed, I hardly recognized them in the early years of our
marriage. Her mother and father might have been more appropriate targets—they were the ones who treated Madonna as a mirror to reflect their own glory from the moment of her conception. She was never able to see Lourdes
and Melvin Clifford as her enemies. On the contrary, they
were always her loyal allies in the long battle against, as
she saw it, the real problem: her inept and inadequate husband.

How does a husband become adequate in a conflict
with a wife filled with unperceived self-contempt? And how
does a father prevent such self-contempt from being
transmitted to his daughter? For Melissa Jean was designed to reflect Madonna's glory in the same way Madonna reflected Lourdes's glory. What else does one do with
a daughter?

Yet I did fail Madonna. She came to marriage seeking
value as a person, though she would not have said that. She
did not find it. For that I am to blame.

I never did court her or propose to her in the conven-
tional sense. I had been her number-two beau through the
high school years, to be called on without apology when
Ron was unavailable. She cried on my shoulder, not his.
And she sought my advice when she was uneasy because of
his roving eye.

Since two beaus were required for each "deb" (the
word was never used), I was her second escort at the first
Presentation Ball, a Catholic cotillion set up in opposition
to the Passavant Cotillion. It seemed to Ron and me that it
was a dreary and pompous affair, justified by frequent references to the "Mrs. Frank J. Lewis Milk Fund" for whose
purposes it was alleged to be directed. Madonna accepted
readily enough our contempt for the heavy solemnities and
at the same time accepted her mother's ecstatic protestations that the day Madonna was accepted for the Ball was
the happiest day in her life.

We were buddies and friends, a more relaxed relationship than lovers. "I don't know what I'd do without you, Brendan," she said after a long and tearful session about rumors that Ron was weary of her.

"You'll never have to do without me," I said manfully.

I can't say that I was in love with her in those days. I wasn't in love with anyone in the sense of being emotionally preoccupied with them, except for Eileen during the prom weeks. My group was a locus of commitment rather than a source of satisfaction.

Not being able to write to Ron at the seminary, she poured out letters from school to me, long, witty, painful letters. She was homesick, the other girls were snobs and immoral besides, the teachers were drips, the rules were outrageous, the nuns were pathetically old-fashioned. I suppose the truth was that at St. Mary's she was merely another freshman and not the center of everyone else's existence.

Gradually, when it became reasonably certain that Ron would stay in the seminary, we became lovers, not, heaven save us as good Catholics in those days, that we went to bed together. Our exchanges of affection became more passionate—making out, necking, petting, as such activities were called in those days. I enjoyed such interludes enormously, more, I confess, than much of the sex that took place between us after marriage. At first I was the initiator, a young male animal on the prowl. Then gradually Madonna became the aggressor. Her lips were warm and demanding, her body firm and eager, the line beyond which we could not go increasingly flexible and porous. She was hungry for as much love as I could give. And then some.

We confessed our sins on Saturday so we could receive Communion on Sunday, dutifully promised the priest we'd stay away from the occasion of sin, and fell from grace in a final frenzy of affection as she boarded the South Shore at 111th Street for her return to her hated college.

So it came to be taken for granted that we would marry. While I did not formally propose and was taken aback when Lourdes Clifford began to discuss the size of the wedding party at dinner in September of 1962 (Madonna, having kept her promise of two years of college, was now free to work in her father's office, and we were celebrating her "joining the team"), the picture of life with Madonna was so attractive that I saw no reason to object. My only stubbornness was that we would not be married till I graduated and that I had a military obligation.

No one seemed to mind. Only many years later did I come to understand that in the Clifford house, the wedding as a festive celebration was what mattered, not the physical or personal relationship that came after.

My parents and I were swept, unprotestingly, aside as Lourdes and Madonna planned the production—twenty-six in the wedding party, a bouquet of roses affixed to every pew, seventeen priests, including five monsignors, in the sanctuary, trumpets and violins in the choir loft, a papal blessing to be announced by the pastor, bridesmaids in pink, groomsmen in pink-tinged summer formals, over a thousand guests at the South Shore Country Club, a wedding not to be forgotten.

Heavily girdled and smelling of a mixture of strong gin and stronger Chanel, Lourdes charged through the preparations, wedding protocol book in one hand, checkbook in the other, with a martyred weariness that said someone had to assume responsibility lest both families be humiliated by gaucherie.

It was hard to tell who was the audience for which the spectacular was being staged. To whom was it necessary to prove that the Cliffords were paragons of taste, sensibility, and etiquette? To listen to Lourdes and her flustered, harried daughter, one would have thought that the jury was the whole city of Chicago, all of whose citizens were watching with a jaundiced eye for the slightest breach of propriety or the faintest hint that cost was an important consideration.

In fact, the audience was the wives of the Neighborhood and of Dr. Clifford's colleagues, who had already decided from advance reports that the Clifford/Ryan nuptials would be a tastelessly extravagant binge and came seeking only evidence for this prejudice. They were not disappointed.

Time forces charity upon me. The nouveau riche are nouveau because they have just made their money and they are not altogether sure they will keep it. When Mel Clifford was growing up in the 1930s and struggling through medical school while he worked a largely mythical sanitary district job, the family did not have a bathtub or a shower in their apartment in Bridgeport. They used the single old-fashioned tub in his grandparents' flat on the first floor. The doctor's mother and father never moved away from that building. One of the first things Mel did when he came home from the war, wounded on Guam (according to a rumor, by falling out of a jeep), was to buy a totally new plumbing installation for the building.

We were the children of the professional generation that started late because of the Depression and the War and then in a few short years became richer than they had dreamed possible at places like Guam, where it did not seem they would live till morning. Their displays of wealth (and most were not as egregious as the Cliffords') were meant for themselves more than for others, as proof that finally after decades of trying, the Irish had become respectable.

It took another generation to realize that respectability wasn't worth the candle.

We who were their children presented them with a dilemma. On the one hand, spectacles like the Presentation Ball and Madonna's wedding demonstrated to the whole world that the Irish now had a bathtub in every dwelling unit and more besides. On the other, there was the gnawing worry that, not having been forged in the crucible of the Depression, we would not understand suffering and not have the strength of character that had been necessary for our parents' climb to affluence and success.

No one dared to say publicly what my father said privately one night to Ned Ryan on one of those rare occasions when the "other" Ryans supped at our house:

"Not many of these folks can admit that they lucked out because they happened to be the right age in the right time and place."

"Not luck but pluck." Kate Ryan grinned over her sherry glass.

"Not Catholics but Calvinists," Ned sighed. "Well, it's a lot easier to admit that your parents were lucky."

I suppose, finally, the "other" Ryans (who were not invited to our wedding; neither Lourdes nor Madonna would hear of it) were the ultimate target of our production. We would show those rich Irish who had a generation head start on us that we were as good as they were and that we were catching up with them.

Unfortunately for the satisfaction of my in-laws, the "other" Ryans didn't know there was a race.

There was nothing in the protocol books that prohibited the Shannon Rovers Irish Warpipes band from escorting us into church, or green, white, and orange ice cream representing the Irish tricolor in addition to the wedding cake for dessert, or the Notre Dame victory march as the bride and groom progressed to the head table at the reception. Nor did the books prevent Notre Dame motifs in the dining hall decorations—banners, flags, seals, pennants, even though I had gone to Loyola and Madonna had quit St. Mary's in disgust without finishing her exams at the end of the sophomore year.

Nor did the books dictate that the Cliffords ought not to leak the week before to everyone who would listen that the cost of the wedding was in excess of $20,000.

My bride was a frazzled emotional disaster area the last weeks of our courtship. Like her mother, she suggested by her frantic behavior that it was necessitated by my family's lack of concern for what "people will say."

We saw little of each other in those final weeks; Madonna was so angry at my irresponsibility that she would not speak to me at the rehearsal and the rehearsal dinner.

Did I have any second thoughts during these frenzied preparations? No more, I suppose, than most young men would under similar circumstances. I enjoyed wonderful fantasies of Madonna in bed, fantasies in which my partner was completely different from the pale, chain-smoking young woman whose mother had driven her to daily attacks of nausea. I consoled myself with the bridegroom's usual self-deception that after marriage I would not have to share my wife with her mother. I considered with grave face and little thought my father's delicate question of whether this was what I really wanted. Eileen was already married to Red Kane, hastily enough to cause uplifted eyebrows among Madonna's friends. What else or who else might I have wanted?

I knelt in the rear corner of St. Praxides for Eileen's wedding. Redmond Kane did not look eight years older than Eileen. He was handsome, attentive, and hopelessly in love with her.

I mentioned my secret presence to Eileen a few weeks ago at lunch.

"Oh, there was nothing wrong with Red. The problem was always me. For twenty years. I'm making it up to him now, poor man."

"Does he accept that scenario?"

Her gemlike green eyes softened. "He thinks it the other way around, poor misguided soul." She chuckled. "It makes for interesting times . . . and elderly pregnancies."

With Eileen married, there seemed no reason not to proceed to the altar with Madonna. Perhaps I was trapped by a series of decisions I had previously made—or more precisely refused to make. The point is that if I was trapped, I wanted to be trapped. Or more accurately did not want not to be trapped.

The Church was no help. The parish priests, having decided long before the day of our monstrosity that they lacked the conviction and the stamina to resist nouveau riche brides and mothers, did their best to avoid Lourdes and Madonna whenever they saw them bearing down on the rectory with tight lips and fevered eyes.

We attended a pre-Cana conference, by way of marriage preparation, at which a priest preached abstract theology, a doctor spoke of technical sex, and a married couple reported with cloying sweetness how much fun it was to have children. Madonna wrote out lists of things to do, and I delighted in convoluted images of Madonna undressing. We hurriedly filled out the ecclesiastical forms in the rectory the night of the rehearsal, having dragged a curate away from his Young Christian Students meeting with insincere apologies and the excuse that there had been no other time for these formalities. He was barely civil to us as we assured him separately and together that we were entering marriage freely, that we understood its nature and purpose, that we had never been married before, that we intended to have children, and that we would not practice birth control.

Madonna was still not speaking to me. Hence she could only sigh noisily when it developed I had not brought my baptismal certificate, which had been mailed from England. I promised to produce it before the ceremony in the morning. The priest was so upset with us, doubtless with reason since the rectory had been inundated with Clifford family phone calls for the last several days, that I could see a flickering temptation in his ice blue eyes to threaten to call the whole affair off if I forgot the certificate again.

He resisted the temptation, fearing, I suspect, that Lourdes would storm the Vatican palace itself.

And I thought that if I could be sure the wedding would be canceled I'd lose the proof of my baptism.

The marriage was a spectacular success for everyone but Lourdes who would barely speak to me all day, and refused to dance with me, because my military guard of honor did not clash their swords at the proper time. My bride, now soft and submissive, and I danced to the music of *Hello, Dolly!* and *Fiddler on the Roof*, interrupted periodically by Dr. Clifford's insistence on the Notre Dame Victory March.

Patsy was unable to be matron of honor because she was too far along in her second pregnancy (in three years of marriage). Ron was forbidden by seminary rules to participate in the wedding party. He assisted at the altar, handsome and virile among the collection of rather decrepit lapdog clergy that Dr. Clifford had assembled to represent the Church's approval of the occasion.

King was the best man, strained and puffy in his tight-fitting summer formal. He had been wiped out at the Board of Trade and was setting himself up with his father's money in a big auto dealership in Joliet.

"No problem," he assured me, using his favorite expression, "no problem at all. This way Patsy and the brats will be only twenty minutes away from work. Maybe when the brats are older I'll go back to the Exchange. Exciting place. Can't beat it for action."

Something had changed in King nonetheless. His eyes danced with cheerful mischief as they always had; but behind them there now seemed to lurk a hint of doubt or fear or perhaps resignation, a tiny but insidious worm. Despite my wedding day happiness, I began to worry about him.

"Was it rough down there?" Madonna's brother asked.

"No problem at all." He waved his hands as if performing a magic rite over his lost capital. "A piece of cake." He snatched another glass of champagne from a passing tray.

We were married, then, with what the Cliffords were certain would pass for high good taste in the neighborhood at that time, and with no preparation for either the sex or the conflict of married life.

The wedding night was a disaster. My bride, who had been so ready and even eager to give me most of her body, was quite incapable of giving me all of it. My dreams of a naked and aroused woman were quickly destroyed by Madonna's timorous—and faintly nasty—prudery.

Our honeymoon, on a damp and misty Maine island (Madonna's hitherto unsuspected fear of flying scrubbed our planned trip to Ireland, though officially that was blamed on my military obligations), was not much better. Sexual release was granted me, but no sense of manly mastery. Madonna seemed sexy, but in the actual physical union of our bodies, she went no further than toleration. Even then there was the implication that it was somehow my fault. Our sex life was foredoomed to failure because by definition I was an inadequate male lover.

The affectionate foreplay that was the barely tolerable preparation for marriage permitted us by the Church (and then only if we confessed it) was banished from our life. Now it was supposed to lead to intercourse, and Madonna didn't want much intercourse. Only in bed and only at night with the lights out. And only as an obligation that could be quickly fulfilled. Otherwise no "fooling around." Good Catholic wife that she was, she would not run the risk that we might have complete fulfillment in an improper manner.

Occasionally there was more than sexual release—mostly when Madonna had had several drinks. On such nights, one during our honeymoon, the pleasure between us was so overwhelming as to threaten to tear apart my sanity. Madonna was capable of ecstasy and in the midst of it capable of piercing cries of satisfaction and fulfillment. Deep within the St. Mary's of Notre Dame prudish matron there was a brazen, bawdy, lascivious woman, inaccessible, unfortunately, when she was sober. She would not discuss such interludes the next morning and indeed resolutely refused to discuss sex with me at all.

"Your mind is obsessed with dirt, Brendan," she would say, dismissing my plea that we ought to talk to someone about our marriage or at least talk to each other. "I'm not going to entertain you or some voyeuristic shrink talking about my sex life. There's nothing wrong with our marriage."

There was a lot wrong, however. I see now that we were out of "sync" from the engagement announcement on. Madonna wanted to be married, I wanted a wife and lover. We never had a chance to straighten it out. Years ago I blamed her family and the Church for our woeful lack of preparation. Now I realize that few Catholics of my generation stumbled into marriage with any notion of what they were doing. The family and the Church cooperated in the conspiracy to keep us ignorant, but they were only part of a larger conspiracy which hid both the conflict and frustration and also the possible pleasures and rewards of married life from the young.

It was sink or swim on your own.

We never learned to swim.

Can a husband jolly a passionate but prudish wife into being a good partner in bed? Now I would say "yes, surely" to that question. But then I didn't know how. Or perhaps I did and lacked the courage to face the devastating barrage of ridicule which flattened my hesitant attempts at mastery.

"Who ever told you that you were a great lover? Come on, don't play around with me; get it over with."

Madonna was soon suffering from the coming of Jean. I was busy with my Pentagon duties. In long and tearful phone conversations with her mother, she blamed me for her exile in Arlington—previously my service commitments were pertinent only because they made possible a military wedding. Lourdes was convinced that if I were willing, Dr. Clifford had enough influence to have me reassigned to Chicago.

God help me, I was willing. Dr. Clifford's clout, however, was weak. I was blamed for the failure of the transfer to materialize. If I really wanted it, it was darkly hinted, I could get it. "Daddy" couldn't do it all himself.

By the time I left for Vietnam, we were both relieved to be rid of each other.

When I came home, shaken by a sexual experience that revealed other possibilities, nothing had changed. We settled down to separate lives, marked by occasional excruciatingly pleasurable encounters and long periods of silence. I lost myself in work and school and later in the law, my boat ("Dirty little thing!" Madonna sneered contemptuously), and my various intellectual hobbies. Madonna devoted herself to punctilious housekeeping; the education of Melissa Jean (who became "Jean" by her own stubborn decision when she went to high school; "Everyone is Melissa," she said truculently, "except the Jennifers and the Micheles." "It was your father's idea," her mother replied, dismissing the issue with little regard for the truth); to elaborate social obligations in which I was only a necessary symbolic presence, as I had been at the wedding, and to occasional bursts of short-lived enthusiasms—art, charity, health foods, and finally watered-down feminism.

I think she marched once or twice in protest against "your goddamned war," and more recently in some of Father Ron's antinuclear demonstrations, but she was not part of the radicalism of the late sixties and early seventies. Her enthusiasms rarely tended toward political or social relevancies. Indeed, while we were at the upper end of the sixties generation, neither of us was ever really part of it. I was too busy with work and school. Madonna was too busy with her social life (on the North Shore, since it was unthinkable that we not live close to her mother and father; when I came home from the war the house had already been picked out) and with making Jean the perfect daughter. History, like married love, passed us by.

I told myself it would change when I graduated from law school or when I became a partner or when Jean went away to college.

We watched the events of our generation as spectators, the way most of my age group participated, I would imagine. The Free Speech Movement at Berkeley, Selma, Martin Luther King, the assassinations, the Conrad Hilton riot, the Beatles, the Rolling Stones, Woodstock, Altamont, *Hair*, Kent State, the marches on Washington, burning draft cards, acid, pot, protests, Watergate, Jesse Jackson swinging from the banners at Miami Beach, McGovern a thousand percent behind his vice-presidential nominee, Chappaquiddick, Abbie Hoffman, priests and nuns marrying and turning Marxist, the Berrigans, English Mass, the birth control encyclical—all were things to be read about in the *New York Times* or to listen to as described by Walter Cronkite.

We felt the Big Chill a decade before its icy fingers touched most of our generation.

Some of my contemporaries were involved in the struggles of the late sixties. Nick and Eileen, both U.S. Attorneys, were gassed in front of the Hilton. Catherine Collins left her religious community, married a priest (temporarily), and was tortured in a prison in South America. Red Kane, Eileen's husband, covered every important event from King's "I Have a Dream" speech to the Tet offensive in Saigon (in which his brother was killed and he barely escaped death). I realized that history was passing me by. I was content to let that happen. Perhaps if my marriage had been happier, I would not have cut myself off from the world beyond my Indian paths. Or maybe I am the sort of man who lives in the midst of history and fails to recognize it because he finds the past more stimulating than the present.

I have my regrets. I also have my memories of a couple of days in Vietnam in the spring of 1966 that still hallow my life. My most treasured recollections of the sixties and early seventies are not of frustrated dreams and failed idealism, but of adventure, sharp, quick, terrifying. And ambiguously successful.

At Jean's graduation Mass, I felt maudlin. From 1960 to 1982 is a short time, yet the length of a generation more or less. What did I have to show for my generation? A few shining hours in war with a tragic after effect, a couple of million dollars, a sailboat, a handful of close friends, a lot of useless knowledge, a wife who does not love me and perhaps never did, and a daughter who does not know me very well and does not like the little she does know. At the end of the day I would lose the last two.

Yet the night before Jean's graduation we had a spectacular sexual encounter, this time both of us cold sober. Madonna was seductive, audacious, irresistible. And I prolonged her pleasure till she screamed for release. We huddled in each other's arms afterward as we had when we were teenagers necking in the forest preserve.

I thought we had turned an important corner. The next day she ordered me out of the house.

I still cannot comprehend what that night of love meant in her scenario—if it meant anything.

And she seduced me one night during the divorce proceedings. She had berated me for my failures in her lawyer's office. Then we waited in hostile silence for the elevator in the lobby, each pretending that the other did not exist. As soon as the door of the elevator had closed on us, however, she whispered, "I'm sorry for being a bitch, Brendan. Can I buy you supper?"

Yes, she could. And caress me lewdly during the meal. And strip for me like a reckless tart in the hotel room afterward. And smother me with affection and love.

Her exercise and dieting had at that time honed her body to perfection and not yet turned her into a possible anorexic. She was a luscious sexual prize. Or maybe I was the prize.

As I sank into a deep and complacent sleep, I was sure the marriage had been salvaged. The next morning she said that we were going ahead with the divorce. "A romp in the hay doesn't mean a thing."

I have often suspected that I probably could have had more of those per year after the divorce than I had before. As mistress and lover, Madonna and I would have been a great pair. Maybe I should have settled for that.

I console myself with the thought that I lost her to her family, that I was doomed to lose any conflict with Lourdes and Melvin (both of whom enthusiastically endorsed the breakup of our marriage). I suppose that such an excuse has some validity. Clearly I lost the fight with them. Whether I had to lose it is another matter.

Just as clearly I lost the feeble battle I waged for Jean. Her debut in the Presentation Ball the year before last was a replication of her mother's debut at the first ball in 1960. "The happiest day of my life," Madonna said in unconscious parody of her own mother. And when I foolishly attempted to moderate the size of our "Pres Ball" party, mother and daughter turned on me with the same vengeful fury with which Lourdes and Madonna had dismissed my hesitant question in 1964, "Does the wedding party have to be so big?"

"You want to take every joy out of my life, don't you?" Madonna hissed.

"You're such a nerd," Jean ranted, as she plunged into tearful hysteria.

I read over these pages and say that I am still unfair. Madonna was sensitive, fragile, intelligent, enthusiastic, gifted. I failed her, even if I'm not quite able to put my finger on precisely the nature of the failure. Our circumstances were, perhaps, not the most conducive to a happy marriage. Yet who does enter marriage without the odds being heavily against happiness? Many overcome the odds. We didn't. I don't want to exculpate Madonna. She didn't give me much help, God knows. But I don't want to exculpate myself either.

Msgr. Blackie Ryan, when I finally spoke to him after the dreadful occurrences I am about to relate, disagreed. "You will not permit yourself the humility," he shook his head disconsolately, "of conceding that perhaps it was all beyond your powers."

"I blew it," I responded. "With the right man, Madonna could have made it."

"What would he have done?"

"I don't know." I buried my face in my hands. She had been so sweet in my arms in the summer of 1963, just before Kennedy had been killed.

"Precisely."

"I can't forgive myself," I sobbed.

"You'd better start trying," the monsignor warned ominously.

10

Our lips touched tentatively, two wary forest animals not yet sure they trusted each other. Then the kiss became firmer, warmer, more demanding as passion melted our suspicion and fear. I took her in my arms, and after a moment of hesitation, her arms encircled me.

She moved back her head. "You're a terrible man, Brendan Ryan, kissing a poor woman in front of her apartment building where the whole world can see."

Before I could reply, her mouth returned to mine, she now more the attacker than I. We slipped into a languorous swamp of pleasure, soothing, relaxed, reassuring. Why fight it? Indeed, what was there to fight?

My program for seducing Ciara Kelly was ahead of schedule. I was not so sure, however, that her program for seducing me was one minute off its schedule.

Was now the right time?

I had slept little the night of the *Rite of Spring* concert; Madonna haunted me; what right did I have, after such a disastrous failure with one woman, to pursue another? Would I fail with Ciara as I had with my wife? When I finally drifted into sleep, I had made up my mind: no more women and particularly no more Ciara Kelly.

The next morning the sun came up over the lake with a burst of spring enthusiasm, the sky was radiantly blue, Grant Park was more lushly green after the rain, and a light lace was beginning to appear on the trees on Michigan Avenue.

Ciara Kelly was back on my agenda. Definitely.

That night we ate scallops creole and drank Jesuitengarten wine at Jackie's on Lincoln, where no one knows me. I explained how the commodities futures market worked; she listened intently and asked a few intelligent questions about "leveraged purchases."

"It's a gambler you are, Brendan Ryan." She winked at me over her white wine. "In the biggest casino in all the world."

"I don't even play poker." I found myself blushing at her cool, appraising gaze. "I'm not a competitive man. I don't even race my boat."

"Don't you now? Sure, that was the great fun of it for me. I guess I'm a competitive woman, though I've never thought about it. What else is it then, if not gambling?"

A woman had never stared at me so frankly before, stripping me psychologically and examining me with the detachment of a lab technician considering an interesting and not unattractive but rather odd species of bug. I was embarrassed, uneasy, and flattered.

"I'm matching wits with the economics experts." I sipped my wine very deliberately, keeping my cool at all costs, if you take my meaning.

"Sure." She laughed delightedly—the bug pleased her. "But you're not a competitive man."

I choked on the wine, tried to explain, and gave it up in the face of her continued laughter.

"You're not trying to understand, Ciara Kelly."

" 'Tis more fun to misunderstand, Brendan Ryan. Here, have some more Jesuit wine. You're so red in the face I think you need it."

We went across the street to watch Brian Friel's condemned IRA men excavate Wood Quay in Dublin. We did not hold hands. Ciara was silent and withdrawn after the play and pleaded to be taken right home. Nonetheless, she did not object when my lips brushed against hers at the end of the night.

The next day, Saturday, even more wondrously springtime, we wandered through the massive Chicago International Art Expo at Navy Pier. I was uneasy that my love might not be interested in art and thus lose some of the perfection I had found in her. She enjoyed it, however, even more than I did, reveling in the delirious panorama of shapes and colors under the white steel girders of the old pier. The Expo itself, Ciara averred, was a work of art—"late surrealism," she decided.

She turned up her nose at the new German Expressionists; marveled at a million-dollar Picasso; examined with intelligent skepticism the Russian Reconstructionists; laughed at the twenty-eight-foot sculpture of used shopping carts at the end of the pier; admired the city skyline ("not Georgian, but nice"); prowled the prestige galleries under the pier rotunda; tickled little babies, speaking to them in French or German where appropriate; and chose as her favorites two local artists, James Winn, an Illinois prairie painter in the Frumpkin and Struve exhibition, and Michael Casey, creator of Chicago neighborhood scenes in the Anne Reilly alcove.

"This is your country, isn't it?" She studied an Illinois field in January. "And a nice country, too, for all that."

"Have you been in it long?" I asked, hunting cautiously for information.

"Not to say long." She turned to a painting of an industrial park.

In the Reilly exhibition she stood transfixed before a haunting oil of a neighborhood street corner—church, tavern, and undertakers—shaking her head slowly as though she understood what Mickey Casey (whose mother was Ed Ryan's sister) was saying.

"Former police superintendent," I said. "Sort of a relative of mine. His mother was a Ryan. The gallery owner is his wife."

Neither Anne nor Mike was there. If they had been I would have steered my prize away without an introduction.

"Poor wee man sees it all," she said mysteriously. "The bitter and the sweet and the mixture, if you take my meaning."

I didn't quite.

"Poor wee man" was one of her favorite expressions. It was used for me at least once an hour. It conveyed in mixtures appropriate to the context admiration, affection, sympathy, pity, and, I think, prayer for the grace of a happy death.

We also glanced at the sunbursts and female nudes of Catherine Curran in the Reilly alcove. "Ah, erotic beauty without exploitation. Sure, the poor woman is good, isn't she?"

"She's done a book about Catholicism and the human body. A reformed Enthusiast, or maybe just a disciplined one. Had a big argument with Cardinal Sean Cronin at the Archdiocesan Art Commission's last public meeting. The cardinal said he wouldn't try to debate a woman who loved God more than anyone else he knew."

"A grand man your cardinal. I've read her book. How old is she now?"

"Turning forty and pregnant."

"Bless her heart." The asthmatic sigh—yearning to be pregnant herself. But she was, wasn't she? With my child.

"Started painting nudes as a kid transforming *Playboy* centerfolds. She'd certainly want to paint you if she ever met you."

Ciara blushed to the roots of her hair and down to her neckline. "I wouldn't want to be hanging naked in this great drafty hall, now would I? I suppose she's another relative?"

"Kate Ryan's niece, God be good to her."

"You Ryans are everywhere."

When we escaped the mile of art—biggest expo in the world, I told her proudly—I was asked would I ever take her to the beach. She would never dare go by herself. "That nice Oak Street place."

Before I could offer to walk her back to her apartment, she arranged that we would meet at Oak and Michigan in fifteen minutes. She appeared promptly, wearing slacks and a T-shirt over her swimsuit, which proved to be a uselessly modest navy blue maillot. I tried not to gape too obviously.

I was permitted to rub liberal amounts of Hawaiian tan cream on her back, a task of mind-bending pleasure. "This sun is not good for Irish skin at all, at all," I was informed. I was also permitted to buy her a hot dog and a Coke. "Only small ones, mind you."

After she had consumed two of both, and large ones at that, she announced her intention to take a wee swim in my lake.

"You can't, Ciara," I protested. "The water temperature isn't much over fifty."

"Sure." She wrapped a towel around her neck. "It's

warm by Irish standards." She loped across the beach, a playful forest antelope, hardly pausing when she hit the cold, deep blue water and dived into the first small wave. She surfaced with a powerful crawl kick and swam out twenty yards or so, then returned, uttering not a single cry against the cold.

Still, she was shivering as she raced back to where I was waiting. She wrapped the blanket around her and discarded the wet towel.

"Ah, you can't beat it," she announced through clattering teeth. " 'Tis the most refreshing thing in the world."

"A good cure for concupiscence, I imagine."

"We don't have any of that in Ireland. And speaking of that, Brendan Ryan, you're staring at me like I wasn't wearing any clothes at all, at all."

"Sorry," I mumbled, feeling my face burn.

"Ah, don't be sorry." She jabbed my arm with an icy finger. "A woman is flattered when a man she wants to look at her that way looks at her that way, if you take my meaning." She was seized by a fit of laughter.

I wasn't sure that I did. "Does that mean I can go on looking?"

"In moderate amounts, as the priest used to say in secondary school." Yet another fit of laughter.

She didn't say what priest or which secondary school. Anyway, I went on looking. And imagining and fantasizing and daydreaming.

"We have a book of modern Irish art at the store," she told me as we left the beach in a golden haze of sunlight. "Some of them are quite talented, you know. Sure, none of the Dublin galleries could afford a place at your grand Chicago Expo. And your modern Irish artists having just one thing on their minds . . ."

"I take your meaning, woman. But I thought that you didn't have any of that in Ireland."

"We had it once and then it went out of fashion." She poked my arm again. " 'Tis coming back in again, or so I'm told."

Yet she was too shy to go to the beach by herself.

That night we listened to Solti conduct Mozart's no. 25

and no. 40, and to Peter Frankl play the Piano Concerto in A. We held hands by mutual and implicit consent. Afterwards, as we walked down Michigan Avenue and then ate a late supper in a Szechuan restaurant, Ciara bubbled like fresh champagne.

Winter returned on Sunday—gray sky, cold, twenty-knot winds, surly lake. Montrose Harbor was virtually deserted. Indeed, only a few hardy sailors had put their boats in the water, so dubious was the city about whether spring would ever come. Ciara, in jeans, a sweatshirt, and a thick dark blue Windbreaker, considered the *Brigid* carefully, touching the gleaming wood hull, feeling the polished teak fittings, sliding the neatly arranged sheets through her fingers, and pronounced *Brigid* a "proper" boat.

She also observed, so softly that I had to ask her to repeat it, that she imagined I had spent more time and energy on the *Brigid* than I had on my wife.

She did not seem daunted by the small-craft warnings and the threat of rain showers. I was not about to call it quits in the presence of a foreigner, and a woman at that. So we prepared the rigging of the *Brigid* and, using our twelve-horsepower auxiliary, steered out into the restless gray lake.

Ciara watched me carefully, and when I nodded, she clambered deftly to the cabin roof and hauled up the mainsail. She didn't wait for my instructions to raise the jib.

It was the kind of weather for which my poor old *Brigid* was made. Sensing that she was in skilled hands, she dug her nose into a wave and skimmed southward on a broad reach with the offshore wind pushing us toward Jackson Park and the University of Chicago.

Ciara stood next to the mast, one hand on the neatly fastened jib sheet, the other in her Windbreaker pocket, her jet-black hair tense in the wind like geese flying south in autumn, her face exultant, her shoulders thrown back defiantly—Grace O'Malley, the pirate queen of old.

She saw me admiring her again, flushed, and shouted, "Not a bad wee lake you have here."

"Not quite Galway Bay," I shouted back, "but it will do."

She shrugged, not committing herself to whether she had actually sailed on Galway Bay.

A good sailor she certainly was, the best crewperson I had had on the *Brigid* for many years, better even than Ron Crowley. We turned around at the Jackson Park point, after I had shown her in the binoculars the captured German submarine next to the Museum of Science and Industry, and began our run back. The wind had risen, rain was falling steadily, and we were bouncing on following seas. We donned oilskins and pulled up the hoods. Ciara, protesting how much she was out of condition, scampered gracefully about the boat, ready for but not anticipating my commands. So exhilarating was the run and so easy was it to work with Ciara, that I almost forgot my desire for her.

"You're daft, Brendan Ryan," she yelled happily when we finally turned into the entrance of Montrose Harbor and she began to wrap the sails—neatly and carefully, I noticed (and without any complaints of the sort that usually mark the final phases of a sailing venture). "Taking a poor woman out on this crazy lake in the rain."

"You're daft for coming with me, and yourself an experienced sailor."

"You're talking like me." She flushed and smiled as I helped her off the cabin roof, all too briefly holding her solid waist muscles in my hands. " 'Tis a bad influence I am."

We ate ham and roast beef sandwiches in the cabin and drank Beaulieu cabernet sauvignon (George Latour special reserve), which caused her to lick her lips appreciatively, took a brief nap—fully clothed and in opposite bunks—and then departed in my Mercedes (about which she made no comment) for the late afternoon Mass at Holy Name Cathedral. We knelt in the corner at the back so our sailing clothes would not cause too much shock to the devout parishioners.

"A nice wee priest," she said as we left. "And himself a good preacher too. I'd never heard the story about the Caravaggio painting with the risen Jesus as a teenager at Emmaus. Would you be thinking, Brendan Ryan, that's what Heaven is going to be like? All of us as teenagers? Were you happy as a teenager?"

"Yes, very happy. And you?"

"No." She jammed her hands into her Windbreaker pockets. "Not a bit . . . who is that nice wee priest?"

"Monsignor John Blackwood Ryan, rector of the cathedral, alter ego to Cardinal Cronin, and allegedly the brightest priest in the archdiocese."

"Such a harmless seeming wee man. Sure, you'd want to pat him on the head and take him home to his mother."

"So inoffensive that you wouldn't even notice him on an elevator, right?"

"One of the 'other' Ryans, is he?"

I had talked about myself, my family, my neighborhood, my life, incessantly through the weekend. Ciara Kelly had been told all there was to know about Brendan Herbert George Ryan, all except my adventure on that hot tropical day on a nameless tributary of the Mekong. Only after much more intimacy would I risk myself in that story, which no one had ever heard before.

And I, for my part, had learned a lot about her.

She said the Rosary every day and considered herself a loyal and devout Catholic, but she refused to take "them" (said with a slightly contemptuous jerk of her head in the general direction of Rome) seriously when they made rules, particularly about sex. "Poor dear men mean well," she observed, "but, sure, they don't know what they're talking about, do they now?"

She seemed to own only a few dresses, some blouses and slacks, and virtually no jewelry. Her makeup, even for dinner and concerts, was at most perfunctory—not that she needed much.

Only now that I have lost her, I note with astonishment that Ciara Kelly seemed incapable of complaint. Never once did I hear her complain about anything.

She was fluent in English and French and also, she assured me, in Irish. "Kind of half my first language." My name, I was told, meant " 'little king.' Brendan the Little King. Not," she said with a shy, wicked grin, "meaning anything pejorative by the expression, mind you." Then, realizing she might have hurt my feelings, "It refers to geography and not stature."

"I'm not sensitive about being five foot eight and three-eighths inches tall, Ciara," I said lightly. Well, not too sensitive.

"Well, you shouldn't be, with that darling silver hair and those wondrous silver eyes."

"I think it's my turn to blush."

"Good enough for you."

She did not smoke and, despite the two Jameson's at the Cliff Dwellers, drank very little. Her strongest language was "bloody hell." She was fiercely Irish nationalist. "The Brits don't belong on our island. And it's one island, not two." The fighting would stop finally, she insisted, when London made up its mind that it had to stop.

Yet she was also passionately pacifist. The terrorists in the North were "psychopathic killers"; the Dublin government, pathetic politicians devoid of integrity and courage; the English, unspeakable imperialists who would not abandon their belief in the inferiority of the Irish.

These convictions were stated in a tense whisper and accompanied by small, sharp hand gestures and fire sparks in her big gray eyes. Like most Irish political positions, hers did not seem totally consistent. My Ciara was a different woman when she talked about Northern Ireland—tense, abstracted, almost haunted. So I did not press her for clarification.

She seemed detached from material possessions. She praised the *Brigid* and ran an approving hand over the exterior of my Benz. Yet she moved in expensive restaurants as though she were untouched by them and immune to their supercilious atmosphere. She kidded me about my fashionable suits and recreational clothes. "Sure, that man looks like a page in *Esquire*. Or maybe like a male model in a page of *Vogue*."

"With a female model in tow."

She responded with one of her many laughs, explosive, not exactly raucous, uninhibited yet somehow melodious, a waterfall crashing through melting ice. "That'll be the day."

I gave her no presents, God forgive me; and she didn't seem interested in them anyway—though I'm sure she would have accepted them, poor wee woman. Never once did I hear the expression "I want" on her lips. She wanted me all right; and she knew I was wealthy. If that made any difference at all to her, it was counted against me.

"You wear those fancy clothes," she said, pointing a finger at the clothes I wore on the *Brigid*, "to make women think you're sexy." The charge was what Kate Ryan called "half fun and full earnest."

"Do they do the job?" I helped her into the cockpit.

"Like a lily needs gold leaf." She kissed me. "Still, I suppose they don't do any harm."

She had strong opinions on other matters, too, but these were articulated with intelligence and modesty, and she seemed capable of changing them when faced with a good argument. Her artistic tastes, I discovered at the Art Expo, were eclectic and sound, though perhaps modestly conservative. She thought an Italian sculptor, one of my favorites, "probably needs a good therapist, poor man." But when I explained and defended his work, she reconsidered his exhibit and admitted, "Well, I might change my mind about him, but not just yet."

She possessed enormous physical energy and a fierce appetite for food after exertion, whether walking the floor of Navy Pier or sailing on the lake. She promised that she would start exercising again soon, lest "all this Yank food turn me into a fat West of Ireland cow." She did not respond to my suggestion, innocent enough, that she might want to swim in the pool in my building.

She could nap at the wink of an eye—in my car between Chestnut Place and the harbor, in the boat after lunch, on the way to the cathedral—and then awaken fully on instant notice and be ready for action and fun. When challenged or excited, she was always good-humored and frequently exultant.

Her hair hinted at her disposition. When it was tied back, she was serious, intellectual, responsible. When it hung loose and flowed behind her in the breeze, she was impish, reckless, a little zany. When it was piled on her head, she was preoccupied by a strain of dark melancholy about her that was a little daunting.

"Pay me no mind, Brendan. I'm in one of my mauve moods. It'll go away. It always has. It's not your fault."

"Whose fault is it?"

"That's a long story with which I won't bore you." Said in a tone so positive and an accent so American that one knew one damn well better not push.

She would not tell me about herself. I learned from being with her that I was pursuing a passionate, lively, intelligent, and beautiful, if faintly haunted, woman. But I found out nothing about her family, her background, her life story, the reason she was living in Chicago and working for what must have been very little money at Dufficy's Irish Store.

Tactfully, or so it seemed to me, I did not ask questions about these matters; and she volunteered nothing. I suppose I should have been wary. Most of us, even the shy and the modest, are willing to talk about our families. Ciara's silence on the subject was mysterious and perhaps threatening. I wanted her so badly that I didn't care. That she was an admirable and brilliant woman seemed to be enough. The past didn't matter.

Not till it came back to haunt us.

What did I want from her? It should be obvious—sex. I wanted her naked before me. I wanted her in bed with me. I wanted to caress and fondle and squeeze and kiss her most intimate secrets. I wanted to be inside of her, shouting with triumphant male pride at my conquest. I wanted to hold her, sleeping peacefully and contentedly, in my arms. And I wanted all these pleasures not just once but scores, hundreds of times in as many different places and in as many different positions as time and ingenuity and self-control would permit.

Adolescent? I admit it. However, it was spring and I was hungry for a woman and falling in love with this woman. At least I thought I was falling in love. I told myself that she was a mystery it would take a lifetime of pleasure to solve and that my horniness differed from that of an adolescent in that I was more concerned about her happiness than a teenager would be about the happiness of a girl he wanted to screw.

I was pursuing my Holy Grail, seeking not only love but happiness, my elixir of youth, my leprechaun's gold at the end of the rainbow, or wherever else this woman leprechaun had hidden it. Later, after I lost her, I told Blackie Ryan that it was too much to expect that a woman could be all of these things.

"It seems to me that is what they are for." He rolled his nearsighted eyes. "So I am told at any rate. In the absence of a grail to pursue, life becomes tedious."

I didn't want a grail, only a woman in bed with me. Or so I thought.

Yet I wanted to make Ciara Kelly happy. I also wanted to screw her. Were not the two compatible? Why worry about it?

Because I worry about everything, that's why.

I wanted to fill her, impregnate her, fertilize her, bring my child to life inside her—even as I knew that before we had made love she was already carrying my child.

That was absurd psychic drivel that I still could not drive out of my head. I cannot expel that conviction even now, when I understand how impossible it is.

I was not, mind you, merely seeking a wild sexual fling, though I certainly wanted that too. I wanted a woman and a child, a family, a community. I might intend to use Ciara Kelly, always respecting her, I told myself, but I surely would not use her and discard her. Marriage? Well, why not? But no rush about that. The Roman Catholic Church had been no aid to me before, during, or after my first marriage, which it had in its wisdom recently decreed was null and void from the beginning. I did not want it mucking around in my sexual relationship with this new woman.

The Church was not totally responsible for the disaster between me and Madonna, but it was not innocent of blame either. I would not sit in an uncomfortable chair in a stuffy parish hall with Ciara beside me giggling uncontrollably and listen to the inanities of another stupid pre-Cana conference. I would not try to stifle yawns of boredom in a rectory office while an overeducated young priest or an undereducated older nun prated about the theology of matrimony. I would not fill out forms, hunt down certificates, make promises, wait for the appropriate delays, touch all the canonical bases, fulfill all the ecclesiastical requirements, merely to permit the Roman Church to bless my union with Ciara. If it wanted to be involved in my love for her, it could damn well do so on my terms and not on its own.

What would happen if I stormed into the cathedral rectory and delivered this ultimatum to Blackie Ryan, the beloved "Punk" of his siblings?

I could imagine.

He would mumble incoherently, shuffle absentmindedly out of the office, return a few minutes later with a somehow camouflaged bottle of Jameson's, and pour a stiff one for the three of us.

The goddamn Roman Catholic Church would own me again.

I pondered the scene with some satisfaction. He would toast our health and future together and quote, in the original, some Gaelic poet, to Ciara's delight.

Oh, yes, that's what my cousin Blackwood would do. It was no creepy, problematic psychic revelation. It was a certainty. Like the rising of the sun in the morning.

And it could wait until I was good and ready.

Or so I thought, as Ciara's lips reluctantly detached themselves from mine and her arms gradually released me. She did not, however, try to evade my embrace, but rather leaned her head, wearily and submissively, against my chest.

"The man tries to seduce me with a storm on a lake," she giggled, burrowing against me.

"Who's seducing whom?" I released her, swatted her rump lightly, and guided her through the door of the Chestnut Place. "I'll talk to you tomorrow."

She nodded dully, her eyes, heavy with both sleep and desire, resolutely refusing to acknowledge the presence of the doorman, and ducked around the obelisklike object that the architect had deposited in the middle of the lobby.

"We're probably the tenth couple he's seen make out tonight," I whispered into her ear as the elevator door opened.

"Would the other nine have been as good as we were, do you think?"

It was cold, not cool, on State Street—not much above

the middle forties—and a persistent drizzle stung at my cheek. It did not matter. I was walking on the outer fringes of the garden of paradise.

I might have pressed for love tonight. She would not have refused. We were both tired and it was late. Tomorrow would be better. I would be a thoughtful and considerate lover.

As I walked down the Chestnut Street ravine, by the old Quigley Seminary (a gaunt gray imitation of the Sainte-Chapelle in Paris) where Ron had gone to school for a year; across from Crickets, in the old-fashioned red-brick White-hall Hotel, where I must take her to eat as soon as our romance was public; past the 111 Chestnut building, where Jane Byrne was licking her wounds and awaiting a chance to throw another monkey wrench into Chicago politics, I started to have doubts.

It had been too easy. I had known her for less than a week. I had no facts about her background or her past. We had had four dates and a day on a boat. There had to be something wrong. Lovely and gifted women like Ciara are spoken for. They do not appear at the whim of a lonely, unhappy man and surrender after minimal effort.

I should rethink the whole matter. Find out more about her. Call my friend the consul general of Ireland. What did he know of a certain Ciara Kelly?

From the window in my own building, I looked down the quaint little ravine of Chestnut Street, with the bright lights of the Margarita Mexican restaurant creating mysterious shadows on the canyon walls. Somewhere in that wave-shaped red and beige brick building—not only late Harry Weese, but decadent Harry Weese—my true love would be sleeping.

Tomorrow night I could be sleeping with her. She was mine for the asking.

I didn't even know her apartment number. Or whether it might be on the other side of the building. Or her phone number. I knew practically nothing except that I wanted her and she seemed to want me.

I would wait a few days, however. For appearances' sake. So I would not seem too lustful.

And so I could find out more about her. Who, for example, was Ciara Kelly really?

All excellent intentions.

11

The next morning I had a thousand reasons for hesitation. It was too soon. I hardly knew her. She would not tell me anything about her origins. I was acting like an old fool. Or worse, like a teenage old fool. I had failed once in love. I would look ridiculous trying to make love to a woman almost ten years younger than I was. Vanity of vanity, as the man in scriptures says, and all is vanity.

I placed a call to the Irish consulate about Jean's trip. Might I ask if he knew anything about Ciara Kelly? Only a cad would do that. Well, a man who was worried about an Irish mystery might too. Well, I wouldn't do it regardless.

My virtue was unnecessary. The consul general was not in. Would I talk to the vice-consul? I thought not. Would you have him call Brendan Ryan? Of course, Mr. Ryan.

Then Jean phoned from Stanford. She was sorry she'd behaved like a little brat at dinner and was grateful that I'd sent her the books in the mail. What was this Dufficy's Irish Store anyway? I'll have to take you there when you come home. Kind of interesting. When I return from Ireland, do you think I could work for a couple of weeks? Yes, Daddy, *work!* I know it sounds strange coming from the spoiled brat of the Western world. Where? Could you find me a job at the Board of Trade? A runner or something like that? Well, I think maybe I might make a good trader. Don't laugh, Daddy, it's not funny. Well, I guess it is. Oh, I could be a photographer and a trader, too. They stop working early, don't they?

You really think I might be good at it? And you'll talk to your friends? Out of sight!

Speaking of coming home, might she stop in Tucson on the way to visit Grandmother and Grandfather Ryan? Did I think they'd mind? Would I call and ask them? She didn't want to intrude.

"Would I get in trouble again, Jeannie, if I asked about airfare?"

"You'll never get in trouble again, Daddy," a sunny laugh, "when you offer me money. I have enough for the trip, but if you want to, like, reimburse me when I come home, that would be groovy."

"Groovy?"

"Old word that's come back. Would you please call Grandmother and Grandfather?"

"Immediately. I'll call you back."

My parents were astonished but delighted. Should we repaint the guest bedroom? my mother wondered.

"Don't be ridiculous, Mom. She means that she'll show up tomorrow. Lay in a new bottle of sherry and make a reservation at El Charro."

"Actually, we're rather seriously into margaritas," she admitted. "I'm afraid I've gone native."

Only in a very proper, very thoughtful, and very English way. Ah, the burden of empire.

What was going on inside Jean's pretty little head? The Board and my parents. Two mystery women to worry about.

What would Jean think of Ciara? Another reason to hesitate. If they didn't like each other, I would be caught in dangerous cross pressures.

"Mrs. Kane is here with a gentleman," my secretary informed me.

The gentleman was a process server with a summons bidding me to prepare myself to testify for a grand jury currently in session in the United States Federal Court, District of Northern Illinois, on or about June 1. Eileen must have left word at the switchboard to head him off so that she could be present when it was served. She seated herself comfortably in one of my easy chairs.

I thanked the gentleman for the document and poured Eileen her herbal tea. Another mystery woman. Not mine to worry about.

"You're looking quite content with yourself this morning, Brendan." She peered at me intently, green eyes magnified now by unifocal contact lenses. "Good sail yesterday?"

"Excellent. You and Red must come with me some Sunday. We could sail over to Grand Beach."

"On his stomach? And what if he likes it? You know his enthusiasms." She continued to examine my face. "You're not in love, are you, Brendan? You look so happy. And this subpoena doesn't seem to bother you at all."

"I'm not in love," I lied, mentally cursing perceptive women. "I'll start worrying about this," I tossed the document at her, "when you tell me to. Are you sure about the plea bargain?"

"As far as I know," she rose thoughtfully from the chair and placed the empty teacup neatly on its rack, "there are some rumors on the street that King Sullivan is up to some new kinkiness. If he gets caught between now and his trial in another caper, he'll do time in Lexington."

For which, I thought, I would be blamed.

I called Jean back and told her that her grandparents would be delighted.

"Will they mind if I ask about the war?"

"No. They're not great storytellers like our cousins, but they're not embarrassed by their heroism."

"Really. Caitlin says her grandfather now thinks he sank the whole Japanese navy."

Ah. The Ryan granddaughters were swapping World War II stories. No harm in that, as far as I could see. No worry required on that count.

The pool in my building was closed on Monday evenings. I decided at lunchtime to walk over to the Chicago Athletic Club, the last of the men's athletic clubs on Michigan Avenue, for my daily swim. Virtue is to be found in exercise. Basketball as an antidote for horniness, as we learned on our high school retreats.

I would not go so far as to experiment with Lake Michigan as a remedy for concupiscence.

Coming out of the showers I encountered King Sullivan, a towel wrapped around his ample but diminishing stomach. His once lean and distinguished face now looked like that of a consumptive cherub. One would never have imagined from his cheer that he had stolen a million dollars from me.

"Hey, Brenny, great! You're as trim as ever. I'll catch up to you soon." He patted his stomach. "Notice how much I've lost? Not a drop of the sauce for two months. No problem. Did you get one of those subpoena things? Don't worry about it. All taken care of. Just go in and tell them the truth. No problem."

"I heard you were in the hospital for some tests."

He dismissed the biopsies with a wave of his pudgy paw. "No problem. Routine checkup. Everything is fine. You know how Ron and Patsy are. Worry about everything. Hey, let's get together for some golf this summer. What 'ya say?"

I agreed that it would be a great idea.

Did he know that his wife and his pastor had both pleaded with me to try to duck the grand jury appearance? He might and he might not. But it wouldn't matter. No problem.

Nevertheless, the little worm of worry that always lurked behind King's cheerfully dancing eyes seemed to have grown bigger. Was the grand jury responsible, or the biopsies?

I felt depressed as I walked back to my office. Spring does not come to Chicago with any delicacy or decency. It rather tumbles toward maturity with the heedless speed of a fourteen-year-old boy racing toward manhood. Dandelions erupt overnight, leaves smash out of the delicate buds of trees, acrid smells—the last rottenness of winter, perhaps—fill the humid and oppressive air. Heavy clouds roll in without warning, seeming to push down on the land to slow, if it be possible, the pell-mell rush of spring. Life is purchased only at a heavy price.

God in heaven, what prices Patsy and King had paid! What kind of price would I have to pay for Ciara Kelly? It would not, I thought, as I considered the return message from the consul general, be worth it. I crumpled the pink slip and tossed it into the wastebasket. I had an afternoon of appointments.

The last of the appointments was canceled. So I pondered the problem of trading in futures on the Standard & Poor's Stock Index or the Chicago Board Options Exchange. Last month there had been some fiddling with the April call option, either a sophisticated new game of arbitrage between New York and Chicago or, more likely, a subtle new form of crookedness.

As I jotted numbers on a piece of paper, I realized that there was an even more subtle kind of dishonesty that no one had discovered yet. Trading on stock index futures was a new brand of gambling, and many of the possibilities for kinkiness remained to be discovered.

I played a couple of games with my PC XT on past option calls. Sure enough, I could have cleared a quarter of a million without being caught. This time.

I flipped the papers into the same wastebasket that contained the consul general's return call. For fifteen years I had been devising cleverly dishonest ways to beat the commodities market. It was an amusing game. I had not the guts to play it for real. I'd make my money within the law or not at all. And enjoy my secure self-esteem and virtuous self-righteousness.

I turned off my PC XT and looked at my Casio watch. Five forty-five. It was safe to walk across the Loop and down Michigan Avenue to my apartment. Dufficy's Irish Store was closed.

As a punishment for my sins, I was caught in a wild thunderstorm and soaked to the skin. Every cab in the Loop was occupied. So, bedraggled, disheartened, and feeling very old, I trudged home, convinced that spring was a trick to blind us to the inevitability of the passing of time and the coming of death.

I crossed to the east side of the Magnificent Mile and did not even look across the street at Dufficy's Irish Store. That, too, was a trick.

I showered, donned a clean terry cloth robe, cooked some frozen asparagus in the microwave for supper, and sat down at my manuscript about jury selection in medieval England.

Out over the dark lake there were flashes of light, another weird psychic phenomenon with which I had long since learned to live. As far as I could understand them they were auras of future dangers. But since they rarely had any content, there was no way to avoid the danger of which they warned. So I mostly ignored them.

Ciara Kelly was at least one danger I had escaped in the nick of time.

12

The next morning I stood across the street from Dufficy's Irish Store with what I'm sure was a smirk of amused self-confidence. I had made a fool out of myself, but at least I was wise enough to stop before my folly became a public fact at which all might laugh.

The storm had wiped away the smell of dirty and heavy air. A light east wind blew off the lake, and the sky was crystalline, the air sparkling and clean. The skyline of Chicago glowed with three-dimensional clarity, a photographic art magazine day.

I was caught again in the rite of spring, still pursuing the Holy Grail.

I would look into the shop for just a minute. Say hello to her. No reason to be rude. Oh, no. No reason at all.

I hesitated at the curb, ducked through the traffic, and decided on the east side of Michigan Avenue that I would drink a cup of tea at the Marriott before venturing into Ireland. I even took two steps in the direction of the hotel.

My feet betrayed me. I found myself inside the shop gaping at Ciara Kelly. More precisely I was gaping at her wondrous breasts.

"You were going to show me that book of modern Irish artists," I said, forcing my eyes to concentrate on hers.

"Was I now?" She was wearing a red and white candy-striped shirtdress that seemed to float around her like a morning breeze. Her hair hung loose, a sign of a giddy, girlish mood. New dress, inexpensive but attractive. Bought for me? A little angry at me? Ah, well, what did it matter?

She found the book on a counter and opened it for my inspection. I stood next to her as she turned the pages.

"One thing on their mind, indeed," I said lightly.

"This is Jim Fitzpatrick, a wee red-haired man. Does wonderful posters of mythic heroines." I noticed for the first time how long and elegant were her fingers. Did she play the piano, or perhaps the violin?

"I know his work. This one looks like you."

"Too skinny by half—the goddess, that is."

"I don't agree." My fingers touching hers.

"You didn't call yesterday, Brendan Ryan." So soft I had to guess at the words.

"I lost my nerve."

Short laugh. "A good thing. I lost mine too."

We were in each other's arms, laughing at our joint idiocy, lovers who have escaped a minor quarrel without even quarreling. Then our laughter transformed itself to fierce hunger. Our lips, our bodies, our total selves pressed against each other in an implacable demand for unity.

"Oh, God, you're a desperate man, Brendan Ryan," she murmured, and then sought my lips again.

Every part of her body that touched mine, breasts, belly, thighs, said surrender. So easy a conquest. Not clear who the conqueror is. Doesn't matter.

I pushed the dress back off her shoulders. Boldly my hand seized a lace-protected breast. My lips moved across her chest, my teeth nibbling her smooth, warm flesh.

With considerable difficulty she pushed me away. "Not in the shop, Brendan . . ." A small chuckle. "Mind you, it's an interesting idea . . ."

Reluctantly, my breath coming in compulsive gasps, I permitted her to escape from my arms. "After work?"

She nodded, rearranging her clothes with clumsy and trembling fingers, shy and embarrassed now.

"Your apartment or mine?"

"Yours."

I kissed her again. Once more the dance of passion swept through us. She pushed me away.

" 'Tis a terrible hungry man you are; you'd not let a

poor honest working woman," she was laughing happily, "earn her poor honest living. Get along with you to your plush law office and spend the day in dirty and obscene thoughts."

"If you're in them, they can't be dirty."

"Go along with your nonsense."

At the door I steadied myself for reentry into the sunlight of Michigan Avenue and reality.

"Brendan Ryan."

"Ciara Kelly?"

"I love you."

The cliché did not even stick in my throat. "Not half as much as I love you."

I struggled through a heavy day of appointments, most of them designed to keep the IRS raiders at bay. When I wasn't fighting off distracting and intensely perverse images of Ciara, I was praying for tax simplification—even if it did put me out of business.

I forgot that it was the day of my weekly lunch with the Kanes and Currans at the Chicago Club, a generous but barely disguised custom that began two weeks after Madonna threw me out of the house. Nick had to come to the office to drag me away.

Catherine Curran, always a clown, despite her sufferings in Costaguana, started in on me as soon as we were seated at our table. "Brenny's in love, guys," she announced brightly, her brown eyes dancing impishly. "What's she like, Brenny? Will she pose for me?"

Catherine, like Eileen, was bursting with life. In a pink sundress with a short white jacket, she looked like a personification of healthy spring. What would it be like, my corrupted imagination wondered, to be in bed with two pregnant women, two of the favorites from your harem? Did Catherine and Eileen realize they created such fantasies in the imaginations of some men? Maybe most men?

I was sure that they would be delighted if they did know. However, it was not my job, Heaven save us all, to inform them.

"What makes you think she's the sort of model you like?" Her husband took her hand. "And why would he introduce her to us, anyhow?"

My new group, more protective, less demanding than the old, but still determined to push their way into my life. Not yet.

"I'll make no comment," I said airily.

"You don't have to when you order a Jameson's for lunch," Red Kane said. "Pay no attention to them, Brendan. All Irishwomen are matchmakers."

"I won't make any decisions about matches till we meet her." Eileen's green eyes glinted. "Which had better be soon, counselor, do you understand?"

I took refuge in another "No comment."

I assumed, however, that the next week or the week after she would be the sixth at our lunch table. In the warmth of my friends' affection and concern, and in the vitality of the two women in pastel maternity dresses, content and complacent with their carrying of life, I slipped deeper into the life-giving and life-absorbing rhythms of the spring ritual. I would soon drink from the Holy Grail. Lunching with them and making love with Ciara were part of the same prodigal, renewing ritual.

Catherine would definitely want to paint her.

Later, when I thought my sanity was slipping from my fingers, I asked my friends if they remembered the luncheon banter. They did indeed. "I was sure that you were going to spend the night with a woman, and a good woman at that, in both senses of the word," Eileen said. "She was real enough to you that day, Brendan. I can't imagine her not being real."

Yet there was then not the slightest evidence that she had ever existed.

She was real enough when I took her arm outside the Irish Store at 5:30, her hair unaccountably bound up. Serious business ahead of us. We walked silently down Michigan Avenue, oblivious of the rest of the world, expectant, nervous, eager, uneasy. Above us the sky had become ominous, dusty pink and soiled lemon, soiled bedsheets, with rapidly scudding low clouds.

"Tornado warnings are out," I remarked.

"Ah, is that what you Yanks call it?" Nervous snigger.

My arm around her waist, solid, substantial, unquestionably real and of this earth, it seemed, we rode up in the parking lot elevator to avoid contact with the doormen and neighbors.

"I hope you're calm and confident, Brendan Ryan," she murmured tensely, "because I'm scared half out of my mind."

"Not to say scared." I patted her rear end, also notably solid, affectionately. "Don't worry. It's not like Olympic gymnastics. Little men won't hold up cards with numbers on them when we're finished."

Our embrace began halfway down the corridor to my apartment. The fires of the spring rite burn not only for the very young. Inside the door we did not even try for the bedroom. The beige couch in the parlor seemed comfortable enough. I began to unbind her hair, the first step in making her my own.

The bedding of Ciara Kelly was an odd, if satisfying, experience. She was not exactly a virgin, it seemed, but with little sexual experience—even less than I—and much sexual fear and ambiguity. Her courage failed her almost at once.

I had pushed away the top of her dress and was caressing her still-covered breasts, as gently as my frenzied state would permit. Her arms draped with the dress, she put her knotted hands in my way, as though she were praying to me. "Please, Brendan."

Outside my window the thunderstorm had begun. Jagged flashes of lightning clawed at the gloomy sky, thick curtains of rain dashed across the city, obscuring whole neighborhoods as they hurried toward the skyline and the lake.

"The woman has the right," I clenched my teeth, withdrew my aching fingers, and quoted the columnist Ellen Goodman, "has the right to say 'yes' and then change it to 'no.' But the woman had better make up her mind."

" 'Tis a terrible thing for a woman to have to take off her clothes." Her face was contorted in misery, her body tense and withdrawn. "And in broad daylight too."

I eased the dress off her arms and returned my fingers, feather light, to her breasts.

"I'll not make love, woman, to someone as beautiful as you in the dark. Seeing you naked is part of the game."

She glanced at the window and the city stretching beyond. "Anybody could look in."

"At this height, only God."

"Could we wait till later?" She sighed with pleasure as my fingers found the flesh of her breasts. I took firm possession of them.

"It's now or not at all," I said, astonished at my own fierceness. I kissed her chin. "Yes or no?"

"I don't know, Brendan, I don't know. Oh . . ." She drew in her breath sharply as my fingers very carefully toyed with her breasts, staking a claim on them but not yet claiming to possess them. "Don't . . ."

"Yes or no, woman?" I demanded, my fondling becoming more imperative. Her heart was pounding wildly. Under the lace I found a slowly ripening nipple.

She closed her eyes and gritted her teeth. "The woman," she spoke through tight lips, "wants a good loving from you the worst way in the world. She's terrified out of her empty mind. And ashamed like she was a First Communion girl naked in church. Stupid Irish prude."

"I'm not accepting excuses." My fingers went to the front hook of her bra. Her hand intercepted mine.

She took a deep breath, eyes still shut. Then a slow grin. "The woman gives Molly Bloom's answer and serves notice that any later retraction should be treated as null and void." Her eyes opened, gray fields soft with love. "Clear enough statement to justify your actions, counselor?"

She undid the hook herself.

Has not every man dreamed of what I had—a license to sweep away reluctances and resistances? "You're enjoying every second of this, aren't you?" she complained.

"I sure am. And so are you, woman."

She was and she wasn't. Our lovemaking was a mixture of comedy, struggle, and passion. With comedy and passion slowly overwhelming the struggle.

"We must have music," she announced abruptly. "Let me go, you monster rapist. This is not an excuse."

I had all my clothes off, and Ciara was clad only in her panties—plain, unadorned cotton. She was utterly delicious. Vulnerable but glorious. There was no need for music.

But music we were going to have. She pulled a cassette out of her purse, fiddled with my stereo, and popped in the tape.

"The *Rite of Spring*?"

"Not Solti's, but at the moment it doesn't seem to matter."

"You want to make love to Stravinsky?" I reached for the elastic on her panties. She tried to dodge me.

" 'Tis better than Ravel altogether," she sniggered. "If you take my meaning. Now get on with your evil designs."

So we continued with a background of Igor Stravinsky and tornado-force winds shaking the windows and forcing the steel girders in the building to moan and groan with agony.

The music was a burst of bravado, a gesture of wild Irish flair. She was still frightened. What were the terrible demons that haunted her? I wondered as our union progressed—half wrestling match and half athletic coupling. It did not matter. My task was to overcome the demons and admire her courage for daring to try.

Finally, as the orchestra's music swelled to the mad crescendo of the sacrificial dance, I lost the remnants of my self-control and claimed her completely. My brain was clogged with an insane image of her body swelling with the shape of my child within. Spring, fertility, love, life all rushing together to create unbearable pleasure. Ciara by then was able to reply, an aroused, passionate woman as out of control as I. Our own rite of spring was accomplished. We drained the Holy Grail together.

We did not even notice when the music stopped.

13

"The great fat Irish cow gave you a hard time on your ride," she said bitterly.

We were lying on the floor of my living room, underneath the Picasso print, sweaty and exhausted.

"You're not fat," I said, truthfully enough. Naked, Ciara was slender to the point of thinness. The fullness of her body came from bones and shape, not from weight.

"God, I'm sorry." She was weeping bitterly. "And yourself such a wonderful lover too."

To tell the truth, as she would have said, I thought I was a pretty wonderful lover, too, especially for the little practice I'd had through the years. I had captured the woman and, to judge by her sighs and moans and then sharp shrieks of pleasure, she had enjoyed the experience.

"You weren't all that bad yourself, once you got started." I patted her approvingly.

She was not ready for consolation. "I'll make it up to you, Brendan," she promised grimly. "I swear I will. Oh, my darling, darling Little King Brendan." She attacked me with kisses, manic, tearful, adoring kisses. "Poor, dear, wonderful man."

Then she went into Irish endearments, whose tender affection needed no translation.

"You'll be the death of me, woman," I murmured. "Give me a chance to breathe."

"Only one breath," she said, leaning over me, marvelous breasts against my chest, her face intent on making me happy.

"Come on." I struggled away and took her hand. "We do have a bed in this house."

Dutifully she followed me into the bedroom and waited till I drew the blinds and climbed into bed. Then she slipped in beside me and resumed her Gaelic endearments and her determined kissing.

"A man doesn't have a chance to get his second wind with you, Ciara Kelly," I protested, insincerely and not altogether accurately.

Much later, she awoke me to say she should go back to her apartment. It was almost midnight.

"Is that necessary?" I yawned.

"It is," she said positively.

So I dressed and escorted my babbling lover through the Chestnut Street ravine and kissed her, positively but briefly, before turning her over to the sleepy doorman.

"I'll see you tomorrow?" she asked dubiously.

"Damn well better believe it."

The demons were scurrying around the fringes of the canyon on my return walk. I ignored them.

So began my love affair with Ciara Kelly, a passionate and sometimes inhibited woman, who made love to Stravinsky and adored me more than I possibly deserved.

Just the kind of woman I would create for myself if I were the hero in a novel I was writing. Presumably no mortal woman would think of making love with the *Rite of Spring* roaring ecstatically in the background; no mortal woman would have ivory thighs and generous hips and swelling breasts like hers, not really. Or if there were such a beautiful woman, why would she fall in love with me?

So Ciara Kelly, fact or fiction, is gone. If she does actually exist somewhere in the world, I'll never find her, never pin her unpredictably unresponsive body to my bed again.

So be it. At least for a time I knew her and loved her.

For the next two weeks she was the only reality in my life. I went through the motions of practicing law and watching the S&P Index call options at the CBOE. I ate the weekly meal with the Kanes and the Currans, and merely smiled wisely when the two women demanded more information about "her."

"Will we like her, Brenny?" Catherine demanded.

I merely laughed. They damn well better like her. How could they not?

I talked on the phone with both my parents and Jean about her pilgrimage to Tucson, which had apparently been a huge success.

"Such an intelligent and self-possessed young woman," my mother said, as though she could not believe it. "One would almost think she were English."

"Awesomely neat," was Jean's terse judgment. "Isn't it exciting that they're writing their memoirs?"

Which was news to me. And indeed exciting. But not as exciting as Ciara Kelly.

While it lasted, life with Ciara was delightfully erratic. She was a West of Ireland faerie spirit, a manic, half-pagan, partly savage lover, whose intermittent loss of nerve was balanced with a brazen, comic eroticism of which most men fantasize but which, after some years and some experience, they come not to expect in their women. You almost didn't notice that while she was giving you herself unreservedly, she was telling you nothing about herself. Gift, but no self-revelation. I was too bemused, too sotted with desire to care.

We were lovers for only a couple of weeks. We made love, however, more often than Madonna and I had in the last decade of our marriage—sometimes, especially at the beginning, serious, almost somber love; other times, particularly during our last days together, we were comic lovers. I told myself that she would wear me out, but I managed to hang on to the roller coaster I had set in motion, often just barely.

One night, after I had walked home with her to her apartment building, I tried to make a written accounting of the woman. I threw away the balance sheet after an hour of work. As I remember, however, I saw her as naive and sophisticated, innocent and earthy, transparent and mysterious, terrified and trusting, fun-loving and deadly serious.

You get the idea—I was in love. Looking back at those weeks, however, and taking into account both my adolescent fixation on her and the mystery of her departure, I nonetheless still feel that she was a puzzle, a riddle, an enigma.

I tossed my balance sheet, "In re: Ciara Kelly," into the wastebasket because I loved her too much to care about the bafflements. Anyway, everything seemed to fit together in perfect harmony, logical and psychological, when I was with her.

There were times when she was an elegant, gracious lady, a woman of the world, a Parisian countess; and other times, by her own description, a bitchy Irish prude; yet other times, a madcap, erotic imp. Like piloting a boat in heavy seas, one learned to ride with the waves.

There were yet other times when she would be so inexplicably angry at me after love that she would lie on the opposite side of the bed rigid and silent like a kidnapped slave girl who had been forced to submit against her will. Then I would awake not a quarter of an hour later to find her clinging to me desperately, as though she were afraid I would slip away. Her favorite position seemed to be huddled in my arms like a frightened child seeking protection.

She was irresistibly affectionate. "Trouble with you, Brendan Ryan," she told me as she hovered, bare-breasted, over me, long black hair brushing my chest, caressing my face with delicate fingers, "is that you're a great, powerful lover and marvelous good at all the prior activities too, but you're almost worthless at accepting mild affection. Well . . ." watching me with eyes so filled with admiration as to make me want to weep, ". . . if you continue to be involved with me, you're going to have to learn to sop up affection when I offer it. Now hold still while I sing to you till you're ready to be loved again."

She sang what sounded like a Gaelic lullaby, but then all Irish songs sound like lullabies.

"Translate it for me?" I begged.

"Sure, I will not. The words are too gross altogether."

At first I found it hard to submit to such, it seemed to me, time-wasting nonsense. I learned quickly enough to enjoy it. Time stopped, the world stood still. I would let her minister to me forever.

I drove her out to the Neighborhood, through the curved streets and the wooded hills of that magic community, the highest elevation in Cook County, a little bit of woodland still surviving in our prairie city. I showed her Glenwood Drive, the Maze, the Courts of St. Praxides, Louis's drugstore. Perhaps she would not see them all as magic like I did.

"It's a great, powerful place altogether," she said thoughtfully.

"Great, powerful" (her alternative to "Great, fucking" she told me once) was best translated as "fine," but with many nuances, not all of them non-ironic, depending on the context.

For the first time, however, the Neighborhood made me sad. It was no longer the paradise garden of my youth and adolescence, but the origin of so many blighted dreams and frustrated hopes, the starting point of so many senseless pilgrimages, the beginning place of so many messed-up lives, the locale of so many ghosts that emerged not only on Halloween but every day of the year.

She sensed my melancholy as we stopped for a few moments in front of the stained-glass window of St. Prax's—depicting that saint with a great, powerful ax (Prax's Ax, to one and all) setting forth to chop the wood from which the Bethlehem manger would be built. (Or was it a boat for St. Christopher? It was always a matter of debate among the nuns.)

"Ah, my poor Little King Brendan." She drew my head to her bosom. " 'Tis a terrible heavy sadness that weighs on you here. The magic doesn't have to stay sour, you know. Some dreams do come true after all."

It was a remarkable reading of my mood. I was perilously close to tears. I vowed to myself that eventually Ciara Kelly and I would move back here and begin life again. I almost stopped at the "other" Ryans' house on Longwood to introduce her to Ned and Helen, his second wife. And then we could have gone next door to the lovely Eileen's sister, Mary Kate Murphy, the Freudian analyst, and her husband, Joe Murphy, the Jungian from Boston.

I drove by the Ryan compound without stopping. Save that pleasure for later. That afternoon I took her for a Wendella cruise on the Chicago River and along the shore of the lake, managing to get slightly seasick, as I usually do when I'm not at the helm of a sailboat but wallowing, even ever so slightly, between waves. I overcame my nausea by concentrating on Ciara's comparison of Chicago from the lake with the strand at Inch on Dingle Bay—"The two places in the world closest to Heaven," she shouted wildly over the wind. "Sure, the trip would be shorter than from anywhere. I think I want to die either at Inch or on one of these boats. Faith, it would be a hop, skip, and a jump to Heaven."

"We'll visit Inch someday."

"And make love on the beach." We were the only customers on the boat, and the crew too far away to hear. "Do you think it would be difficult? Would sand be a problem?"

It was a problem to be discussed seriously and responsibly. No joking around about screwing in the anteroom of Heaven.

"Not if you had a big enough blanket."

"You're daft, man." She hugged me. "Altogether daft."

She had learned my moods quickly. And also my fantasies, as she demonstrated the next day when we were on the *Brigid*, sailing north with an east wind on a fluffy day with ice cream cone clouds.

" 'Tis said that some American women strip to the waist on boats when they are far enough offshore," she announced suddenly.

"Doesn't happen in Ireland, I guess?"

"Not with the Irish male's great, terrible breast fixation. I don't suppose it's ever happened on this boat."

I could hardly believe my ears. The night before she had protected herself from my gaze with a sheet held underneath her chin while she lectured me again about the politics of Northern Ireland, not a word of which I understood.

"Not to my knowledge."

"Not even your wife?"

There were occasional questions about Madonna, shrewd, cautious probings of my marriage. She was trying to calculate, I guess, what went wrong. Fine. When you find out, tell me.

"Madonna rarely came on the boat. She didn't approve of nakedness."

"Poor woman," she said, pulling the sweatshirt over her head.

It was not a sight with which I was totally unfamiliar. A bedroom is one thing, however. A thirty-foot boat at flank speed is something else. I lost control of the tiller, and *Brigid*, jealous perhaps of a rival lover, heeled dizzily.

"Tend to your steering," she shouted, hands defiantly on her hips. "The scenery is meant to be admired not pawed . . . for the moment."

"Admirable it is," I gasped, bringing the boat back into line. "And delightful too."

"I want to delight you," she exulted, arms stretched triumphantly over her head. "I want you to be able to think of nothing else but me. I want to drive you out of your mind with desire. Now mind what you're doing with the poor boat."

She could not keep her distance for long. Within a quarter of an hour she was snuggled in my arms in the stern. "Trouble with bare tits on a day like this is that it's cold."

"There are a number of approved and recommended ways of keeping warm."

We made love leisurely in the cabin, anchored not in the harbor but behind the Navy Pier breakwater, with the skyline watching, I imagined, in surprised amusement. Ciara avowed that boat cabins were the best place in the world for loving, though I was sure she'd never had the experience before.

I didn't bring her to the weekly lunch with my new group. Our relationship was still too private, I told myself, too new, too fragile. Moreover, she had told me nothing about herself, despite my increasingly obvious hints that I wanted to know more about who she was and where she came from.

Sometimes she would weep in my arms, protesting that her tears were from "too much happiness altogether." There was happiness in the tears, all right, but something else, too, that I did not quite understand and was not sure I liked—a kind of frightened hopelessness, as if she were sure that it would all have to end.

Could she, I wondered, have a husband somewhere else? It didn't seem likely. Even an unhappy marriage would have involved more sexual initiation than she seemed to have received.

I persuaded her that she might swim in the little-used pool in my building. She carried her swimsuit from the Irish Store.

"You'll not wear that terrible ugly swimsuit in my pool," I insisted, giving her the almost weightless little Lord & Taylor plastic bag I had been carrying.

She removed the floral print bikini (relatively modest, all things considered) with feigned dismay. "Ah, one of the great, powerful, immoral things the bishops are after warning us about." She inspected the size and colored. "Bloody hell! You've been measuring me, Brendan Ryan. Shame on you."

"Put it on, woman," I ordered.

"I'll do no such thing." She faded into the bathroom and emerged a minute or two later, awkward and uncertain. "Ah, there's too much of me and not enough of it."

"That's the general idea." I put my arms around her. "It's a grand suit altogether."

"Stop talking like me," she sniffed. "And keep your hands to yourself, man. We can't make love and swim both."

"Why not?" I demanded, my hand already underneath the bikini.

"Swim first." She drew in her breath and her head tilted as the pleasure chemicals rushed into her blood.

"No way. The nice thing about this design is that it comes off so easily."

When we finally made it to the pool, she swam for forty-five minutes with a relaxed, confident kick that effortlessly ate up the laps.

"Well, at least the wicked thing stays on in the water. . . . Keep away from me, Brendan Ryan. Not in the pool we don't."

Riding the elevator back to my apartment, still gasping for breath, she observed, "It's a terrible thing for a woman to let herself get so badly out of condition. I've fallen apart altogether. Sure, I won't be able to work tomorrow. Lucky we did the loving beforehand."

"Did we now?"

"Stop talking like me!" She poked me, hard. "Brendan, not in the elevator."

So I waited till we were back in the apartment. Then I waited till she had showered to clean the chlorine from her hair. Showers had become part of routine. "Loving isn't dirty, but I am," she asserted. "And they'll be private showers for the moment, do you take my meaning?"

I admitted that I did.

After she emerged from the shower, hair limp and loose, wrapped in a yellow towel, I agreed that we both needed a glass of Jameson's to warm us up, though I was more than warm enough.

We frolicked with one another, made love, and napped. I awoke to find my naked woman standing by the bed with the Jameson's bottle and two clean tumblers. "Another drop won't do us any harm," she informed me.

So we lay under the rumpled sheets in the darkness of my bedroom, the smell of shampoo still on her, and watched the lights of the jets dotting the night sky like fireflies on the approaches to O'Hare and drank our Jameson's—straight up, naturally—settled and self-satisfied companions in passion.

"You were in the war, Brendan?" she asked suddenly.

"I was, before it really was a war. I came home in 1966."

"Did you shoot at anyone?"

"Yes."

"Kill them?"

What a strange line of questions. Why did she want to know?

"I suppose so. I didn't stop to make sure."

"How do you feel about it?"

"Sorry if anyone is dead. Glad that I'm still alive and the others I was protecting."

"It was self-defense, was it?"

"You better believe it. Protecting the innocent even."

She was quiet in the darkness next to me.

"Do you talk about it much?"

"Not ever, not to anyone. Except my father and mother, who were in the Second World War."

"Your mother?"

"Both."

"Do you want to talk to me about it?"

I did indeed want to talk about it, to tell Ciara Kelly about a different Brendan Ryan from the one she knew. And the third woman in my life. Yes, I wanted to tell Ciara Kelly about her too. Regardless of what she thought of me after the story was finished.

"Very much. May I put my arm around you while I talk?"

"After I fill your glass again."

14

Red lights flashed around the house as our boat, the advance party for Operation Dakota, slowed down and turned toward the riverbank.

"Did you see any red lights, Corporal?" I said to the kid who was driving the launch.

"No, sir," he said. "They don't have traffic lights up in this part of the country, sir."

"I am well aware of that, Corporal."

"Yes, sir."

The lights were my own internal warning signals, my erratic psychic sense foretelling, accurately if imprecisely, the dangers that were to come. The psychiatrist I would see after the disappearance of Ciara Kelly and the other springtime disasters was perfectly prepared to admit that I had hallucinated her. But he brusquely denied the existence of psychic powers and extrasensory phenomena.

"Dere iss no such ding as ESP," he assured me dogmatically. "Iss a scientific impossibility."

"A scientific impossibility," Blackie Ryan would comment yet later, "that affects three-fifths of the people in the country. The good doctor would have voted for the conviction of Galileo."

On that hot, humid night in up-country Vietnam during the spring of 1966, I knew little about ESP, but enough to realize that the warning lights were not required to tell me that it was a stupid mission.

Then I saw Guy and Marie Tho on the veranda of their bamboo house, built on stilts so that part of it extended over the river, and forgot about dangers. Marie was the sort of woman who without even trying makes you forget everything else in the world.

The official histories of the war mention our mission, but in cautious and obscure words. I suppose that it is still cloaked in security wraps to protect any of the survivors who may still be working in Vietnam—for the CIA. Who else?

Or maybe the secrecy is to protect the geniuses who devised the project, some of whom went on to become very important members of the military establishment.

So I will be properly judicious in my description.

Someone had a very bright idea about intelligence gathering in the months after the 1966 election, when, as we knew in Nam but as the American people did not yet know, there would be an enormous buildup of American military power.

The idea did not have a chance to work. Worse, by sending small American teams into that particular part of the country, it was likely to provoke Viet Cong reaction, causing considerable risk to the team members and the native personnel.

In any case, I was the second in command of one of the teams, chosen not because of any talents of my own, but because they thought they needed someone who was Catholic and spoke French. (My mother had taught me French when I was a kid by talking to me in that language for half an hour every day.) I also suspect that the man I replaced had the kind of clout that Dr. Clifford thought he had. My predecessor was on his way back to the Pentagon, and I was dragged from my analysis desk in Saigon and converted from a chair-bound officer to a command officer.

Under a major who was an old OSS hand and now in the final stages of dementia.

Marie Tho made me forget about him too. She was about thirty then, the mother of four children, including a lovely baby daughter, perhaps four months old, named Emily. I was six years younger, over a year and a half away from my wife, and suddenly aware, in the presence of that slender, elegant woman with high, conical breasts, deftly curving hips, trimly sculpted legs, and exquisite face, how deep and powerful were my unacknowledged sexual hungers.

The Thos were educated Catholics from the North, members of the mandarin class that had been civil servants for the French empire, like President Diem, whom Cabot Lodge seems to have had murdered. They and their community had migrated to the South after Dien Bien Phu and established a rubber and rice plantation in this remote upriver jungle district. Hard working and industrious, more Chinese than Tonkinese, it seemed, they had prospered and now faced with stoic resignation another migration, another new beginning.

They had agreed enthusiastically to help "the Americans," believing that we might protect their community, their church, their priest.

Soon they would learn better.

"Lieutenant Ryan? So nice to have you. You will be welcome to stay here in our house. We will be honored if you take your meals with my family. May I present my wife, Marie?"

Her almond eyes locked with mine. She moved her head slightly, disconcerted, as I was, by the electricity between us. "Welcome, Lieutenant Ryan," she murmured, lowering her eyes.

Guy Tho was a handsome little man with silvering hair at his temples, a smooth blend of French and Asian intellectual. We became instant friends and spent many long hours discussing Napoleonic and Anglo-Saxon law and Thomistic philosophy on his veranda as the radio crackled next to us. I'm sure that in those days he found me a naive young cub. Yet he was unfailingly courteous and respectful, treating me like a learned senior colleague.

There was little to do but talk and make sure the daily patrols poked through the thick, steamy, sweet-smelling jungle beyond the plantation perimeter. It was an exercise we performed because sending out patrols was what armies did and not because we had any hope of finding the Viet Cong before they decided to sweep down from the mountains in the distance and wipe us out.

I had come to Vietnam with the "pay any price" idealistic faith of the Kennedy years, though in my case it was always a soft-spoken and slightly skeptical faith. "Wars are won," my father had told me long before, "by the side that makes fewer mistakes. Pray not for good leaders but for leaders who are less stupid than the leaders of the other side."

Six months in Vietnam had convinced me that the

other side would have to be monumentally stupid to be worse than us. We were, I thought then and still think, the good guys. Read any newspaper account of the current situation in Vietnam and learn that poverty, corruption, and tyranny are at least as bad if not worse than they were when our side was running Saigon. There was hope in those days, and there is no hope now.

Regardless of who was good and who was bad, who was the lie and who was the half-truth, it was clear that Program Policy Budgeting System, Robert McNamara's contribution to military theory, could not be transferred from Ford Motor Company and Pentagon management to fighting a war against a tenacious Asian enemy.

I'm not sure today whether we could have won if we'd done it right. Nor do I know what doing it right would have meant. But I was certain as I sat on the Thos' veranda, ogling Marie, arguing philosophy with Guy, and worrying about my lunatic CO, that we were going down the path to sure defeat.

My Kennedy idealism faded quickly in Vietnam. Pragmatic American enthusiasm was not subtle enough, perhaps not cynical enough, to cope with the twisted and historically rooted complexities of Southeast Asia. We had blundered in with our "can do" spirit, our massive technology, and our Harvard Business School management techniques, and were in the process of making a bad situation worse, expanding the size of the sinkhole with our every move. Southeast Asia would have been better off if we had not become involved.

Later I would make the same decision, not without some ambiguity, about my involvement with the Thos and would go home reluctant to leave my observer's position on the banks of the river of the human condition. Ordinarily, it seemed to me, you only made things worse when you became involved, whether as a nation or as a person. Even when you had behaved bravely. Perhaps especially when you had behaved bravely.

The junior officers in my team, most of them ROTC-trained like me, in the air-conditioned basements in Saigon, poring over data sheets on their cheap metal desks, were unanimous in this viewpoint about the war. Which is why we were sent home to be replaced by more brilliant analysts, West Point careerists who understood that you told superiors what they wanted to hear instead of what they ought to know.

The war would soon be in the hands of the professionals, men like my CO, though not as berserk, who were skilled at the bureaucratic game of getting their "ticket punched" with a Vietnam tour and incompetent at fighting the kind of war in which we were engaged. Probably any other kind of war too.

Not many of them went as far toward the deep end as my CO, who would take his machete in hand each morning, sling an M16 over his shoulders, and stride out into the jungle to "kill me some Charlies." One of our noncoms told me that the major chopped the tops off bamboo plants and fired his automatic weapon into rice paddies.

We could tell when he was coming back; the sound of gunfire in the distance meant that Major Schilling was mowing down imaginary Charlies.

"How will we know the difference," the noncom asked, "when the VC really attacks?"

"We hope it's after the major comes in."

I realized that we were the forward outpost, the first one that the VC would attack should they decide to come down from the mountains and clear us out of the province as an object lesson to the local people and to exiled Catholics from the North that they would only make matters worse for themselves by cooperating with the Americans.

Our unit, two officers and a dozen enlisted men, would have to sound the alarm for the other stations. Thus, for all practical purposes, the fate of a hundred or so Americans and about the same number of Vietnamese Catholics depended on a CO who later might easily have made the cast of *Apocalypse Now*. If he should be out with his machete and his M16 shooting up imaginary Charlies when the real ones showed, I'd be in charge.

I reviewed the tactics courses I'd had in ROTC at Loyola and concluded that if the VC came down the river— which would be what I would do if I were in their position—the only proper response would be what we euphemistically called "redeployment": getting the hell out of there as quickly as we could.

When my supercharged imagination was not preoccupied with fantasies about Marie's charms, I tried to figure how I could, as an inexperienced first lieutenant, give the orders for a redeployment and how we could fend off the VC while we were waiting for the cavalry to come riding over the hills.

Our operation should have been called Little Bighorn.

I studied the tactical layout of our situation almost as intently as I studied the relationship between Guy and Marie. He was older than she, perhaps in his middle forties, although the childlike faces of the Vietnamese made it hard to guess age. There was obvious affection between them, but, it seemed, not much passion. Guy was a dry and pedantic if charming man. Marie was devout and pious—she made the sign of the cross whenever she passed one of the many statues in their house—but also deeply sensuous. Moreover, she seemed more fatalistic than her husband, certain that the atrocities which had wiped out the other members of her family would eventually claim her too.

"I do not care," she said one night, bouncing the infant Emily on her knee, "if they bury me up to my head in the sand and permit the ants to destroy me as they did my little sister. I hope that this one," she poked a finger at the happily gurgling little girl, "somehow survives and escapes to America."

Her husband gently but firmly reprimanded her for lack of faith.

We spoke rarely to each other, implicitly agreeing that the energies that raced back and forth between us were dangerous.

One afternoon I was poking around in the river ponds, downriver from their house. I didn't permit myself to realize that I was looking for Marie.

I found her, as I thought I would, bathing in one of the pools, playing in the water with the delighted Emily.

"You shouldn't be here, ma'am." I tried not to look at her olive skin, long black hair, and small, high breasts—a delicate Asian water deity. "If there's an attack, you'd be in serious danger."

She held Emily close to her body, a symbolic protection of modesty. "I will die, then, with my little girl."

"Guy would say that was lack of faith."

"Faith did not save my parents or my sisters."

"I think you'd better permit me to accompany you back to the house, ma'am."

She shrugged her delicate little shoulders. "Am I permitted to dress?"

"Certainly, ma'am."

"Then you will hold the *enfant*?" She passed the smiling child—she always seemed to smile—to me, revealing, as she stepped out of the pool and onto the rock at the edge of the pond, her full womanly beauty.

An innocent movement for a Vietnamese? A tease? A natural gesture? An invitation?

Probably all four in some complex mixture. I turned away and played with the delighted Emily while she dressed. We walked back to the house in silence, my own embarrassed, hers, as far as I could tell, perfectly self-possessed.

I told myself that if I were a little more certain of her invitation, neither the commandment against adultery nor the obligations of hospitality would have stopped me. Looking back, there was no reason to doubt the invitation. I was too well indoctrinated in virtue, or perhaps too inhibited, to respond. Later I would love her too much to exploit her weakness.

We were visited one afternoon by a brigadier general, a lean, dour, hard-bitten man, who viewed our post with an expression of distaste that indicated either a bad ulcer or horror at the lunacy of Operation Dakota.

He ate lunch with the Thos, the major, and myself. The major, perfectly sober in the presence of the brass, raved about the opportunities for "killing Charlies" in our zone.

As he was boarding his helicopter, in a clearing I had ordered in the rubber plantation about twenty yards behind the house, he sent the major back for a map case that had been left in the house.

"What do you think, son?"

It took me several seconds before I realized he was talking to me. ROTC officer that I was, I spoke the truth. "It should be called Operation Little Bighorn, sir."

"Humph . . . Are there evacuation plans?"

"None that I know of, sir. And, if there were . . ."

"The major would not activate them, right?"

"Yes, sir."

He thought for a moment.

"When I get back to HQ, I'll create such a plan. Helicopters. We will call it . . . let me see, Red Baron. I'll inform the major." He glared at me significantly. "You will know the code too."

"We'll remove the Vietnamese personnel?" I was thinking of Marie. And Emily. No anthill for that cheerful little girl, if I could help it.

"Negative," snapped the general. "We cannot assume responsibility for them."

"With respect, sir . . ."

"Yes?" he barked irritably.

"If we do not take care of them," the answer sprang to my lips without thought, "we will confirm the enemy propaganda that it is not safe to trust Americans."

He thought about it. "Right," he spat out finally. "Good thought, son. We'll get them out too. . . . You from the Academy?" He glanced at my hand to see if I was wearing a West Point class ring.

"Loyola University in Chicago, sir."

"More like you," he grumbled, "and we might win this war."

"Yes, sir."

The major never told me about Red Baron, but the next day I began building a small perimeter around the house and the landing pad: foxholes, barricades, fire points. The major was too busy on his hunt through the plantation for Charlies to notice.

Marie emerged from the house late in the afternoon with the grinning Emily in her arms.

"I would respectfully submit, ma'am," I could on occasion sound like I was a West Point grad, "that it is unwise to return to that pool."

"For me or you, *mon capitaine?*" She smiled enigmatically.

"For both of us, ma'am." I managed to force the words through my tight throat. "In different ways, perhaps."

She laughed softly and slipped down the path, her slim hips swaying under her tight-fitting dress with slit sides, like a young tree in a strong breeze. That's the way they walk all the time, I told myself.

In addition to constructing a perimeter from which we could be evacuated, I began to explore upriver in our small launch, assuming that the VC would strike at dusk, when it would be difficult for our air support to be called in.

For a week nothing happened, then another week. Marie and I did not speak. Guy and I discussed Jacques Maritain and Etienne Gilson, French Catholic philosophers. The radio crackled every day. The mid afternoon rain became heavier, the sun hotter. I counted the days until my return to my wife and daughter. Only another month. My men—they were mine now—swam in the river. The major continued to shoot up the plantation. Emily continued to laugh.

Then another week.

And three days into a fourth week.

My sergeant and I were returning in the boat, a little earlier in the afternoon than usual. Half a mile upriver from the Thos' house, an automatic weapon opened up on us—like a string of firecrackers on the Fourth of July, with phosphorescent flashes dashing over our heads.

I pushed the throttle full forward and raced away while the jungle behind us exploded with noise and fire and bursting white lights.

The VC made mistakes, too, almost as many as we did. If someone had not been trigger-happy that day, all of us would have been dead in a few hours.

I ran the boat into the landing beneath the veranda of the Tho house at full speed, calmly ordered my men into position, and warned Guy to prepare his family and dependents for evacuation. The world went into slow motion, frame after frame passing before my eyes, so that I had plenty of time to see what was happening and make my decisions.

Much later I read an article by John Brodie, quarterback for the San Francisco 49ers, and apparently also a psychic, in which he described the same phenomenon occurring during (some but not all) pass plays. He could see the defensive patterns developing like a frame-by-frame slow-motion film and "check off" his pass at the last fraction of a second to select a secondary receiver who was in the clear.

Obviously, I thought in my slow motion, that kind of firepower meant a major attack. I turned on the radio transceiver and reported, "Red Baron. I repeat, this is Operation Dakota. Red Baron. Red Baron."

The major appeared on the veranda and tried to take the transceiver away from me.

"We're going to have a feast of Charlies tonight," he ranted.

None of the men was watching. I coolly slugged him with the butt of my M16.

"Corporal," I ordered a man who came rushing up the steps, "the major seems to be a casualty. Remove him to the perimeter."

"Dakota, we acknowledge," the transceiver crackled. "Red Baron. Your lucky day. The air force has some ordinance in the area."

In later days in Vietnam, coordination between ground and air was often disastrously bad. It was indeed our lucky day—or so it seemed at first. The other side had blown its cool; then F104s tore the VC's sampans to pieces before they could turn the big bend in the river and descend on us.

The enemy was swatting a pesky fly with a howitzer.

See, General, I was right. The Catholics are important to them.

It was sixty miles to our base. If the choppers were on their way at once, we would need only half an hour. Ignoring the screams of the Vietnamese, which I couldn't understand anyway, I formed my tiny command into its defensive perimeter and waited for the enemy.

They came almost at once, not from the river but through the neatly ordered lanes of the rubber plantation, a score or so of little men in black pajamas, appearing like make-believe ghosts in the fading light, firing automatic weapons, throwing grenades, and screaming like lunatics.

If we had not been prepared, we would have fled in panic and been cut down.

As it was, we were prepared and they were the ones who were cut down. I squeezed the trigger of my M16. Oddly enough it worked. I had won the marksmanship prize in my ROTC company. And in man-to-man combat too. I'd sworn to myself that I would never use either skill to kill.

They crumpled like rag dolls at the edge of the rubber trees. What did they think in their last seconds of life? Were they dying for Karl Marx, for a socialist Vietnam? Or because their commanders would kill them if they did not charge?

A handful of them raced back down the lanes, firing wildly at us.

"Hold your fire," I ordered, realizing for the first time that I had never ordered my men to open fire. I must have started to shoot and then they joined me.

"We slaughtered them, sir," yelled the sergeant triumphantly.

"Yeah," I said, feeling no enthusiasm for what had happened. "They'll be back."

They were back indeed. In fifteen minutes, I suppose, though it seemed like a couple of eternities. They were more cautious this time, hiding behind the trees and firing at us intermittently. Testing our defenses and carrying off their dead.

If they'd been any good at their work, they would have discovered that our defenses were pretty weak. Their commander would wait till dark—dusk was already thick around us—and wipe us out.

Then we heard the sound of choppers, huge khaki dragonflies hovering protectively above us.

Two of them settled quickly onto the landing area. No fire from the enemy. Surprised and uncertain, perhaps.

"One more craft coming," an officer on the lead chopper shouted.

I ordered the civilians onto the first chopper and the still unconscious major and the Thos onto the second.

"Marie!" Guy screamed at me, his face twisted in anguish. "She is not here."

"I'll find her," I replied, still cool and confident. "You get out of here with the others. We'll be in the last chopper."

"She is my wife!" he pleaded, tears streaming down his grief-stricken face.

"I'm in charge," I said, surely the most foolish words I've uttered in my whole life. "I'll bring her out. Now get on that helicopter. That's an order."

I must have sounded terribly military. He did as he was told.

There were six men left besides me when the two giant dragonflies lifted off the ground and disappeared quickly down the river.

"Give us five minutes, Sergeant," I said quietly. "If I'm not back by then, leave without me."

He hesitated.

"That's an order."

"Yes, sir."

I never told Madonna about that act of madness. A husband and a father recklessly playing hero for a provocative Asian woman.

In any case, it was more than ten minutes before the third chopper arrived. By that time the VC had brought up their mortars and were zeroing in on the landing area.

Stumbling over roots in the twilight, I rushed through the underbrush toward the pool, not reflecting until I was almost there that if Marie had not returned to the perimeter behind her house, the reason was that the VC had already captured her.

I crawled the last twenty yards through the brush and peered cautiously at the dusk-shrouded pond. They had her, all right, and if they had not been so busy at their work, they would have heard me.

She was tied naked to a tree with a knife at her belly. Two of the men were peasants in black pajamas, indistinguishable from any rubber plantation worker. The third, the man with the knife, was dressed in white shorts and shirt, an officer or a cadre. It was not rape they had in mind. Not yet. They wanted information. Why were the Americans ready?

One of the other men pulled a small wailing object out of the water. What could it be?

Emily.

I thought of Melissa Jean back home in Chicago, calmly switched my weapon to manual fire, lined up the man with the knife in my sights, and with now the slowest of slow motion put a bullet in the back of his head, smashing it like a grapefruit. Then, with what seemed like infinite leisure, I shifted my gunsight to the man who had been dunking the poor little girl and killed him. Emily fell back into the water.

The third man turned in my direction and raised his AK-47. Much too late. I had blown his head away before he was able to aim.

These were the first of the enemy I was certain I had killed. The only emotion I felt was fury at what they were doing to Emily.

I heard, as if from a great distance, the sound of an incoming chopper and the muffled flumps of mortar rounds. I ran around the pond, snatched the fiercely protesting Emily out of the pool, cut the rope binding Marie to the tree, and ordered her to stop vomiting and follow me.

She obeyed.

We reached the perimeter just as the chopper disappeared above the trees. Mortar rounds were exploding all around us, sending up little balls of silver smoke and dirt.

A naked woman with a trickle of blood running down her belly, a hysterical little girl, and a now thoroughly frightened first lieutenant, who knew with total certainty that soon he would die.

I had saved Marie's life. Now she saved mine.

"We must go down the river in a sampan," she said softly. "Come with me."

The mortars stopped as abruptly as they had begun. I imagined the enemy creeping through the trees for their final attack. "Come with me," she repeated.

My terror ebbed. I followed her into the house.

Quickly she found black coolie pajamas and broad hats for the two of us. "You must wear the hat over your face," she said. "You are short enough to be a Vietnamese." She jammed food and a wad of money into two baskets, presented me with the somewhat placated Emily, and led the way to the boat dock beneath the house. We boarded a sampan, perhaps fourteen feet long, with a small cabin in the front. She skillfully poled us out of the dock and into midriver. We turned once in the current and then began to drift almost casually downstream.

The mortars resumed fire. Marie's house erupted in a cloud of incandescent smoke and then burst into flame. She did not even look back.

During the voyage down the river, a bizarre mixture of terror and quiet restfulness, Marie was the pilot and the commanding officer who steered us through the swift currents and the slow, and poled us away from the tangled jungle at the banks when we drifted too close. She decided when we would paddle way into shore and hide till dark. She gave the instructions on handling the boat. She talked in the local dialect to the uneasy and suspicious people we encountered. She slipped into a village one night to buy fruit.

Her orders were always given as a polite request, as if she were asking me for a favor. She spoke and acted as though she were devoid of emotions. "It would perhaps be useful, *mon capitaine*, if you remained very close to me when we pass that sampan, so that they will look at my face and not yours."

You bet, honey.

VC patrols roamed the area, making sure that there were no Americans left and collecting taxes (tribute) from the peasants. We hid in a small stream for two days, waiting till she learned from the natives that it was safe to travel downriver again.

Every sound in the jungle made me reach for my M16. Finally, Marie told me somewhat impatiently that she'd let me know when it was needed.

We slept during the day, huddling in the stifling heat under the bamboo cover that was our cabin, pressed close together in what was even in those circumstances a delightfully sensuous embrace. Emily, merry little child, created no fuss as long as her mother's breasts were available when she was hungry.

Only once did Marie show emotion. I woke late one afternoon, soaked in sweat and with a terrible headache, to hear her crying softly.

She was worried about Guy and the other children. I assured her that they were safe and held her in my arms while she cried herself back to sleep. Whatever hesitancies there had been in my love for her disappeared. In a twinkling, love became adoration.

Later that night, after she had nursed her daughter, half asleep, I reached for a breast. She smiled benignly and guided my lips to first one nipple, then the other. Her milk was sweet and warm, her body firm and restful, her eyes, just visible in the moonlight reflected on the water, were soft and big with pleasure.

I did not ask her to nurse me again.

Six days after we had fled, we were picked up by an armed patrol that stumbled on us without warning just as we had paddled ashore at dawn.

I shoved my weapon into the wide sleeves of my pajamas while they pulled Marie out of the boat and knocked her to her knees. They wore American-made uniforms and carried M1s. Government provincial troops who, from the point of view of the peasants, were as much a threat as the VC.

They pushed me in the direction of their lieutenant, who had already pulled back the shoulder of Marie's black jacket and was admiring his prize. I buried the muzzle of my weapon into his belly and told him, in the GI language he would understand, that he was one step away from being a dead motherfucker.

They apologized profusely, doubtless expecting to be executed, and led us to the nearest American outfit, a marine patrol. The gyrenes were impressed by how tough I looked, and even more impressed by Marie. They took us back to the headquarters of Operation Little Bighorn.

"You didn't make love to her?" Ciara asked, her eyes staring off in the distance, seeing something that was far away.

"I could have. Easily. She didn't desire me the way she'd done the first day at the pool. Yet she would have given herself to me for the asking. Out of gratitude and affection. I adored the woman. She was so brave, so smart, so good. We told each other our life stories while we floated down the river under the stars. I have never had a closer friend. I wanted her more than I have wanted anyone till I met you. Somehow it didn't seem right. Now I wonder. Maybe drinking her milk was as bad. I've never had pleasure quite like it. Typical male fantasy, I suppose."

"Sure, you have no monopoly on it." Ciara jabbed my ribs playfully. "We're nursed and weaned, too, you know."

"I don't even want to think about the kinky fantasies that makes possible."

"You do too." She kissed me reassuringly. "There's nothing wrong with fantasies."

"Do you think I was a coward because I didn't make love to her?"

She rested her head on my chest. "Ah, sure, you did the right thing altogether. Still, I wouldn't have thought less of you if you'd made love to the poor woman. And herself wanting it, too, I suppose. You're a great, powerful hero you are, Brendan Ryan, and a noble one at that."

"I'm not so sure," I said. "When we finally reached the base we learned that the second chopper had been hit by enemy fire and crash-landed at the base. The major, Guy, and two of the kids had been killed. I got a medal."

"Glory be to God." I felt her tears on my chest. "Still you did the right thing, Brendan."

"Did I? If I had not ordered Guy out, he might have lived. If I had ordered them to wait for us, the VC might not have hit them. We mucked up going into that place, and I mucked up getting out."

"You can't torment yourself that way," she insisted.

"I should have locked the woman in the house. Or warned her husband to keep her away from the pond." I went on remorselessly with accusations I had never spoken to anyone before. "I wanted to keep open the possibility of going back there and making love . . ."

"Hush," she ordered weakly. I hushed.

"They're all dead now?" she asked, stroking my cheek gently.

I watched the lights of a jet gliding through the darkness toward O'Hare. It was easy to fly a plane. You follow the instructions and it takes off and lands. You program the automatic pilot and the plane goes where it is told. Not so easy to pilot your life. "Oddly enough, no. No thanks to me. I couldn't deal with her grief, so I went back to my basement in Saigon after I kissed her and Emily good-bye. She married an American navy commander six months later. Somehow he managed to extricate her whole community, priest included, and ship them to America."

"A bad man?"

"No, a hell of a nice guy. Marie didn't choose her first husband. She was smart enough to make the right choice the second time around. A good Catholic like she is, kind of conservative but flexible and pleasant. He retired as a rear admiral. They live in San Diego now. She owns a string of Chinese restaurants—high-class places."

"You see them, then?"

"Occasionally. When I'm on the West Coast. Not too often. It wouldn't be safe. I love her. I always will."

"She loves him?"

"Very much."

"Does she still love you?"

"Yes. In a way."

Ciara kissed me gently. "Terrible question. Lucky Brendan. If you had made love to her, she wouldn't dare still love you."

I'd never thought of it that way. "Perhaps."

"No perhaps about it."

"Oddly enough, it turns out now that the Holy Roman Church has decided that Madonna and I were never married. It would not have been adultery to make love to Marie. I could have brought her home as my wife."

"It wouldn't have worked out and you know it." Her lips roamed about my face. "Besides, then you wouldn't have noticed me in the Irish Store."

"There's that." I held her tightly. "You've been worth waiting for, Ciara Kelly. . . ."

"Go 'long with you." Gently she pushed me away, but the kisses continued. "And the wee lass?"

"Emily?"

"And who else would I mean?" She stopped kissing me to indicate her response to such a stupid question.

"That's kind of strange. She's at Stanford. Valedictorian in her class at some Catholic school in San Diego. Very lovely kid. Completely American."

"And she and your daughter are good friends?"

I swatted her lovely rump in mock displeasure. "You're an incurable romantic, woman. I don't think she and Jeannie know each other."

"You didn't tell your daughter?" Ciara turned on the bed lamp so she could examine me in angry disbelief. "What kind of a 'quare crayture' are you, Brendan Ryan?" Her accent was West of Ireland again, a mixture of shock and incredulity. "What are you afraid of?"

"Messing in people's lives," I said. "And messing them up."

She stared at me, considering me again as if I were some newly discovered and baffling form of animal life. Will she kiss me again, I wondered, or reach for her panties and bra and ask me to take her back to Chestnut Place?

Irishwoman that she was, she did both.

And invited me to have supper there on Sunday night, after sailing.

I had been judged and found not guilty by reason of insanity, and then committed to tender care to see if my sanity might be restored.

It had not been a bad night after all.

15

"There'll be no sailing today." Ciara pointed at the limp mainsail. "Ah, well, there's an ancient Irish adage to cover the situation." She giggled. "In fact there's an ancient Irish adage to cover every situation."

She jumped into the cockpit, agile and graceful in white shorts and red sweater, inexpensive recent additions to her meager wardrobe.

We drifted lazily five hundred yards offshore. The sky-line was wrapped in tissue paper haze under a bright sun. An occasional ripple in the water, changing its color from dark blue to dark green, was the only sign of a breeze. For a sailor, a disappointing day. Summer doesn't last long; every weekend is precious.

"What's the old Irish wisdom?"

She furrowed her lovely forehead. "Let me think now. Ah, it goes something like this: A bad day for sailing is a good day for loving."

"Let me drop the anchor first."

Our bodies were becoming familiar with each other and loving it. Ciara was telling me none of the secrets of her life—a mysteriousness that made her all the more desirable. But she hid nothing of her growing sexual passion.

With some embarrassment I would undress first. Embarrassment and also, to admit the truth, a growing masculine vanity that my woman was so quickly turned on by my body. It was supposed to be the other way around, but there was nothing wrong, I told myself to drive away my initial shame, with it happening both ways.

I had just finished Leo Steinberg's wonderful book about the sexuality of Christ in Renaissance art. He noted that in a few paintings of the Resurrection the risen Lord is depicted in a state of sexual arousal to symbolize power and vitality. I didn't know whether this was blasphemous, but it was surely true that to be sexually aroused in the presence of Ciara made me feel more powerful than I ever had before in my life. Power over her? Rather, knowing that my sexual arousal had the power to arouse her and that I could satisfy her desire and make her content, complacent, happy. Knowledge which, in its turn, increased my own arousal so that my body seemed to be charged with tremendous electrical energy.

The most delicate of all the phases came next. Ciara would be temporarily caught in a conflict between her own hungers and the residue of her prudishness and fears. She would clench her fists, not in anger, but in a determined effort to restrain them from resistance to being disrobed. Once her clothes were off she was a wanton, but the process of being stripped was both painful and pleasurable for her.

Perhaps painfully pleasurable would be a better way to put it. When I slipped away her panties, it was as if she'd crossed the line between scrupulosity and bawdiness and was free to go on to more forthright, not to say brazen, pleasures.

That morning on the *Brigid* she resisted more than usual, perhaps because her businesslike underwear had been replaced by bits of mostly transparent lace—the result, doubtless, of the same frugal shopping expedition that had produced the shorts and sweater.

"Dear God in Heaven, Brendan Ryan," she sighed as I finished my undressing task, "I don't know why you tolerate me, I really don't. I'm such a great, powerful puritan about all this."

"Tell you the truth, I rather enjoy it."

"I'm sure you do. Fantasy that you're raping the poor captive . . . terrible Viking carrying off a nun. . . . Oh, Brendan, don't stop."

So it went. That morning lovemaking was particularly good. I was learning that more rewarding than to pleasure yourself with a woman was to pleasure her so that her body was shaken by deep and cataclysmic joy, ecstasy that subtly addicted her body to yours.

I needed Ciara like I had needed no one before in my life. She needed me even more.

That time, as was often the case, at the very height of my satisfaction, I saw her body growing large with my child.

Which, as I told myself while I stroked her reassuringly afterward, is what the rite of spring is all about.

"Should we abandon this craft for the sun and sand of Montrose Beach?" I asked her sleepily.

" 'Tis a wonderful fine place, save for one thing." She pronounced the word "ting," deliberately, I suspected, manifesting the Irish "th" problem. (There's no "h" sound in their language. Ciara did it because she knew it was one more aspect of her that turned me on.)

"And that is?"

"Sure, we can't make love there, can we?"

"You're insatiable, woman."

"You have no one to blame but yourself for that, Brendan Ryan. And yourself such a gorgeous man." Her lips began to explore my face, my chest, my body. "Well, one more time and then the beach. Have to save something for tonight."

"It may take a while . . ." I protested.

"Not at all, at all."

I tried at such times not to be shocked by the discovery that I was a sex object being used, however lovingly, by a woman for her own pleasure. "Hold still, Brendan." She shook her head, sending her long black hair tumbling behind her shoulders. "I'm not finished with you yet, at all, at all. . . . Saints preserve me, Brendan, I love you so much, every last wonderful bit of you." Sweat poured from her body and dripped on me as she did breathtaking things to me and moaned ecstatically in pursuit of her own delirium.

"You terrible, wanton thing," I groaned.

"Terrible altogether," she sighed in return, and then, as her body arched backward in convulsive spasms, she cried out in pure animal joy. Again and again and again.

Orgiastic sex with a vengeance, yet somehow innocent and graceful. Her hunger for me was simple, uncomplicated, childlike; and her happiness afterward reminded me of a little child at the Christmas tree. Brendan Ryan, great seducer of the Western world, became a present Santa Claus had brought to a wide-eyed little girl—a girl who studied the reactions of her new toy very carefully indeed, so she would know exactly how it worked.

You're going to have to be good to keep up with this one, Brendan Ryan. You've transformed a spring breeze into a hurricane.

Later, I turned on the auxiliary motor and pointed the bow toward the harbor. Ciara lolled in the cabin, contentedly naked.

"Haven't you forgot one important thing, Captain Brendan Ryan?"

"What would that be?"

"Isn't my swimsuit at my apartment?"

More questions in response to questions. Deliberate now, at least half the time.

"'It's not, not at all, at all. Look in the cabinet."

"Glory be to God," she exclaimed. "Do you want me to appear on the beach worse than naked?" As if to protest the very thought, she pulled a blanket around her body and hugged herself to fend off both immodesty and cold.

"Not quite."

"Sure, it's Montrose Beach, not the Copacabana. And I'm not one of your Brazilians. I won't wear it."

"You will, woman. Now put it on and stop arguing with me. If there's one ting I can't stand 'tis an argumentative woman."

She slammed the cabin door shut with a derisive bang. A few minutes later she emerged in a white outfit that indeed would have done very well in Rio.

"I don't know, Brendan." She was still glowing from sexual pleasure but awkward and uncertain.

"I do."

"You'd just be wanting to show off your prize, wouldn't you?"

"Would I now?"

"You would indeed. Well . . . are you sure?"

"Quite sure."

"All right." She agreed half dubiously and half happily, and pulled on her sweater and shorts. "The nuns at my school would be horrified."

"What school?"

"My school in Ireland."

Still the woman of mystery.

As we were leaving the *Brigid*, she carrying the lunch basket, I returned to the cabin and stuffed her bra and panties into my Windbreaker pocket.

"Give them back to me, you terrible man," she demanded, face flaming.

"I can't have such things lying around my boat. Sure, it would shock the occasional priest that uses it."

"You're teasing me."

"I am. But if you're good, as hard as that is for a woman from the West of Ireland, I'll give them back at the end of the day."

"It's a word that can have many meanings, isn't it now?"

I shoved her rear end off the boat, and she swung a
strong arm in my direction.

Montrose Harbor is created by a hooklike landfill that
pushes out into the lake. Its point separates from the shore
by the fifty yards or so of harbor mouth that is further nar-
rowed by two concrete breakwaters. It is a snug little harbor surrounded by beach and sloping green lawns. Ciara
found a spot on the lawn near the outer breakwater that reminded her of Ireland despite the Chicago skyline which
loomed directly to the south of us. I spread our blanket and
we set up camp.

It was an idyllic day. Ciara swam for half an hour, pro-
nouncing the lake much warmer, and attracted attention,
as she walked back to our blanket, both for her hardiness
and for her well-displayed beauty.

"They're all staring at me," she whispered.

"Because you're glowing so brightly."

"It's from the waters of the lake."

"Certainly it is."

We covered each other with suntan lotion and lay on
the blanket holding hands while the perspiration rolled off
our bodies. It was uncomfortably humid, but that suited
the dissolute, desert-island mood we were both in—
lethargic, languorous, complacent, deeply and abidingly
satisfied with our love.

"All we need is a troop of hula dancers."

"Would you listen to him now? One woman isn't
enough for him?" She poked my ribs, gently enough.

"Hey, I didn't specify only women dancers!"

"Sorry." She giggled and kissed my shoulder. "I'm not
much good at mind reading."

We ate lunch and drove back to my apartment, where
we showered (independently still), cleaned the dishes from
our picnic ("I'll not be having you think I'm one of your
sloppy Irish housewives"), and strolled down Michigan Avenue, people-watching and noise-listening—auto horns,
lovers' conversation, chattering kids, crying babies,
reproving mothers. She must have packed spare lingerie in
her bag, because she made no attempt to recapture my
prizes. At Superior Street she protested that she was "destroyed" from all her "exertions" and didn't have "a hope"

of walking another block. We returned to the little square around the water tower and relaxed on a bench. I was dispatched to buy ice cream cones, even though it would do terrible "tings" to her figure. "I won't be wearing that terrible indaycent bikini for long, at all, at all, if you keep making me eat your American ice cream," she claimed, capturing a large glob of chocolate that had escaped to the corner of her lips. "Then you'll lose interest in me altogether."

"I will indeed."

She was too busy with the cone to poke me.

We were even fellow chocolate freaks.

Ciara inspected every baby and small child who passed, flirting with the little boys, playing with the little girls, and complimenting the mothers of both with outrageous blarney in her thickest West of Ireland accent.

She should have children of her own. She would soon. That's what spring is all about.

I returned to our bench with the popcorn she had requested. "I've always thought that this little square was kind of like something you might see in Paris."

"Paris, is it?" She glanced around the square. "Sure, 'tis easy to see you haven't been to Paris."

"Not as good?" I stuffed some popcorn in my mouth.

"Not as good, is it? Glory be to God, Brendan Ryan. What little square in Paris would have something as wonderful as that?" She gestured admiringly toward the soaring John Hancock Center. "Or that?" She pointed at the Olympia Center, known to everyone in Chicago as the Needless Markup Center because of the presence of Neiman-Marcus in the building. "Paris doesn't have any quaint little squares with cute nineteenth-century water towers and Skidmore Owings and Merrill prizewinners for a backdrop. It's a wondrous meadow in the high mountains."

"With the Chestnut Street ravine feeding into it . . . You sound as though you like Chicago."

"It's a great, powerful city. And beautiful besides."

"And yourself planning to stay here, is it?"

She jabbed at my arm with her popcorn box. "Stop talking the way I do. One of us is enough. Maybe too much."

End of discussion.

We ate supper at Jerome's on North Clark, after I had persuaded her that she did not need to dress for it. "Your legs will earn us a good table in their outdoor café," I insisted.

The maître d' was a woman, but she sized up Ciara admiringly and did indeed give us a corner table, at which we could eat and from which we could continue to people-watch. If I observed a young woman for what Ciara deemed was an inappropriately long period, she would reprimand me, "half fun and full earnest."

"Love with one woman," I sighed, mocking her sigh, "makes you notice all women."

"It's not the noticing I mind." She was polishing off an artichoke in lemon butter with great relish. "It's the devouring of them. You might at least leave the poor tings their clothes. Anyway, you should do it like I do," she winked mischievously, "with more taste and discretion."

We ate Alaskan rockfish and drank a bottle of sauvignon blanc. Ciara insisted on chocolate mousse for dessert and a "wee drop" of Baileys Irish Cream. Three glasses of Baileys later she was delightfully giddy.

"It's been a grand day altogether, Brendan Ryan. No one will ever say you're not good to your women."

A lot of people had said it, but I wasn't about to argue.

It was eleven o'clock when I finally dragged her away from several conversations with other patrons of the restaurant. "I didn't embarrass you, did I?" she asked anxiously.

"You couldn't possibly embarrass me, Ciara Kelly. Every man in that place envied me." I guided her to the door of my car. "Take you back to your apartment?"

"Have you lost your ardor altogether?"

I found an empty parking lot and demonstrated, with few preliminaries and considerable vigor, that I had not.

"Have you ever done it that way before?" she asked me when we were done.

"I've never had a woman who drove me to it before, Ciara Kelly."

She giggled in satisfaction and snatched her bra and panties from the pocket of my Windbreaker.

"Not that I mind," she giggled again, "but I don't have all that large a supply, if you take my meaning."

Looking back on that incident, if I had kept her undergarments, I might have had some evidence. But then, perhaps you can't have evidence of someone who doesn't really exist, not, at least, in the same time and space that you do.

At Chestnut Place she insisted that it was not necessary for me to get out of the car, which meant that she didn't want me to. We were still protecting the poor doorman from scandal.

"See you tomorrow night." She turned away. Then she turned back to the car, eyes filled with tears. "Dear God, I love you, Brendan Ryan," she said in her thickest brogue and softest whisper. "I know I'm fluthered, but it doesn't matter. I'm out of my mind with love for you."

"Isn't it risky to tell a man that?"

She kissed me with enough tenderness to break my heart. "I don't care at all, at all." Then she ran to the door, leaving me with visions of a life in which every day would be as blissful—and as unpredictable—as that day.

There was no question of Ciara sailing with me on Sunday. I was invited to her apartment for supper, and the supper had to be well prepared. "When you're after a meal," she proclaimed, "you should be doing it right!"

I sensed, or perhaps only hoped, that our relationship would change that Sunday. Perhaps I would be invited not only into her apartment but into her life.

I sailed in the morning, worked on my manuscript in the afternoon, and set forth down the Chestnut Street ravine at five o'clock, carrying two bottles of Baileys and two dozen roses. The doorman rang apartment 960, and I was shown the way to the elevator.

"You're on time." Ciara glowered at me from the doorway, a saucepan in her hand. "You were supposed to be late."

For a moment I was quite speechless. Ciara had designed the night to make more explicit the gift of herself she had promised. She had even gift-wrapped herself. She was dressed in a lilac nylon and lace lingerie arrangement that would have stopped any man cold. More of the J.C.

Penney's shopping expedition I thought, and instantly reprimanded my snobbishness. She was dazzling regardless of how little money it took to make her dazzling. Her hair was burnished and lustrous, black lava on new-fallen snow; her face carefully made up; red stones, rubies, I thought, on her ears and at her neck—the family jewels, doubtless, or all that remained of them. Her body radiated an enticing scent. Her gray eyes were both easing and inviting.

She knew she was devastating and was embarrassed, for the record anyway.

"Well, what are you standing there staring at?" she demanded, the corners of her mouth struggling unsuccessfully against a grin. "Are you going to come in and give me those gorgeous roses, or are you going to stand there and stare?"

"Can I come in and stare?"

"You're a terrible man altogether, Brendan Ryan." She brushed my cheek with a quick kiss.

"Jesus and Mary be with this house," I said as I entered.

"Jesus and Mary and Patrick be with you," she replied promptly. "And there's a wee jar of the creature on the coffee table for you while I'm finishing the stew."

Her studio apartment, weirdly shaped like a bent corkscrew, was like a hotel room—utterly devoid of the slightest imprint of her personality. No photographs or drawings, only a handful of paperback books, some in French; a tiny transistor radio; a black-and-white portable TV; the simplest and most inexpensive furniture, drapes, and bedspread; functional beige walls and carpet. The occupant, you sensed, had only touched down for a few hours and then would be on her way.

"You get a nice view of Washington Square Park, the Newbury Library, and the Montgomery Ward building out the window." She sailed back in from her tiny kitchen, amid the rustle of fabric, with a plate of hors d'oeuvres concocted from cheese and ham. "Don't eat too much of them or you'll spoil your supper."

How to reconcile the flair and energy of the occupant with her bland dwelling place? I felt vaguely uneasy. While she was in the kitchen, I quickly wrote down her phone number and slipped it into my pocket.

"Woman of the house?"

"What would you be wanting?"

"You."

"I'm cooking your dinner, you idjit."

"Come have a wee jar with me."

"I can't do two things at once," she exploded in a burst of temper.

"Cool it, woman!" I shouted in return. "Or I'll come out there and take the back of my hand to you."

Silence. Then a shamefaced Ciara, mixing spoon in hand, appeared at the kitchen door. "I'm sorry, Brendan darling. When I was a little girl, I swore I'd never do that to a guest. It was good of you to call me on it. Just a second and I'll be with you."

In only a few seconds she was seated on the chair across from me on the sofa—the only furniture in the room besides the bed. She took a deep breath and relaxed. "An Irish fishwife, and I'm not even a wife. Slainte to you anyway, Brendan Ryan, failte and slainte."

"Slainte to you, too, woman of the house." I toasted her gravely.

"I'm sorry I was so rude." She put down the drink, Jameson's, and made a face. "I know a happy hostess is better than an efficient one. Damn it, I want to be both."

"You look wonderful."

She stirred uneasily. "I'm not sure that I'll ever be any good at this seduction business. I feel . . ." she waved her hands awkwardly ". . . silly."

"It's my impression that women enjoy dressing that way. What do you call it?"

"A teddy and a wrap coat . . . and a garter belt too." Averted head and blush.

"Even more than we men enjoy them dressing that way."

She considered me very carefully. "You're a very clever man about women, Brendan Ryan. And yourself not having much experience with them. Remind me to be careful with you. Anyway, you're right save for the first attempt, when the woman feels clumsy and silly."

"You don't look silly. Maybe you'd relax if you sit next to me and let me kiss you. It's not a proper way to come into the house, not kissing the woman of the house."

"You'll never get your supper," she warned.

"Only a kiss for now."

It was, however, a very intense kiss, driving down into the depths of her soul. Her jaw sagged, her eyes blurred, her head rested against my chest.

"Ah, you'll be the destruction of me altogether. Truly if you want to eat, I'd better go back to the kitchen."

She was, in addition to everything else, a good cook— Caesar salad, prosciutto and melon, a California white, and, true to her promise, lamb stew, indeed the most skillfully seasoned lamb stew I'd ever eaten, accompanied by Beaulieu cabernet sauvignon, George Latour special reserve.

Poor woman shouldn't spend her few dollars on expensive wine.

All by candlelight and WFMT music and witty conversation—in which nothing at all was said about her past.

I helped her clear the table, a gesture that caused a flicker of amusement in her astonishing gray eyes.

"Sherry trifle for dessert, and cappuccino," she announced.

"Ciara Kelly for dessert."

"Brendan . . . no . . . I've worked hard on the sherry trifle. You Yanks don't know how to make it. Oh, God . . . no . . . *Brendan!*"

"Two desserts."

"Sherry trifle first . . ."

"No." This time her clothes, such as they were, came off first.

She giggled merrily as my fingers fumbled with slippery fabrics and unfamiliar fastenings. "Sure, you're tickling me, you clumsy oaf."

I wasn't, but I liked the suggestion. A new kick. She shrieked in outrage, but she liked it too. Our sex was turning away from serious passion and in the direction of play. It was even better that way.

It was also prolonged and sensitive and deeply rewarding. We both knew we had crossed the mountain range. It was no longer an affair, not as far as our bodies were concerned. Whatever we might think in our heads, our loins had already decided: Ciara and I were now one flesh. For keeps.

Then we ate the sherry trifle, drank the cappuccino, and sipped our "wee jar" of Baileys. In fact, I ate two helpings of the sherry trifle and admitted that, indeed, we Yanks did not know how to make it.

"I'm thinking you liked it better than you liked me," she protested.

"Do I have to choose?"

"Course not." She had put back on what might, I suppose, be called the robe of her ensemble—not that it made much difference in the scenery. As we drank the Baileys, she seemed abstracted, far away. Perhaps drifting further away.

I would marry her. That was that. The sooner the better. So questions must be asked.

"Who are you, Ciara Kelly?"

She jumped up from the sofa, startled and angry.

"Not who you think I am, Brendan Ryan." The brogue was now almost undetectable. "I'm not the charming Irish innocent you've created in your fantasy, not the sweet superannuated virgin whom you've seduced and intend now to redeem."

"Huh?"

"Get out of here!" she screamed at me. "I never want to see you again!"

"What did I say?" I stood up, prepared to leave.

"It's not what you said, it's who you are—a smug, self-important little bourgeois hypocrite."

I sat back down on the sofa. "I'm not leaving here till I receive an explanation."

"You can stay all night. I won't say another word to you." She flounced into the bathroom and returned in an aged and tattered bathrobe.

"At least you didn't put your hair in curlers."

A small smile, quickly repressed.

"You don't mind if I get myself mildly fluthered on your Irish Cream?"

"It's yours, you brought it."

"You already broke your word that you wouldn't say another word."

She closed her eyes. Her face became a mask of pain, as though someone were squeezing the life out of her.

"All right." She opened her eyes and crumpled into the corner of her chair. "You have a right to know."

She had graduated from secondary school at the age of sixteen, highest honors in her class and a university scholarship. Not that they would collect any money for it. Her father was a prominent lawyer, wealthy by Irish standards, and well known. He was a stern man, harsh and demanding of his children and narrow in his views. Ciara was to be a nurse and that was that.

She thought she might want to be a nurse, as a matter of fact, but she resented that she was being given no choice. Of all the children, she was the only one with the nerve to tangle with her father.

Either nursing, he said, or you go to work as a shop girl.

So she defied them all and signed up for a year of volunteer service as a nurse's aide with an Irish missionary community that maintained a hospital in the Congo. Her father could hardly refuse her permission to go to Africa. Ireland was heavily involved in the U.N. peacekeeping mission in the Congo. It was a matter of national pride. Nor could he stand in the way of a possible religious vocation for his daughter. After all, one of his principal charities was a hospital administered by nuns, and he had praised their work publicly as a sign of stability in a foolishly changing Church.

He warned her, however, that she was a rash and disrespectful young woman and that God would punish her terribly for her imprudence. Which indeed He did.

Africa fascinated and overwhelmed her. She was appalled by the poverty and sickness, charmed by the patients at the hospital, exhausted by the heat and the string of tropical illnesses which were part of acclimating, intrigued by the nuns' courage and cheerfulness, and repelled by the rigidity of their community rule. Their hospital was near Lubumbashi (formerly Elizabethville), far away from the region of Katanga where the violence had been and where the Irish troops had died. The nuns insisted there was no danger in their part of the country, and so she wrote dutifully every week to her mother. There were no replies because her father had forbidden the rest of the family to write to her.

Then there were rumors of a rebellion at the other end of the province—a group of unpaid soldiers (the central government at Kinshasha had plenty of money but did not seem to be very skillful at paying its troops in the outlands) who had drifted across the border into the former French Congo, which had gone Marxist. The Russians paid them, equipped them with guns and munitions, and sent them back as "patriotic socialist revolutionaries." The troops called themselves Simbas—lions.

"They won't come here," Mother Superior said confidently. "Even if they do, they won't hurt us. The African people love us."

The Simbas came early one morning, crazed with drink and drugs (also furnished by the Russians). They bayoneted all the men patients, and the women too, after they'd raped them. They gathered the nuns and the nurses in the courtyard and amused themselves with them till daylight, and then killed them, as slowly and painfully as possible. Some survived, screaming, until the end of the day, when the Simbas finally blew their brains out with automatic weapons.

They spared Ciara and two black girls who were nurse's aides because they were young and pretty and could offer amusement for several days. Ciara lost track of the number of times she was raped and degraded. After the first day she prayed for death.

The Simbas, who seemed to have a plentiful supply of drugs and drink, often threatened them with death, pointed the guns at their heads or their bellies or their sex organs, and pulled the triggers. They found it greatly amusing when the young women screamed in anguish and then discovered that the guns were not loaded this time.

Then one morning they cut off the breasts of the two black girls and stuck bayonets up their wombs until they bled to death, laughing crazily all the while. The sergeant in charge of the execution swaggered to the post to which Ciara was tied, drained a bottle of liquor, smashed it against a tree, and raised it to her face. She prayed that she would die quickly.

There was a short burst of automatic weapon fire and blood poured out of the sergeant's stomach as he tottered and fell. Paratroopers from the French Foreign Legion had arrived. About the same time they saved most of the foreigners at Lubumbashi. Ciara, or what was left of her, was the only one they saved at the mission station. The Simbas, too drunk to fight, quickly surrendered.

When the Legionnaires saw what had happened to the patients and the nuns and the nurses, they executed all the Simbas, most of them with machine gun bullets fired into the groin. At the end of the day, Ciara, hysterical with fear and humiliation, was the only living being left from the hospital and invading force.

Sure, the Africans loved them. Many of the people whom the nuns had healed shouted with glee as they were tortured and killed. The Legionnaires killed many of them too. One can't blame all Africans, not even all of those in the mission area. Who does not do what they think the men with the guns want them to do? Yet every time she sees a black man, she remembers the Simbas and is afraid. She's ashamed of her reaction. It's not fair. She goes out of her way to be friendly. But she can't forget the Simbas. Or the man in whose badly cut arm she had put stitches only a few days before. He laughed enthusiastically and taunted her in broken English as she was raped.

She was only turned seventeen. She knew nothing at all about sex.

The Simbas were no worse than most men in conquering armies. Most Americans don't know what happened in Stuttgart in 1945 when the American army captured the city. Men have raped women for the whole history of the race because they are stronger and have the weapons. What are the statistics in America? A third of the women in the country have been raped, most of them by men who had some kind of power over them—husbands, lovers, fathers, brothers, uncles, friends. What right did she have to be immune from the ordinary lot of womankind? Rape doesn't happen in civilized countries? What country is civilized? And how thin is the line separating civilizations from barbarism? The world will be civilized only when women are safe from the men with the weapons and from the relatives who have power over them.

She came home a heroine. A survivor of martyrdom. No one was supposed to know what had happened to her. Everyone did, naturally. It was just not discussed in the Ireland of the late 1960s. Her father told her it served her right for her disobedience and pride. She cursed him and said she would never set foot in his house. She went to see him when he was dying, and he refused to see her.

I filled both our glasses when her story ended. My stomach was knotted, my throat tight with fury, my hands clenched. I had to be careful of what I said.

"So what?"

My words stirred her out of her reverie. "What do you mean, so what?"

"I don't mean so what about your pain or so what about the memories that torment you. I mean, so what about us?"

"No man wants a woman who has been soiled that way."

"Now who's the male chauvinist?"

"It's true."

"It's not true. I grieve with you, Ciara. I admire you even more for the strength it took you to bounce back . . ."

"I haven't bounced back." She drew her old green robe more tightly around her.

"Bullshit. As I was saying, I grieve for you. I will suffer with you. I admire you for your guts. I'll help you fight off the fears when they return. I'll not let you use this to put me off."

"Get the hell out of here," she screeched hysterically.

"You said that before. Drink your Baileys."

"You want to make me fluthered so you can rape me like they did."

"You're too smart to say something dumb like that, Ciara. The whole point of this crazy dialogue is you want to know whether a man can make effective love to you after he knows what the Simbas did to your poor young body. It's a fair question. I propose to answer it for you."

So far so good, Brendan Ryan. Nick and Eileen would be astonished at how good you are in court.

"You can't make me."

"I'm not trying to make you do anything, Ciara Kelly. You've challenged me and I intend to respond to your challenge."

"I won't fight you off," she said with infinite sadness. "Do whatever you want to do. I won't enjoy a second of it. That's all over for me."

Which was absolute nonsense. As the two of us proved in rather short order.

Then there were many tearful apologies.

"I didn't know I was testing you, Brendan darlin'," she said, sniffling in a tissue. "I mean I suppose I was doing that, but I didn't mean to. You poor dear man, what a terrible thing to have happen the first night you visit a woman's apartment. Sure, you should walk out and never come back again."

I held her close and stroked her thick black hair. "I didn't and I won't, I hope that's clear enough."

"I'll make up even worse stories if you love me the same way after them." The woman leprechaun was never too far away, not even at the most painful moments.

"I'll always love you, Ciara Kelly. I don't like the tests, but you're entitled to as many as you want."

"There'll be no more of that." She sat up straight and pounded her bed—onto which we had moved earlier in the process. "I'm yours, Brendan, my dearest," she bent over me and kissed me, her breasts firm against my chest, "for as long as you want me, any time you want me, any way you want me, any place you want . . ." the inevitable laughter, "even in your car parks, oops, parking lots."

I felt, poor fool that I was, that I had won. No longer a loser, Ron Crowley, but a winner.

"That's a gift, woman, that I'll not be refusing." She lay

in my arms, quiet, passive, a pure gift. Her gray eyes were solemn and liquid. I kissed both of them and laid her back in bed.

"Completely yours," she whispered softly.

I covered her with the sheet and thin blanket. "You need a good night's sleep."

"The house is a terrible mess," she protested. "I can't have you leaving thinking I'm a slob."

"I'll clean up."

"A holy martyr," she sighed peacefully.

It was no great task to dispose of the remains of a dinner for two, especially since the wine and Baileys bottles were quite empty. I turned on the dishwasher, scrubbed the pots and pans, cleaned off the sink and the stove, polished the glasses while the dishwasher hummed happily in the background.

Ciara and I had both been activists, I reflected as I put the glasses in her small but fastidiously neat cabinet. Not quite like the protesters of our generation—and we did overlap the activist generation, one of us at either end of it—but young people who were firmly convinced that we could make a difference. I would be an intelligence officer in Vietnam, as my father had been in Europe, and help make Southeast Asia safe for democracy. She would follow in the wake of fifteen centuries of brave Irish missionaries and heal and convert the pagans of Africa. We both had failed. We both had come to understand after painful losses—much more painful for her than for me—the futility of trying to solve the twisted problems of humankind and rebuild the world with such poor tools as generosity and enthusiasm. We had, perhaps necessarily, withdrawn into our narrow private lives. Now we had each other. Could it be that with each other some of the old generosity might be reborn? We would be more cautious. No more Congo or Vietnam, but carefully thought out enthusiasm and rationally controlled generosity. With frequent sips of the Holy Grail of our springtime passion for each other.

Looking back, I realize how much of an idjit, to use her word, I revealed myself to be in such reflections. Men in love never think very clearly.

"Sure, you'd make a grand wife," she said as I turned off the kitchen light and crept into the parlor.

"Go to sleep, woman." I kissed her gently. She watched me with a smile that I can only call adoring. "No more talk."

"Yes, Brendan."

I tucked her in and kissed her again. "Pleasant dreams."

"I love you, Brendan."

I suppose I rode down the elevator. I was so happy, however, I'm sure I could have floated to the ground.

There were uncertainties, but only sounding in the recesses of my brain like a bell tolling at a great distance. She had told me nothing about the sixteen years since she'd come home from Zaire. How had she managed to climb out of her tragic suffering and become the mature woman she was?

And what was a woman who could read modern French novels doing working as a sales clerk?

Those issues were minor, I assured myself. We'd clear them up in the next few days.

The Chestnut Street ravine was crawling that night with demons and shades, warnings and threats, dangers and dooms. I paid them no attention. Psychic manifestations were unimportant when compared with the woman whom I now planned to marry.

I showered in my apartment and sat for a few moments staring out at the lake, savoring my joy. Ciara Kelly was mine.

What enormous willpower it must have required for her to recover from the terrible traumas of the Congo, and to risk a love affair with me, and to make of herself a trusting and generous gift. Ah, my Ciara, you're a woman with a heroine's strong will.

And stubbornness.

Still, I'm pretty good at coping with you when you're stubborn.

I saw a jetliner catch fire in the sky, streak across it like a meteor, and plunge into the lake. Then another liner followed it. Shaken, I turned on WBBM, the news station, and listened for fifteen minutes. No report of any plane accidents.

Another psychic kink. I tried to dismiss it, but couldn't quite banish the picture of the flaming light slicing across the sky. A death symbol, perhaps.

I concentrated on Ciara's slow and magic smile, and the image of the fire disappeared.

I would probably have to tell her about the peculiar psychic things that happened to me. Unlike Madonna, she would notice them.

I slept peacefully and well, and awakened at five, still blissful. The night before at her apartment had not been a dream. Indeed, I *had* won Ciara. I went back to sleep and did not wake till nine o'clock. So besotted with love that I had not set the alarm. I shaved quickly, swallowed half a cup of tea while I was dressing, did not bother to turn on the radio or glance at the paper for the morning news, and dashed for a cab so that I wouldn't be too late for my 9:30 appointment.

It was a quarter to ten when I jumped out of the cab at 211 West Jackson and rushed for the elevator.

On the third floor I nodded briefly at the receptionist. Oddly enough, she screamed. What was the matter with her? I wondered, as I rushed down the beige-carpeted corridor to my office. Heart attack? Maybe I ought to go back and check.

Someone else must have heard her.

My secretary was not at her station, which was unusual. And my client was not in the office. Strange. He was a compulsively punctual man. Had he left already? That would not be like him.

I pulled his folder out of my file drawer.

"My God . . . !"

It was Eileen. She and Nick were standing at the door, pale and stricken. Like they'd seen a ghost.

"You're dead, Brendan," she said in a weird, choked voice.

"Blown up early this morning," Nick agreed.

three

THE
DANCE
OF
SACRIFICE

16

"**I** don't care what was on the radio," I said with elaborate casualness as I poured out two cups of hot water and put the herbal tea bags in them. "I am not dead. I am very much alive. I was not blown up last night. As in the case of Mark Twain, reports of my death are greatly exaggerated."

"God . . ." Eileen breathed softly. "But who? . . ."

Nick shook his head, as though trying to clear away mental cobwebs. "What made you think I was dead?" I asked amiably, relaxing in my judge's chair.

"Your boat blew up last night."

The tips of Nick's fingers touched his forehead as though he were desperately trying to recapture his sanity.

"The cops are all over." Eileen frowned deeply.

"The *Brigid*?" Now I was shocked and incredulous.

"Two people on it," Eileen said.

"A man and a woman," Nick continued.

"The man was tentatively identified as you. Who else would be on your boat?"

I felt like I was watching a late-night TV movie, one that was running in the wrong direction.

"I don't understand . . ."

"What the fuck are you doing here alive?" At the door of the office stood a tall, lean, bald man in a gray suit with angry darting eyes.

"Lieutenant Samuel Norton of Homicide." Eileen waved a casual hand. "Like most cops he thinks that obscene language establishes his masculinity."

"Where the fuck have you been?" The lieutenant's voice was thin and piercing.

"The rotund spear carrier behind him," Eileen continued dispassionately, "is Sergeant O'Connor. It's not clear whether he can talk."

"I said where the fuck have you been?" Norton was paying no attention at all to Eileen.

"Either you keep a civil tongue in your head, Lieutenant," her green eyes sparkled dangerously, "or my client will have nothing to say to you."

The lieutenant turned menacingly toward her. "What do you mean 'client'?" he snarled.

Nick Curran eased out of his chair and stood toe to toe with the lieutenant. "What does a lawyer normally mean by the word 'client,' Lieutenant? And how tall was the male deceased who was removed from the boat early this morning?"

"Over six feet," Lieutenant Norton said grudgingly.

"As you can see, Lieutenant, Mr. Ryan is no taller than Sergeant O'Connor, a little over five foot eight. That's the first stupid mistake for the Chicago Police Department. Why did you tell the press that you suspected the body was Mr. Ryan's without making the obvious inquiry about his height?"

"We're checking dental X rays." The lieutenant backed off from his eyeball-to-eyeball confrontation with Nick. Just as well, for if his violent temper had caused him to lay a hand on Eileen, Nick would have broken his back. And Sergeant O'Connor's, too, for good measure.

"You can forget about Mr. Ryan's dental X rays," Nick said easily. "I think we can assure you they won't match the teeth of the deceased."

"Where were you at midnight?" The lieutenant turned abruptly on me, the veins in his forehead standing out like mountain ridges on a topographic map.

"In my apartment."

"What time did you go into the apartment?" He sounded like a prosecuting attorney closing in on a victim.

"Red? Eileen." Eileen was speaking into my telephone. "We have a resurrection on our hands. He's alive and well and looking fit. God knows who was in the boat. We have a cop from Homicide with a foul mouth here in the office. Name of Norton. You know him? Huh? Well, spread the word to the press that Brendan Ryan is alive and the homicide officers of the Chicago Police Department neglected to call his apartment on the off chance that he might not have been the body on the boat, a body which, by the way, is several inches taller than Mr. Ryan. Got it? Thanks. Love you."

"You bitch." He hissed at her.

"Get out of here." Nick stepped toward Norton, who backed up another step.

"Nicholas!" Eileen said imperiously. "We have witnesses, and we'll take it up in due course with Internal Investigations in the police department. For the moment I would suggest that Mr. Ryan answer the lieutenant's questions."

"I returned to my apartment about eleven-thirty." I still felt like I was watching a late-night movie, but now that I was somehow inside the television screen. "I chatted briefly with Charlie, the doorman, went up to my apartment, and promptly went to bed. I overslept and came in to the office late without listening to the radio or television this morning."

"Had you been on your sailboat at all yesterday?"

"In the morning and early afternoon, till about two o'clock."

"And what were your actions after that?"

"Just to establish the ground rules, Lieutenant," Eileen drummed her fingers on my desk, "my client, who may very well have been the target of a murder attempt, does not have to answer any of your questions. He's answering them now out of a spirit of cooperation, which is more than your attitude merits. Don't push us."

"I worked in my apartment till about five in the afternoon on a manuscript." The words flowed automatically. "And then I had supper at the apartment of a friend. . . ."

The lieutenant was about to ask the name of the friend, so I answered his question before he asked it.

"Her name is Ciara Kelly. She lives at the Chestnut Place, apartment 960, and she works at Dufficy's Irish Store on Michigan Avenue."

"We'll check into all of this," Norton snarled. "You better be telling the truth. Come on, O'Connor."

The two men left our office, a storm system receding.

"Charming man," Nick observed lightly.

"I'm confused." I felt like I was coming out of anesthetic after an operation. "Will someone please tell me what the hell is going on."

"The *Brigid* was seen leaving Montrose Harbor a little after 11:30 last night." Nick was ticking facts off on his fingertips. "As you know, there aren't many boats in Montrose or any of the other harbors yet, but somebody with a berth near yours recognized the *Brigid* going out and assumed you were on it. There wasn't much of a breeze so the boat was under auxiliary power, even after it left the harbor entrance. The other sailors said that it was perhaps a hundred fifty or two hundred yards beyond the harbor mouth when there was a flash, like an explosion in the cabin, and then the ship was engulfed in flames. Luckily, I suppose, the Coast Guard cutter was coming down the shore at just that time, having picked up two kids whose fourteen-foot Boston Whaler had run out of gas early in the evening. They used their fire equipment on the flames and managed to get a line aboard. Then they towed the craft into the breakwater and secured it there while they extinguished the fire. Otherwise the water from their equipment probably would have sunk it. They pumped out the hull and found two bodies in the cabin, both 'scantily clad,' to use their words. Somebody on the police force called Mickey Casey, and he called Ed Ryan, who got me out of bed at about six this morning. I went over to the morgue." He hesitated briefly. "It wasn't very pleasant, even for a scene in the morgue. The bodies were burned completely beyond recognition. I was too dumb to think about height. . . ."

"The Coast Guard," Eileen continued remorselessly, "thinks that there was arson involved, though they're not quite ready to say that to the press yet."

"Arson?" I was clutching for rationality as a drowning man clutches at a life jacket that has been thrown to him.

"Perhaps," she filled her cup with hot water and immersed a new tea bag in it, "some kind of radio-controlled mechanism. If the Coast Guard cutter hadn't been on the spot, the *Brigid* would have burned to the waterline and sunk. By the time the divers would have had a chance to look at it, there might not have been any evidence. Maybe no bodies either."

"But who were they?" I exclaimed. The incredible enormity of what had happened was finally beginning to affect me. "Who would have taken the *Brigid* out?"

"They were running it from the cabin, apparently." Nick was staring out the window but seeing none of the traffic on LaSalle Street below him. "The people in the harbor saw the lights on in the cabin, and that's where the bodies were found. You lock your cabin, I suppose?"

"Of course."

"Who has a key to it?"

"No one!"

"I hate to have to say this, Brendan," Eileen rose and stood behind my judge's chair, her hand on my shoulder. "Perhaps you could phone your friend Miss Ciara Kelly and see . . ."

"And see if she's still alive," I said hollowly.

From memory I punched out the number of Dufficy's Irish Store. "This is a recorded announcement . . ." A sweet and melodious Irish voice, but not Ciara's. "Dufficy's Irish Store is closed today. We'll be open tomorrow from nine o'clock in the morning until five-thirty at night. If you have an important message for us, please leave your name and phone number and the message after you hear the sound of the beep."

"The store she works at is closed." I was trembling like a mainsail luffing in a heavy breeze.

"Her apartment." Eileen's hand tightened on my shoulder.

I fumbled with my wallet, groped for the slip of paper on which I had written her phone number the night before, tried to punch the number, and could not make contact between my fingers and the buttons on the phone. "Here," I gave the number to Eileen, "you do it."

Nick pushed the buttons and gave me the phone. At the other end there was no answer. I let it ring twenty, thirty times, still no answer. Ice cold, I put the phone back in its cradle.

"No answer," I said unnecessarily.

"Is Jean home from Stanford yet?" Eileen asked suddenly.

"Oh, God," I moaned. "And Madonna too . . ."

"Their number?" Nick asked crisply and punched it in as I gave it to him. The line was busy.

"Dear God in heaven, poor Jeannie will be out of her mind with worry and grief."

"Red will have the word out on the news stations in a few more minutes," Eileen said reassuringly, her fingers still digging into my shoulder. "You're still alive, Brendan. That's what matters. That's our starting point. Everything else is going to be all right."

Nick rang the Lake Forest number again. "What do we do now?" I groaned.

"We first of all try to learn who those poor people were and figure out why the boat caught fire and who, if anyone, was responsible for it. But before any of that . . ." She released my shoulder and opened the top-secret liquor cabinet in my credenza and removed an almost full bottle of Jameson's. "All three of us need some of this."

"The line's ringing." Nick jammed the phone into my hand.

"Jean Ryan," said the tearful and woebegone voice at the other end.

"Thank God, Jeannie. It's your father. I'm alive. I wasn't on the boat. We don't know who the people were. I didn't have the radio on this morning. No one called the apartment. I found out only when I arrived here at the office a few minutes ago. I'm alive, Jeannie. It's all right. It's all right!"

I listened to her convulsive sobbing and sipped from a very large shot of Jameson's that Eileen had poured for me. I gave Jeannie plenty of time to regain control.

"I was so afraid that I had lost you, Daddy." It sounded like the croak of an old woman. "After I'd only just found you. I'm so glad. . . ."

I felt the sting of tears in my own eyes. At first, embarrassed, I tried to stop them and then I realized that with my friends Nick and Eileen that was not necessary.

"We have lots of time to become good friends, Jean. Lots of time. Everything's going to be all right. I'm terribly sorry that you had to suffer all the unnecessary worry. Stay there at the house. I'll be up in an hour or an hour and a half." I glanced at Eileen for approval and she nodded. "Have one of your friends come over. Don't go outside and don't say anything to reporters. Hang up on them if they call you."

We spoke for a few more moments, promising that we'd spend a lot of time together in the next few weeks, and then I hung up, feeling that I was beginning to take charge of the bedlam in which I had suddenly found myself.

Ciara. Oh, God!

I punched the number of Dufficy's Irish Store. The same recorded message. Then her apartment. Nothing.

"Maybe Brendan and I could drive up to Lake Forest." Nick was thoughtfully polishing his thick horn-rimmed glasses. "We might stop at Montrose Harbor and take a look. The fire department arson investigator and the Coast Guard might be able to tell us something. Eileen, you could make a few phone calls so that our friend Norton doesn't silence them."

"A good idea. Get Brendan the hell out of the office and away from the working press. I'll let my husband, the distinguished national columnist who doesn't have to work for a living, be our spokesperson. He'll love it."

Eileen reached for the phone but it rang before she

could lift it. "Brendan Ryan's office. . . . Oh, sure, honey, your dad's right here."

"Daddy." Solemn, somber, horrified. "Mother isn't here."

"What! Oh, my God, no!"

"I got home from Tucson yesterday and there was a note for me saying that she had a headache and was going to bed early and I would see her this morning. You know how late she sleeps when she takes those sleeping pills of hers. I . . . I . . . I didn't want to wake her when the news came over the radio. I mean, I didn't know how to tell her. Then when I talked to you and found you were still alive, I went down to her room to give her the good news. . . . And Daddy, she wasn't there. It looked like her bed hadn't been slept in."

"Nick Curran and I will be right up, Jeannie. We're leaving this minute."

I was immobilized, paralyzed, frozen.

"Brendan . . ." Nick shook me vigorously. "Brendan, what is it?"

"Madonna. She's not at the house, hasn't been there since yesterday afternoon."

For what seemed like half of eternity, my office was as quiet as a mausoleum. Then Eileen picked up the phone. "Yes? Oh, Mike . . ."

"Mike Casey?" Nick asked. Eileen nodded.

"I'm sorry we didn't call you, but it's been crazy here in Brendan's office. You've heard the good news? It may take me a long time, Michael, to forgive you for not getting rid of that so-and-so, Norton, when you were acting superintendent. . . .

"I know, but it's going to be unpleasant enough as it is. Anyway, I don't want to call him with this information, because God knows what he'll do with it. But talk to some of your friends in the department and tell them they should begin to compare the woman's dental work with the X rays of Madonna Clifford Ryan, the estranged wife of Brendan Ryan. The same dentist, Brendan?" She glanced at me and I nodded. "She hasn't been home since yesterday afternoon. As far as we know, she didn't have a key to the boat." An eye cocked in my direction for support. "And she didn't like sailing, but she's definitely missing. I'll be at my office here at Minor Gray and Blatt. Nick and Brendan are driving up to Lake Forest to protect poor Jeannie from the vultures. Stay in touch."

Nick made a quick call to Catherine that heralded my resurrection. Before we left the office I tried Ciara Kelly's apartment again. Still no answer.

On the way up the drive I said to Nick, "Turn off at Chicago. She lives at Chestnut Place."

Nick maneuvered over to Chestnut and stopped in front of Ciara's apartment building. I dashed in the door.

"Is Ms. Kelly in?" I breathlessly asked the doorman.

"Who, sir?" He looked puzzled.

"Ms. Ciara Kelly." I gave him the apartment number.

"I think that apartment is vacant, sir. Just a minute." He thumbed through a worn sheaf of pages, reached the end, and thumbed through it again. "Yes, sir, it's vacant."

An icy chill raced through my body. I was dead and Ciara didn't have an apartment in this building?

"I must have the number wrong then. Ms. Kelly's apartment."

"I don't think we have a Ms. Kelly, sir." He started to thumb through the sheets of paper again.

"Let me look." I yanked the pages away from him.

There was a Kafer and a Kennelly, but no Kelly.

"Thank you," I mumbled. "Sorry to have disturbed you."

"Find her?" Nick watched me anxiously as I jumped into the seat next to him.

"She doesn't live here, Nick." I shut my eyes, confused, exhausted. "Apparently has never lived here. I think I'm going mad."

"Nonsense," he said confidently. "It's a very bad day, but tomorrow will be different."

Had my hyperactive psychic sense created her out of my own frustrated sexual longings?

Was such a thing possible?

Maybe.

17

The *Brigid* was a scorched and twisted wreck, her remnants being probed and tormented by fire department and Coast Guard technicians.

"A clumsy job," said the new fire lieutenant, huddling in his black jacket against the blustery east wind that was beating against us off the gray and dangerous lake.

Eight-foot waves, I mentally noted, not that it made any difference.

"It's so damned easy to convert ordinary walkie-talkie mechanisms to radio-controlled bomb detonators. Every two-bit crook thinks he's a frigging mechanic."

"Definitely arson?" Nick asked.

The young man looked up from the hulk of the *Brigid*. "Don't quote me," he said cautiously, "but hell yes. A detonator that kicked off a tin of gasoline underneath the bed blew the two of them in an instant. No wonder their bodies were so fried."

I turned away from the boat and into the fresh slashing of the wind, lest I become sick and perhaps even collapse on the spot. Dear God in Heaven, no!

"Not all that bad an idea," the fireman went on thoughtfully. "If the frigging Coast Guard," he jerked his head contemptuously toward a petty officer who was poking around in what had once been the *Brigid*'s bow, "hadn't come along when they did—the first time the frigging feds have ever been around when anyone needs them—we might never have found any of this stuff."

"Any hope of tracing the equipment?"

"Nah. Buy it in any Radio Shack store in town."

I was numb, dazed, incoherent, a zombie going through motions, a principal lead in a tragedy, who had forgotten his lines. What to do about the *Brigid*? She was insured. Not that insurance could restore anyone's life. Rebuild the boat? With all the memories that were attached? An unlucky boat on which death had occurred? Who would ever want to sail it? I wanted to shout out horrible curses at the murderers who had destroyed my beloved *Brigid*. *Brigid*, however, was only a thirty-one-foot sailboat. Who were the humans who died with her? And who were the fiends who sent them to God's judgment seat while they were making love on the same bunk on which Ciara and I had made love a few hours before?

Was Ciara one of the victims? Or Madonna? Or someone else? When would the terrible uncertainty end?

Jean's eyes had been dry and her face composed when we arrived in Lake Forest. The young priest from the parish, two of her girlfriends, and a handsome, wiry black Irishman were in attendance, fierce guardians ready to repel any invaders. Without makeup, dressed in a simple skirt and blouse, Jean looked thirteen instead of nineteen.

"It was her, Daddy," she said, her hands folded quietly in her lap. "I know it was."

"We can't be sure, Jeannie." I put my arm around her. "Your mother hated sailing. Don't forget that."

"I don't care." She squeezed my hand tightly. "I *know* it was her. Oh, Daddy, how terrible!"

The slim young man, perhaps a year or two older than Jean, had been introduced to me only as "Tim." He had shaken hands with me briskly and flashed a beautiful set of gleaming white teeth in an appropriately brief smile of acknowledgment. I noticed that he and Nick seemed to know each other, then I realized that it was Tim Murphy, Mary Kate Ryan Murphy's second son. Mary Kate and her daughter Caitlin had wasted not a moment in calling out the reserves.

It was decided that, accompanied by her entourage, Jean would go to the Cliffords' house to be waiting for them when they returned later in the day from their medical convention in San Diego.

"They'll need me there to help when they find out," she said dully.

The police department, Eileen had told them in a hurried phone call, already had collected the X rays and the charts from our dentist. It would be some time before they could make a certain identification, but in a few hours we would learn, unofficially and off the record, the truth.

I hugged Jeannie fiercely, and she hugged me back with equal fierceness. "Take good care of her," I said to the priest and to Tim Murphy. "Don't let anyone hurt her."

With those two determined young men as her escort, I doubted anyone would try. In the back of my head, however, there was a terrible fear: If it is Madonna, Jeannie will blame me.

Before Nick and I left the house to drive to Montrose Harbor and then back to the offices, I tried Ciara's number again. Still no answer.

Madonna or Ciara? I didn't want it to be either, but if I had to choose, it would not be a difficult decision.

"What do you think, Brendan?" Nick was wiping raindrops off his glasses as we stared at the ruined boat. "Damned good thing you weren't in the boat, eh?"

"A bad thing for them. A good thing for me."

"I wonder if you were the target?" He put his glasses back on and eased me away from the breakwater and toward the parking lot and his maroon Chevrolet Celebrity (no Porsche or Benz or BMW for Nicholas B. Curran). "Did the arsonist want to kill you or the people who were actually killed?"

I was thunderstruck. "It never occurred to me that I might be a target. I thought Eileen said that to fend off Sam Norton! Who would want to kill me?"

"King Sullivan?"

"That's absurd, Nick." I paused and looked back along the breakwater towards the ruins of the *Brigid*. It would have to be a new boat, perhaps custom-made, to have some of the *Brigid*'s characteristics. "King wouldn't be capable of something like that, and besides, he's set with a plea bargain, isn't he?"

"I know." Nick again took my arm and drew me away from the breakwater and the scorched hulk of the *Brigid*.

"My point is that we're not sure yet who either the real or the intended victims are."

If Ciara wasn't the woman on the boat, then where was she? And how might she have been involved in the explosion off the entrance to Montrose Harbor?

I was still too dazed and too shocked to put my anxieties and questions and doubts in any sensible order, but I did know in the pit of my stomach that I had lost Ciara.

At the Minor Gray and Blatt switchboard we were told, in tones that admitted of no possible dissent, that we were to go at once to Mrs. Kane's office. Eileen was sitting behind her desk, pale, preoccupied, thoughtful. At the coffee table was a young black associate of the firm, Art Savage, who looked like a college football linebacker, which was precisely what he had been at Iowa State.

"Art is joining the team on this case." Eileen spoke like an archduchess who has made decisions that are not to be discussed. "In addition to his talents at litigation he demonstrated in the Hurricane Houston case, he will restrain Lieutenant Norton, should such restraints be required. Is that clear, Nicholas?"

"Yes, ma'am." Nick flopped into an empty chair and grinned. "Anything you say, ma'am."

"It's because I'm bigger and stronger and faster and better than you are." Art laughed, a pleasant young man who simply hadn't been mean enough to make it in pro football.

"Younger, at any rate," Nick agreed ruefully.

Eileen poured me the ceremonial cup of apple cinnamon tea. "No word on tentative identifications yet." She settled wearily into her chair. "Now about Ciara Kelly, Brendan."

"Yes?"

"We've been trying to find her, as you can imagine." Her voice was carefully neutral. She fiddled with a photograph of a Minnesota winter scene done by her son, John Patrick. "But we were able to reach Martha Dougherty, the owner of the Irish store next to Stuart Brent's. Apparently they proclaim holidays more or less to suit their convenience. She tells me that no one named Ciara Kelly works for them or has ever worked for them."

"What!" I was as astonished as I had been in the morning, when I heard about the explosion on the *Brigid*. "But that's impossible . . ."

"We spoke with the management at Chestnut Place. They have no record of anyone named Ciara Kelly ever living in the building. Moreover, apartment 970 has been unoccupied for the last three months."

It had seemed the night before—was it only the night before?—that the apartment was barely lived in. "I was there with her last night, Eileen," I said, burying my head in my hands. Good God in Heaven, was I losing my sanity too?

"We called the number you gave us, and it's not in service."

"But it was in service when I rang this morning . . ."

I reached for the phone and punched out Ciara's number. I heard the annoying musical beep and then the computerized voice telling me, "The number you have dialed is not in service. Please check your directory . . ."

I punched the number again and smashed the phone down in its cradle as soon as I heard the beep. "I know the phone rang this morning."

"Perhaps you were ringing the wrong number, Brendan." Her green eyes were sad and sympathetic. "The telephone company tells us that the line has not been in service for the last year. Do you have any other leads that we might follow?"

"She was an immigrant," I blurted desperately. "She told me she had a green card. I'm sure the Irish consul general knew about her. . . ."

"Art." She turned to the young associate. "Would you call the consul general and check it out? Also, see if there's someone in the building who has a good contact over at the INS and determine whether they have, indeed, issued a green card in anyone's name that is even remotely like Ciara Kelly."

"Yes, ma'am." Art bounded out of his chair like he was blitzing the Illinois quarterback.

"I don't understand, Eileen." I heard my own voice quavering. "I've dated her for the last two weeks. She was as real as you and Nick are. I . . . I was in love with her. . . ."

"It's a strange one, Brendan." She nodded sympathetically. "I don't doubt you for a moment, but it would certainly be a big help if we could find her or figure out what's happening. Norton's undoubtedly making the same investigations and he will create a big fuss about an alleged alibi that doesn't exist."

"Am I a murder suspect," I shouted, "merely because my boat exploded and I had the good fortune not to be on it?"

"Not a real murder suspect," Nick said soothingly. "Rather, a newspaper suspect for an ambitious, angry, and not-terribly-bright police lieutenant. We're not pleading before a jury now, we're pleading before the people who read newspaper headlines and listen to ten-second clips on the five o'clock news."

"We'll beat 'em, Brendan. Don't worry."

The phone next to her elbow rang, interrupting her encouragement.

There was something wrong with the narrative I had just heard, a piece that didn't fit, an element of information that didn't make sense. I reached for it in the dark basements of my brain and it slipped away from me. Until the Memorial Day weekend I continued to encounter it, flitting across my path like a bat at sunset.

Finally Blackie Ryan caught the elusive piece of the puzzle, as obvious once one saw it in daylight as it was obscure before it was seen.

"Mrs. Kane . . . Yes, yes. Put him through. This is Eileen, Michael. Any news?"

What little color there was left in Eileen's face drained away. Her eyes closed, her jaw tightened. "There's not likely to be a mistake about it, is there? . . . No. Surely, we'll be ready for them. Thanks much for calling. Give my best to Annie."

"Madonna . . ." I said in a hoarse whisper.

"That was Mike Casey." Eileen's eyes were still closed. "Even a retired deputy superintendent can have powerful connections in the police department. They have a tentative identification based on dental X rays." She opened her eyes and sighed deeply. "I'm terribly sorry, Brendan, terribly, terribly sorry. They won't have a confirmation on it till tomorrow sometime, but Mike says there's no chance of them being wrong."

She opened her eyes and regarded me with infinite sadness. "Sam Norton is on his way over here. He doesn't have anything but nasty innuendos. Let me call the tune and give short legal answers to whatever questions he asks. Grief comes later? All right?"

I nodded dumbly. Love for Madonna had ended long ago, and yet I once had loved her, or thought I loved her with great tenderness and affection. I remembered the tall, slender blonde fourteen-year-old spiking a volleyball and shouting her team to victory. Dear God in Heaven, please. Please what? Just please!

"Nicholas," she said softly. "Go find Art. He will intimidate our friend Norton into something resembling civilized behavior."

Sam Norton, accompanied by Sergeant O'Connor and another policeman who was never identified, arrived at the office doorway at the same time as Nick and Art Savage. Norton glared balefully at the young associate and did not introduce the third policeman, and Eileen countered by not introducing Art.

"Your wife was murdered on that boat, Mr."—he said the word with disdain—"Ryan. Do you realize that?"

"Do sit down, Lieutenant Norton." Eileen gestured towards a chair. "What you mean is that Mrs. Ryan was killed in the explosion on the boat, at least if the tentative identification is correct. You have no conclusive evidence yet that there was a murder."

"There goddamn well was a fucking murder." The lieutenant exploded, as he sat tentatively on the very edge of the chair. The two cops stood silently behind him.

"Savage," Eileen tapped her blotter thoughtfully with

a pen, "would you be so good as to take notes of this conversation so that we have appropriate evidence when we lodge our protest with the Professional Practices Board. Now," she said, leaning forward, pointing the handle of a letter opener at Norton, "let's be clear about what's happening here, Lieutenant. There is a strong reason to believe that Mr. Ryan's wife died in an explosion on his yacht, off Montrose Harbor early this morning. You have come here, as I understand it, to ask Mr. Ryan some informal questions. At this point, you are not even certain that a crime has been committed, and you're in no position to make formal charges. My client will be happy to cooperate in responding to your question, subject to my decision as to whether the question is appropriate. I reserve the right to terminate the interview, should you become abusive. Is that clear?"

"Did your wife have a key to the boat?" Norton flipped open a large spiral notebook.

"Don't answer that, Brendan." Eileen's eyes blazed as she half rose from her desk. "Are my conditions clear, Lieutenant Norton? Answer me or we will adjourn this meeting now!"

"Yeah, they're clear." The lieutenant sneered at her.

Art Savage was on his feet, and halfway across the room.

"Sit down, Savage," Eileen ordered him. "Your job, for the moment, is to take notes. You may answer the question, Brendan."

"To the best of my knowledge, my wife . . ." My voice faltered. "My late wife did not have a key to the cabin of the *Brigid*. She was not interested in sailing."

"Then how did she get on the boat?" he asked contemptuously.

"I have no idea."

"You and your wife were divorced, weren't you?" He made it sound like divorce was a crime.

"That is correct," I said, trying to remain cool and keep my temper.

"Then you have an ecclesiastical annulment," he continued, as though that were even worse a crime. It dawned on me, in a fleeting irrelevancy, that Sam Norton, like everyone else in the room with the exception of Arthur Savage, was a Catholic.

"And there was a very large divorce settlement?"

I glanced at Eileen, and she nodded imperceptibly. "Approximately two million dollars, Lieutenant. It's a matter of public record."

"And that divorce settlement was not final yet, is that not correct?"

"I had not thought of that, Lieutenant." By desperate effort I kept my voice even. "I once loved my wife very much. I have fond memories of our marriage. I have not thought about the divorce settlement."

"That two million dollars reverts to you, does it not?"

"Lieutenant," Nick Curran interjected, "you haven't come over here to inquire about the fine points of divorce law, have you?"

"And the trust fund you've set up to guarantee the alimony payment for your wife and daughter, that reverts to you, too, doesn't it?"

Eileen hesitated, but flickered an eyelash of instruction in my direction. "It does."

"And you recently lost a large sum of money in commodities speculation, didn't you?"

"The matter is pending before a grand jury." Nick's fists were clenched, his thin face fiery red. "In point of fact, the money was removed from Mr. Ryan's account by his broker."

"Regardless." The lieutenant smiled cheerfully. "Within the last few months, Mr. Ryan, isn't it true that you've lost a million dollars, and this morning you got three million dollars back?"

"I would not accept that formulation," I said, now strangely bold and self-possessed again.

"Your formulation may not matter," the lieutenant said triumphantly. "You needed the money and you profited from your wife's death. Wouldn't you agree that you had excellent motive for blowing up that sailboat this morning?"

"You can't get away with a question like that, Lieutenant, and you know it."

Art Savage was on his feet again, looking rather frighteningly like Mean Joe Green.

"Sit down, Savage," Eileen barked.

"What's the matter with you, man?" Norton spat out. "I'm not black, but I wouldn't let that white bitch call me a savage."

Art grinned beatifically. For the first time I knew what Eileen's game was. " 'Cause that's my name, Lieutenant Norton. Arthur Savage."

"You must remember him, Lieutenant," said the unintroduced cop. "He was a linebacker for the Cincinnati Bengals."

"Only for the exhibition season." Art slipped back into his chair, almost gently.

"Any more questions?" Eileen said with ice in her voice, knowing that she didn't even have to mention a formal complaint to the Professional Practices Board.

"Yeah," the lieutenant bellowed angrily. "Where is this Kelly woman that you dreamed up as an alibi? We haven't been able to find any trace of her."

"That will be quite enough, Lieutenant." Eileen rose majestically. "We have no proof yet that a crime has been committed. The client is not charged with or even suspected of a crime. He does not need an alibi. The whereabouts of Ms. Kelly are not at the present time relevant."

"He damned well is going to need an alibi soon," Norton snapped, and stormed out of the office, his two henchmen in tow, the unintroduced one grinning openly behind his boss's back.

"Nice mousetrap, Eileen," I said wearily. "That may slow him down a bit."

"Rather the opposite, I think," she said, sinking back into her chair and looking now every day of her forty-three years. "It's enough to get him off the case over the long haul, but for the next few days we're going to have to put up with him. . . ." She drew large circles on her desk blotter as she pondered intently. "Brendan, you wouldn't have any objection to a lie detector test, would you?"

I was sinking deeper into a nightmare swamp. My wife was dead, my love had vanished, and now I was, for all practical purposes, a murder suspect. "Not if you think it advisable. Let me say for the record, by the way, that I didn't kill Madonna or whoever was with her on the boat last night."

My three colleagues laughed in nervous unison. "We're sorry, Mr. Ryan," Art Savage said. "The thought that you might have simply would never have occurred to any of us."

"There's no way to avoid it," Eileen continued thoughtfully. "The newspaper headlines tomorrow morning will say, 'Police question lawyer about wife's death in boat blast.' The only way we can undercut that even a little is by announcing that you have volunteered to take a police-supervised lie detector test. Are you willing to do that?"

"Certainly."

"Good. Arthur"—and she smiled at the young man with maternal affection—"by the way, you were wonderful. Just magnificent . . . When little Redmond here," she patted her stomach, "shows up, you're going to take over all my cases. Your histrionics are better than mine will ever be. Anyway, get on the horn to the state's attorney's office, talk to the first assistant, and find out whom they're going to assign to the case. Tell the assistant and tell the prosecutor that a police officer was here in the office making wild and unfounded accusations against Mr. Ryan and that, to clear the air, we are formally offering to take a lie detector test."

"Yes, ma'am." Art Savage bolted enthusiastically from the office.

"Will they go along do you think?" I asked.

"Rich," Nick said, meaning Richard M. Daley, the state's attorney, the son of the later mayor whom everyone on LaSalle Street called by his first name (except Ned Ryan, who always called him "Mr. Daley" because he had called the late mayor "Dick"), "will think about it overnight, cautious, careful man that he is, and then insist that our offer be accepted. He's not going to permit the state's attorney's office to become a tail for Sam Norton's kite."

Eileen picked up the ringing phone. She listened patiently, glowing with pride and affection. "Redmond Peter Kane," she said firmly, "you are fifty-three, going on fifty-four years old, you have three going on four children." She patted little Redmond. "You are a distinguished, internationally syndicated Pulitzer Prize–winning columnist. You absolutely will *not* punch anyone in the mouth! Besides, if there's any reprisals necessary, I can take care of myself. Thanks for the offer anyway. Should I ever need that kind of help, you'll be the first to know about it!" Her smile was broad and happy now. "Bye-bye, darling."

When she'd hung up, I staggered to my feet, feeling like a zombie, a man at the most only half comprehending, slowly weakening in my struggle to break out of a nightmare.

"Where are you going, Brendan?" Eileen asked gently.

"Back to the apartment, I guess." I turned around, not altogether sure where the door to her office was. "Jeannie is taking care of Madonna's family. My parents are staying in Tucson. I need a good night's sleep. I suppose we have to make the funeral arrangements tomorrow. The wake will be the next day and then the funeral. Somehow I've got to get through those days and then do your lie detector test."

"Will you make the funeral arrangements?" Nick asked, standing at my side as though he were a guardian angel still in charge of me.

"I don't suppose so. Jean and the Cliffords will probably take care of things. I don't imagine the Cliffords will want me interfering."

"Are you sure you don't want to go home with one of us?" Eileen was standing on the other side of me. Two guardian angels now, shepherding me toward the elevator.

"No, I think it best to be alone for a while. . . . I'm terribly grateful to the two of you for your help. . . . I have no right to friends like—"

"Nonsense," Nick said crisply. "It's our privilege being able to stand by you."

"You're a good man, Brendan," Eileen added. "You deserve better than what's happened to you today."

"I don't deserve friends like you." I was getting sentimental, maudlin; that had to stop.

"You never have understood, have you, Brenny?" Eileen asked. "You never understood why people like you."

"Mrs. Kane, your brother's on the telephone," her secretary said as we moved into the corridor.

Eileen took the call at the secretary's desk. "Punk? Thanks for calling. Pretty shook up . . . but doing well, all things considered. What?" Again the color drained from Eileen's face. She leaned against the secretary's desk, badly shaken. "You can't be serious. . . . Oh, my God . . ." Her jaw sagged, and again her eyes closed. Nick jumped to her side, steadying her. "Yes, yes. Certainly. I'll put him on. . . ." She looked up at me. "It's my brother Blackie, Brendan; he'd like to talk to you."

I took the phone from her trembling hand, wondering what new disaster had happened. It really didn't matter. The swamp in which I was caught couldn't become worse. "Good afternoon, Monsignor. This is Brendan Ryan."

"My deepest sympathies, Brendan." A vague, ineffectual, but unquestionably sincere voice. "You deserve better."

"That's what your sister said," I replied listlessly.

"I very much regret having to make this call. . . . Cardinal Cronin asked me to do it, however. The published reports say that you have no recollection that anyone else besides yourself had a key to the *Brigid*. . . ."

"Yes, that's correct. Madonna didn't like to sail."

"But surely Father Ron Crowley had a key, didn't he? As I recall, he sailed with you several times each summer?"

"Oh, no," I gasped.

"You see," Monsignor Blackie Ryan said apologetically, "the associate pastor at St. Jarls called the cardinal an hour ago. No one has seen Father Crowley since late yesterday afternoon, when he left the rectory in sports clothes, dressed, as a matter of fact, as though he planned to spend some time on Lake Michigan."

18

Melvin Clifford's fists beat ineffectually against my chest, like those of a child pounding playground equipment in a temper tantrum. "Murdered our daughter," he screeched, as the flashbulbs popped around us. "You ruined her life, you ruined her marriage, and then you killed her!"

Behind him Lourdes Clifford screeched hysterically while Joan, their dumpy, tublike unmarried daughter, tried to console her, despite her own convulsive sobbing. Damien Clifford, squat, balding, and, as always, frantic, struggled to pull his father off me.

"Get away from him, Daddy. He'll try to kill you too!"

A long time ago Clifford had been my height but had seemed taller because of the ramrod-stiff military posture that he had affected ever since his service with the First Army in the Second World War. Now that he was shriveled and withered and old, a fragile leaf just fallen from a tree, he seemed several inches shorter and had to reach up to try and pound my face. I raised an arm in gentle self-defense.

"You should be castrated," he screamed, sounding like a martinet on temporary release from a home for terminally ill, retired military officers. Damien—Damie to all who knew him—finally pulled his father away. Damie had never been good enough for anything. He had failed at two American medical schools and finally had barely made it through a Mexican university. Haplessly determined to be a great surgeon like his father, he was bounced from his surgical residency after six months of blundering. Now he earned his living by working the night shift in the emergency room in a fading inner-city hospital. Neither he nor Joannie would ever have to worry about money, however; arrogant, domineering, inflexible, Mel Clifford had been fortunate in his choice of investment advisers. The fact that his investment man had been a colonel in the war prevented Mel from meddling in his work the way he had destructively meddled in the lives of his children.

Having dragged his father off me, Damie renewed the assault on his own initiative. "Castrating you would be too good for you, you murdering bastard," he yelled, flailing at my stomach as more flashes exploded all around him.

I pushed him away but he returned to the battle. I was still among the living dead, a zombie, living off crackers and Jameson's. Dr. Clifford was an old man who had lost his beloved daughter. I could hardly hit him back. Damie was what Jean would call a nerd. I cocked my fist with a blessed sense of relief. Finally, I could strike out against those who were assaulting me.

Mike Casey, former deputy superintendent of police, looking like a well-dressed Basil Rathbone, intervened quietly. "Please, Dr. Clifford, this only makes things worse."

Damie Clifford was quite prepared to make things worse, but he was incapable of resisting Mike Casey's iron grip on his shoulders. He permitted himself to be led away and ushered with his parents into the undertaker's office.

The reporters turned on me. "Do you have any reply to Dr. Clifford's charge?"

"Have you really agreed to a lie detector test?"

"Who do think killed your wife and Father Crowley?"

"Do you think it's good taste for you to come to the funeral?"

"Is it true that you knew Father Crowley in the first grade?"

"Do you agree that Father Crowley's murder was political assassination?"

Mike threaded his way through the reporters, quietly and effectively. "Mr. Ryan doesn't have any comment, fellows."

Somehow it had been arranged that Mike would take charge of me through the wake and funeral. A lawyer, a retired deputy superintendent of police, and a painter, he had married a few months earlier Anne Reilly, a glamorous art dealer who was listed last year as one of the ten most beautiful women in Chicago. Anne and Mike had been grammar school sweethearts. Her marriage, like mine, had been annulled, but for me there was no grammar school sweetheart because I had already married a grammar school sweetheart, whose body was in the closed casket at the front of Sheean's funeral parlor.

Casey was the son of Ed Ryan's late sister, an extremely effective cop and the author of two scholarly monographs on police work. The Ryan family, having made a collective decision to take care of me, apparently had assigned Mike to watch over me. Still staggering through a world in which a nightmare of dreams and reality had blended, I offered no objections.

The newspaper headlines were shattering:

DR. CALLS EX-SON-IN-LAW KILLER!
SUSPECT IN PRIEST MURDER CASE TO TAKE LIE TEST
CARDINAL PERMITS MASS FOR PRIEST, WOMAN FRIEND
POLICE 'NEAR SOLUTION' IN DOUBLE MURDER CASE
LAWYER SEEKS 'MYSTERY WOMAN' FOR ALIBI

The Caseys had picked me up in midmorning and driven me to the funeral home in Highland Park from which the casket containing Ron Crowley's body was to be brought to St. Jarlath's for the parish wake. It had been arranged that we could visit the casket privately before the procession to the church. I would be spared the press while paying my last respects to the man who was, I suppose, the closest friend I ever had. Cardinal Cronin, Mike Casey told me, had authorized Church funerals for Ron and Madonna with the terse announcement "We leave the final judgment to God." The cardinal had "no comment whatsoever" on published reports that Father Crowley and Mrs. Ryan were "scantily clad" when fire swept the *Brigid.*

"Apparently the apostolic delegate," Mike shrugged his shoulders, implying that the apostolic delegate was about as important as a Chicago alderman who was not also a ward committeeman, "or I guess they call them papal nuncio now, raised hell with Cronin. I hear the cardinal told him to 'stuff it.' "

The three of us now stood quietly in front of the bronze casket in the empty funeral parlor, all that remained of Ron Crowley. Images raced through my clouded mind, like a freight train roaring past on a foggy night: Ron hitting a home run in a softball game when we were ten years old—scoring at home by sliding under the catcher's tag; Ron scoring a winning touchdown for St. Ignatius in a Catholic football game; Ron and Madonna making out in the back of the car at the McAuley High School prom; Ron informing us that he was quitting Notre Dame to enter the seminary; Ron's moving and brilliant talk at his first Mass banquet at the Martinique on a scorching hot June Sunday; Ron at an antiwar protest march in the early seventies; Ron, haggard and bearded, brought home from South America against his will because of failing health; Ron, flushed and over-weight, the last time we met. Dear God, I prayed, please try to understand him. Ron did not choose to be a hero. We all cast him in that role, his family, his friends, his teachers, his admirers. He tried hard. He wanted to be a good priest. Forgive him whatever sins he committed. Grant him peace somewhere else that he was never able to find here.

I was distracted while I was praying by the thought that, if I were to judge by Jean's report, the people of St. Jarlath's would not greatly grieve for their new pastor. For them he had not been a hero at all. Perhaps, after a life of struggling to be an all-American, the Reverend Ron Crowley had wearied of the game.

Curiously enough, however, in death he had achieved what had escaped him in life: all the newspaper stories had described him as a "consensus high school all-American" and said that he had given up certain "all-American status" and "probable success as a pro" to become a priest.

And some Catholic left-wing groups condemned his death as "political murder" and "a CIA assassination." These groups (most of whose members seemed to be intense and angry nuns, if one was to judge by their TV appearances) contended that Father Ron Crowley was a martyr, liquidated on orders of the Reagan administration because of his bitter opposition to the United States' involvement in El Salvador and other Central American countries. Father Crowley was, they said in tones that admitted of no disagreement, "a hero of the people and a saint whom we will not forget."

As best I could remember, Ron had not been involved in a demonstration or a march for the last eighteen months, since shortly after his appointment to St. Jarlath's. Either the Catholic radicals did not know of the transformation that occurred after he was assigned to St. Jarlath's or they didn't care about it. "They're more interested in TV exposure for themselves," Mike Casey had said tersely, "than they are in mourning Father Crowley."

We left Ron's wake in somber silence and went on to the funeral home in Lake Forest, where, because of unhappy chance, I arrived at the same time as my in-laws, or ex-in-laws, as the newspapers called them.

By unspoken consent, the Cliffords stood at the left of the casket to receive sympathies of mourners first, and I at the right of the casket to shake hands with anybody who was willing to be seen speaking to a murder suspect. Jean arrived with a grim-visaged Tim Murphy in resolute attendance. She stood in front of the casket, a bit to the left side, and hence somewhat closer to her grandparents than to her father. She smiled wanly at me from a distance but did not draw close enough for us to talk. My brief adult friendship with my daughter, I concluded, was yet another casualty of the explosion on the *Brigid*. How could it be otherwise, after she had spent a couple of days with the angry and hate-filled Cliffords?

Irish wakes are usually complex mixtures of grief and joy, of mourning and defiance of death, but something about the multiple tragedy of this particular wake seemed to suppress the Celtic propensity for defiance and joy. The line of mourners passed by the ornate, gray-tinged casket in heavy, stricken silence, their faces betraying bafflement and horror at the possibility of murder, suicide, revenge, adultery, sacrilege. Condolences were whispered in undertones that could hardly be heard. There were no noisy gatherings at the back of the parlor or in the lobby of the funeral home. Mourners were in a hurry to escape this wake, where the contaminating touch of evil seemed to linger.

Madonna, I thought, would not very much like this wake. Indeed, if she were alive, she would certainly not come to it.

The only ones who seemed inclined to keep alive ancient and pre-Christian traditions of wake-as-festival were the Ryan clan. They turned out en masse. A quick consensus had doubtless been reached in a series of phone calls. Madonna had never liked any of them and they were scarcely good friends with the Clifford family, but fourth cousin or not, Brendan Ryan was still "family." He might need support at the wake, though to tell the truth, he was well rid of the woman; so the Ryans would be there, paying perfunctory respect to the Cliffords, hugging and kissing Jean, who was being squired by one of their own, and lingering with me, to demonstrate that they thought the hint of murder allegations in the press was ridiculous. Their handshakes were firm and brisk, their hugs tender and reassuring, their words of sympathy brief and poignant. Only the Ryans brought me close to tears during my wife's wake.

A strange, quixotic bunch, a throwback, perhaps, to more ancient Irish days of loyalty. The Ryans had family problems like all families; at various times many of their marriages were in jeopardy (including her own, according to Eileen's brief hints). They knew, as do all families, the meaning of suffering, tragedy, and premature death. But unlike most of the South Side Irish of our generation, the Ryans did not approach life with cautious prudence. They did not minimize the risks or hedge the bets or play the conservative percentages. They did more than meet life halfway—they charged into it aggressively, embracing every possibility, every challenge, every opportunity that came anywhere near them. As my mother had once remarked long ago, "They're a bit much, but they're never dull."

Eileen seemed to have lost all the aura of tough, aggressive defense counsel that she radiated at the offices of Minor Gray and Blatt. With her big, genial husband's arm around her, she was an attractive, pregnant matron, a sensitive and vulnerable wife and mother, mourning a woman who was, perhaps, not a close friend, but nonetheless someone she'd known most of her life and with whom she had skipped rope almost every day in the pigtail years. Her eyes were red and her face stained with tears when she rose from a kneeler and embraced me. "I'm so sorry for you, Brendan," she murmured through her tears. "Sorry for you, sorry for Madonna, sorry for Jean, sorry for everyone."

"It'll be all right, Eileen." I held her in one arm and shook hands with her handsome husband with the other. "Nice of you to come, Red. I really appreciate it."

"We Ryans have to stick together." Red's affable face broke into a broad grin. "And God knows you've been nice enough to the woman down in the office."

"The woman's not a bad lawyer." I felt myself grinning in reply.

"Not a great lawyer," he said, "a good one. A very good one, but not what you'd call great."

"Ah." I found the brogue coming on me, too, and thought fleetingly of Ciara Kelly and how she would like Red Kane. "Not to say great. Sure, and hardly the kind that would win the Pulitzer Prize if they gave it for briefs."

"I take your meaning."

"You're both male chauvinists, that's what you are—genetically bred into Irish males, I guess. You're not really all that much to blame."

So, for a few moments, the pall lifted and I could think of Ciara Kelly and at least hope that I would see her again.

"The lie detector test is tomorrow at eleven?" I released the Kanes from my embrace.

"Right. I noticed our friend Sam Norton and his henchmen loitering around the door." Eileen jerked her head in their direction. "Doubtless waiting for you to break down and confess. He doesn't want the test at all. He claims he has enough of a case for an arrest and an indictment and that a lie detector test would be a waste of time."

"Does he?" I said, feeling the kind of fear in my stomach that I had not known since Vietnam.

Eileen shook her head impatiently. "He wants to position himself so that if the murders aren't solved, he won't be blamed. Rich Daley wouldn't hear of any other steps until a lie detector test is over.

"You have to understand," Eileen continued, her husband's big strong arm holding her close, "you're the only one they know who would have a motivation. But they have no evidence to link you to what happened and, as a matter of fact, no certainty about who was the target. If it was a professional contract, and it looks like either a contract or a terrorist caper, they probably never will find out who did it. Norton wants to be able to blame it on someone.

"I don't think he'll try anything here, with Mike Casey around." Eileen squeezed my arm as she and her husband prepared to make room for Mary Kate and Joe Murphy, Tim's parents. "Mike still intimidates cops, even though he's retired. Besides, politics change and Mike may well be back in power in another couple of years, a thought scary enough to make Norton think before he opens his mouth."

"I still can't believe it all," I said. "I keep trying to focus, to think intelligently about it all. It is as though some-body threw a circuit breaker in a part of my brain that does the thinking."

"Don't worry, Brenny." She departed with a dazzling smile of reassurance. "Until things get better for you, your friends will do all the thinking that needs to be done."

Friends? Why should anyone like me have such good friends? How would I ever be able to repay them?

By a quarter to ten, the flow of mourners had diminished and the Cliffords stalked out with the dudgeon of a jury that has just delivered a murder verdict. Jean said something to Tim Murphy and then walked across the room and stood next to me.

"After living with those people for two days, I can al-most sympathize with her." She embraced me and rested her head against my chest. "Oh, Daddy, they are such terri-ble people!"

So I had not lost my adult daughter/friend after all.

"You have to understand their past." I stroked her short, fine brown hair. "The transition from Depression to prosperity was a lot tougher than people realize."

"You're always making excuses for other people, Daddy." She sighed. "Face it: Mom was a bitch on wheels. She cared about you only because you made her life-style possible. And she cared about me because, as long as I was the perfect Barbie doll little girl, people praised her. I think she brought me into the world principally so I could be in the Pres Ball. When that was over, as far as she was con-cerned, I didn't exist!"

"That's too harsh, honey." I tilted her head up so I could look at her tearstained face and study her sad eyes. "Your mother had a very hard life. You've only had to put up with your grandparents for two days; they dominated every breath she took for forty-two years."

"She wanted it that way," Jean replied bitterly. "And if she'd lived long enough, she would have ruined my life the way they ruined hers."

"She's dead now, Jeannie," I pleaded. "Please forgive her."

"She would never forgive you or me, never!" Jeannie argued stubbornly.

"You know better than that, kid."

"I'm sorry, Daddy." She pulled a tissue out of her purse. The black suit she was wearing, I thought, was utterly appropriate for a Barbie doll mourner. "I forgive her; I hope she's happy; I hope she finds the happiness that she missed out on here on earth. It still makes me mad that you have to suffer so much."

I thought to myself that if I didn't deserve friends like the Ryan family, I didn't deserve either a daughter like Jean, who suddenly and unaccountably had become fiercely loyal to me, almost as though I had borrowed her temporarily from the "other" Ryans.

"Timmy seems to be a very nice boy." I took her arm and walked toward the door of the funeral parlor, where that handsome young black Irishman waited for her.

"He's all right." She blew her nose and reached for another tissue.

"Just another boy, or someone special?" I asked lightly.

"*Well*," she considered thoughtfully, "he's not *really* just another boy, but he's not someone special yet either."

"Your friend Caitlin has lent him to you on approval?"

She laughed in spite of herself. "Daddy, you're so funny!"

I kissed Jeannie, shook hands with Tim, and bid them good night. Back in the room with the casket, I saw a priest standing unobtrusively at one end of it. He was short, pudgy, and wore an ill-fitting clerical suit that may very well never have been pressed. He was staring grimly at the casket, his nearsighted eyes blinking rapidly behind thick, rimless glasses; indeed, so innocuous that you would hardly notice him, so apparently a cipher that he could drift into the funeral parlor and not be seen, rather like a contemporary Father Brown.

But there was anger in his eyes, and fury in his knotted fists. I thought of Chesterton's Father Brown, and then thought of a line from another one of Chesterton's works, which seemed much more appropriate for Monsignor John Blackwood Ryan: "It is Richard, it is Raymond, it is Godfrey in the Gate!"

At what was he angry? The Cliffords and the whole post–World War II new-rich suburban Irish culture that had ruined so many lives and about whose responsibility, I was quite sure, Monsignor Ryan had not the slightest doubt. But also, I suspect, angry at all the evil energies and forces in the world that keep us from being the kind of creatures God wants us to be.

"Thank you very much for coming, Monsignor," I said, standing behind him.

He looked around, startled, and seemed at first neither to recognize me nor to realize who I was. "Brendan Herbert George Ryan," he said. "Never underestimate the immensity of God's mercy or the lunatic passion of His love."

"I'm sure that's true, Monsignor; but I still don't understand why God does something like this."

There is considerable debate in the Ryan family as to where Blackie received his middle name. Some argue that he is named after an Irish revolutionary chieftain of the 1700s named Blackwood, who was allegedly one of the leaders of the "Whiteboys," a remote ancestor of the IRA; others in the family, thinking that "Blackwood the Whiteboy" was a mischievous family joke, argue that Kate Collins Ryan had made a blackwood convention in bridge the night her son John was conceived.

"The youngest first-grader in Holy Name Cathedral doesn't call me Monsignor," he began, his eyes blinking rapidly. "And I don't accept that God is responsible for the tragedy of Ron Crowley and Madonna Clifford. He wanted their stories to be very different, and He was unable to write them the way He wanted. I reject all other explanations."

"But what does that do to God's omnipotence?"

"Omnipotence be damned!" As he talked, Blackie Ryan was exploring his pockets, apparently searching for his car keys. "Anytime the necessities of Greek philosophy force us into a position that is at odds with the scriptural self-revelation of God, I say reject Greek philosophy. But we have raised generation upon generation of Roman Catholics to believe, not because of the scriptures, but because of Greek philosophy, that everything that happens in the world is directly attributable to God. That, it seems to me, is patent nonsense."

"You mean that there are some evil things that God would like to prevent but can't?" I could no more focus on philosophical discussion than I could on the urgent task of organizing my thoughts and my life.

"Precisely. God is the great improviser, the great player-by-ear. When bad things happen, or we do bad things to one another, He simply adjusts His game plan and achieves His goals by an alternative path. Humans are responsible for the death of your wife and your friend. God isn't."

"Oh," I said, wondering if all priests of his generation so abruptly dismissed Aristotle. "That's Whitehead, isn't it?"

"Didn't Professor Whitehead himself say that his philosophy was the first one to be directly inspired by scriptures? . . . At any rate," he finally discovered the car keys in the pocket of his trousers and switched them to the pocket of his coat, "I searched our parish census files for a record of Ciara Kelly. I'm afraid I didn't find her."

"I'm beginning to wonder whether she's a figment of my imagination."

"Oh?" He peered at my face intently, as though he were trying to recall who I was. "I can't imagine anyone, Brendan, anyone less likely to create an imaginary woman. No, Ciara Kelly lives, and she is the most interesting part of this whole mystery."

"I was in love with her, Monsig . . . er, I mean Blackie."

"All the more reason for finding her. . . . You'll excuse me, but I must return to the cathedral. My Lord Cronin will need someone to listen to his tale of the doings over at St. Jarlath's."

"A madhouse?"

"To put the matter mildly." Blackie rolled his eyes. "The grief of the parishioners was underwhelming, to say the least, and their outrage over the pickets protesting political murder has already notably surpassed their grief at the loss of a pastor none of them liked. My Lord Cronin quite properly bemoans the harm done to the diocese and to the Church and to the priesthood by this unseemly mess."

"Ron was not well." I was defending a priest to another priest, the same way I defended Madonna to her daughter.

"Indeed, yes." The priest began to search for his car keys again. "He had promised my Lord Cronin to seek psychiatric help and then repeatedly reneged on the promise. A bad choice, if I may say so."

"Do you think that what happened to Madonna and Ron was something they chose? Were they responsible for it? Will they be punished like they were responsible?"

"Ours is a God of love, not justice, Brendan Ryan, a fact for which we should all be profoundly grateful. I will do neither Ron nor Madonna the discredit of suggesting they were not, in some fashion, morally responsible. I also refuse to believe God did not and does not love them." He shrugged his shoulders helplessly. "On some later occasion the two of us can challenge the Great Improviser and suggest that in these particular circumstances His improvisations were not all that impressive. Sometime after all of this settles down, you must come see me."

"To talk about the Great Improviser?"

"Of course not. To talk about Ciara Kelly. What else?"

It is hard not to like Blackie Ryan, and even harder to disagree with his theology when he begins to talk about it. But I did not want to seek counsel from him now or ever about the mystery of Ciara Kelly.

The Caseys were waiting for me in the parking lot. Sam Norton, Mike informed me, had long since departed. "I think I make him kind of nervous."

They drove me back down the lake shore to the apartment. I watched the passing Chicago skyline, glittering and peaceful in the gentle warmth of the starlit spring night, and felt myself drifting away from my problems and achieving a sense of serene unity with the quiet stability of the city at night.

Only after my shower, as I sat in the usual terry cloth

robe, sipping my final Jameson's of the day and watching the reflection of the stars on the lake, did I remember Blackie Ryan's conviction that somewhere there was a Ciara Kelly whom I had to find.

I had found her once, I could find her again.

But look at what the result of finding her had been. Might not another search for Ciara Kelly produce even greater disasters?

Suddenly I had an inspiration. The floral-patterned bikini that Ciara wore in the pool—it was always neatly folded and placed in a bathroom cabinet. It should still be there.

Despite the numbing effect of the Jameson's, I jumped out of my chair and ran to the bathroom and threw open the cabinet. The place where her swimsuit had been was empty, but the towels that had been piled on that place were still stacked on a higher shelf. Ciara Kelly's bikini was not in my apartment, but there was a hint that it might have been there once. Perhaps that hint would be a starting point for the search that Blackie Ryan had demanded.

19

"Please answer yes to this question: Are you a woman?"

"Yes," I responded, knowing that they wanted to test my reactions to a lie. "I am a woman."

"You were born in 1942, is that correct?" The woman's voice whined like that of a perpetually angry schoolteacher, perhaps a nun who was unhappy in her religious order.

"Yes, I was."

"How many traffic citations have you had in the last three years?"

"None."

"Have you ever been arrested and charged with speeding?"

"Yes, I have."

"When?"

"About twelve years ago, I believe." My head felt like someone was working a jackhammer on it. I still could not focus on the murder of my wife and best friend. Was he really my best friend? Had he ever been? The circuit breakers in my brain were flipping back and forth as the woman police sergeant, who was the lie detector technician, mixed routine questions with questions about the murder.

"Did you yourself install the incendiary device in your yacht?"

"No, ma'am, I did not."

"Did you pay someone else to do so?"

"No, I did not."

"Did you love your wife?"

"That's a tough one." I hesitated. "I was very angry about the divorce. I still cared for her. I suppose I experienced a sense of relief, however, after the marriage was over."

"Are you happy that she's dead?"

"No, I am not."

"Do you have any idea who killed her or Father Crowley?"

"No, I do not."

"You say you met Ciara Kelly in Dufficy's Irish Store?"

"That's right."

"You became very friendly with her?"

"Yes, I did."

"You claim you were with her the night of the explosion on your yacht."

"Yes, but I believe I had left her apartment before the time of the explosion."

"Were you intimate with her?"

"Yes."

"How often?"

"I didn't count."

"Did you ever cheat on your wife?"

"No."

We were in a windowless room in the police headquarters at 11th and State. I sat at a table strapped to a machine that measured the reaction of my body to questions and answers. One technician was monitoring the machine while the other, the woman sergeant, was asking the questions, a mixture of those given her by Sam Norton and approved by Deputy Superintendent Cosmo Gambino and routine questions that enabled them to monitor the responses of my body when I had no reason to lie. Behind me, watching the output, were Norton, Gambino, a young prosecutor from Rich Daley's office named Joe Urbanik, Eileen Kane, looking pale and exhausted, and Mike Casey. Gambino obviously disliked and feared Casey.

"You don't work for the police department anymore," he said ungraciously. "You've got no right to come in here."

"Ah, Cosmo." Mike's frosty blue eyes glinted cheerfully. "As unperceptive as ever. I am a practicing attorney, am duly certified by the Illinois Bar Association. Mr. Ryan is a client of mine, and if you try to exclude me, I'll have to drag your ass over to superior court and have a judge put an injunction on you. Nothing would make me happier."

"I'm not so sure about that," Gambino grunted pugnaciously. "If I say you can't come in here, then you can't come in here."

"Don't be an asshole, Gambino." Joe Urbanik was no more than twenty-five years old, perhaps only a year out of law school, and arguably the toughest person in the room. "If you try to exclude Mr. Ryan's attorney, the state's attorney's office will withdraw from this whole procedure. We'll tell the press why. Do you want to call Mr. Daley or should I call him? Or are you going to wise up and realize the Supreme Court interprets the Constitution and you don't?"

Gambino muttered incoherently but raised no more objections to Mike Casey's presence.

"Was your wife unfaithful to you?"

"I did not think so until the time of the divorce. She claimed then that she had been unfaithful. I'm not sure that I believed her."

"Did you know that she was having an affair with Father Ron Crowley?"

"I did not know that, and to this day I do not know it."

"You have how many children?"

"One."

"A daughter?"

"Yes, Melissa Jean by name, usually called Jean."

"Where does she attend school?"

"Leland Stanford Junior Memorial University."

Not even a trace of laughter in the droning female voice.

"Was Father Ron Crowley really your closest friend?"

"I had thought of him as such for many years. I suppose in the last few years we drifted apart."

"Did you suspect that he was having a love affair with your wife?"

"I did not suspect that, and I do not now know it to be a fact."

"Did you murder your wife and Father Crowley?"

"No, I did not."

"Did you arrange for their murder?"

"No, I did not."

"Do you know who is responsible for their deaths?"

"I do not."

"You still insist you were with Ciara Kelly at the time of the explosion?"

"No, I was not with her at the time of the explosion. I was with her before the explosion. At the time of the explosion, I was in my apartment."

"Did you purchase the remote control materials from which the incendiary device in your yacht was made?"

"I did not."

"Do you know who did purchase them?"

"I have no idea."

"Do you think Ciara Kelly was involved in the murder of Mrs. Ryan and Father Crowley?"

"It's a possibility, I suppose." And one that had occurred to me a couple of times, but which seemed madly improbable. But then, Ciara's disappearance also seemed madly improbable. "I have no reason to think so, however."

And so the questioning continued for two and a half hours. I wondered how a body that was as weary, as heartsick, and as physically ill as mine could possibly give the sorts of signals to the polygraph from which the technicians would be able to make any sense. I felt like a character in a Franz Kafka novel, or perhaps an inhabitant of purgatory, destined to spend all but a few moments of eternity answering the same questions.

Finally, however, the sergeant said, "That will be all, Mr. Ryan. Thank you very much."

With businesslike efficiency she removed the tentacles of the machine from my arm and shoulder and wrist and chest. Her pale and not unpretty face was an expressionless mask. "Would you step into the next room please. Your attorneys will join you shortly."

Eileen, I thought, looked relieved as I walked unsteadily into the next room, and Mike Casey managed a quick, covert, thumbs-up sign. However, it was half an hour later before they did join me, both of them looking angry. "We're all right," Mike said. "Let's get the hell out of this place before I vomit."

We hurried down the corridor and into the elevator, Mike acknowledging with a curt nod the friendly greetings from his former staff members. There wasn't much doubt whom they wanted as superintendent of police. And there was also, I thought, not much doubt that Mike Casey was happy he'd made the transition from being a cop to being a lawyer and that he would not make the return pilgrimage.

The sky above State Street was overcast, rain threatening again, the temperature near ninety, a debilitating, oppressive Chicago summer day, even though it was still the month of May.

"I never thought I'd be so happy to get out of that place," Mike said grimly. "What assholes, you should excuse the expression, Eileen."

"My sentiments precisely," she said through tight lips. "Oh, it's all right, Brendan. You came through with flying colors. Sam Norton tried to intimidate that poor young woman into saying that the test was 'inconclusive.' She wasn't buying it. At first Gambino tried to lean on her too . . ."

"A cheap trick from a deputy superintendent, if I ever saw one. I wanted to tear those three stars off his uniform," Mike Casey said bitterly.

So finally Gambino agreed to make the usual announcement that there was nothing in the test to implicate

Mr. Ryan in the crime, and to add that the investigation would continue and that no one had been cleared of suspicion.

"That dumps the ball in Rich Daley's court," Mike concluded. "Norton will press for an arrest and an indictment. Some people over there at the state's attorney's office will say 'Hey, we might get lucky with a judge and jury and get a conviction no matter how thin the evidence is.' There will be a big fight over it. Rich will sit and listen. They'll adjourn without a decision."

"That may be, Brendan," Eileen concluded, as she opened the door of the Volvo, "where things are going to remain."

"I don't understand," I murmured. "I thought I passed the lie detector test."

An elderly cop, whose job it was to preside over the parking lot, came up to shake Mike Casey's hand. The brusqueness Mike had displayed with police staff members inside the building vanished. He chatted amiably with the cop and offered to bet him five dollars that the Cubs would finish higher than the White Sox.

"My five bucks against one of your paintings, Mickey," the old Irishman said with a laugh.

"You'd have to be dealing with my new wife on that one, and she's a sharp trader, she is." Mike poked him in the ribs. "See you soon, Marty."

In the car Eileen explained the situation in which I was trapped. "Let me continue Mike's scenario: there'll be another meeting over there at the end of the day. You're the only suspect they have, Brendan, and you're obviously not a very good suspect. Gambino will hedge; Norton will urge an arrest and an indictment. Some of them will repeat their point from previous discussions: with the right judge and the right jury and some bad mistakes by Eileen Kane, your defense attorney, they might possibly be able to get a conviction. The more cautious people from the state's attorney's staff will say 'Who the hell are you trying to kid? It's a rotten case, and even if she's a nursing mother, Eileen Kane isn't going to blow one that easily.' Rich Daley still won't say much. He'll take the lie detector output home with him, and tomorrow morning there'll be a cautious announcement from the state's attorney's office that there's no reason to seek a grand jury indictment at the present time. As far as they're concerned that's the end of it for you."

"The cops," Mike went on, "will have more pressure on them than the state's attorney's office because of the media. So the police department will say that the investigation is continuing, that there are a number of suspects, and that you can no longer be considered the principal suspect. And that's the way it'll be, maybe indefinitely. Norton will try to strong-arm some of the people from Montrose Harbor into saying that they saw you fooling around the boat. He'll have his stooges poke around radio supply stores to see if they can find out where the equipment for the incendiary device was purchased. They'll lean on a few of their softer mob stool pigeons to learn what the word on the street is about the contract. But Norton won't spend much time on it because he'll figure there isn't a payoff in pursuing it."

"So that's the way it will be, Brenny." Eileen stared straight ahead. "The murder will remain unsolved, and the cloud of suspicion over you will never dissolve completely. Oh, sure, you passed the lie detector test and people will remember that. Your friends will be convinced you're innocent, but still you'll be three million dollars richer and people will whisper about that."

"You're even more cynical than I am, Eileen," Mickey Casey said with a thin laugh as he stretched his long legs in the back of the Volvo.

Eileen turned right at Roosevelt Road and edged over toward Michigan Avenue.

"Even though I'm a lawyer, I guess I'm kind of naive. Where does justice fit in all of this?"

"Justice," Eileen exclaimed impatiently, braking just in time to obey a red light. "No point in violating traffic laws so close to 11th and State. Justice mostly doesn't figure. The police department and the prosecutors are both worried about the unsolved crime rate, their conviction percentages, the negative reaction to a rich man escaping indictment, and their media images. Justice only computes after all the other factors are taken into account."

"Then why don't they go for an indictment? That would be a lot of good publicity for them, wouldn't it?"

"Not if a judge directed a not-guilty verdict. Besides, we lucked out in one important respect: the state's attorney is a decent man. Of the whole crowd that's going to be involved, Rich Daley is the only one for whom justice is the decisive issue. He'll study the lie detector output carefully and conclude that you didn't kill your wife and Father Crowley, and that it would be unjust to seek an indictment."

"Maybe Joe Urbanik too," Mike Casey remarked.

"Maybe, maybe not."

We stopped at Monroe Street, between the Art Institute and Orchestra Hall; young women in sundresses were streaming by in both directions on Michigan Avenue. I thought of Solti's *Rite of Spring* and wondered again about Ciara Kelly.

"So the system works, if it works at all, because there's an occasional decent man in a decision-making position?"

"And each year," Mike Casey said sadly, "there seem to be fewer such men around."

"One thing would make Rich hesitate." The light changed and Eileen eased the car forward. "Norton made a big point about your responses concerning Ciara Kelly."

"Was I lying then?" All the circuit breakers in my brain were suddenly in the on position, and for a moment I was thinking clearly again.

"No," Mike said. "The machines showed that you were telling the truth. Norton argues that there obviously is no such person as Ciara Kelly and that proves you are such a sophisticated liar that you were able to fool the machine. Stephansky, the woman who conducted the test, stood right up to him and said the only correct conclusion was that you believe she does exist. Norton didn't like that at all, and he's going to continue to chew at the Ciara Kelly element. Unless I completely misunderstand our state's attorney, it will worry him a little, too, but not enough to change his mind."

The circuit breakers in my head began to flip on and off randomly again. "Not a very bright picture you paint for me, is it?"

"It'll get better," Mike Casey said. "It'll take time though."

"And your friends will stand by you," Eileen agreed. "Speaking of which, I suppose you've forgotten that this is the day for the Ryan family lunch. Anne and Mike are going to join us. We'll take a vote later to see whether they get permanent invitations. Me, I'm afraid it will turn into a discussion of art between Mike and Cathy Curran."

"Let me have a rain check," I pleaded. "Next week will be fine. Today I just want to return to my apartment and sleep for about eighteen hours."

"Sure," Eileen said. "But don't think we're going to forget about you. Next week, you'd better be there."

"You know, it's funny," I said, sounding rather wistful. "I had sort of intended to bring Ciara to the lunch today."

Both my friends were silent. So they, too, were dubious about the existence of a Ciara Kelly. I could hardly blame them.

They dropped me off at my apartment building, her green eyes and his blue eyes both soft with affection and concern. I didn't deserve friends like that. I didn't want friends like that. I wanted to be alone, forever if possible.

20

I became a vegetable, existing but barely living, absorbing nourishment but refusing to think, continuing with life, surviving from day to day but avoiding any plans for tomorrow or the next day or the day after.

Vegetables don't indulge in self-pity and I did. It became the dominant, indeed the exclusive emotion in my life: Brendan Ryan as victim, as outcast, as martyr, betrayed by his wife, by his friends, by his community, by his lover. I felt no grief over the loss of Madonna and Ron, no pain for Jeannie, who had lost her mother, no compassion for the battered remnants of the Crowley and Clifford families, not even any concern for Ciara, for which God forgive me. I stayed away from the office, unplugged the telephone in the apartment, ignored messages from Nick and Eileen, avoided the Caseys, whose gallery was just down the street from my apartment, and declined a weekend invitation to Grand Beach. I did not make my bed or clean the apartment, and survived on fruit, crackers, and half a bottle of Jameson's a day, nursing my grudge against the cosmos because, innocent and honest man that I was, I would be forever tainted with the suspicion that I had murdered my wife and my closest friend.

The house in Lake Forest was empty now. The Cliffords had gone back to Florida, Jean had been carried off to Grand Beach by Mary Kate and Caitlin Murphy, and Madonna was dead. I realized that I had to do something about it. I certainly did not want to move back, yet Jean would need to have some kind of home for her vacations from Stanford. My apartment was hardly big enough for the two of us, and I could not expect her to stay at Grand Beach all summer long, however much such an arrangement might delight young Tim Murphy.

Although I had declined the Grand Beach invitation, I envied Jean her opportunity to go there, not so much wanting to deprive her of it but rather wanting to feel sorry for myself because I had never been permitted summer resort excitement when I was her age. My parents much preferred to put a pool in their backyard in Chicago, and while the "other" Ryans would have been delighted to share with me the sand and water and sun of Grand Beach, my group abominated the place and I accepted their decision. It seemed, as I tried to drown myself in the pathos of self-pity, that I had spent my whole life accepting the decisions the group had made for me. Now there was a new group, Nick Curran, Eileen Kane, Mike Casey, and their spouses, who were ready to replace the old and deprive me again of my free will.

God damn it, I would not permit that to happen!

Nick Curran sent a hand-delivered message to my apartment, reminding me of my grand jury subpoena on Monday morning of the next week. I plugged in the phone, called Nick, pretended that I was self-possessed and cheerful, and assured him that I would be there to talk to the grand jury. "Just give me till the end of this week, Nick," I said, trying to sound refreshed and businesslike, "and I'll be back at the office as good as new."

"I'm glad to hear that." He sounded dubious. "You won't be up at Grand Beach this weekend?"

"Give me another week," I pleaded.

It was already 5:30 in the afternoon—how had the day slipped away? In fact, what day was it?

I poured myself a glassful of Jameson's, ate an orange, cut myself some cheddar cheese, finished my supper with cheese, crackers, and Irish whiskey. Another furious late-afternoon thunderstorm—it seemed to have been the pattern the last few weeks—lashed against my apartment building. It reminded me of the night that Ciara and I had first made love.

Ciara? I had not thought about her for several days. She was gone from my life, never to return. It was probably just as well.

The phone rang. Damn, I forgot to pull the plug. Well, let it ring. Perhaps it's something important. Nothing much could be important. Perhaps it was another disaster in my life. That I didn't want.

Nonetheless, forty-two years of a responsible life compelled me to pick up the phone. "It's Mary Kate Murphy, Brenny. There's nothing to worry about. Jean is fine. I thought I had better call you and tell you that we had a bit of an accident here this afternoon."

All the circuits in my brain were suddenly activated. Terror had sent a flow of energy into me that overrode all the disconnected circuit breakers. "My God, Mary Kate, what happened?"

"Jeannie's been taking long walks these days, getting her head screwed back on, she tells us. She was going down a hill over in Michiana—you know the one, Dogwood and Ridge—it fills up with water every time it rains."

"I'm afraid I don't . . ."

"Anyway." Mary Kate doubtless assumed everyone in the world was well-informed about the roads in Grand Beach and Michiana. "A car went out of control at the top of the hill, skidded down toward her. Fortunately your daughter is a good athlete; she dived off the road and the car missed her. She picked up some scratches and bruises and bumped her head a little, so we put her in St. Anthony's Hospital for the night. Joe and Timmy are with her. . . ." Mary Kate laughed. "So if she needs any Jungian psychotherapy, my husband will be glad to oblige."

My body sagged against the couch in my parlor. "Thank God everything's all right. . . . What about the driver of the car?"

"He didn't stay around, kind of hit and run, except that he didn't hit anyone. We reported it to the Michigan state police, but he'll be pretty hard to find. All Jeannie remembers is that it was a black car. She was too scared to remember the license number."

"Well, I'm glad she's all right." The circuit breakers flipped off, and I prepared to hang up the phone. "Thanks for calling me."

"She's in room 314 at St. Anthony's Hospital—that's area code 219-472-3600."

The clear implication was that if I didn't call Jeannie I would have to answer to Mary Kate Murphy and probably the entire Ryan clan, even unto the third and fourth generations.

"Thanks a million, Mary Kate. I'll call her right away."

"You'll be up here with us for the Memorial Day weekend."

"Is that an order?"

"It's an imperial rescript."

Dr. Mary Kate Murphy never denied that she was the empress of all the Ryans, even third and fourth cousins.

I called Jeannie at St. Anthony's Hospital. She sounded woozy and distracted but was delighted to hear from me. "I'm surprised the driver of the car didn't come back to help you," I said after she had assured me in five different ways that she was feeling "fine."

"Oh, he did back up, fast too, then another car came around the corner and he took off. I'm sorry I didn't notice the license numbers."

"You'll be up there all week?"

"Uh huh—they'll probably let me out of the hospital tomorrow after they do a few more tests, and I'll stay here for the weekend. Then I'll come into Chicago and stay at Connie's house and drive up with you next Friday afternoon."

"It's been decided that we're driving up on Friday afternoon, has it?" I managed to laugh. "Dr. Murphy doesn't take no for an answer?"

"No way, Daddy; we're going to stay with the Currans, and I will help Aunt Catherine with the kids and the cookout."

All neatly prepared. My new friends were, if anything, more efficient and better organized in taking charge of my life than were my old friends.

I lay back on the couch, a cracker in one hand and a half-empty Jameson's glass in the other. Something was wrong with the story of the near-accident in Michiana.

One of the circuits in my brain began to work again, slowly, laboriously, nonetheless effectively. I didn't know Mary Kate's number in Grand Beach. Whom should I call? Mike Casey directly? Probably not a good idea.

I dialed the number of Holy Name Cathedral and asked for the rector. "Ryan." A mild and inoffensive voice.

"You heard about Jeannie's 'accident' in Michiana this afternoon?"

"Indeed, Brendan. A curious incident, was it not?"

"Do you think I'm wrong to be frightened about it?"

"Not in the least. I, uh, have already made certain preliminary investigations on the subject."

"Would you call Mike Casey for me and tell him it seems suspicious to me and that perhaps they might keep a close eye on Jean this weekend—not let her go out walking by herself, for example ..."

"I believe that some protestations in that direction have already been made. I'll tell the responsible parties that your concern merely reinforces my own—not that they take the matter lightly."

"Why, Blackie?"

"I must confess that I know of no reason that anyone would wish to endanger you and your family. However, it does not at all seem unreasonable to me to suppose that you

212 ANDREW M. GREELEY

and, uh, Ms. Kelly—was that not her name?—were the real targets of the incendiary device in your yacht. There's no reason to believe that your late wife and Father Crowley used the craft often, indeed if ever before, and at a distance, at twilight, I would have thought that whoever operated the remote control mechanism could not have perceived that it was not you and, uh, Ms. Kelly on the yacht."

"That's interesting." Worn out from disuse, the active circuit in my brain ceased to function. "I suppose I'll see you there next weekend?"

"Saturday, surely, unless I want my family membership card to be revoked. I'll come back here for Masses on Sunday and then return in late afternoon. And the search for Ms. Kelly?"

"There isn't any search, I'm afraid, Monsignor Ryan."

"Ah!"

I passed the weekend in a pleasant, soothing state of nirvana in my air-conditioned apartment, away from the heat and the humidity that had settled into the city and which, punctuated occasionally by thunder showers, threatened to become the pattern for the summer. I did manage to put in half an hour in the pool, and also to sneak out of the building and watch the first two-thirds of Robert Redford's *The Natural* at the Water Tower Place. I left before the end because my soggy mind was not capable of comprehending the symbolism of the story.

However, at ten o'clock the following Monday morning, clean-shaven, dressed in somber color-coordinated gray, smelling of my expensive cologne, I presented myself at the appointed grand jury room at the Everett McKinley Dirksen Federal Building. I listened and nodded at Nick's brief instructions, asked a few intelligent questions, and then entered the hallowed chamber of the Grand Jury of the Northern District of Illinois, which was investigating the commodities market actions of John King Sullivan.

The Assistant United States Attorney for the Northern District of Illinois who was to question me was young, blonde, and very pretty. To my surprise I found myself thinking that when she was finished with her apprentice time working for the government she would certainly be welcome at Minor Gray and Blatt—and this before she had asked me a single question.

Male chauvinist, I denounced myself mentally. Eileen would be furious if she knew I was thinking such thoughts in the hallowed precincts of a grand jury room. So would Ciara.

Ciara.

Questions began about my relationship with John King Sullivan. In addition to being young, blonde, and pretty, the Assistant U.S. Attorney for the Northern District of Illinois was very feminine in her mannerisms and very, very smart. Oh, yes, we needed her at Minor Gray and Blatt.

Ciara.

I explained, in response to her question, that "taking a position" meant, in my case, a long-term estimate of whether the economy would move forward or slow down over a six-month period, an estimate I would back up with a leveraged purchase of government bond contracts.

"By leveraged, you mean, do you not, Mr. Ryan," she asked demurely, "your actual payment is only a small proportion of the market value of the contract?"

"Yes, that is correct."

"So if your guess seems to be going wrong, you will be called upon to put up additional funds in the course of the position?"

"I wouldn't use the word 'guess,' Counselor."

She blushed—very prettily, I may add. " 'Informed estimate'? Or perhaps 'calculated risk'?"

"Something of the sort. But to answer your question, Counselor, it would have been subject to margin calls if the price of a contract with the Chicago Board of Trade had increased. You see, I hold futures contracts at the market price on a given day. This means that if the price of the contract has diminished, then I abandon my position and purchase the contract at that price in order to deliver the contract, which I sold at a much higher price, and the difference is my margin of profit."

"A good deal of money was involved, was it not?"

"About a million dollars," I said mildly, noting the raised eyebrows, the shocked expressions of the good working-class and middle-class people on the grand jury.

"Your informed estimate turned out to be correct, did it not, Mr. Ryan?"

"Yes, it did."

"In fact, your informed estimates have usually been correct, have they not?"

"More often than not," I admitted.

"So if your money had been invested as you directed your broker, Mr. John King Sullivan," she glanced at the papers in front of her as if she didn't know full well that that was the name of my broker, "you would have by now realized a substantial profit?"

"Yes, ma'am," I said, "a very considerable profit."

Her eyes, gray like Ciara Kelly's, glinted with amusement. Ma'am, indeed, she seemed to be saying teasingly. How could I explain to her that I had no idea what her name was? If Nick had told me, or if she had mentioned it, I had completely forgotten.

"Can you describe to us in your own words what happened to your money?"

"I discovered, quite by accident, in a conversation with a floor trader, that Mr. Sullivan had invested very heavily in the opposite position, that is to say, he had sold government bond contracts to a bond contractor at approximately the same price at which I had purchased them, expecting a sharp increase, I presume, from the economic indicators, and perhaps a renewal of inflation."

"At that time you questioned Mr. Sullivan about this matter?"

"That is correct."

"And did you find his answer satisfactory?"

"No, I did not."

"Did you report your suspicions immediately to the Commodities Future Trading Commission?"

"No, not immediately."

"How long did you wait?"

"Several days."

"May I ask why?"

"Mr. Sullivan and I had been lifelong friends. First of all, I wanted to be sure that the violations had indeed occurred; secondly I wanted to be sure that other investors had also been . . ."

"Victimized?"

Gray eyes like Ciara Kelly.

"I suppose so, yes."

Ciara Kelly.

"In other words, you were willing to absorb your own enormous loss in the name of friendship, but you could not permit other investors to suffer losses?"

Ciara Kelly. Ciara Kelly. Ciara Kelly.

"Mr. Ryan?"

"Ma'am?"

She considered me curiously for a moment. "Should I repeat the question, sir?"

There was a faint tease in the word 'sir.'

"Would you please, Counselor."

"I asked whether your attitude at the time was that you would absorb your own financial losses but that you could not permit other investors to be defrauded of their money?"

"Yes, that is correct."

Ciara Kelly. Ciara Kelly. Ciara Kelly.

She was in enormous danger. Not the leggy, gray-eyed blonde who was questioning me and flirting mildly with me—perhaps in response to what she saw as my own initiation of flirtation—no, she wasn't in danger at all, but Ciara Kelly was.

"Mr. Ryan?"

"I'm sorry, Counselor." I felt my face burning. "Would you mind repeating the question?"

"We understand that you've had many serious problems on your mind recently, Mr. Ryan. Did Mr. John King Sullivan attempt to dissuade you from reporting his violations of the Commodities Future Trading Act?"

"Yes, Ms. Kelly. Only once, however."

The young woman grinned broadly. "Kennedy, sir."

"Yes. I'm sorry, Miss . . ." I saw the wedding ring on her finger. "I'm sorry, *Mrs.* Kennedy."

And so it went. The information that would constrain

the grand jury to indict John King Sullivan was gently but firmly drawn from me by a very clever young woman who, understanding my own confusion, deftly adjusted her interrogation style to make me look good before the grand jury.

There was enough testimony, should the reported plea-bargaining deal break down, to send John King Sullivan, my lifelong friend, to a federal correctional institution for a good long time.

And Ciara was in danger, grave, grave danger. From whom? Where? No answers, but about the danger I had not the slightest doubt.

When I was excused at the end of my testimony from the grand jury room, Mrs. Kennedy made a charming little speech. "We're very grateful to you for your cooperation, Mr. Ryan. We understand how painful this matter must be for you. You've been very frank and forthright and helpful to us."

"Thank you, Mrs. Kennedy," I murmured, and quickly escaped from the grand jury room.

"How did it go?" Nick Curran asked breathlessly.

"We'd better hire that woman when she leaves federal service," I responded.

"Every law firm in the Loop," Nick said with a grin, "will want her."

"A job for Eileen, then."

"I agree completely."

"Well, you're enough yourself again, Brendan, to react positively to pretty and smart young women."

"How long has it been, Nick, since you've known me to react that way? Maybe I'm just the opposite of my ordinary self."

Before Nick could respond, we encountered, lounging in the corridor outside the grand jury room, Lieutenant Samuel Norton of the Chicago Police Department.

"Looking for a traffic violator, Sam?" Nick asked sharply.

"Nah." Norton jingled the coins in his pocket. "Looking for a murderer. I know you killed them, Ryan, and I'm going to get your ass in the electric chair if it's the last thing I ever do."

"You just added one more charge to our complaint to the Professional Practices Board," Nick snapped.

"I don't give a fuck about your charges," Norton sneered. "You won't dare bring them when I get the goods on this motherfucker."

"Don't say another word to him, Brendan." Nick turned on his heel and dragged me along with him. "He has no right to harass you."

"I didn't say a word, and wasn't planning to," I observed mildly.

"Eileen'll go through the ceiling when she hears about this." Nick was furious.

"Are we really going to file a complaint against him?"

"You damned well better believe we are. The asshole thinks we're afraid to risk more newspaper coverage on the murder; in fact, when we're finished with him, we'll have the truth in the papers: the police department in the person of Lieutenant Samuel Norton was so busy harassing you that it did not seriously search for the real killers."

Who were the real killers? Were they the ones who had endangered Jeannie's life last week? And were they the ones who were threatening Ciara Kelly? And how could someone be threatened who apparently did not exist?

"Have a bite of lunch?" Nick asked, as we emerged in the scathing sunlight of LaSalle Street—high noon, the only time the sun shone in the LaSalle Street ravine.

"I'm not quite up to it yet, Nick," I pleaded. "I'll take a rain check till next weekend at Grand Beach."

"You'll be staying with us, I'm told." Behind the thick glasses, Nick's eyes seemed to twinkle.

"Someone, someday, ought to do a study of how the Ryan family women arrive at their collective decisions."

"ESP!"

Ciara Kelly was in danger.

"You're looking good," Nick continued somewhat dubiously. "The Crazy Mal business in the paper didn't bother you?"

"Who's Crazy Mal?" I began to walk north on LaSalle Street, and Nick tagged along. "I'm afraid I haven't been reading the newspapers the last few days."

"Sam Norton got the word from one of his Taylor Street stoolies that a contract had been put out to a scumbag—the police term for him—named Cesare Malocha, otherwise called 'Crazy Mal.' He's a minor hit man that some of the lesser lights in the outfit occasionally hire when they need a job done that doesn't require too much finesse. He's called 'Crazy Mal,' one gathers, because his contracts tend to be a bit reckless and amateurish. Some of the top people can't understand why the police let him roam the streets." Nick smiled thinly. "They don't have a very high regard for law enforcement in this city, I guess."

"So what happened?" I was more concerned with what threatened Ciara Kelly than I was with Crazy Mal.

"Norton sweated him," Nick said with a shrug, "or tried to sweat him. Pretended that they already had a link between him and you. Mal listened to it for a while, called his lawyer, and is out walking the streets again, much to the dismay of the top brass in the outfit."

"But if he's the killer, why can't they arrest him?"

"It's one thing to know from the word on the street that he did the job, and quite another to prove it. The cops know who most of the hit men are in mob slayings, but there's never any proof that would stand up in court, so the hit men go free unless they make a mistake or somebody squeals on them and stays alive long enough to testify."

"And then he goes off and leads a new life, courtesy of the United States government—sometimes even committing crimes that the FBI won't let local authorities prosecute."

"When Eileen and I were working for the government," Nick said—we were standing at LaSalle and Madison, Nick's internal gyroscope tilting him back toward his offices in the Minor Gray and Blatt Annex on Jackson, mine tilting me toward my apartment and the Jameson's bottle—"we defended the Informant Protection Plan as the only way to convict someone in the outfit. Now I don't know. Anyway, Sam Norton didn't lay a glove on Mal, and I think that's the last you're going to hear of it. . . . Incidentally, the Continental Bank Building still seems to be standing there, doesn't it?"

"Why wouldn't it?"

"You really aren't reading the newspapers; the feds bailed Continental out the other day to the tune of seven billion dollars; they're looking for a merger—maybe Morgan Guarantee. . . . Banking, I guess, is too important to be left to the bankers."

The disappearance of the Continental Illinois as a separate entity would be an enormous blow to Chicago's pride and independence, far worse than losing the *Sun-Times* to Rupert Murdoch. It would also be a severe shock to Minor Gray and Blatt, which handled much of the Continental's business. I felt guilty for nurturing my own self-pity and distracting the attention of Nick and my other friends from the firm's serious problems. I was sure that he had better things to do that morning than to sit outside a Dirksen Building grand jury room waiting for me or, for that matter, standing at LaSalle and Madison trying to tempt me back into the cold waters of the rushing stream of life.

"I better let you get back to the offices. I imagine the senior partners are having fits."

"One more thing." Nick paused and jammed his fists into his pockets, a gesture that indicated he was spoiling for a fight. "The money in the trust fund you set up for the alimony is yours to do with whatever you wish. After all, the trust fund was your idea. The divorce settlement monies are another matter. Technically, the divorce wasn't final, so you have the right to the money. But the Cliffords have hired a lawyer, who has gone into court with a petition to appoint them Jean's guardians on the grounds that you're unfit to be a guardian of an innocent girl. They've also asked that, as guardians, they have control over the divorce settlement money until Jean reaches her majority. It's pure, gratuitous nastiness."

"But Jean's nineteen years old!"

"And well able to take care of herself without Mel Clifford messing in her life like he messed in her mother's. They can't hope to win. It's a form of harassment, an opportunity for the Cliffords to attack you in public. We will beat them, but it's one more burden you don't need right now."

"I don't suppose there's any compromise possible?"

Nick regarded me curiously, still incapable of understanding that some men were not as competitive as he was. "We can explore that, but I don't see any. A monetary settlement wouldn't be appropriate. And in any case, the Cliffords don't want money, they want a chance to attack you."

"You're sure I won't lose?"

"Lose?" Nick exploded. "You're the girl's father, a distinguished lawyer and civic leader. You have committed no crimes. You weren't the one who went to bed with the priest. . . . Sorry, Brendan."

"Not at all. I guess I feel guilty. I feel that maybe I'm not a fit father for Jeannie. I haven't done a very good job at fatherhood, God knows."

"That's not what Jeannie thinks," Nick argued hotly. "In fact, if this thing ever gets to a court hearing, the judge will throw it out as soon as we put Jeannie on the stand."

"I don't want Jeannie on the witness stand!" I shouted at him.

Nick laughed at me. "Brendan Ryan, when will you ever learn? Whether you want Jeannie on the witness stand makes not the slightest difference. She knows about the Cliffords' petition, and according to my Grand Beach sources, she's furious. She's Irish, Brendan, and like all the other women in the family, the Archangel Gabriel couldn't keep her off the witness stand."

"My mother isn't Irish."

"No." A whimsical smile spread across his lean, elegant face. "She's Scottish. They're the worst kind of Irish."

We shook hands and went our separate ways, Nick back into the maelstrom of trying to save the seventh largest bank in the country, with assets of over forty-two billion dollars, from its own folly, and I back to my beloved Jameson's bottle. I didn't care what happened to Continental Illinois, and I was confident that Nick could protect Jeannie from her grandparents. There was, nonetheless, one point about which Nick had not been completely honest. Cesare Malocha was a scumbag with an alibi and a high-priced outfit attorney. There was no reason for him to sing with lyrics provided by Sam Norton. Not yet. But if Crazy Mal should stumble, and even the outfit's overlords were surprised that he had not, and the police department arranged a plea-bargain deal with him, he would sing any tune that Sam Norton devised for him. Then there would surely be an indictment and a trial. Presumably Eileen Kane would tie both Norton and Malocha in knots on the witness stand, and presumably I would be acquitted. But not necessarily. Plea-bargained informants had sent innocent men and women to jail before—no one yet to the electric chair, but I did not relish the prospect, however remote, of being the first.

The murderer of my wife and friend had to be found, even if I must do it myself. But later. First to my apartment and the Jameson's bottle.

Ciara Kelly. Ciara Kelly. Ciara Kelly.

An oppressive fear pervaded my soul, weighing me down, slowing my footsteps as I trudged doggedly along Madison Street toward Michigan Avenue. Dark, somber clouds, matching the psychic energies that were bombarding me, were slipping over the city, obscuring the top half of the Sears Tower. The thunderstorm would come early today.

Some of my psychic kinks, like those of others, according to the literature, are visual: I actually see the garrison leaving Fort Dearborn, the flashes of fire over the lake, the dark shadows in the Chestnut Street ravine. Other phenomena seem to be purely intellectual, at least initially. I *knew* that Ciara Kelly was bearing my child, even before the first time I made love to her and *saw* her body blossoming with my offspring. Still other happenings are somewhere in between, emotional but not visual. I *feel* an event, neither seeing it nor comprehending it. The emotions of the event take possession of me but tell me nothing of what is happening or where it is happening or whether it is a past or a present or a future phenomenon.

My terror for Ciara, as I walked home under the glowering gray clouds, was in the last category. Ciara's emotions had become my emotions—the terror, shame, degradation, humiliation, revulsion at being used and abused. Torment, pain, a desire that death terminate suffering. Despair.

222 • ANDREW M. GREELEY

Ciara being raped by the Simbas—a recollection of the past, memory traces still lingering from the night at her apartment?

An apartment in which she had never lived.

Partly. But also partly the present, and mostly the future. Ciara was being threatened. The emotions I was experiencing were either in the present or in the immediate future. Those who wished to torture and destroy her were at hand. She needed my help and protection.

The feelings were overwhelming, the most vivid psychic vibrations I had ever experienced. At the Chicago River and Michigan Avenue I leaned against a pillar of the bridge in the shadow of the rain-drenched Wrigley Building. It was raining now. I had hardly noticed it. Beneath me one of the Wendella excursion boats bobbed on the windswept river. Ciara needed my help.

Then slowly the emotions ebbed, leaving me drained and uncertain. As I have noted previously, my psychic sensitivity is erratic, unpredictable, and mostly useless. Nor can I ever be certain that I am not producing the vibrations myself unconsciously. Had I created peril for Ciara Kelly because if she was in peril, she was real? Her danger was a confirmation that my love was not self-deception.

I was drenched from the rainstorm, which now had moved out over the lake, to be replaced by thin clouds and a sizzling sun, angry that its domination of the city had been temporarily interrupted. Thick waves of steam rose from the puddles on the Magnificent Mile.

Did I really want to go to Grand Beach? Did I want to trust myself to the enthusiastic and affectionate ambience of my new group of friends, pushy and uninvited friends?

It was too late to answer that question. I had agreed to go to the beach for the Memorial Day weekend because my daughter wanted me to. I owed poor Jeannie at least that much.

Sometimes psychic experiences linger, and other times they disappear completely. I must note very carefully here that my fear for Ciara was in the latter category. By the time I had reached the Water Tower, there was not a trace of it. Indeed, I could, with minimal effort, persuade myself that it had not happened. Moreover, and I must insist on this too, rarely do such phenomena pile on top of one another. I cannot recall an occasion when there has been more than one such event in a given day, at least not more than one intense event.

I therefore supposed that the psychic phenomena were finished for the day and perhaps, given the strength of the terror that had left me shivering on the banks of the Chicago River, finished for several days.

Exhausted, and eagerly expecting my bottle of Jameson's, I nodded to the doorman and rode the elevator up to my apartment.

If I had not been so careful about bringing Ciara into my apartment through the parking lot, the doorman could now have solved my problem.

Was I careful because I did not want the doorman to report that he had never seen a woman with me?

Because there never had been such a woman?

Or was she, like Billy Wells in Fort Dearborn, a woman from another era, another world?

I unlocked the door, walked in, and found Madonna waiting for me on the couch.

21

The woman who sat on my couch, wearing a white sports dress, relaxed, even casual, but infinitely sad, was not the praying mantis whom Ciara and I had encountered at Orchestra Hall, not the corpse burned to a cinder off Montrose Harbor. She was a young Madonna, not an adolescent, not a young bride—more like the beautiful wife to whom I had come home from Vietnam, but with none of the petulance of the woman who had welcomed me back with notable indifference.

Two comments seem appropriate here: first of all, it was an experience of considerable duration. When my Great Aunt Heather had "checked out" with me at the moment of her death, it had been a brief and phantasmagorical interlude. In the books I've read on the subject, it appears that some men and women are the ordinary "check out" points for members of their families who are dying. (No one even begins to explain the reason for this rather peculiar family role.) Such experiences, which are almost routine in their lives, are much like those with my Great Aunt Heather—brief, somewhat mystical, problematic in their content.

There are, according to the literature, other interludes of apparent contact with the dead, incidents of some duration in which the person encountered seems *physically* present, not perhaps quite the way the person was present when alive, but still not hazy or ectoplasmic. It was to this latter variety that my meeting with someone who seemed to be Madonna must be assigned.

Moreover, there was nothing uncanny or frightening about my experience of Madonna. It was not the raw material for a ghost story. She was not haunting me. Most psychic experiences, by the way, are uncanny perhaps in the telling, but not in the experience. They seem ordinary, matter-of-fact, commonplace.

So the presence of my murdered wife, reclining with mild suggestiveness, seemed neither unusual nor disturbing. It was almost as though a friend had stopped by my apartment unexpectedly and waited until I came home.

Did we talk to each other? That is a question I cannot answer. As best I can remember the interlude, words were not exchanged, but we communicated, we absorbed emotions, we understood. At the time this emotional communication seemed rich, complex, and important. When I set it down on paper, it reads like a commonplace, a cliché: we grieved over the lost opportunity of our life together, we forgave each other. We mourned our own suffering and that of our friends. We looked forward. . . .

I'm not sure what we looked forward to. Nothing explicit. But there was a very strong sensation that Madonna and I were not finished with each other. There was work yet to be done, difficult, painful, arduous work. We had no

choice in the matter. That work would be done. More than
that, there would be joy mixed with the pain of doing it.

My wife surely did not seem to be one of the damned.
Neither did she seem to be one of the saved. She was sad,
hurt, wounded, but not unhappy and certainly not without
hope. She also seemed to say that I was much too hard on
myself, that I blamed myself far more than I should, that—
was there a hint of laughter here?—that I was far more critical of myself than she had ever been.

Then she was no longer with me and I was sobbing con-
vulsively, like a little boy who is lost in a department store.

The reader will be skeptical, and indeed should be, for I
am skeptical myself. I was troubled, anxious, guilt-ridden,
devastated. I needed and wanted absolution. I yearned for a
sign of hope that all was not totally lost between me and
my wife. I desperately wanted an indication that, indeed,
somehow, some way, the group with whom I had grown up
and which had played such an important part in my life
would be given one more chance. I wanted to believe that
Madonna had survived. I wanted to believe that she was
once again the lovely young woman for whom I had
yearned so intensely, both before our marriage and while I
was in Vietnam. I wanted to believe in a loving God who
did provide second and third and fourth and fifth chances.
The wish, as Madonna might have said herself in her fondness for clichéd proverbs, was the father of the thought. As
the psychiatrist would tell me caustically a few days later,
"Yah, you wanted to believe dat your wife was still alive so
you hallucinated her."

I wanted to believe that she was still alive, I wanted to
see her again, I wanted a promise of a new beginning, and
the peculiar kinks of body and/or soul that constituted my
psychic sensitivity gave me the tools to temporarily recreate her. Hardly had my weeping stopped when the ra-
tional, civilized, cautious lawyer in me took over and dis-
counted the experience.

Later, however, Monsignor John Blackwood Ryan
would peer through his thick prescription sunglasses ("Uncle Blackie won't wear contact lenses," Caitlin proclaimed,

"because then he wouldn't be able to blink his eyes and pretend that he's Father Brown!") at the procession of cabin cruisers bumping along, perhaps a quarter mile offshore in the bright blue glory of Memorial Day, and murmur, "I don't understand, Brendan Herbert George Ryan, why it is necessary to determine whether the experience was 'real.' " He glared in some confusion at his empty Jameson's glass, baffled as to how the precious brew had disappeared. "Or indeed, how one can ever know whether such experiences are 'real.' Is it not more pertinent to inquire as to the validity of the message than as to the nature of the phenomenon?"

I admitted that I didn't quite understand.

"One either lives in a universe where absolution and new beginnings are possible, indeed a matter of commonplace occurrence, or one does not. The burden of your interlude was that you and Madonna could still forgive each other and still begin again despite the absurdity of death. It is surely not the first time you've heard that message. If the message is true, then all things are possible. But the issue—is it not?—is whether the message is true and not whether a particular phenomenon is possible, a phenomenon which, in the nature of things, does not admit of easy falsification or verification."

As usual, Blackie Ryan was right. However, by his own admission being utterly devoid of psychic sensitivities, he did not know the anguish, the delight, and the bafflement of such a message being communicated by someone whom you have every earthly reason to believe you have lost.

There was also a later experience for which there was at least a hint of verification.

While my mind attempted to disprove the reality of my experience of Madonna, I went to the swimming pool and swam for forty-five minutes. Then I phoned a local pizza house, very much like an adolescent, ordered a large sausage and cheese pizza. I consumed it as though it were the first food I had eaten in a week, which for all practical purposes it was, and washed it down with the last bottle of Perrier water in the icebox. I resolved that I would have a good night's sleep without the assistance of John Jameson's nectar, and that the next morning I would begin the search for Ciara Kelly.

22

The air conditioner in Dr. Otto Freihaut's office rumbled busily, but either the machine, which seemed to be at least as old as the bald, gnomelike doctor, had long since ceased to provide effective cooling or my emotional unease canceled out its effects. Sweat was pouring off my face, and my shirt clung limply to my chest and back.

"Yah, ve vill haf no talk in dis office about dat gottdam ESP," snorted the doctor, brushing cigar ashes off his soiled brown vest. "Dat is all gottdam nonsense! Ve vill acknowledge dat ve vere hallucinating, *nein?*"

I expected the doctor at some point to say to me, like the Gestapo interrogators in late-night films, "Ve haf our vays."

It was Friday morning before the Memorial Day weekend, just a few days ago, though so many things have happened since then that it now seems a couple of lifetimes ago. Jean was to pick me up at my apartment building at two o'clock so that we could escape the rush-hour traffic on our pilgrimage to Grand Beach. I had a terrible, trapped feeling that I would never escape from Dr. Otto Freihaut, that he would lock me up in an institution and throw away the key. Or perhaps sell me to a traveling carnival as a third-rate freak, a psychic equivalent of the bearded lady. The doorman at my building would tell poor Jean that her father was in the loony bin and she could only see him with Dr. Freihaut's permission, *nein?*

"Ve must admit dat ve haf a wery serious problem. Ve are haffing schizophrenic delusions mit paranoidal overtones, yah?"

"If you say so, doctor," I agreed mildly. After all, there was a very strong possibility that the doctor's diagnosis was right.

Impulsively, late in the previous afternoon, I had asked one of my colleagues, who did considerable tax work for the psychiatric profession, if he could make a referral for me on an emergency basis. The colleague was overjoyed, doubtless convinced that I had been a sick man for a long, long time. Dr. Freihaut had a cancellation on Friday morning, and there I was in his office, trying to explain about two women whom he promptly dismissed as schizophrenic fantasies—Ciara Kelly, who had never existed, and Madonna Clifford, who did, but who was dead and could not come back from the dead.

It was necessary for me to acknowledge my sickness, to admit my systematic schizophrenic delusions, to seek admission to the appropriate psychiatric institution as soon as possible before "you do serious harm to yourself, *nein?*"

I had not intended to tell Dr. Freihaut about the interlude with Madonna, since I was very dubious myself about the reality of that incident, but he demanded that I explain to him why, after more than a week of ignoring the problem, I had suddenly begun my search for Ciara Kelly. I suppose the model in my mind was my confessor when I was a boy. If Father asked you a question in the confessional, you tried to tell him the truth, no matter how ridiculous the truth might sound. So if the psychotherapist asked you a question, you tried to respond truthfully, even if it meant saying that you began your search for a woman whose existence everyone else denies because an encounter with your dead wife gave you hope for forgiveness and renewal.

I thought the outraged little Black Forest elf would swallow his cigar. (If you objected to cigar smoking in the therapist's office, you could avail yourself of someone else. If you wanted Dr. Freihaut, you meekly accepted his cigar, *nein?*) "Iss de vorse kind of schizophrenic delusion!" he gurgled. "Iss sign werry sick man!"

I suppose so. If I were a psychoanalyst, I guess I would be driven to the edge of apoplexy by a patient who claimed to have communed with a dead wife. Such communications were, as a matter of scientific definition, impossible, and therefore the only alternative explanation was that the patient was a sick, quite possibly dangerously sick, person.

Blackie Ryan's reaction to my description, a few days

later, of the conversation with Dr. Freihaut was interesting. He mercifully spared me the question why, with psychiatrists in the family, I had not sought their recommendations for a therapist. "*Herr Doktor*'s reasoning is utterly appropriate," he struggled in vain to squeeze suntan cream from an empty container, "save in one set of circumstances."

"And that is?"

He paused long enough in his struggle with the suntan cream to gaze at me in surprise. "In circumstances where the client actually has interacted with a dead spouse."

"I'm afraid the doctor believes that that is impossible."

"How does he know?" Blackie Ryan asked blandly.

My two-day search for Ciara Kelly had been brisk, efficient, businesslike. I assumed the role of a man who is trying to clear up some minor misunderstanding, just to keep the record straight. I was not desperately searching for a woman who apparently did not exist. Rather, I was trying to comprehend how this bizarre event had occurred. I resolutely refused to give up this pose, even though my respondents were embarrassed by it.

"Ah, sure," said my good friend Seamus O'Rafferty, a blond giant who looked more like a professional rugby player than the Consul General of the Republic of Ireland, "we've been friends ever since I came to Chicago, Brendan. I'd be wanting to give you every possible help, but we have no record of any Irish immigrant named Ciara Kelly. If she were here on an Irish passport, mind you, we'd know about her. And when the matter came up a few days ago, I checked with people that make it their business to be in contact with the immigrant community. No one had ever heard a word about her at all, at all."

"Perhaps she came in on a British passport," I suggested tentatively.

"Well, now, that would be a possibility, though I did call my colleague the British consul general at the time, just to be certain. Sure, he had no record of her either. Mind you, now, it's not definitive. People come in through Detroit, for example, and we have no record of them. It's a big city, and someone can be here for a long time and go unnoticed. But, sure, weren't you after saying that she worked at that Irish store down the road? Ah, it would be hard to miss someone like that."

"She's a very well educated woman," I said. "Trinity College, at least, and probably some sort of graduate school—literature or history or something of the sort."

"Did your immigration service or your state department know anything about her?"

They did not. No green card, no work permit, no tourist visa, nothing. If Ciara Kelly had come to the United States of America—under that name, at any rate—neither the Republic of Ireland nor the United States of America knew anything about her.

"That might not," I observed in the tone I normally used with the better class of IRS agents, "have been her real name."

Everyone tried to be extremely helpful, indeed so helpful that at times I suspected a massive cover-up. The manager of Chestnut Place permitted me to interview his doorman, who had no recollections of either me or Ciara Kelly at the door of the building every night for a couple of weeks. Then the manager brought me up to apartment 960. It was empty and dusty, the walls and the carpet blue instead of beige, as they had been when I had eaten dinner and made love to Ciara in the apartment. Even the disconnected telephone was blue instead of white and a push button instead of a rotary phone, nor was the number on it the same one I had written down when Ciara had gone into the kitchen for the steaming Irish stew.

Yet, for several hours in the morning after the *Brigid* caught fire, that phone number had rung somewhere. Then, in the afternoon, a computerized voice had begun to inform me that the line had been disconnected. At one time, then, the phone number I had jotted down in my wallet was real. Had it rung in this apartment? If it had, then everything else might be fakery. The different color scheme, the new phone number, the bland assertions of the manager and the doorman that they knew nothing of Ciara Kelly. Dr. Otto Freihaut said all of this was paranoia. Perhaps it was. But what if it was not?

The staff did not remember her at the Cliff Dwellers, nor at the Hunan restaurant, nor at Jackie's, nor at

Jerome's, nor at any of the other restaurants or theaters where I asked my polite questions. Gary Jensen, the nasty little gossip columnist who had been Madonna's escort at Orchestra Hall, denied that he'd even seen me there that night.

After a day and a half of determined and systematic searching, I had found not the slightest trace of Ciara Kelly.

Finally I tried Dufficy's Irish Store. Mrs. Reardon, who was in charge of the store, was huffy and uncooperative. She had been asked these questions several times by the police and by private detectives (undoubtedly hired by Nick and Eileen). Really, she had better things to do with her time than to pursue such a ridiculous subject.

I was patient and polite and deferential. Finally I was told that there were four women who worked in the store, Ms. Hurley, Ms. Creaghan, Mrs. Farrell, and Mrs. McCarthy. The former two were in their twenties, the latter in their forties, and only Ms. Creaghan was an immigrant, and there she was, herself, rearranging the Waterford on the other side of the store.

It seemed to me that the whole inside of the store had changed. When I was courting Ciara I'd paid little attention to the distribution of knits and tweeds and plaids and prints and books and crystal; yet when I had entered for my awkward conversation with Mrs. Reardon, I had had the sensation of walking into an entirely different establishment.

I asked if the book on modern Irish artists was still in stock and was assured, after an impatient search (Mrs. Reardon demonstrating the enormous virtue of her patience in seeking an answer to such a frivolous question), that the book was not in stock and never had been but that, if I wished, she would be happy to order it for me.

I turned to leave, discouraged and defeated. Then I stopped and stared in astonishment at the full-length painting that hung behind the Waterford crystal. It was Ciara, beyond any doubt, in the formal evening dress of perhaps 1840.

"What is that painting?" I asked, straining to control my fascination.

"Ah, it's lovely, isn't it? It was painted by one of the

most promising Anglo-Irish artists of the first half of the nineteenth century. It was said that he was in love with the woman; Constance Keenan was her name. She died at the age of thirty, under mysterious circumstances, at her husband's manor, Castle Keenan, near Westport in County Mayo. It is said that she still haunts the house."

I was thunderstruck. "The woman has been dead, then, for over a century?"

"Closer to a century and a half." Mrs. Reardon seemed to be doing arithmetical calculations in her head. "Her husband was never brought to trial, you know; everyone thought he killed her because she'd been unfaithful with Rory Conley, the painter. But there was no proof. Her boat tipped over on the lake, don't you see. Her husband was twenty miles away, hunting pheasants. So he couldn't have killed her, could he?"

Only after I had left the store, shaken and, to be honest about it, frightened, did it occur to me to ask whether Constance Keenan had produced any children.

Mrs. Reardon, who had warmed a bit while describing the painting, lost both interest and patience when she decided that I was not about to pay $3,000 for it.

Sometime later, perhaps, when I'd abandoned completely my search for Ciara Kelly, I might want the painting, not so much to remind me of her as to remind me of her unreality.

Again the thought flickered in the back of my head: there's something wrong with this whole picture, a piece missing, the perspective tilted at an odd, indeed impossible, angle.

I grabbed for the bat in the back rooms of my brain, but it flitted by me and away into the twilight.

Could I have seen that painting behind the Waterford crystal in Dufficy's Irish Store and in some bizarre and demented twist of my psychic kinkiness invested the woman in the painting with life?

A man who can create, from out of his psychological kinks, an image of his dead wife, smiling sadly on the couch of his living room fifty-five stories above the city of Chicago, is capable of any self-delusion.

"Yah," observed Dr. Freihaut, "you created delusions. You saw de voman in der painting *und* you made her real in your imagination. Ve need no gottdam ESP to explain dat."

I finally escaped from Dr. Freihaut, the stench of his cigars, and the inefficient rumblings of his air conditioner, by promising that I would come back "first ding" on Tuesday morning, and only after I agreed that the doctor would not be responsible for any harm I did to myself or to others over the Memorial Day weekend. He made me feel like I was an epileptic driver insisting on racing in the Indianapolis 500.

It would be a deadly weekend all right. In that respect, at any rate, *Herr Doktor* had been an excellent prophet.

I was willing to promise almost anything to be able to flee from his office before he summoned the men in white with the large syringes filled with powerful tranquilizers. I would talk to Mary Kate or Joe Murphy at Grand Beach this weekend, I told myself, with little conviction.

My first session with that psychiatrist, I knew, would be my last. I had read enough books on the subject to realize that the "gottdam ESP" was a reality in the lives of the majority of the American population. Whatever tricks my psychic kinkiness might be playing on me, I was not going to entrust myself, and certainly not at $150 an hour, to someone who rejected in principle the possibility of my experiences.

As I walked out of the office building into the rainy mists of Michigan Avenue—Jeannie had assured me it would clear up by early afternoon and be a "glorious" weekend—I wondered ruefully what Dr. Freihaut would have said if I told him about my encounters with the Fort Dearborn garrison.

"A perfectly proper decision," Monsignor Ryan agreed later, having borrowed a suntan tube from a passing unidentified niece and begun to smear the gooey white lotion on his arms and neck, with only minimal effectiveness. "Patently, *Herr Doktor* has considerable anal retentive rigidities. . . . Not that I know what that means, but I'm always impressed when my sister, the good Mary Kate, speaks that phrase trippingly on the tongue."

"Let me rub it on the back of your neck, Uncle Punk." The blonde niece removed the tube from his willing fingers. "You always forget that you can get sunburned in back as well as in front."

After the niece was appropriately thanked with a "Bless you, child" and had affectionately ruffled her uncle's hair, Blackie returned to the question at hand. "It would seem that no one, not Dr. Freihaut, nor my sister, nor the good Eileen, nor the inestimable Counselor Curran, nor the superlative sometime Police Commissioner Casey, is willing to face what I take to be obvious about Ciara Kelly."

"That she never existed?" I asked hopefully. If Blackie Ryan said so, then I would be dispensed forever from further questing.

"Oh, no." His pale, nearsighted eyes widened in surprise. "Quite the contrary. I take it as self-evident that she did and does exist."

23

"I hope you don't mind the car, Daddy." Jean was sitting in the driver's seat of her mother's black Mercedes Benz 250SL convertible with white leather seats. "I kind of hesitated at first, and then I decided, gosh, it's only a car, and I don't really believe in psychic vibrations."

Oh, don't you, my child?

"A car is a car." I climbed in the front seat with her. I supposed that, should I have asked her, my anti-psychic daughter would have advocated the reconstruction of the *Brigid* too.

Madonna's car had been found several days after the killings in a parking lot on Broadway and Montrose. The police speculated that Madonna and Ron had either walked from the parking lot to the harbor, or hailed a taxi on Broadway. Since they were unable to locate the taxi driver, they concluded that the couple had walked. I found this extremely unlikely. For all her pathetic addiction to exercise,

Madonna did not like walking and I could not imagine her strolling for half a mile burdened with sailing gear, food, and drink. Nor, for that matter, could I imagine Ron Crowley, overweight and worn out, negotiating such a distance. Not that such speculations mattered.

"Do you mind if I drive?" Jean was wearing a khaki miniskirt, a red and green striped T-shirt, and expensive-looking German sunglasses. Her hair was tied back with a green ribbon that matched the green in her T-shirt. She was barefoot, as was appropriate for the official beginning of summer.

"It's all right with me. If I knew we were using the convertible, I'd have brought a ribbon for my hair too."

"Silly!" She smiled affectionately. "Hey, don't I get a kiss before we start?"

"Sure." I touched her lips affectionately with mine.

"Not bad for an old daddy." She turned on the ignition of the car and we began the trip. "I think we'll go right over to the expressway and avoid the mess your friends in city hall have made at the 'S curve' on Lake Shore Drive."

"They're no friends of mine. . . . What's new in your world?"

"Well." Jean drove skillfully and confidently in the crush of near-north traffic, hardly a reckless teenage driver. "Not all that much; my Cubs are still in first place, and the Edmonton Oilers, with that darling Wayne Gretzky, finally won the Stanley Cup."

"Did they?"

She took her eyes off the traffic for a fraction of a second to glance uneasily at me. "Don't you read the newspapers, Daddy?"

"I guess I must have missed the hockey play-offs. What do you think the Cubs' chances are? Are they going to fold in July?"

Until that moment, I had been unaware my daughter was a sports fan. Had she always been? Or was this one more dubious influence of the "other" Ryans?

She outlined for me, not without some sophistication, the sad collapses of promising Cubs teams in the heat of the summer in other years and analyzed the prospects for the present surprising Cubs. Her conclusion was that, yes, they would probably fold, but that the team was young and showed promise for the future, even though their pitching was terribly weak. "Anyway, they're exciting and they're doing *so* much better than the dopey White Sox this year. It keeps those crazy Sox fans at Grand Beach in their place."

Ah ha, the "other" Ryans were Sox fans. Somehow I had not realized that either.

I felt traces of Ciara Kelly's fear. I was unsure how I should respond to the fear. What could I possibly do to help her? Was not becoming involved in her life, if she really existed, like my involvement in the life of the Thos? I was still shaken by my interview with Dr. Freihaut. Perhaps I did belong in a mental institution. Not one where he was on the staff, however.

We drove south on the expressway, passing on the right the boundary of the royal borough of Bridgeport, with the impeccably neat old frame bungalows and streets so clean that it was, indeed, credible that housewives scrubbed the sidewalks every night. Then we slipped by the fringes of Englewood and Woodlawn, with their ravaged two-flats and apartment buildings, as devastated as any air-raid landscape.

We left the Dan Ryan, breaking, as it were, with the city of Chicago, passed briefly over Studs Lonigan's neighborhood and onto the battered Chicago Skyway, which carried us briefly through the aging steel mill community of Eddie Vrdolyak's tenth ward, and entered the Indiana Tollroad. The oil refinery haze of Hammond, the fires and chaste white smoke of Gary, the great black steel mills, seemed a surrealistic painting on the sky over Lake Michigan and under the implacable May sun, an intensely vital kaleidoscope of color, light, and energy.

Jean explained for me, with considerable enthusiasm, the arrangements at Grand Beach. The "Ryan compound" consisted of three homes: "Old House," where Ned Ryan and his second wife, Helen, and their four children—three teenagers and twelve-year-old Trish—("The last but hardly the least," Ned would say admiringly of that irresistible bundle of energy)—lived with implicit protection from the rest of the clan for their peace and privacy. Next door, in the middle of the compound, was the "New House," where Mary Kate and Joe Murphy presided over their own family and over the clan's swimming pool and recently added Nautilus equipment. Next to the Murphys' was "Cathy's Place," the new and ultra-modern home that Catherine Curran had designed and built after she'd sold her family home, some distance down the beach, to Eileen and Red Kane. The splendid garden that surrounded the Curran home was the locale for the family cookouts. Ned and Kate Collins Ryan's other children (Patrick "Packy" Ryan and Nancy Ryan O'Connor) were some distance from the central compound, for reasons of chance, personal finance, and a desire to be close but not too close to the rest of the family. We were to be assigned, for the weekend, to the Currans, because Catherine had cunningly designed her guest suites to provide a maximum of privacy. Father Blackie, who was passed from house to house, unprotestingly, would be staying with his father and stepmother.

"Nautilus?" I asked.

"Well, Nautilus and weights. Caitlin runs courses for everybody."

"Does she now?" That sounded like Ciara Kelly. "Are they obligatory?"

"The only rule the Ryan family has is that nobody has to do anything. All the women take the course, though, even Aunt Cathy and Aunt Eileen, but they do special exercises because they're pregnant."

"I've noticed. The doctors call them 'elderly' pregnancies."

Jean giggled. "They seem to love it. It's kind of nice for us younger women, because it shows us that pregnancy doesn't have to be terrible."

My little daughter thinking about pregnancy? How dare they!

"At any rate," I sighed with relief, "I won't have to do any iron-pumping."

"C'mon, Daddy, you must do a lot of exercise to keep in condition like you do. It's a good example for me."

"*You* pump iron?"

"Don't look so shocked. Everybody does nowadays. It's good for your build."

"Are you planning to be a linebacker?"

"I just want to preserve my figure."

"There's nothing wrong with your figure, at the risk of repeating myself."

"There's nothing wrong with it and I intend to keep it that way. C'mon, Daddy, you read all those books about evolution. So you know that we evolved as a creature that collected its food by hunting and gathering. So we had to be good at short-distance sprinting—not jogging, which is, like, totally bad for you. And by bending over hundreds of times every day and picking up roots and berries and plants, and then carrying them back home in big bundles. Well, we don't do that anymore, so we lift weights and work out on the Nautilus instead."

End of lecture for reactionary father who had yet to learn that neo-feminism meant "getting built"!

"Women exercising is probably the best thing that could possibly happen to the men of your generation!"

"You're an old male chauvinist, Daddy," Jeannie sputtered through her laughter as we slowed down for a toll-gate. "Actually, girls my age are in much better condition than the boys. I suppose that's because the boys drink a lot more beer. Poor dears, being away from home at college is so much harder on them that I suppose they have to indulge in oral dependencies."

Not only a Cubs fan, not only an admirer of that "darling Wayne Gretzky" of the Edmonton Oilers, not only a devotee of "getting built," but the stranger who was my daughter could speak psychoanalytic jargon without dropping a syllable. What, I wondered, would she think of Dr. Otto Freihaut?

"Is Catherine Curran painting this summer," I inquired, "despite her pregnancy?"

"*Certainly*," I was informed in a tone that indicated I had asked a perfectly stupid question. Why should pregnancy interfere with painting? "Anyway," Jean said lightly, as she pushed the Benz up to the fifty-five-mile-an-hour speed limit, "I'm posing for her."

"Nude?" I sounded, even to myself, like a shocked and outraged Victorian grandfather.

"How else?" Jean snickered. "I'm not a sunburst. Are you shocked?"

"In theory, no." I rubbed the sweat from my forehead. "In practice, yes." I thought to myself that if Madonna were alive, this would never have happened. "It's up to you."

"Don't you want to know what it feels like?" She chuckled knowingly.

"Afraid to ask."

"Well . . . At first it was kind of scary and kind of silly. Then, Aunt Catherine is so professional, it just seemed perfectly natural. You can be modest with your clothes off just as easily as you can be modest with your clothes on."

"Uh huh."

"Then, when I saw the portrait—Aunt Catherine shows it to you and discusses it with you as she goes along because she says the model is kind of the co-painter—then it got kind of exciting. Not sexually exciting, particularly, but just exciting. I realized how beautiful the human body is, especially a woman's body, and how it was designed to be beautiful and how its beauty can be depicted in such a way that it's erotic, all right, but not obscene or exploitive. Aunt Catherine's work is feminist, just like the photographer Rena Small's. A non-exploitive painting of a woman is a judgment against all the exploitive pictures."

"Uncle Nick tells me" (was I really calling him "Uncle Nick"?) "that she was repainting *Playboy* centerfolds when she was a teenager."

"Aunt Catherine says," I was now being treated to the Aunt Catherine lecture, "that the difference between exploitation and non-exploitation is frequently a facial expression, the angle of an eye, or even a few strokes of the brush."

"A lot of people think that a portrait of a naked woman is a portrait of a naked woman."

"The kind of people who see no difference between Eve in Michelangelo's 'Creation,' " she slipped by a large semi-trailer whose driver greeted her with an admiring hoot of his horn, "and a *Playboy* centerfold: we shouldn't pay any attention to them. Any more than to that geek in the truck."

"Right!"

"And, as I look at the painting," she moved back into the right-hand lane, "I realize that I was designed by God to be attractive to men. . . ."

"She did a good job."

"So I figure that if I find a career at which I'm good and learn a few more things and acquire a touch of wisdom, *well*, I might just make some guy a pretty good woman."

"Indeed you will," I said fervently.

"You're putting me on." Her jaw tightened, hinting at anger.

"No way. Even as you are now, you'd make some guy a hell of a fine woman. And if you work your way through that agenda, you'll be irresistible. . . . Make sure he's as strong as you are."

"Yeah, I know. Still, I'm clinging by my fingertips, Daddy. Remember what a little bitch I was at Les Nomades? And I almost did it again, damn it." She pounded the leather-coated wheel of the Benz.

"When can I see the painting?"

"Oh, you can't see it!" She was shocked, horrified, appalled. "You and Timmy and Uncle Nick can't see it until it hangs in the gallery. Then when everyone else looks at it, you can look at it too."

The logic of that constraint escaped me, but I knew better than to argue. "Your mother's parents will be horrified." I tried to sound casual about it.

"Geeks."

"Jean." I did my best to sound disapproving.

"Well, I don't care, Daddy, they are, like, *totally* geeks. I mean, when I was a little girl, they always brought me presents, designer dresses and things like that, and I thought they were the greatest grandparents in the world. Now I realize they were buying me off, just like they bought poor Mom off. I tried to be nice to them when they came in for the funeral because I felt so sorry for them. They were just horrid. Just horrid."

"How so?"

"The big thing was that I had Ryan blood in me and that's dangerous blood. I had to be very careful or I'd end up like you—a warning every hour on the hour. I felt sorry for them because they were so old and so unhappy so I didn't argue. But never again."

"You know, I suppose, about their legal petition?"

"Uncle Nick," she said decisively, "says we'll bury them."

And that, I guess, settled that.

"You're a very tough young woman, Jeannie." I studied the sharp outline of her jaw. Was it Madonna's or Jocelyn's? "You must fit in with all the Ryan women at Grand Beach very nicely."

"I'm a lot tougher than they are, Daddy. They're all really very vulnerable. Even Aunt Eileen, who pretends that she's such a fierce courtroom fighter, is a pussycat. I guess I've had to be tougher than they are. I'm not so sure it's a good thing, but that's the way it is."

We then discussed her photography, and I was told to look under the jacket in the backseat for her portfolio. It was a collection of portraits of El Capitan in Yosemite National Park, imitating and sometimes making fun, with infrared lens, of the Master. The folio was kooky, comic, loving, and oddly moving.

Then we turned to her plan to work at the Board of Trade when she came back from Ireland. I discovered that her math scores were in the ninety-eighth percentile, that she received A's in computer science, and that she liked to make up her own computer games—all positive indicators for the new breed of commodities investors. I told her a little bit about the imaginary larceny I practiced on my PC XT and she listened with interest and appreciation. And a warning, "Don't ever tempt me with those games, Daddy. I might want to play them for real. Especially when I'm down on myself."

Clinging by her fingertips.

An altogether fascinating young stranger, this daughter of mine, part little girl and part perceptive, mature woman of the world. Catherine, I presumed, would capture all that in her painting. It would be a fascinating work of art.

How had Melissa Jean, now simply Jean, become who

she was, more clear-headed and less self-deceptive than Madonna and more forceful and determined than I? Madonna had failed to turn her into a clone. I had been of no help to her at all. She had become who she was pretty much on her own. It would be nice to know her better.

That would not happen. She would go back to Stanford, stay in San Francisco, or move to Los Angeles or New York in pursuit of her photographic career, and perhaps never return to Chicago, or if, as seemed only a remote possibility, she should marry Tim Murphy, she would become thoroughly integrated into the Ryan clan and remain a stranger to me. Either way, this ride to Grand Beach was probably the only serious talk we would have for many years, indeed, perhaps the only serious talk ever. The moments were precious. I felt the sands of time slipping through my fingers as we turned off the expressway at the Michigan City exit.

"Hey, isn't this the wrong turn?"

"Nope. We have to stop at Karwick Plaza to do some shopping. I told Aunt Catherine she should stay home and rest."

"That's very thoughtful of you."

We crossed the thin line of scrub trees that separates the spur of the Great American Prairie reaching into northern Indiana from the several-mile-wide strip of forest and dune land that skirts Lake Michigan. The tide of duneland forest has ebbed and flowed as the character of the world's fourth largest lake, basically a melted glacier, has changed through geological eras. Soon we were on Highway 12, the sturdy concrete ribbon at the fringe of the most recent dune forest which, before the tollroads, linked the Indiana and Michigan dunes to the south side of Chicago. Even today occasional shops and houses and farms along U.S. 12 suggest the 1930s and the scraggly, deadening poverty of the Great Depression.

"Aunt Catherine is a totally remarkable woman. Awesome. She's so funny and so happy you can hardly believe that they did those terrible things to her in the concentration camp in South America."

"She was a very vivacious little kid." I was thinking of

another woman who was tortured while trying to help the Third World. "We didn't realize it then, but she has enormous resiliency."

Someone else had enormous resiliency too.

Ciara Kelly. Ciara Kelly. Ciara Kelly.

The terror seeped momentarily back into my body and mind and then disappeared.

"Emily is a remarkably happy girl too."

Zap! You've been mousetrapped, Daddy.

"Emily!"

"Sure, the girl who goes to Stanford with me whose life you saved in Vietnam. I couldn't believe it at first." She laughed self-consciously. "It didn't sound like my daddy, but Emily was certain. Brendan Ryan from Chicago with a daughter named Melissa Jean."

"And that made you decide that it might just possibly be a good idea to reevaluate old Daddy?"

So that was the explanation for the transformation in Jeannie's attitude towards me.

"Were they really trying to drown her?" Jean ignored my comment.

"When I reached the edge of the pool, it was twilight. Darkness seems to come very quickly in those places. I saw one of the men pull a little bundle out of the pool. The bundle wailed, and I knew it was the Thos' baby. She was about the same size and age as you when I'd left you behind in America. Somehow you and Emily became confused with all the other babies that evil men were killing."

I was no longer on Highway 12 but back on a tributary of the Mekong River.

"Then you killed the man who was planning to drown her?"

"No, I killed the man who was holding a knife against her mother. Then the man who was threatening to drown Emily." No reason to mention the third victim.

"And the man dropped her in the water and you dived in and pulled her out?"

"Something like that. She was still breathing, thank God. The three of us redeployed ourselves—that's military terminology for running like hell—and just in time, too."

Jean nodded thoughtfully. "Emily doesn't remember any of it, but she's heard the story so often from her family that it's very vivid for her. . . . Did you love her mother, Daddy?"

"In a way."

Again Jean nodded sympathetically. "I could understand that. She's a wonderful woman."

A very clever young person, my daughter, Jean. Very clever indeed. She might make several fortunes speculating in commodities—and then taking photographs in the afternoon. Too bad it was fated that this might be the only long conversation we would ever have.

We pulled into the Karwick Shopping Plaza, a modest brick collection of supermarket and assorted smaller stores. It was only middle afternoon, but the parking lot was already half filled with cars, prudent shoppers like us getting a head start on the Friday night crunch at the beginning of the Memorial Day weekend.

A small shopping plaza in a resort area, on the eve of one of summer's two beginnings (the Fourth of July being the other) is the center of a festival of hope, like the entrance to a church before a wedding mass—cheerful conversations, happy chatter, enthusiastic greetings for old friends, eager anticipation of the summer festivities ahead.

I must state categorically that my psychic sensitivities, which had worked so furiously in the last several days, erratic as always, gave me no warning of the mortal danger in the Karwick Plaza. There were no threatening flashes of light, no feelings of danger or doom, no clairvoyant anticipation of the bloody drama that would be enacted in a little more than a quarter of an hour.

Jean took charge of the shopping expedition, just as her mother would, but gracing her domination of the event with polite requests rather than orders, and with laughter at my ineptitude rather than waspish criticism.

I was given charge of the cart, and Jean bounced around Jim's Fiesta Villa (as the rather attractive market was called) collecting materials for the hamburger and hot dog roast, which would be the Sunday night meal. "We have the big steak dinner tomorrow night after Mass, when everybody's in the mood for a huge meal to celebrate the beginning of summer. Then on Sunday night, we have a simple meal, a kind of a picnic, because folks will straggle in at different times. Monday night we'll have sandwiches and potato salad and ice cream for those who are going to stay around till Tuesday morning. Like us."

"I didn't know we were going to stay until Tuesday morning."

"Well, Daddy dear," she poked my chest playfully, "now you do!"

Four nights of Ryan enthusiasm. I was not up to it.

"What if it rains?"

"Aunt Mary Kate says that the only way to react to rain at a summer resort is to ignore it, and that anyway it's wish fulfillment to think that summer begins the last weekend in May."

Hope and wish fulfillment are almost the same thing, aren't they?

"I think her psychiatric colleagues would call that denial."

"That's what *she* calls it, and she's arguing with Uncle Joe, poor dear man."

I was sent back to the mustard shelves twice before I produced the correct brand.

"Everybody, except nerds, uses Grey Poupon mustard, especially if they drive Mercedes cars."

She had to explain to me that it was a joke about a TV advertisement.

The shopping cart, jammed with condiments, charcoal, soft drinks, and enough hamburger meat to have required several steers, was pushed to what seemed to me to be a somewhat longer checkout lane than the others. I shared that observation with Jean.

"Sure it is, but I want to talk to Marilyn about her golf game. She's the captain of the golf team at Marquette High School. The *men's* golf team."

Marilyn and Jean chatted happily about golf. Did my daughter play golf? I did not know. I reached for my checkbook. "I hope they'll take a check."

"They will, but not your check." She tilted her nose into the air like a mock archduchess. "My treat."

She filled the check out with a flourish, presented it to

Marilyn, and promised that she would see her at the dance later in the evening.

"First that I've heard of a dance."

We unloaded the cart into the backseat of the Benz, since the trunk was filled with my small duffel bag and three large garment bags belonging to Jean, who apparently was bringing enough clothes for several summers.

A battered Saab, of dubious vintage, pulled up next to us with a noisy blast of the horn and a rather vulgar squealing of tires.

"Hi, Uncle Brendan," said Caitlin Murphy, her eyes shining wickedly. "Welcome to Grand Beach!"

Caitlin emerged from the car and kissed me vigorously. Like Jean, she was wearing a miniskirt, white, with a broad red belt and a short-sleeved white blouse. Caitlin had the aloof, long-haired blonde beauty of a professional model, the self-possessed grace and balance of an athlete, and the mobile but always beautiful face of a queen of clowns. It was an understatement to call her stunning. Caitlin would bring the Indianapolis 500 to a dead halt!

She was accompanied by a little slip of a girl dressed in a seersucker blue summer uniform of the United States Coast Guard. As best I could remember the navy insignia, she was a petty officer/3d class—a corporal. She looked like she was perhaps thirteen years old.

"This is Petey's Cindasoo," Caitlin announced, rolling her wonderful blue eyes. "She's in the Yewnited States Coast Guard."

"Right proud t'make ya quaintence." Cindasoo extended a tiny, but firm hand.

"She talks real funny," Caitlin said in a noisy stage whisper. "Don't call her a hillbilly or a redneck. Them's ethnic slurs. She's an Appalachian—A-p-p-a-l-a-c-h-i-a-n— Uncle Brendan."

"I do know how to spell Appalachian, young woman," I said. And turning for a closer look at Cindasoo, "Watch out for the Chicago Irish, Cindasoo. They're strange folk."

"Ah'm Irish, too, Mistah Ryan." A glint in her brown eyes suggested Cindasoo could take care of herself. "Mah folks came over after the battle of Culloden Moor, same as the folks of that fella down in 'Ssippi who wrote all them books."

"Faulkner?"

"Yassah, old Billie Faulkner."

"And then moved out west?"

"Yassah. Beat Dan'l Boone by twenty years. Place called Stinkin Creek. Nobody never done left since. Ah joined the Yewnited States Coast Guard to see the world."

Cindasoo was a forest creature, a pretty wraith gliding noiselessly through the valleys and the hollows of the Appalachians. She was also a pixie, her thick auburn hair in a pixie cut, her solemn face barely hiding pixie laughter, and her lovely pixie body teasing you with a tiny shoulder movement. No wonder she and Caitlin seemed to be buddies. Pete Murphy had himself a handful.

"Is Michigan City, Indiana, the world?"

"Beats Stinkin Creek," she said solemnly. "Not by much though."

I suspected that her Appalachian dialect was like Ciara Kelly's Irish brogue, a wild card to be played when and as desired.

Ciara Kelly. Ciara Kelly.

"I hear you're engaged, Caitlin." I turned to the blonde Celtic goddess, who was jiggling coins in the pocket of her miniskirt. "Congratulations."

"Not to say engaged, exactly." She rolled her eyes again. Ciara Kelly. Ciara Kelly.

"Practically engaged," Jean corrected me.

"Hasn't got him hog-tied yet," Cindasoo observed.

"The man," Caitlin said demurely, "is taking his time. He's entitled to that for maybe another week or so."

"He really is a farmer?"

"Yep." Caitlin tried to look woebegone, a virtually impossible task. "Grandfather says we're going from bog to bog in five generations."

"He teaches at Valparaiso Law School too," Jean insisted.

As we were chatting in lighthearted anticipation of the fun of a Memorial Day weekend at the Ryan compound, I noted a black car, an old Ford, I thought, which had halted between the lanes of parked cars, just a few yards away. I heard the click of an opening door, rather than saw it, was aware before I heard a sound, of a moving burst of light. Caitlin. . . .

"Brendan Ryan! Brendan Ryan!"

Not exactly a familiar voice, but demanding, surely someone I knew. I turned in the direction of the voice.

Once again, John Brodie's slow motion, the first time since the Viet Cong opened up with their automatic weapons upriver from the Tho house. The man was wearing a baseball cap, white Windbreaker, white sweatshirt and slacks, and a handkerchief with holes cut for eyes, hanging down from the cap over his face. As I watched, frames slowly unrolling one after the other, he reached under his Windbreaker and leisurely removed a small-caliber pistol, almost a toy. The .22, favorite weapon these days of outfit hit men. Cesare Malocha.

With casual patience and care, it seemed, as the frames moved slowly before my eyes, he aimed the pistol at my head. Like John Brodie "checking off" a receiver, I ducked at the moment I saw his finger tighten on the trigger. Unperturbed, he adjusted his aim and squeezed again.

This is the end of my life, I thought calmly, waiting patiently for the slow movement of the bullet from the muzzle of his gun into my head. The white burst that had swept by me was suddenly next to him. Caitlin, the flat edge of her hand slicing down on his shooting arm, hitting it just as he squeezed the trigger.

The bullet whipped by my head like an angry mosquito. An anguished cry of pain from the gunman, the black car behind him began to move. Another slash of Caitlin's hand and the gunman toppled in agony on the asphalt. My dormant psychic sensitivity suddenly began to work. I knew who the driver of the car was. I comprehended what I must do to protect Jean and myself and to exorcise the demon of Sam Norton. The black Ford slipped down the lane between the two rows of parked cars. I heard screams of fright all around, including those of two kids who, paralyzed by the sight of the gun, were in the path of the moving Ford and barely escaped it. I ran after the car, caught it before it reached the end of the lane, and yanked open the door on the driver's side. The person at the wheel was also wearing the absurd handkerchief mask. I grabbed one arm and pulled the driver away from the wheel and out of the car, a short, pudgy, squirming figure. We both fell to the asphalt and the car careened past a couple of shopping carts and smashed into a post in front of the supermarket. The driver squirmed out of my grasp, jumped up and swung an arm towards me. Only then did I realize that the right hand of the driver had grabbed a huge carving knife as I was pulling my enemy out of the car and the knife was arching toward me in implacable slow motion.

Again, a heavenly angel materializing from nowhere, the white burst of Caitlin Murphy appeared next to me. She slammed the edge of her right hand into the driver's neck. The knife spun out of my attacker's hand and before Caitlin could strike again, the driver collapsed against the rear of a BMW and toppled to the ground knocking off both hat and mask in the fall.

I did not even have to see the twisted angry hateful face to know that it was Patsy Sullivan.

I turned around to see what had happened to Crazy Mal, a few yards behind us. He was struggling to stand up, his right arm limp, his left hand groping under his Windbreaker.

Cindasoo had captured his pistol and, squatting in the approved pistol-fire position, was holding it extended in front of her with both hands. "Stay war you are, varmint, or I'll put a bullet plumb through your head."

She seemed a ridiculous, pathetic little figure in a make-believe sailor suit, a child with a toy gun acting the part of Calamity Jane in a school play. Cesare Malocha must have thought that she was ridiculous. He jerked his second pistol from under his Windbreaker and fumbled with his left hand as he tried to aim the gun at her.

So Cindasoo did exactly what she promised: she shot him right between his eyes.

four

THE
QUEST
FOR
CIARA
KELLY

24

*M*alocha lay sprawled on the pavement, a neat hole drilled in his forehead. Cindasoo was babbling incoherently. Caitlin was muttering over and over to herself words that I could not understand. Later I decided that it must be the Act of Contrition, possibly in a post-conciliar form with which I was not familiar. The crowd that had gathered was mumbling and rumbling, dangerously close to panic of its own.

I took charge of the melee with the same detached calm that I had displayed during the Viet Cong attack eighteen years before.

"Please stand back everyone, don't touch," I ordered. "Don't touch the knife or the guns or the bodies. The police will be here shortly. The man is dead. The woman is still alive."

Dutifully the crowd fell back, forming a tight circle fifteen or twenty yards from the two prone bodies. Jean was sobbing hysterically against my chest, and Caitlin, pale but dry-eyed and quiet, was consoling Cindasoo, whose shapely little body heaved with anguished vomiting.

254 • ANDREW M. GREELEY

"I'll stay with her for a few minutes, Caitlin," I whispered. "Slip over to the public phone and call your parents and the police. . . . And Caitlin," the wonderful violet eyes now devoid of their usual vitality swept across my face, "thanks a lot."

"Anytime, Uncle Brendan." A slight hint of a smile as she ran, or perhaps I should say danced, through the crowd towards the telephone. It must have been only a few minutes though it seemed like hours before the various relief expeditions arrived. God knows my own little Fort Zinderneuf needed relief. I could do nothing to revive Patsy or quiet Jean or calm the desperately sick Cindasoo, although the latter two clung to me as though I were a salvific angel.

The Coast Guard arrived first: a young, slim, black ensign with a Coast Guard Academy ring and three ratings, all very young, two men and one woman. The convulsive retching that was shaking Cindasoo's body diminished as the ensign put his arm around her and the woman rating fiercely gripped her hand. "Ah shot me lots of varmints down by the crick," Cindasoo sobbed. "Never killed me a human before. I shot him daid as four o'clock."

I made a mental note to ask later what that phrase meant. Everyone was still babbling.

Then the Ryans arrived in selective but not massive force, in an aged dark blue Volvo station wagon. How do they assemble the proper team in such a short period of time?—Ned Ryan, the white-haired patriarch and naval hero, a political lawyer with ice-blue eyes and a strong, soft voice that commanded attention; Mary Kate Murphy, a handsome, statuesque psychiatrist with gold and silver hair and enough nerve for a regiment; Mike Casey, cop and lawyer; and a red-bearded, freckled young giant, who needed only a pike in his massive arms to be an ancient Celtic pirate.

Then, last of all, the police, Indiana State and Michigan City police, lights flashing, sirens chirping. Five cars and a couple of vans roared into the shopping plaza parking lot, scattering temporarily a crowd of goggle-eyed bystanders who had been staring in grim fascination at the lifeless remains of Cesare Malocha and the pathetic little form of Patsy Sullivan.

"The damned fools could kill someone," Mike Casey murmured through clenched teeth.

At first the police characteristically made things worse instead of better, shouting orders, pushing people about, cursing vigorously. They turned my orderly crowd back into a melee, threatened to arrest almost everyone, and fought among themselves. A lieutenant of the Michigan City police and a sergeant of the Indiana State police were more interested in squabbling with each other over jurisdiction than determining what crimes had been committed. A fat, officious Michigan City sergeant, apparently informed by someone in the crowd that Cindasoo had shot the dead man, approached the small knot of Coast Guard persons and proclaimed to the accompaniment of florid obscenities that they were going to haul her little ass into jail on a murder charge. The black ensign twisted the cop's arm behind his back and forced him to his knees, as quick as an eye could blink. "Over the dead bodies of the United States Coast Guard, you fat, stupid son-of-a-bitch."

Clearly Cindasoo was the pet of the Michigan City station.

"Let 'im up son," Ned Ryan said quietly, somehow managing to sound like a retired admiral. "He'll apologize later, when the commandant gives Cindasoo a medal for bravery."

"Who the fuck is this dead motherfucker?" demanded the Michigan City lieutenant, pulling the bloody mask off Cesare Malocha's face.

"I wouldn't touch him, Lieutenant." Mike Casey moved into the confusion. "Wait till your technical people come and finish their work. His name is Cesare 'Crazy Mal' Malocha. He's a fourth-rate hit man on the fringes of the Chicago mob. He attempted to kill Mr. Ryan," he nodded his head toward me, "and his daughter. That woman," he pointed at Patsy, who was slowly reviving in response to Mary Kate Murphy's ministrations, "was driving the automobile, the black one piled up against the supermarket. Ms. Murphy, the girl in the white miniskirt, disarmed him. When he tried to draw another weapon, Petty Officer/3d Class McLeod shot him with his own gun."

McLeod? That seemed a fitting surname for Cindasoo.

"No shit!" the cop said in astonishment. "Hey, who the hell are you?"

"Casey. I used to be with the Chicago Police Department."

"*Mike* Casey?" The cop was appropriately awed.

Mike replied with a terse nod of his head.

For all practical purposes, he then took charge of the investigation. Patsy, who was now babbling hysterically, was placed in the van and, with Mary Kate in attendance, driven to St. Anthony's Hospital in Michigan City. The crowd was dispersed. A yellow rubber tarpaulin was placed temporarily over the body of the unfortunate Cesare Malocha. I was interviewed briefly by a very nervous patrol officer. Caitlin, who'd been holding hands with her red-bearded giant, Jean, and Cindasoo were excused to be interviewed later.

"It might be a good idea to impound and seal that vehicle," Mike said to the lieutenant. "Mal Malocha has been questioned about a double murder in Chicago, and I wouldn't be surprised if you found some materials related to that crime in the trunk. Lieutenant," Mike permitted himself a thin smile, "Sam Norton of Chicago Homicide would be very interested in anything you find."

Cindasoo and her Coast Guard escort, still fiercely protective enough, I thought, to fend off the entire Russian army, were entering the nondescript blue U.S. government car in which they'd come. I hurried over to them.

"Petty Officer/3d Class McLeod?" I tried to sound like the officer I had once been. "Can I say I reckon that I'm right grateful to you?"

A wan smile creased her face, which was still as white as a summer dress uniform. "Yassuh, I'm proud I could be of assistance. We Coast Guard persons are taught to be *semper paratus*, suh. That means always ready."

Incredulous laughter from her colleagues.

"*Semper parata*," I corrected her, "if the ready Coast Guard person is a woman person."

"Tell her, sir," said the ensign, "that she's not ready to go on duty tonight."

"Ensign, I am not Petty Officer/3d Class Cindasoo

McLeod's commanding officer, for which I'm deeply grateful. As it is, I wouldn't try to tell her anything. She's Irish, you know."

"I'm goin on dudda," Cindasoo said flatly, in the midst of the laughter.

"I guess that settles that."

The ensign touched his forehead in a brief salute and drove off. Cindasoo, at any rate, was in very safe hands.

"Four o'clock means 4:00 A.M., Uncle Brendan." Caitlin was standing next to me, her giant in tow. "Incidentally, this is Kevin Maher. The name begins with an 'M' just like Murphy, so that's convenient, isn't it?" The red-faced barbarian blushed even more vividly. "Anyway, four o'clock in the morning is either the deadest time of the day or the time when the dead are most likely to wander, so, in Appalachian English, to kill someone like four o'clock means to kill them real dead. I thought you might want to know."

Then, and only then, as I watched the blue Coast Guard car being waved out of the parking lot and saw the first faint touches of color returning to Caitlin's magnificent face and noted the quiet and steady breathing of my daughter, who was still hanging on to me for dear life, did I comprehend fully that these two young women had certainly saved my life and probably Jean's too. Spontaneously, reflexively, they'd intervened and become involved, much the way I had in the Mekong River Valley but with even less time to think about what they were doing than I'd had. They could have easily and safely stayed on the banks and watched the river rush by. Instead, they'd plunged into the icy water, snatched Jean and me back to safety, and had terrible images burned into their memories for the rest of their lives. Would they ever wonder if they'd done the right thing?

Those two? Don't be absurd. Some kinds of generosity or courage, blessedly, never question themselves.

"I am happy to meet you, Mr. Maher." My voice broke. "I'm told you teach tax law, which happens to be my specialty." I couldn't possibly be crying. "I hope you don't mind if I hug your wonderful girlfriend. She just saved my life."

"Be my guest." The red-haired giant grinned.

So Caitlin Murphy and Jean and I wept and hugged one another in the Karwick Shopping Plaza, and I grieved, paradoxically and characteristically enough, not for what had been lost that day, but for what might still be lost in my life.

25

The Currans and I sat in reflective silence, like monks after vespers have been chanted, on the long balcony around the second floor of their house, watching the rising moon paint the waters of Lake Michigan a creamy white. "Cathy's place" was an ingenious blend of New England and prairie, of Cape Cod clapboard and Frank Lloyd Wright. Nicole, a vivacious clone of her mother, and Jackie, the family mystic, had both gone to bed, not without considerable protest. Her eyes still red, and with several assurances from me that I did not mind, Jean permitted Tim Murphy to drag her off to the young people's dance at the community center. Tim and his older brother Pete had been racing their Hobie Cat on the lake at the time of the "shoot-out at the Karwick Corral" (as it was now being called). They were experiencing powerful guilt feelings because they had not been present when their womenfolk needed them. Pete had already departed for the U.S.C.G. station in Michigan City to "kind of wait around" for Cindasoo. The whole Ryan compound seemed momentarily peaceful, a rare enough situation, I would learn in the course of the long weekend.

Mary Kate Murphy, in blouse and slacks, walked quietly onto the porch. "Mind if I sit here for a while?"

Eileen had told me once that she and her Junoesque sister had had a "classic sibling rivalry for all our lives." Her older sister was, according to my colleague, the "goddamn matriarch of the clan." She was entitled to it, Eileen supposed, by reasons of age and wisdom and psychiatric training. "The bitch is almost always right. For twenty years she's told me how to deal with Red, and finally, without much choice, I did what she suggested and I've never been so happy." A crooked grin. "Wouldn't that frost you?"

Conscious of her power, Mary Kate played the role of the low-key, laid-back precinct captain, a pose no more effectively deceptive than her brother's Father Brown mask.

"Patsy?" I asked anxiously.

"Acute, manic-depressive psychosis," she replied listlessly. "A very, very sick woman. The mania has peaked, and she's about to go into a very deep depression." Mary Kate shrugged. "I'm not sure she'll ever come out of it. If she does . . . Well, it would be a long time before that happens. Her husband has terminal cancer, you know."

"Oh, my God!" Catherine said softly.

"I don't suppose she'll ever stand trial," Nick said.

"Despite the policewoman in her hospital room taking notes, most of which probably wouldn't be admissible as evidence anyhow, I can't imagine a court ordering a trial. A preliminary psychiatric hearing ought to settle it. Will it be in La Porte or Cook County, Nick?"

"It may be one of the rare cases where both counties want the other to assume jurisdiction. All that could be charged today is attempted murder. Over in Chicago there would be a murder-one charge. I imagine her family lawyers, whoever they are, would rather a Cook County court order a psychiatric institution for her than an Indiana court."

"How long does King have?" I asked.

"A few months at the most. He's over there now, being very sweet and kind to her. A little late, if you ask me." Mary Kate stood up, hands in the pockets of her tailored jeans. "One way or another, it's all over for the two of them."

"And the kids?" I asked.

"They'll be parceled out among grandparents and in-laws, I suppose." Mary Kate shrugged glumly. "Some of them will make it, Brendan, and some of them won't, and there's not a damned thing that any of us can do about it."

We all stared quietly at the shimmering lake; for all practical purposes I was the only survivor from my grammar school and teenage group.

"Caitlin was wonderful." I tried to change the subject.

"That child will be the death of me," her mother observed proudly. "And she'll be the death of that red-bearded pirate if he doesn't work up enough nerve to give her a ring in the next couple of weeks. Isn't it ironic, Brendan? For twenty-five years of marriage I've called my poor Joe 'the pirate,' and he really doesn't look like a pirate at all, not even when he wears a beard. So my firstborn child falls in love with someone who really does look like a pirate. Joe loves it, the so-and-so. He claims it proves that there really are Jungian archetypes."

"And you say all it proves is an Electra complex." Catherine laughed.

We stared quietly at the somber waters, wishing perhaps that the tragedies of the day could be blotted out and knowing that they would always be part of our memories. We would go ahead with the festivities of the weekend, for the children and for ourselves, too, pretending that the world was normal again.

"You're staying till Tuesday morning?" Mary Kate asked. "For all the festivities down to the bitter end?"

"It has been decreed by the women in the Ryan family that that's what I must do, so that's what I will do."

We all laughed then, and continued to pretend that the tragedies of the day were wiped off the agenda. Joe Murphy appeared with martini glasses for himself and his wife, Catherine found some Jameson's for Nick and me, and a glass of orange juice for herself, and we toasted the moon and the beginning of summer.

"Caitlin says you're a modern Finn MacCool, Brendan." Joe Murphy peered at me with his kindly blue eyes. "A modern Celtic folk hero."

"I smell a Jungian lecture," his wife scoffed, and at the same time laid a hand on the thigh of his white jeans. "Take notes for the test, Brendan."

Joe was a slender man with white hair, white beard, a youthful face, and the manner and appearance of a very holy Trappist abbot.

According to family legend, he and Mary Kate Ryan began to fight the first day of her clerkship at Little Company of Mary's psych unit, in which Joe was the senior resident. They contended day and night for two months. Finally, it is said, on the last day, he said something unguarded and very un-Jungian like "It would take a lifetime in bed with you, Miss Ryan, to begin to reduce the sexual tension you generate."

And Mary Kate had replied simply, "All right."

"Was that an acceptance?" he is reputed to have asked.

"Was that a proposal?"

"I can't believe my good fortune."

Mary Kate claims that her answer was the wisest sentence she ever spoke: "I'm the lucky one."

Sometimes she adds, amid much laughter, "Fortunately the tension has not yet been reduced." So the battle, finding its origins in deep and powerful love, was not a new one.

"Well, since no one else will ask," Mary Kate continued on the porch at Grand Beach, "I'll be straight person again, Dr. Murphy. Who is Finn MacCool?"

"Finn MacCool, Dr. Murphy, was an Irish Ulysses, Agamemnon, Achilles, and Aeneas all rolled into one, with a bit of Childe Harold and Robin of Locksley thrown in. He led a group of fellow berserkers called Fenians, and they went around bashing heads of the bad guys, of whom there were more than a plentiful supply. Like all mythological heroes, he incarnates a certain dimension of the culture that creates him, in this case the wandering, invulnerable, generous, slightly demented warrior, an Irish version perhaps of a Samurai in a Kurosawa movie. Mifune perhaps."

"Brenny a Samurai?" Cathy Curran, again the imp girl of her youth, giggled. "With a broadsword or a pike like the one Mary Kate keeps in her living room?"

"The point my school would make is that your man Finn MacCool represents a model that is present deep down in the soul of most Irish males. We fantasize about playing the role. Occasionally we're given a chance, and we either blow it or don't."

"I think you might make a good Finn MacCool," Mary Kate admitted. "But you'd really have to be pushed. Same for Brenny. Pushed real hard."

"I can't imagine it," I insisted, not wanting to think of my Finn-like escapades in Vietnam.

"Did Finn have a breast fixation?" Nick Curran asked.

"He was an Irish male, wasn't he?" Mary Kate tilted the martini pitcher in my direction, then, remembering my form of weakness for the creature, replaced the pitcher on the table and lifted the bottle of Jameson's.

I begged off a second drink. "I've had a tiring day." Everyone seemed to think it was a remarkably funny comment.

"He really is Finn MacCool," Cathy commented as I slipped away. "I think he could be very dangerous."

I thought perhaps I should be offended.

The weather the next morning was perfect for a holiday weekend, warm and clear. Only an occasional fluffy cloud trailed its shadow across the calm green waters of the lake, drawing on it a fluid, inky design. A light breeze carried the Hobie Cats and the windsurfers (most of them in wet suits, because the temperature in the lake was still in the fifties) across the waters at moderate speeds. The TV minicams, probing for news about the shootout at Karwick, were kept at bay by a combination of Mike Casey's "No comment" (with a special smile reserved for mention of Sam Norton) and a bland refusal of wandering Grand Beach urchins to admit to the press that anyone named Ryan lived in the community. The swimming pool and sun deck at the Murphy House swarmed with children and adults. Uncle Brendan was very much in demand, doubtless as a result of some decision made by the collective Ryan consciousness.

"Would you like some lemonade, Uncle Brendan?"

"Come on out on the Cat, Uncle Brendan!"

"Would you put suntan oil on my back, please, Uncle Brendan?"

"Would you like a hamburger and a Coke, Uncle Brendan?"

"Please come play volleyball with us on the beach, Uncle Brendan."

"Would you tie my straps please, Uncle Brendan?"

"Come on in the pool and swim, Uncle Brendan."

"Uncle Brendan, will you come with Jean and me to water-ski at Pine Lake?"

"Want to play tennis, Uncle Brendan?"

Uncle Brendan knew he was a victim of a conspiracy but went along willingly. Why not cram into one weekend all the neglected weekends of the past?

So Uncle Brendan did go out on the Hobie Cat and did play tennis and did swim forty lengths in the pool and did eat several hamburgers and did indeed go with his daughter and his "nephew" Tim to Pine Lake, a small lake in La Porte, fifteen miles inland from Lake Michigan, which my mother would have called a "proper" Midwestern lake because it looked like it had been designed for a picture postcard or maybe as part of a set for a 1930s romantic film—weeping willow trees, tiny piers, and floating rafts in front of freshly painted cottages, roadhouses that once must have been speakeasies across the highway.

The Ryan clan kept a boat (with a 155 horsepower engine) in a marina on Pine Lake so that its water-ski enthusiasts would not be dependent on the vagaries of Lake Michigan. I had never water-skied before and was constrained to accompany Jean and Tim on the grounds that they needed a third person to be the "observer" on the boat. I was not, however, completely surprised when my daughter insisted, after she and Tim had sped skillfully (on one ski, needless to say) on the glass-smooth waters of Pine Lake, that I "totally" had to try it. I was even more astonished than she was that I got up the first try and even stayed up for a commendable period of time. Moreover, having lost all my common sense and against Jean's anxious protests that I didn't want to wear myself out, I tried it a second time and performed even more acceptably.

"Gosh, Uncle Brendan," Tim Murphy said as I climbed into the boat and tried to pretend that I was not utterly exhausted, "you're real good for a beginner. You ought to come up here every weekend during the summer. With a little practice, you'd be better than Jeannie."

"And you could keep Tim company while I'm in Ireland," said Jeannie, devastating in the most minimal of string bikinis, as she threw a towel at me. "Don't catch cold now."

"Growl." Tim revved up the boat. "The lakes are too cold to water-ski in Ireland."

Jean made an impatient face. "I'm going, Timmy, and that's final."

The slim young man shrugged. "I still think that if I asked my mother, she'd let me go with you."

"No way!" Jean exclaimed, with a touch of anger. "Absolutely no way."

"That's what I figured," Tim sighed, not altogether seriously, and steered the boat toward the narrow slip in the miniature marina at the edge of a busy two-lane highway.

So, a minor lovers' quarrel. Jean wanted to go to Ireland without the encumbrance of a knight in armor trudging along after her. She also wanted, I suspected, some freedom from Tim's obvious devotion. Tim, for his part, was being good-natured about the separation, partly because it was his character to be good-natured and partly because, like the rest of the Ryan family, he was one very clever Mick. If they had a fight over it, it would be my daughter's doing—and probably to soothe a guilty conscience about leaving him.

I prudently stayed out of the discussion and told myself that I might be much happier today if I'd had more such lovers' tiffs when I was their age.

We returned to the Ryan compound, our summer resort Camelot. Mass was scheduled for 5:30. I told my daughter and her beau that if I were to survive the hamburger roast, over which Jean was to preside, I'd better take a half-hour nap.

"A half hour?" Jean scoffed. "I'll wake you at five-fifteen. Monsignor Blackie is saying Mass at our house—Aunt Catherine and Uncle Nick's—and you'll need every minute of sleep you can get." She shook her head as one who simply cannot understand the follies of the old. "Old daddies shouldn't try to act like they're teenagers."

As I climbed the staircase from the first level to the second level—in Catherine Collins Curran's house there were levels, not floors—I reflected on how hungrily Tim Murphy's eyes devoured Jean as she lifted her arms to pull on a sweatshirt on the marina pier, a delicious offering of young womanly perfection, and I envied Tim his youth. If not

Jeannie, then some other appealing and satisfying young woman, about whom he had a choice, unlike me.

I was now prepared to admit to myself that I had chosen Madonna only in the negative sense: I had not said "no" to everyone else's foregone conclusion. My fault, not theirs, but I wished I'd had it to do over again.

I did have it to do over again. Maybe. Now, however, it was all my choice. Nobody was constraining me to pursue Ciara Kelly, and she was, was she not, an improbable will-of-the-wisp?

Madonna was waiting for me again in my room, dressed this time in blue. Blessed Mother blue?

I did not believe in her, I did not want to believe in her, I willed her out of my glorious summer weekend. She was dead, as Ron was dead, as King would soon be dead, and as Patsy would be better off dead. Yet she did not disappear and did not even seem aware of my displeasure. The interlude was the same as the last one, only more intense, a kind of bittersweet sorrow, a pained nostalgia mixed with a minute quantity of hope, like a touch of triple sec in a margarita. I had no choice but to give myself over to the emotions that seemed to radiate from her and fill the room.

What was the nature of the greater intensity? I cannot say. Emotions in both interludes were unspecific, generalized, almost cosmic. Yet, when she finally was there no more and the only blue was that of Lake Michigan (also Blessed Mother blue?), I sensed that there was something she wanted me to do or that I was supposed to do or that I should do. It would go far beyond the content of the interlude to say that the woman I pictured or encountered— choose your own verb—in the Currans' guest room was urging me to seek Ciara. Yet she *was* urging me to do *something* which I did not want to do.

I glanced at my watch. Twenty-five minutes, not exactly a transient experience. A nap was now out of the question.

I found the Jameson's bottle in the Currans' liquor cabinet, poured myself what might conservatively be called a double, and found myself a deck chair on the lawn. The drink might substitute for a nap.

Ciara Kelly. Ciara Kelly. Ciara Kelly.

"Hi, Uncle Brendan." Jackie Curran, actually John Blackwood Curran, a wide-eyed, thoughtful, towheaded five-year-old. "Whatcha doing?"

"I wore myself out water-skiing with Jeannie and Tim and I'm trying to rest before Mass."

"O-h-h-h." An unfathomable mystery satisfactorily explained.

"Did you have a good time today?"

"Uh huh. It's going to rain tomorrow."

How did he know? Better not ask.

I swallowed some more Jameson's, savoring every drop.

"Uncle Brendan?"

"Yes, Jackie."

"Did that lady with the blonde hair who was looking for you find you?"

I swallowed a very large gulp of Jameson's. "The one with the blue dress?"

"Uh huh. She was real pretty."

"Yes, Jackie; she found me."

Even the unperturbable Monsignor Blackie Ryan expressed mild surprise at that part of my story. He quickly recovered. "If there is such a thing as ESP, and there's every reason to believe there is, and if my namesake has some psychic sensitivities, which wouldn't surprise me in the least, then it would not seem at all improbable that some of the energies might leap from your neo-Neanderthal vestigia to his."

Perfectly natural explanation.

"Do you want a perfectly natural explanation?"

"Not I."

Blackie was attempting to polish his sunglasses with the tail of his sports shirt (white with a green leprechaun at the pocket). "To me the theme of the message is more important than a metaphysical explanation. I was simply offering you a natural explanation if you wanted one. Do you?"

"I don't know," I said honestly.

Jean found me sitting on the lawn and reproved me for drinking when I needed a nap. I was dispatched to my room to shower and prepare for Mass.

The Ryan clan and assorted neighbors and friends assembled in Catherine's vast "living area level" for the Eucharist. Cardinal Sean Cronin himself was present, accompanied by his sister-in-law Senator Nora Cronin and her second husband, the sportscaster Bob Hurley, her youngest daughter, Noreen, and Noreen's fiancé, Steve McLean (whose mother, Maria Donlon, had recently become the first woman bank president in the Loop); the cardinal, in gray slacks and a blue sweater, shook my hand vigorously.

"You come to Blackie's Mass too?" I asked.

The hoods retracted briefly from Sean Cronin's wild brown eyes. "I have to preach in the cathedral at noon tomorrow. I thought I'd steal some of his ideas. Watch him. He'll putter around up there like a young priest who's only said Mass a couple of times, or an old priest who no longer remembers the ceremonies."

It was a perfect description of Blackie Ryan's apparent surprise at the sight of the altar, the vestments, and the congregation. There was nothing lacking in his sermon, however.

The gospel of the sixth Sunday after Easter depicted Jesus in his Last Supper discourse to his apostles, promising to send them the Paraclete. Blackie shuffled sermon themes like a Mississippi riverboat gambler would shuffle a deck of cards.

"The holy spirit, the Paraclete, God's spirit of variety and diversity, a kind of cosmic Tinker Bell, who flits about the universe bringing splendid new things into existence, is the spirit of courage, the spirit who gave the apostles the fortitude they needed to go forth to preach Jesus to a hostile world. Courage is also the virtue that we honor on this weekend, devoted to those who died fighting for our country in all its wars, but especially the Civil War, which was fought for many reasons but not the least among them the conviction that a nation could not survive half slave and half free. As we reconsider those wars today, it may seem to us that often, if not always, they were foolish and unnecessary, but that does not detract from the courage or the generosity of the men who fought in them, nor from the debt we owe them for their courage and generosity.

"Courage is nothing more than generosity in time of crisis and risk. It is nothing more than powerful hope translated into action when others desperately need our help. We have seen recently a remarkable display of courage from some of our young people. . . ."

One could hear a pin drop in the "living area level." A few younger adolescents stole nervous, admiring glances at Caitlin and Cindasoo, the latter looking even more waiflike in Coast Guard fatigues. . . . "We admire their bravery, but none of us is surprised because we know them both to be generous young women, generous in countless little ways to all of us every day, young women of strong and powerful hope, young women who, we might safely suggest, are in league with, indeed in conspiracy with, the Paraclete. The events in the Karwick Plaza merely demonstrate in a highly spectacular fashion patterns of generosity that are typical of their daily lives. And if, as seems unlikely, praise for their bravery the other day should cause them to suspend their generosity and their hopefulness on the grounds that, well, 'they've already done enough,' one can be certain that the good Paraclete will light a fire under them.

"Their generosity is only secondarily something for us to admire. It is primarily for us to imitate. Life is an exploration of hope, an enterprise of risk taking, a journey of ever-renewed challenge. Generosity, hopefulness, courage are not options on such a pilgrimage. If we wish to be able to respond spontaneously and heedlessly in moments of crisis, as did our two rather interestingly matched young women, then we, too, must develop habits of generosity in our daily lives. We must take out the garbage when we're asked, put gasoline in the car when we're asked, clear off the table when we're asked, help drag the Hobie Cat up on the beach when we're asked, pile up the dishes in the dishwasher when we're asked, and run to the store to buy milk, bread, and charcoal lighter when we're asked. It is of these small heroisms, and sometimes at the moment they don't seem very small, of which great human courage is created."

And as for you, Brendan Ryan, are you ready to be as generous as Caitlin and Cindasoo?

No way. Not yet, anyhow.

When Blackie had finished, the cardinal, who was standing behind me, whispered in my ear, "Well, that's my sermon for tomorrow morning."

At the bidding prayers, after the homily, Mary Kate forestalled any mention of specifics by beginning with, "For those who have died recently and those who are sick, let us pray to the Lord."

Jackie Curran followed with "that the rain not last all day tomorrow." That produced laughter from his cousins, who were confident that there would be no rain at all tomorrow. Wasn't that what the weather forecasters had said?

"For brave young women," Jean prayed fervently.

"And for brave young men who have the courage to risk their lives by giving away diamond rings!" Caitlin Murphy shouted, waving enthusiastically her left hand, on which there was now a diamond ring that would sink a battleship. Or at least a Coast Guard cutter.

The "living area level" was filled with shrieking, cheering, laughing, crying, hugging, kissing, and similar manifestations of manic Irish delight. Kevin Maher seemed even more delighted than his fiancée; since he was receiving less attention, I shook his hand first. "Lucky guy," I said.

"It'll never be a dull moment," he chuckled, shaking the rafters of the room, it seemed to me. "I hope my hospital insurance never gets canceled because of too many broken limbs."

Blackie Ryan stood behind the makeshift altar in his white alb and gold stole, smiling like a benign Irish Buddha who was perhaps not quite sure of the reason for all the merriment but certainly approving of it.

His cousin Brendan Ryan, despite himself, had become part of the celebration. I had sworn to myself, when I reluctantly yielded to Jean's decision that I must come to Grand Beach for Memorial Day, that I would not be seduced by the vitality and the enthusiasm of the "other" Ryans. It had taken them twenty-four hours to capture me—and save my life in the process. Maybe, just maybe, I would water-ski with Timmy every weekend.

Mass continued, Communion was distributed (both the

wafers and the chalice, in what I suspect was a contraven-
tion of the Roman wishes—with a cardinal present at that).
The little Coast Guard waif received Communion like everyone else.

After Mass, I cornered her. "You went to Communion,
too, Cindasoo."

"I asked the cardinal man, and he said 'long as I was
Irish, it was all right.' I dunno. My mammy done warned
me 'bout you papists. She said that you're no count and you
drink too much and you breed like rabbits and 'the first
thing you know,' she said, 'if you give 'em the chance they'll
try to make *you* a papist.' "

"Are they making any progress?"

"Monsignor Blackie, he's a powerful prayin' preacher,
ain't he?—He say that you papists already have enough no-
count white trash and you don't want me." She spoke with
a perfectly solemn face; only a pixie twinkle in her brown
eyes hinted that she was putting me on. " 'No way,
Cindasoo,' he say, 'we gonna let you in.' "

"Are you all right after yesterday?"

"I reckon," she said slowly. "At least I'm fixin' to be."
Ciara Kelly. Ciara Kelly. Ciara Kelly.

Blackie's sermon, Caitlin's engagement, Cindasoo's pi-
quant charm, the graceful courage of my new friends, the
laughter, the good times, the merriment, they almost captured me, a fly yearning for honey.

The next morning, however, the rains that little Jackie
had predicted did indeed come. After breakfast (which, in a
Ryan house you make for and by yourself: "We put out the
makings," Eileen commented, "and let them graze."), I retreated to my room to work on this diary and to acknowledge to myself, if to no one else, that I indeed am faced with
a decision. The issue is inchoate and unformulated, diffuse
and unspecific, as vague as it was yesterday when I imagined I saw Madonna in this very room where I am writing
now, and just as yesterday, I do not want to define a decision, to give it a name, much less to make it.

26

Nicole Curran brought a large pitcher of lemonade and set it between me and Monsignor Blackie. "Mommy says there's not sand in it like there was sometimes when she made it," Nicole giggled, " 'cause I'm a good little girl and she never was. Is that right, Uncle Blackie?"

The priest's eyes blinked rapidly as he tried to switch from whatever deep thought it was that had him staring at the thundering whitecaps on the lake. "That you are a good little girl, Nicole," he said, examining the lemonade as though the possibility that it was not John Jameson's might indicate that it was poison, "is a matter that is quite beyond debate. As to your mother, I cannot recall sand ever being in *my* lemonade. It was always your daddy's. Doubtless he richly deserved it."

Nicole giggled again and fled.

"Where was I?" he sighed, resuming his contemplation of the waves. "Oh, yes, in re: Ciara Kelly."

The winds had whipped Lake Michigan into a furious boil. Even Pine Lake was turbulent, but not so turbulent that I was able to escape another try at water-skiing. After the skiing I returned, somewhat tentatively, to my room to see what if any psychic phenomenon awaited me there. The room was empty, save for this diary, and impulsively I found Nicole and sent her to seek out her Uncle Blackie and ask him if he could come over and talk to me for a few minutes. The conversation, and Eileen's revelation at the end of it, have clarified nothing for me. Spending another day at Grand Beach will only confuse me further. My daughter's plans notwithstanding, I will return to Chicago tomorrow with Jean and do my damnedest to pay no more attention to the Ryans and all they stand for.

"I should think," Blackie sighed heavily, "that the resolution of the issue is obvious."

"Oh?" In addition to being a brilliant painter and an

interesting house designer, Catherine Curran made good lemonade.

"It seems to me patent, self-evident, beyond dispute, that Ciara Kelly is real and is alive somewhere, and that you must go and search for her."

I had intended to make only a few careful inquiries about what the Church thought of ESP and perhaps mention my unpleasant encounter with Dr. Freihaut (how many centuries ago was that?), but Blackie Ryan's attitude of bemused and interested sympathy accomplished precisely what it was designed to accomplish. I told him everything, the retrocognition at Fort Dearborn, the interludes with Madonna, my romance, perhaps imaginary, with Ciara.

"How can you be so sure?"

"I dismiss as ridiculous the proposition," he tasted his lemonade and seemed astonished at its flavor, as though never before had he tasted Catherine's lemonade, "the hypothesis that she is imaginary. You, Brendan Herbert George Ryan, are a sensible and reliable attorney, investor, and civic personage. You may have in your organism some vestige of Neanderthal modes of cognition and communication. These may produce some odd experiences in your life, but I reject as offensive and affronting the notion that you would have a sustained love affair with a creation of those neo-Neanderthal vestigia." He permitted himself a small smile. "Indeed, a sustained love affair in itself, you must admit, Brendan, pushes our credulousness to its outer limits. A love affair with an imaginary woman?" He shook his head decisively. "No, no, that is too much to ask us to accept!"

"But—"

He held up an admonitory hand, a timid traffic cop assuming bravely that a small wave will stop a massive truck. "Moreover, in the extremely unlikely event that you should indeed create a lover for yourself, it is most implausible, you surely will concede, that you would create such a multifaceted and interesting woman as this, ah, Ms. Ciara Kelly. Do you truly expect me to credit that as plausible a

man as you could bring into being such a delightfully implausible woman?"

"I don't know whether you're flattering me or insulting
me," I grumbled.

"Heaven forfend," his nearsighted eyes glinted over the
lemonade glass, "that I should do either. I'm merely suggesting that the delectable Ms. Kelly is beyond imagination, that is to say, real."

"It seems to be awfully thin . . ."

"Moreover," he refilled his lemonade glass, spilling on
the redwood table almost as much as he poured into the
glass, "at the very beginning of this improbable criminal
affair, it seemed obvious that either you or Ms. Kelly was
the target of the crime and that poor Ron and your unfortunate wife were the unintended victims. . . ."

"That's not what the Chicago police thought."

"They erred. Patently. Consider: Father Crowley was a
troubled and disillusioned clerical leftist who, upon being
appointed pastor, shifted dramatically to the right.
Unattractive, perhaps, but hardly a serious candidate for
murder. And your wife, Lord have mercy on her, was a pathetic woman trying unsuccessfully to cope with the middle years of life and aging herself more rapidly than necessary. Again, sad and unfortunate, but who'd want to kill
her?"

"I might want to kill her. After all, men have killed for
less than three million dollars."

"Come now, Brendan." He waved the lemonade glass
in dismissal of my absurd suggestion, spilling more of the
lemonade. "We can reject that possibility out of hand. Anyone with the knowledge of your successful trading in the
bond market would have little question about your ability
to make up your losses in short order. You would match
Richard Dennis's three hundred percent profit margin
rather handily. Indeed, if the police had bothered to check
your other brokers, I'm sure they would have discovered
that, despite King Sullivan's pilferage, you have done quite
nicely in this lamentable situation of failing demands for
notes of government indebtedness."

"How do you know that?" I demanded hotly.

"A good guess." He stared suspiciously at the nearly empty lemonade glass, wondering apparently who had stolen the precious liquid from it. "Let us progress. Just as Madonna and Ron, God be good to them, were unlikely targets for low-quality outfit hit men, so it seems to me that you and Ms. Kelly were much more probable targets. I would have guessed Ms. Kelly, an inclination I doubtless share with her highly skillful protectors. Consider again: there is some doubt as to her actual name, we know nothing of her background save for an extremely unfortunate incident in the Congo some years ago. She is well-educated but impoverished, she gives no account of her family or of her life for the last decade and a half, a mysterious woman, a woman with a past, a woman who must disappear at the first sign of trouble—is this not the kind of person who might easily be a target for an assassination?"

"That's highly speculative . . ."

"Hear me out." Nicole reappeared and filled his lemonade glass and mine again. "Moreover, you are a well-known Chicago lawyer with unimpeachable integrity and with a strong, not to say puritanical sense of professional ethics. That you might have offended someone in the course of your career who wanted revenge is not at all improbable. Therefore, clearly you or Ms. Kelly was the target. Presumably, it seemed to me as I read the papers, Ms. Kelly. I erred, as apparently she did, and those in whose interest it was to protect her. If she and her friends had not made this error in judgment, it seems to me possible that she would not have disappeared."

"Let me see if I understand your argument." I felt faintly dizzy. It was not the logic of the court or the law office that I was hearing. "I don't see how it follows that Ciara is real because either she or I was the target of the killers."

"If either of you was the target," Blackie pointed a pudgy finger vaguely in my direction, "it might make perfect sense for her to disappear. Indeed, that is a reasonable assumption with which to begin, far more reasonable, it seems to me, than the rather naive notion that you created her out of a mixture of loneliness and psychic sensitivity."

"Everyone denies her existence: the Immigration Service, the Irish consul general, the owner of the store at which she worked, the manager and doorman at her apartment building, her neighbors. Doesn't that prove that she's unreal?"

"In the possibility, the very real possibility, that she was the target of the killers, or thought to be the target, it could just as readily prove that there was a conspiracy to hide and protect her."

"A conspiracy *that* well organized?"

"Such elaborate organization only proves," Blackie Ryan shrugged indifferently, "that those who wished to protect her are powerful, resourceful, and strongly motivated."

"I'm still not convinced."

"Brendan." Blackie removed his glasses and peered at me with a sympathetic and kindly face. "Their only serious mistake was the empty apartment."

"Pardon me?"

"You could have checked easily, Brendan. That you did not do so should suggest to you that her non-existence allayed some of your fears of intimacy. In any event, I did check. Chestnut Place has a three-month waiting list for apartments. Our mysterious friends were able to remove her and her belongings from the apartment, repaint it, even change the telephone, but they did not have quite enough time to move in someone else and create the appearance of long residency for the substitutes—a more difficult task perhaps than merely covering one woman's disappearance. Still, candidly, I feel this was rather inept of them."

There was the bat that had been flitting around the dungeons of my brain: of course, there were no empty apartments in our neighborhood.

"We should have thought of that!"

"Perhaps you lacked the perspective," Blackie shrugged indifferently, "to see it. From my roost on the third floor of the cathedral rectory it was, one might argue, easier to see the forest instead of the trees. The 'mysterious friends' probably hoped that no one would think of the waiting lists for apartment buildings." His watery eyes glinted, briefly hard and determined. "Too bad for them."

Right, they'd lost one to Blackie Ryan!

"But who could these 'mysterious friends' be?"

"Patently, men of enormous power and persuasiveness, men who could convince the cast-iron bureaucrats of the INS and your good friend the Irish consul general that it was necessary to deceive you. Men within the American government of very powerful credentials, perhaps working in cooperation with counterparts from other governments."

"Why?" Despite the chill winds off the lake I was sweating profusely.

"Ah, is that not the basic question? Does it not address itself to the heart of the mystery of Ciara Kelly? Is that not indeed what you must learn if you are to continue your quest for her?"

"I haven't even begun such a quest," I protested.

"She must be found, Brendan," Blackie Ryan insisted fiercely, now not a modern Father Brown but once more Richard, Raymond, Godfrey in the Gate. "She is, by your own admission, in jeopardy from the powers of evil and darkness. We cannot let them destroy her."

"What powers of darkness?" I began to understand the reason for Blackie's Father Brown persona. Whether he be Godfrey or Don Quixote, such a passionate contemporary crusader would scare the hell out of you.

"My Lord Cronin, as a punishment for his many sins, has been assigned to preside over the liquidation of the Vatican financial mess. It would appear that the shadow world of terrorism, secrecy, and conspiracy in reality far exceeds that presented to us by such excellent authors as Ludlum or Le Carré. Indeed, the shadow world is so incredible that no fiction writer would dare to describe it as it is, for fear that he would be dismissed as a paranoid. The CIA and the KGB and their counterparts in England, France, Germany, and Israel, for example, are a law unto themselves. But they are more legitimate than some of their occasional allies—the Masonic lodges like Propaganda Due in Italy, the Mafia, international drug traders, brokers in the arms and munitions market, fanatics who work for lunatics like Qaddafi and Khomeini, remnants of the 1968 radical groups like the

Weathermen, nutcakes like the Symbionese Liberation Army that kidnapped Patty Hearst, Turkish revolutionaries, so-called, who also smuggle drugs and arms and do an occasional job for the Bulgarian secret police, like assassinating a pope, international smugglers who occasionally do a job for the Vatican, like smuggling money into Poland for Solidarity or disposing of a pope who is going to sweep them out of power, as I fear John Paul I may have been disposed of, and various other assorted psychopaths, sociopaths, mercenaries, dogs of war, and heavily armed madmen. Not to exclude the ones who started it all and will be playing the game long after the others have finished. The ones who never learn and never forget, and I don't mean the Bourbons."

"The heirs of Michael Collins," I said thoughtfully, referring to the great Irish revolutionary leader from 1918.

"Indeed. And not as clever as Michael Collins, who understood, God be good to the poor man, that there's a time when the game must stop."

"You think Ciara is mixed up in *that* world?"

"Is it not patent that that must be the case?" Blackie drummed on the redwood table with his folded spectacles. "After a time in the shadow world, the game becomes an end unto itself and the goals for which it is played no longer matter, if they're even remembered. Ciara Kelly, if that really be her name, has become, I suspect, a pawn in the game. And those who play it are sufficiently important to be able, very quickly, to mobilize prestigious resources from the United States government. She must be saved, snatched out of the psychotic evil of the shadow world."

"What if she doesn't want to be saved? What if searching for her would endanger her life even more? What if—"

"If she doesn't want to be saved, you should at least hear that from her own lips." Blackie's sigh was almost as loud as Ciara's would have been. "As for your quest endangering her all the more, that is perhaps a risk you have to take."

"It all seems very thin." I emptied my lemonade glass and waved off his proffered refill.

Blackie sighed heavily. "You're probably the only person in Grand Beach besides me who's read Alfred North Whitehead. If you want, I'll be simple: God is engaged in the business of creating beauty by drawing us forth in hope and love. Sexual attraction is but one dimension of hope, the trickiest of the games that God plays with us. It's God's best technique yet to lure us into generosity and risk taking, which are the raw materials of beauty. Bluntly, your attraction to Ciara Kelly is a trick God has played on you. 'Love Ciara Kelly, love Me' is what She is saying to you. 'Pursue Ciara Kelly, the will-of-the-wisp, the Holy Grail, and you pursue Me, the divine will-of-the-wisp . . . "

"And thus be tricked into playing Her game of creating a beautiful universe, no matter what happens to Ciara and me."

Blackie contemplated the ten-foot white waves for a moment. "Will your own life be more beautiful if you search for Ciara Kelly or if you don't?"

"I'm not going to be tricked by Her sexual game!"

"She is pretty tricky."

Eileen Kane joined us, looking tired, distraught, and angry. She poured herself a glass of lemonade and sank into the empty redwood chair between the two of us. "God damn!" She sipped the lemonade like it was vodka.

"You seem troubled, good sister," Blackie commented.

"I am angry, good brother." She drained the lemonade and poured herself another glass. "I am angry at Little Redmond. He's made me awkward, ungainly, and tired, and he is currently behaving as though my insides were a soccer ball. Moreover, I am angry at Big Redmond because I have to carry the child instead of him. I have just had a monumental fight with him, which was about ninety percent my fault. In the old days I never fought with Redmond, and hence never had to apologize." Her sigh reminded me of Ciara Kelly. "Now I must go apologize to him, which will only make matters worse."

"How does Red react to an apology?"

"How does any man react to an apology from his woman?" She glared balefully at me. "It's an aphrodisiac. What else? Just what I need."

"Ah," Blackie murmured. "That is not, however, why you have joined us."

"No." Eileen strove to be her businesslike legal self. "Mary Kate thought of something this afternoon that she thinks is pertinent to the issue of the fire on the *Brigid*. Pertinent, indeed. I don't know why it took her this long to tell me. Typical of the Irish, she wants to tell you indirectly, Brendan, doubtless to escape responsibility. Anyway, one of the things that poor Patsy Sullivan said before she went into her depressed phase: she told Mary Kate, with the policewoman there taking notes, that she did not intend to kill Madonna and Ron. It was you and the woman with the long black hair and the big boobs who she thought were on the boat."

Dead silence on the porch. The wind howled, whitecaps beat against the beach, in the background one could hear shouts of children in the swimming pool next door.

"Indeed," Blackie Ryan said patiently, "Ireland is where the search must begin. I would imagine, Uncle Brendan, that a man of your influence would have no difficulty obtaining a passport immediately."

27

Jean handed me the eyeshades. "People in Ireland are going to sleep now, Daddy. Maybe we ought to do so too."

I had returned to my room in the Curran wonder house at Grand Beach, determined that neither Blackie Ryan nor God would trick me into going to Ireland on a foolish and possibly dangerous search for Ciara. I woke up the next morning, after wildly erotic dreams about her, with the same resolution. Jean and I ate breakfast together at 7:30 because I wanted to be in my office before ten o'clock. I'm not altogether sure what angel or demon invaded me. Without a precise realization of what I was saying, I remarked to her, "Would you mind if I fly over to Ireland with you? I don't belong on your photo tour, but I thought I might hang around Dublin and take a look at how law is taught and practiced in Ireland."

I could scarcely believe my own ears.

Jean swallowed half an English muffin at one gulp and embraced me enthusiastically. "Daddy, how wonderful!"

The month of June had only just begun, and here I was on an Aer Lingus 747 in first class, flying to Ireland, still not quite sure how it had happened.

The search is over now, for weal or woe, and this diary, the last previous entry of which was made on the evening of Memorial Day after my conversation with Blackie, can now be finished.

Jean took charge of my trip, purchasing the tickets, advising me on what and how to pack, rushing a passport through at record speed (activating, I believe, both the United States senators from the Prairie State), and assisting my secretary in canceling all my appointments for three weeks. No doubt about it, the young woman was an extremely able administrator, though her efficiency did not become officious. Her suggestions were careful and cautious, and never did she seem to be giving me orders. I went along with her plans, most of the time anyway, because it seemed the sensible and easy thing to do. Taking orders from Madonna, Lord have mercy on her, as the Ryans would say, was always punishment. Taking orders from Jean was pleasure. How very clever of her.

The only disagreement was whether to fly first class. She was appalled at the suggestion. All that money for a little bit of extra room and some drinks? Anyway, we're not going to drink because we're going to follow Dr. Ehret's Jet Lag Program, aren't we?

"We certainly are going to follow the program," I said, watching how neatly she folded my shirts into the lightweight flight bag she'd purchased. (The only way to travel to Europe, I was told, was with carry-on luggage. You brought a lot of clothes to Grand Beach, only a few clothes to Europe. Why did that seem so strange?) "But I, at any rate, being a tired and elderly man, value that extra bit of comfort enormously. You go coach if you want, kid, I go first class."

"Really. *Well* . . . you're paying for it. Hmmm, I guess we're going to have to take one of these shirts out."

"You expect me to have lunch with Irish lawyers in dirty shirts?"

"They *do* sell shirts in Ireland. Anybody who can afford to fly first class can afford to buy clothes in the country he visits and then give the clothes to the St. Vincent De Paul Society or something like that when he leaves. Right?"

"Right. Naturally."

So we had feasted with the Currans and the Kanes, flew out of O'Hare to New York, where we fasted and saw *Cats*, and then boarded the Aer Lingus 747 for Dublin.

A blurred image of Ciara was never far from the center of my consciousness; with the image there came constant sexual desire. Beneath the exterior image of a sedate middle-aged professional man preparing for a trip abroad with his daughter was an aborigine desperately hunting for his spring woman, lusting for her with savage appetite.

No one but Blackie Ryan was certain why I was going to Ireland, though perhaps the Kanes and the Currans might have guessed. I had no strategy, no game plan. I would go to Dublin, look around, and see what happened, perhaps contact the Irish police or the Special Branch, which was kind of their FBI. However, if Blackie was correct about the shadow world, they would be less than forthcoming. Timmy Murphy was not at O'Hare to bid us goodbye, nor was there any excuse or explanation offered for his absence. I had enough sense not to ask questions.

"Did you know," said my daughter, who was wearing a khaki jumpsuit with a pink blouse under it, "that Baileys Irish Cream, which we are not to drink on the flight over because it will violate the plan, accounts for one percent of all the exports of Ireland, that it is the most popular cordial in both West Germany and France, that it outsells all other liqueurs put together in the United States, and that such distinguished old brands as Grand Marnier have been forced to bring out their own creams to compete?"

"Remarkable," I agreed. Not only was Jean marvelously efficient, she seemed to have acquired, in her nineteen years, a vast collection of useful and useless information.

"And you're wondering why Tim Murphy wasn't at the airport?"

"Was I?"

She nodded her head vigorously. "Yep, you were wondering. We had a big fight."

"Ah."

"You sound like Uncle Punk."

"Don't you think it would be more appropriate if you called him Uncle Blackie?"

She eyed me disdainfully. "Tim and I had a big fight. He's too intense. I can't stand the hungry way he looks at me."

"At the risk of intruding in what is none of my business, Jean, you are a very attractive, indeed sexy, young woman. Moreover, you are smart, personable, efficient at planning projects such as hasty trips to Dublin, and a storehouse of knowledge about such critically important things as Baileys Irish Cream. Any young man Timothy's age, with the standard complement of hormones, would devour you with hungry eyes."

"Hmmph."

"Moreover," I crawled far out on a limb, "you've had some rough things happen to you lately and you might be said to need some male protection. Add that to all the other factors I've just mentioned, and a young scion of the Ryan clan can't help but be intense."

"I don't need protection, I don't want protection," she pounded the armrest, "I won't accept protection."

"Oh."

"That sounds kind of silly, doesn't it, Daddy?" she asked sheepishly.

"Really."

"I can't cope with him, I'm not ready for it. It just wouldn't work."

"Was Tim making demands?"

"Making demands?" she asked scornfully. "You mean, like sex? If he was a Stanford student, he'd be trying to drag me off to bed every time he saw me. That's not how the Ryans and the Murphys act. They protect their goddamned virgins."

"He was being possessive, then."

"Not to say possessive," she said thoughtfully.

Ciara's syntax again. You are alive, my darling, but what chance do I have of finding you?

"No," Jean continued. "Tim isn't the kind of boy who,

like, hangs around and gets jealous every time you look at somebody else or somebody else looks at you. He just wants to love me, like, more powerfully than I want to be loved. He doesn't mean it to be a demand, poor guy. But for me it's a demand just the same."

"I'm pretty far out on a limb now ..."

She pounded the armrest again. "C'mon, Daddy, we've gone beyond the stage where you have to apologize for giving advice."

Indeed, as Blackie would have said. Have we now? as Ciara would have said.

"Neither your mother nor I, Jean, gave you a very good example in this respect, but don't try and do it alone."

"Do *what*?" she asked irritably.

"You know *what*. Make it, survive, grow up, get your act together, find a little wisdom as you yourself described it, whatever."

"Yeah, I know."

And then I was offered eyeshades and told that just because they were playing a movie, it didn't mean that I had to watch it.

The plan does not absolutely require that you sleep at the time that the people in the country of destination are sleeping. You must merely rest, relax, and end all conversation. But I slept like I was back in my bed in the apartment in Chicago. Jean nudged me gently. "Wake up, Daddy. Have you ever seen anything so green before in all your life?"

There was a thin layer of cloud beneath us, and then beneath the clouds the greenest fields I had ever seen, unbelievably, unbearably green, occasionally smeared with ragged gold splotches, like someone had spilled a can of paint, as the sun broke through the cloud layer.

"It must be all the rain," I murmured.

"Oh, boy," Jean said joyfully, "am I going to get the pictures here!"

"Everybody here looks Irish," she whispered in my ear as we waited in line at the Dublin airport customs.

"What else did you expect them to look like?" I asked. "It's almost like being back on the south side of Chicago."

The immigration inspectors managed to process us rapidly while projecting an image of casual unconcern. An elderly little white-haired man, who inspected our passports and stamped them, peered through his rimless glasses at Jean. "And what county would your ancestors be from, young woman?"

"Mayo, God help us," she responded, with her brightest smile.

"Ah, well," said the little fellow with the leprechaun wink, "at least you're honest about it. Take good care of your father now. Make sure he drives on the right side of the road, which is the left side here, if you take my meaning."

"I'll do most of the driving," Jean replied saucily. "Himself is one of your dreamy lawyers, sure, you can't trust 'em at the wheel of a car at all, at all."

And to me, as we walked over to the luggage carousel, "See, Daddy, I told you everybody would know you were my father and wouldn't think you were a dirty old man traveling through Europe with a nymphet. We do look a little bit alike, after all."

I wanted nothing more than to check in at the Shelbourne Hotel and go to bed, but the plan forbade that. This was, however, to be a day of feasting. I had dutifully consumed two cups of coffee before the plane landed. The Shelbourne was a rambling, untidy, and quaint old place, which if it were cleaner might have appealed to Queen Victoria, on the northern edge of Stephen's Green, which at the moment was partly obscured by what our taxi driver called "mists" and what I would have called a "driving rain."

In the mists I saw the image of Ciara. I wanted her so badly that I almost ran out into the rain to search for her. I knew that common sense dictated a day or two of acclimatization and orientation, but common sense was not so powerful in me as it used to be.

Never in my life had I experienced sexual desire so intense, so persistent, so violent.

We had to go at once to the dining room and consume a large breakfast—bacon, eggs, melon, brown Irish bread, and several more cups of coffee. "Your body," Jean said confidently, "will now be convinced it's breakfast time instead of three or four o'clock in the morning."

"Great," I muttered, with more enthusiasm than I felt.

In order to live up to the stern discipline of the plan it was decided that we would, after breakfast, go on a tour of Georgian Dublin. First of all, however, we had to cross Stephen's Green, now wet but glowing, "like, kind of mystical" as Jean put it, in the sunlight, and pay our respects to the black marble bust of James Joyce, donated by American Express, on the south side of the green, across from Newman House, where he'd gone to college. On the front of the bust was carved the words from *Portrait of the Artist*, "Crossing Stephen's, that is my, Green."

"The poor dear man certainly had bad eyes, didn't he?" Jean scurried around the bust, Nikon in hand, trying to capture both Joyce's craggy features and the Georgian building across the street where Joyce had gone to school and where a half century before another unappreciated Dubliner, John Henry Newman, had been rector and had presented the lectures that became *The Idea of a University*. American Express had yet to erect a bust in his honor, however.

Stephen's Green was nothing more than a small park in the center of a city, a park in which Handel and Newman and Swift and Joyce and a couple of dozen other geniuses had routinely walked, across which the British army and the Irish volunteers had battled during Easter week of 1916. If you ignored the history and the literature and Newman and Joyce and the rest of them, it was not a special place. Or so I told myself as my daughter and I paused to admire every little Celtic brat being pushed through the park in a stroller.

I was then dragged to Bewley's on Grafton Street for tea and scones. It was, I was assured, the most famous tea-room in Dublin, and perhaps the best tea in Ireland. Besides, this was our day for feasting.

I was sure that a woman on the other side of the room was Ciara. I excused myself to go to the men's room so that I might see her face.

It wasn't Ciara, but my tumescent imagination wanted to undress her anyway.

I hurried back to Jean, now not only my daughter but also my link with the real world.

We stayed south of the Liffey for the rest of the day, exploring Grattan's parliament building (now the Bank of Ireland), Trinity College, Christ Church and St. Patrick's Cathedral (both Protestant, one early Norman Gothic, the other later English Gothic), Dublin Castle, Merrion Square and Fitzwilliam Square with their classic—and just barely preserved—row houses, and the Custom House and the Four Courts across from the south bank of the Liffey.

Grattan's Dublin may not have been an Irish city, but one could imagine what a smart town it must have been, men and women in expensive clothes, elegant carriages, fashionable furnishings in the homes. All of that was gone. Dublin town was crowded, dirty, and by the standards of a Chicago Irishman, still poor. The people seemed underfed, anxious, subject to premature aging, and badly in need of dental work. My daughter informed me that I sounded like an American snob and that I would probably feel better after I'd had a good night's sleep.

Moreover, she continued, as I knew very well Ireland was deep into the hardest times it had experienced in twenty years. Youth unemployment was close to fifty percent. If I was suffering as much as most Irish people were, I'd look anxious and prematurely aged.

"So would I," she added sheepishly, looking at me out of the corner of her eye as we ended our second visit to Bewley's. On this note, since it was raining again for the fourth or fifth time in the day, we withdrew to the lobby of the Shelbourne to have high tea, which, I calculated, was my fifth meal of the day. I looked around the elegantly shabby room with its canary-color walls, its plush but down-at-the-heels furniture, and its vast fireplace and wondered if I looked as overfed and as arrogantly self-satisfied as the other American tourists, who were devouring pastry like it was about to be banned by either the pope or OPEC.

"You're going to get your old daddy fat in this country," I protested as Jean shoved a cream puff into my all too willing mouth.

"That's all right." She turned to the complex task of

loading her Nikon. "Eat as much as you want today because tomorrow is a fast day. Remember?"

"God forbid," I sighed.

I was permitted to return to my room and read a Dublin guidebook that had been purchased for my edification but was sternly warned not to nap. We ate supper at a restaurant in a little mews down the street from the Shelbourne, strongly and justifiably recommended by Jean's guidebook. My tour guide was uncommunicative and somber as we picked our way through the rain and the mist to the restaurant.

"Can I order some Jameson's?" I asked her.

"Two of them," she snapped. "And make them doubles."

"Is that part of the plan?"

"No, goddamn it. It isn't."

"Phone call from Tim?"

"Mind your own fucking business."

"*Jean!*"

"I'm sorry, Daddy." She grabbed my right hand with both of hers, tears welling up in her eyes. "I'm clinging by my fingernails again. *So* angry and *so* bummed."

"Angry at Tim?"

"Angry at myself. The poor boy called me from Grand Beach to apologize for the fight. Can you imagine that? His mother'll kill him when she sees the phone bill. And he didn't start the fight, Daddy. I started the fight so I was angry at him all over again. Isn't that terrible?"

Terrible it was, but I was too preoccupied with my own problem to be of much help to Jean. My problem was that every handsome woman I saw on the streets of Dublin—there turned out to be more of them than I'd realized at first—reminded me of Ciara.

I wanted to make love with all of them.

Now that I was in Ireland, what was I going to do? Wander through the streets of Dublin and accost every beautiful woman in her early thirties that I encountered?

What the hell was I doing here?

28

St. Kevin's Shrine at Glendalough did not at first seem sinister. It was a quaint and mildly interesting collection of gravestones and ungainly ruins, crude old rock buildings nestled in a valley in the Wicklow hills, which, with some exaggeration, might be called picturesque. A parking lot, or "car park," as the Irish seemed to call them, a somewhat battered and weather-beaten tourist center, where one could get a meal that might have been attractive if there were a famine, and crowds of Sunday tourists reminded me of Starved Rock State Park back in Illinois, an unspectacular tourist attraction to which you drove on a Sunday a quarter century ago when you had guests from out of town and had to be home in the evening.

It was only after I had wandered through the park in the bright afternoon sunlight while Jean joyously scampered ahead of me with her Nikon that I began to be terrified.

I'd slept well the previous night: the plan worked. I had discovered, however, that it was indeed true, as I had read in geography books in grammar school, that the days were long and the nights were short in the northern climes during late spring and early summer. There were a few hours of darkness around midnight, but by three in the morning, daylight was pouring through the holes in the shades in my room, creating patches of light on the worn blue carpet and the badly scratched mahogany-veneer furniture. I remembered Jean's eyeshades, fumbled in my traveling bag for them, and stumbled back into bed for sleep and more dreams of Ciara.

I had to wait until Monday to begin my search. Could I last another week without her? Even another day?

At breakfast Jean enthused about the cloudless blue skies and the green hills of Wicklow in the distance hovering over St. Stephen's Green and the, like, totally wonderful pictures she was going to take today in South County, Dublin. Really.

"Is that where we're going?"

"C'mon now, Daddy; you read the schedule I typed out."

So I had, and we were off to South County, Dublin. After a stop at the ugly nineteenth-century procathedral for the eight o'clock Mass (the pernicious infection of folk music at Mass, it seemed, had spread even to Ireland), we drove south on Merrion Road, crossing the Grand Canal, passing Boland's Mills, where De Valera had held out to the bitter end after the Easter rising, and circled through University College in Belfield, which Jean pronounced, in disappointment, to be "just like any American state university," and then worked our way over to Rock Road, along the edge of Dublin Bay. Jean turned up her nose at the beaches, which were, indeed, rocky, and declared that she, for one, was not going to swim in the ocean when the water was fifty degrees, no matter how many skinny, pale-skinned boys were spread out on the "strand" (which was the proper name for a beach in the British Isles, I was informed). "Yucksville!" she observed. The class passed through Blackrock and Monkstown and detoured to see James Joyce's Martello Tower, one of a series that had been built along the coast of Ireland to fend off invaders in Napoleonic times. "Why would anybody want to live in *that*?" Jean sniffed.

"So he could grow up and write *Ulysses*," I replied.

"Yucksville," she observed again.

We drove through Dun Laoghaire and watched the ferry from Liverpool chug through the harbor mouth like a supercilious elderly matron, pick its way among the yachts and sailboats that were rushing out into the bay, and slide securely into its pier with what seemed to be an enormous sigh of relief.

Several of the young women disembarking from the ferry—probably coming home for "holidays" from their English jobs—reminded me so forcefully of Ciara that only by sheer willpower did I restrain myself from running up to them.

"Maybe we should have scheduled sailing for today," Jean said. "Would you like to go sailing, Daddy?"

I had not, in fact, even thought about it. The memories of the *Brigid* were still too vivid in my imagination.

"Later on, before I leave Ireland. Today I'd be satisfied with Glendalough."

"And Powerscourt."

"Certainly Powerscourt. How could I ever forget Powerscourt?"

"Really!"

Even though we were on the fast day of the plan, I was nonetheless permitted to buy tea in a café at the head of the East Pier in Dun Laoghaire harbor. Jean took off her blue (the color, I was informed, was actually "lilac") sweater. She was wearing slacks that matched the sweater and a lilac-and-white striped blouse with white collar and white cuffs and carrying a white shoulder-strap purse as well as her camera bag. I had raised an eyebrow at such garb for a trip to the Wicklow mountains, but she replied that she wasn't going to walk into an Irish church on Sunday morning in jeans and sweatshirt and there wouldn't be time to stop at the hotel to change. It turned out that many of the local colleens had no such scruples about their Sunday morning garb. The men in the coffee shop could hardly help but notice her. She radiated fresh, young, happy sexuality. Small wonder that poor Tim Murphy had been overwhelmed.

A big brown-haired lad with broad shoulders and thick forearms held the door for us as we left. "Sure, if you don't know my cousins in the States," he said with a wink and a charming grin, "it's a grand misfortune—for them, that is."

"Is it now?" Jean cocked a speculative eye at him.

"You have to admit it's a new approach to getting acquainted." A faint tinge of color rose in his face.

"It's all of that," Jean replied curtly, swinging her rear end, I thought, a little more than usual as we walked away from the pier.

The young man caught up with us. "Am I never, never

to see you again, at all, at all?" he asked. "Ah, sure, won't I
be destroyed altogether if that happens?"

"I've been known to come in and out of the Shelbourne
Hotel," Jean suggested.

"Should I ask for anyone by name?" The young man
grinned broadly.

"Ah, you might, and then again, you might not."

"And your father wouldn't be minding?"

Jean glanced at her father. "Ah, you shouldn't let his
mild manners fool you. He's a terrible dangerous man."

"You're not the kind that gets picked up?" I said, as we
boarded our rented Renault.

"Not to say picked up." Jean laughed cheerfully. "He is
kinda cute, Daddy. Admit it."

"Well, at least I'm happy I don't cramp your style. I bet
he's more pushy than Tim Murphy."

"Tim who?"

And so we went on to Dalkey and Bray, admiring the
sun-drenched blue waters of the bay, which we both agreed
looked like Naples, though only Jean had seen Naples, and
we were intrigued by the elegant and graceful if somewhat
run-down homes of South County, Dublin.

"There are so many writers in this part of Ireland,"
Jean said, "that you have to push your way through them
on the streets."

"You've read so much about this country that you even
talk like the people."

Jean glanced at me curiously. "How many of the people have you talked to, Daddy?"

"Oh, not that many. But you certainly had that young
man's dialect down."

My darling Ciara. When will I find you?

Then we turned inland and drove up the foothills to
Glendalough, a mildly interesting Irish ruin on a bright,
cheerful Sunday afternoon in spring, swarming with visitors, including an alarmingly large number of women with
strollers equipped for two infants.

"I would say they were crazy for having two children
so close together," Jean had just admired two little boy
children, both of whom had flirted with her outrageously,

"but both the kids and their mothers look healthy and happy."

"Maybe they don't know any better," I suggested.

"I want kids," she replied. "I want them in the worst way, but I don't know what kind of a mother I'll be."

"You're doing a fine job of mothering me on this trip."

"Daddy." A hug and a laugh that was almost tears, and despite the swarms of Irish tourists, a very nice kiss. I suspect some of them began to question their original decision that she was almost certainly my daughter.

All in all, it was a pleasant and delightful Sunday with a daughter who was rapidly becoming a friend. It was not the sort of afternoon when one would expect to be suddenly overcome by naked terror.

We were inside the ruins of what seemed to me to be a tiny stone chapel, overgrown with weeds, which the guidebook said was a "cathedral." Jean was photographing the round tower (a lookout and hideaway from Viking pirates) through the door of the ruins because, as she told me, the composition was "just right."

The terror came suddenly, without warning. Unlike my other psychic interludes, this one was uncanny, ghostly, spooky, horrifying.

I slumped into the corner of the old stone church and curled up in a knot. I felt, rather than saw, the clanging of bells, the flashing of swords, burning buildings, screams, torment, death. Death, death, death everywhere, violent, painful, humiliating death. The screams of the wounded and dying were all around, the swords of the enemy slashed through the air above me. The stench of burning timbers filled my body. I prayed for salvation and knew that there could be none. I was being swept into the agonies of hell. The fire, the noise, the smell, the anguish of death grew stronger and stronger, filled me, possessed me, overwhelmed me, dragged me toward the tomb.

"Daddy, Daddy, oh, please Daddy. . . ." A tender, frightened voice from another world. I reached for it but could not find it. This was not Fort Dearborn, not one videotape played on top of another, this was rather a world of darkness reaching up to snatch me and claim me and drag me down.

"*Please*, Daddy."

Jean. Ciara. Eileen. Catherine. Jocelyn.

I reached for the world of light and green and Sundays in spring with boys who followed pretty girls down the streets of Dun Laoghaire and little children in white First Communion dresses and suits.

"I'm okay, Ciara. I'm fine. Just," I managed a weak laugh, "a little bit too much fast on the fast day. Do you think we might go back to the restaurant and have us a wee spot of tea and a scone or two?"

I was helped to my feet by a couple of very anxious young Irishmen to whom I explained with what I hoped was a rueful laugh, "It's what happens to a Yank tourist on jet lag when he doesn't have a big enough breakfast. I'm all right, fellows, I'm fine. No heart attack."

The two young men, countrymen, I thought, perhaps up for a weekend in Dublin, looked skeptical, but a grateful smile and thank you from my lilac-clad daughter reassured them. Fast day or not, I ate two ham sandwiches and three scones and downed several cups of tea while Jean apologized, with less conviction than I might have wanted, for pushing the plan too vigorously.

"Your father is an old man out of condition," I joked.

"My father," she said grimly, "is forty-two years old, in excellent condition, and, if one is to judge from the way these hungry-eyed Irish bitches look at you, damned attractive."

"That's the comparative for cute, isn't it?" I asked.

"Superlative." She pushed my arm. "Should we go back to the hotel?"

"Nonsense," I said. "On to Powerscourt."

We visited the sad, charred ruins of that great manor house, admired the garden, flirted with the children, took pictures of a wide variety of objects, mineral, vegetable, animal, and human, and finally arrived at the Creole Restaurant in the dark, comfortable basement of a house near the harbor in Dun Laoghaire about six o'clock for supper. The psychic vibrations of St. Kevin's Shrine still lingered, but they were not powerful enough to greatly trouble me. We sat in a booth in the back of the restaurant, ordered a bottle of Niersteiner wine, and relaxed.

At any rate, I relaxed. Jean thumbed through the guide-book after she'd returned from the women's room, and found the place she was looking for. "Many people claim that the Shrine of St. Kevin at Glendalough is haunted by the ghosts of the monks who were massacred there at various times during the Danish invasions. Indeed, some psychic researchers say that it's the most haunted place in all of Ireland."

"Considering all the Irish ghost stories, that's a pretty broad claim, isn't it?" I laughed weakly.

"Let's have it, Daddy." She pointed an imperious finger at me. "I want the truth, all of it."

I comprehended clearly for the first time the essential difference between Jean's propensity to "take charge" and her mother's similar characteristic. Jean's determination and efficiency was in the service of love, still awkward and clumsy, perhaps, still searching for nuance and refinement, but not really capable of ever becoming domination. I was relieved and happy at that discovery.

"I said, let's have it, Daddy," she insisted, her voice rising dangerously.

Nonetheless, a very determined young woman. How would she and Ciara get along if she should be Ciara's step-daughter?

"Daddy?" Dangerously close to anger.

"You told me a while back you didn't believe in ESP," I began.

"Maybe now I do. Was that what happened?"

We ordered scallops meunière and drank our seafood soup while I told her of the various strange psychic phe-nomena that were so much a part of my life that I took them almost as much for granted as I did winter colds or blocked sinuses in spring.

Jean became very pale and held my left hand with hers while we both manipulated soup spoons with our right hands.

"My God," she breathed softly. "How awful!"

"Not really, honey. I mean, you get used to it. This is the first time that anyone else would have noticed what was going on. I guess I should stay away from the most haunted places in Ireland, huh?"

"*Dead people*, Daddy?"

"Not very often. I'm not one of those persons with whom everybody in the family seems to check in on the way to Heaven."

"Mom?"

I hadn't told her about the two incidents with Madonna, but I suppose I knew she would ask. So I recited that part of the tale too. I even mentioned Jackie Curran's lady with the "blonde hair and the blue dress." Jean leaned back against the booth, closed her eyes, and drew a very deep breath. "Wow, like *wow*!"

"Monsignor Ryan, excuse me, Uncle Punk, says it's a neo-Neanderthal vestige, a crude means of communication that evolved before we humans had developed more elaborate forms of speech. Some of it still lingers in a few of us. Jackie Curran and I have a common ancestor back several generations. I suppose we inherited it from him, or maybe more likely from her. Other members of the Ryan family may have it too. It's really no great big deal, Jean."

"I'd die if one of my kids was that way." She sat stiff and upright, eyes still closed.

"But you wouldn't die if your daddy was that way?"

She relaxed and laughed. "Am I ever a nerd! It might be kind of fun to have a kid around who's even better at weather forecasting than John Coleman."

"Jackie's luckier than me. I'm not much good at forecasting anything."

"Was it *really* Mom?"

"I don't know. Probably not. But as Uncle Punk said, the message of forgiveness and reconciliation and beginning over again is something I should believe even without such an experience."

"Okay, Daddy." Jean seemed to be checking that item off her agenda. "Oh, thank you very much," to the waitress who filled her wineglass. "Hmmm, these scallops are yummy. Now, Daddy, one more question. You didn't call me Jean back there in the cathedral when you had your fit, or whatever it was. You called me another name."

"Did I?" Rapidly sinking heart.

Jean's brown eyes flashed dangerously. "You sure did. Who is she? Who is Ciara?"

29

So in the Creole Restaurant in Dun Laoghaire, South County, Dublin, a warm, shadowy, pleasant basement room with marvelous scallops meunière, I told my daughter about Ciara Kelly.

"My God, Daddy!"

"As Uncle Punk would say, *indeed*!"

"You went to bed with her," Jean asked incredulously.

"I'm afraid so."

"Don't be afraid about it," she reproved me. "I'm impressed."

"Surprised that your father might be a lover?"

"I, like, totally won't comment on that. And you've come here to Ireland to find her?"

"I guess."

"Like wow. *Wow*!"

"I'm not sure where to begin looking." I began working on my sherry trifle, a delicacy that Jean sternly refused. For her it was still a fast day of the plan. "I'm still trying to figure out what Ireland is all about and where to start— eager and uncertain, I guess."

"You mean, you haven't any strategy at all?"

"Not yet. Maybe tomorrow."

"I'll help," she said firmly.

"No, you won't."

"The hell I won't, Daddy, and don't argue with me. That's settled."

Indeed it was settled with, as it would develop, horrible results for the two of us.

When we returned to the hotel, the young man from the morning, who was named Liam, I was informed in tones which indicated that I ought to know it, was waiting for us. I was sent off to bed while Jean and Liam went forth to explore Dublin pubs.

At breakfast the next morning, while we watched the rain pour down on Stephen's Green across the street, I asked about the pub exploration.

"It was all right," she said without too much conviction, "especially after I drew a few lines."

"Fresh?"

"They certainly move a lot more quickly over here."
She daintily dug out a piece of none-too-tender grapefruit
from its rind. "He made poor Tim Murphy seem slow and
bashful."

"Really."

"They're smooth talkers, and you get so charmed listening to them that you almost don't notice what they're
doing while they're talking. *Well*, I sorted him out, to use
their term."

"And that's the end of Liam?"

"Oh, no, not at all!" she exclaimed in mock horror. "He
just knows what the rules are now."

It was arranged that she would try to photograph
Dublin in the rain and I would explore the Irish National
Gallery, in whose highly recommended restaurant we
would meet for lunch. And so we did; however, Jean had
not been taking photographs.

She was wearing the jumpsuit with the pink blouse
again. She dropped her trench coat and her rain scarf on
the chair between us, sat down, and placed a photocopy of
the *Irish Times* in front of me.

"There she is, Daddy. You weren't kidding. She really
is a knockout. Her real name is Clare Keenan, and her father was a surgeon, not a lawyer. Everything else fits. The
poor woman, she was so young when it happened, younger
even than me."

It was the lead story in the *Irish Times* under the head-
line "Irish Girl Saved by Foreign Legion." The basic facts
were all there just as Ciara—or Clare—had told me. Not a
hint that she'd been raped so often that she'd lost count. In
those days the *Irish Times* would not have reported that.
Presumably everyone in Ireland could read between the
lines and no one would ever mention it.

"A regular Sherlock Holmes," I remarked.

"She might not even be in Ireland . . ."

"There must be people in Ireland who know where she
is."

The restaurant of the Irish National Gallery is in the basement, in a large room painted light green. Everything but the food, which was indeed excellent, reminded me of the dining room at the Art Institute in Chicago. There must be some worldwide rule about gallery eating places. We ate fresh salmon and lamb chops, and I had another sherry trifle and drank a good French wine.

"What next?" Jean demanded briskly.

"It says here that her father, Patrick Keenan, is a surgeon at St. Mary's Hospital in Castlebar in County Mayo and the family lives in Westport. Perhaps that would be the best place to start."

"That was sixteen years ago, Daddy. Maybe her parents are dead. Maybe no one there remembers her anymore."

"Maybe. But do you have any other ideas?"

"I'm going back to the *Irish Times* this afternoon to see what else I can find. See you at supper at the Shelbourne."

"What about Liam?"

"No big deal. He'll come around about half past nine to continue our pub tour. If he doesn't show, well, Daddy, there are a lot of cute boys in Dublin."

I returned to the hotel, huddling under the protection of an inexpensive umbrella I'd bought in a store on Grafton Street, went into the lobby of the Shelbourne, tossed my raincoat on the floor, put the folded umbrella on top of it, and sank into a vast easy chair near the fireplace. It was late for lunch and early for high tea, so I had the lobby to myself to think. A solicitous waiter discovered me and was only too happy to take my order of a Jameson's neat.

Despite the intensity of my love for Ciara, a love that had become an addiction only a few weeks before, she no longer seemed real to me. Ciara was now somehow a mythological figure, someone who must be pursued, indeed, but no longer a real woman whose warm, soft body would open like a flower for me again. No matter what came of the quest for Ciara Kelly—or Clare Keenan—or whatever she was called now, she would never again be my lover. That part of it was finished forever.

Nonetheless, she must be found. Why? Because I loved her and needed her and could not do without her.

Contradictory? Sure. I was in such an advanced state of sexual hunger that I could no longer think logically much of the time.

Most berserkers have suffered a long period of sexual frustration.

The absence of sex in my life had never snuffed out my intellect before.

But I'd never made love to a woman like Ciara Kelly before.

I opened a map of Ireland on one knee and unfolded Jean's photocopy of the front page of the *Irish Times* on my other knee. Clare Keenan's family were gentry, her father a surgeon, her grandfather a lawyer, descendants of the Keenan's Keep in Old Castle on the road between Westport and Newport. So she was a descendant, indeed, of the Constance Keenan whose picture had hung in Dufficy's Irish Store in Chicago, a deliberate attempt on the part of somebody to throw me off the chase. Or maybe an accident or a coincidence. Who could say?

Somewhere the family, which had been Anglo-Irish aristocrats, turned into Irish Catholic gentry, educated professionals whose children went to private schools and then to Trinity College, not University College, Galway, or University College, Dublin. If you were West of Ireland Catholic gentry, you kept one foot in the Anglo-Irish Dublin Protestant elite. It didn't offend your Catholic clientele; and, while the Protestants never fully accepted you, there was still some social prestige in associating with them. Besides, her father probably had a fair number of Protestant cousins.

Your headstrong daughter went off to the Congo and was savagely brutalized. She came home a bit of a heroine but also a bit of a disgrace. What did you do about her? You certainly didn't seek psychiatric help. You've got to pull yourself together, young woman. You have responsibilities. You've postponed your education too long. Now that this missionary fling of yours is over, you should settle down and earn your degree. Yes, Clare, since you can no longer get yourself to a nunnery—for what nunnery would want someone like you?—and since there's enough whispers about what happened to you in the Congo that the eligible young men would tend to shy away, get yourself to a university and become . . . what? A nurse? A teacher? A sales clerk in an import shop?

A somewhat seedy-looking man in a rumpled gray suit, a battered black raincoat with missing buttons, and a gray cap, with a large umbrella in his hand, settled down in the next easy chair. What the hell? He has the whole hotel lobby available and he has to sit near me.

I drank my Jameson's cautiously. The quest was real now, largely because my daughter had made it real. I must clear the cobwebs out of my brain and start thinking again.

Even if I am never to have you again, Ciara Kelly, I am still going to find you.

Where else to pick up the trail but in Castlebar and Westport? Even if her parents were dead, surely there would be cousins or friends or other relatives who might be able to give me hints. What had happened in the life of Clare Keenan between 1969, when she was a young woman Jean's age, and 1984 to turn her into Ciara Kelly?

She was still beautiful and still haunted by what had happened in the Congo. She was also very well educated, self-possessed, desirable, witty, and, after some hesitancies, wonderful in bed. She had shaken off some of the ill effect of what the Simbas had done to her, healed most if not all of her wounds, and become learned and sophisticated in the process; university training, graduate school probably, and some other terrible secret too.

Where else to go but to Clew Bay, the stronghold of Grace O'Malley, the pirate queen? And perhaps something might be learned in Keenan's Keep, now a hotel, on the bay between Newport and Westport. If the ghost of Connie Keenan really did haunt the old castle, and if my psychic instincts were working, perhaps the ghost could tell me something.

It was an absurd notion, but the whole search was absurd. Real now, yes indeed, but not yet urgent.

"The young lass ought not to be searching the files of the *Irish Times*," said the man with the gray cap, which he had taken off. He was lean, not unhandsome, about my age. His eyes were deep brown and intelligent, his high forehead, under a brown-haired, unruly widow's peak, had a permanent bemused frown, his thin face hinted at wit and wisdom, an actor or a writer perhaps, down on his luck.

"Who the hell are you?" I demanded fiercely, an annoyed berserker.

"Finnegan," he said in a brogue so strong that I had a hard time understanding him. "I'm in the Garda, don't you see. James Finnegan." He reached across the fireplace and handed me a warrant card. He was indeed a Detective Chief Superintendent James P. Finnegan. A major more or less, or maybe a light colonel. More cops.

"Do Irish detective superintendents normally tell Americans that they ought not to read back issues of the *Irish Times*?" I demanded curtly.

"Ah, no." You might decide that he was not an actor but perhaps an undertaker, or an out-of-work bartender. Then you would notice the shrewd, hard brown eyes and you would instinctively say cop. "Only in certain rare circumstances, where the Yanks are asking questions that might cause trouble."

"We haven't asked any questions yet."

"That's a fact," he agreed mildly. Even his voice sounded like that of an undertaker or a sympathetic bartender.

"Why should we not ask the questions that you think we're going to ask, Superintendent?"

"Simple enough. They're dangerous questions to ask."

"Have you ever been in a war, Superintendent?"

"No." He raised a bushy eyebrow. "I have not."

"I have, and I don't frighten easily."

"I didn't think the United States of America gave away Distinguished Service Crosses to men who do frighten easily. But would you mind if I gave a small lecture on recent Irish history?"

"Lecture away, Detective Superintendent James P. Finnegan."

"My friends," he sighed the typical Irish sigh, "call me Jaymo."

"Indeed."

"Well," he sighed again, "as you know, there's been

trouble in Ireland for the last fifteen years, particularly in the six counties of Northern Ireland."

"I do read the newspapers, Superintendent; incidentally, I presume you're from the Special Branch?"

"You might say that." He produced a pipe, stuffed it with tobacco as ineffectually as though he were Blackie Ryan, lit the pipe, which created an acrid smell that made me faintly dizzy, and continued. "What you might not know, and sure, there's no reason for you to know it, is that it did not begin with the IRA at all. In the late sixties, Captain Terrence O'Neill, the Prime Minister at Stormont—that was the seat of the Northern Ireland government—and Sean Lemass, our taoiseach, began a series of friendly conversations. Everyone was confident that we were entering a new era of peace and friendship between the two Irelands. That pleased most of us, but it didn't please much a lot of the Ulster Protestants, who voted O'Neill out of office. The trouble was that expectations of peace and equality and justice—all very great powerful attractive things—had been stirred up among the Catholics, but among some other folks, too, particularly in the universities, who thought it was time to bury the past. Do you follow me?"

"I'm not a secondary school student, Superintendent."

Yet another Irish sigh. "Well, the civil rights movement began, modeled after your own American civil rights movement. It was mostly university students, and many, but not all of them, Catholic. They were all young, all enthusiastic, and all convinced, poor daft young ones, that they could do in Northern Ireland what Martin Luther King did in the American South. Sure, it was a grand idea, but they didn't realize that the Royal Ulster Constabulary, and particularly the B Specials, a reserve force dominated by the Orange Lodgers up there, made your man Bull Connor look like a member of the American Civil Liberties Union, and that the London government was not headed by a man like John Kennedy or Lyndon Johnson or even Richard Nixon."

"Bernadette Devlin and her crowd?"

"The very same." He seemed pleased by my knowledge of recent Irish history. "At first it looked like things were going their way. They had great, powerful demonstrations, thousands of people, and your Orangemen were stupid enough to attack them and beat them, which earned them sympathy for their bravery here in the South, and in England, and I suppose all over the world."

"I remember the pictures on television."

"Well, the crowd in Stormont got nervous, and, sure, they behaved predictably. They unleashed the RUC and the B Specials, not only on the civil rights young ones, but on Catholics in Derry and in the Falls Road in Belfast. You could be a Catholic woman or child, minding your own business on the streets of either place, and find yourself banged over the head by a B Specials club. The fools seemed to enjoy especially doing it in front of television cameras, figuring that that would terrorize the Catholics back into passivity."

"Selma all over again."

"That's what the civil rights kids thought, anyway." He sighed, relit his pipe, and admitted to the hovering waiter that he would like a pint of Guinness. "Sure, I'm not exactly on duty, if you take my meaning. Anyway, there was a Labour Party in power in England, and they were half sympathetic with the civil rights kids, even if they were Irish, and it was embarrassing to them, being Leftists and all, for the whole world to see on television police in a province of the United Kingdom acting like they were American rednecks. So they sent in British troops—mind you, to protect the Catholics from the RUC and the B Specials and the Orange Lodge thugs. Paratroopers were cheered when they arrived in the streets of Derry and the Falls Road. Sure, Catholic women ran into the streets to give them cups of tea. The British army, for the first time, had intervened in Northern Ireland to protect the Teagues, as the Catholics are called, from the Prots."

"I vaguely remember that."

"Most Americans do." He considered his Guinness balefully. "Somehow they forget the details of what happened next. At the time the British troops arrived, there probably weren't more than five or six guns in any of the Catholic neighborhoods in Northern Ireland. The IRA was split into two factions: the Officials, who were Marxists, but Irish Marxists, mind you, and the Provisionals, who are anti-Marxists. Your famous Provos. They were busy arguing among themselves. No one took them seriously, and there hadn't been any violence for over a decade. Your civil rights folk were as nonviolent as Martin Luther King and his friends.

"Well, there was a British election. Your wee Bach-playing gombeen-man, Edward Heath, became prime minister, and Reggie Maulding took over responsibilities for Northern Ireland. In three months the British army, which had come to protect Catholics, had been converted into an occupying army that smashed Catholic homes and beat up Catholics in the streets of Derry. They were supposed to be searching for guns, because the Ulster Protestants were convinced that the homes and churches of the Catholics were filled with guns—there'd soon be a Catholic uprising with the connivance of the British army. Heath and Maulding wanted to reassure the Prots they would tolerate no violence from the Teagues. So, typical of everything England has ever done in Ireland, they turned a bad situation into a disaster."

"And the invisible army crawled out of the cellars and the caves."

"Ah." He knocked the ashes out of his pipe and concentrated all his attention on the Guinness. He had still not taken off his raincoat. "You are a quick man, Mr. Brendan Ryan. Jesus, the lads were the only ones who were ready to protect the Catholics. Some of our politicians here on the South shipped guns up to them, not many guns, mind you, but enough to begin the job. There were a lot of folk who thought then and think now that there wasn't much choice in the matter. It was either guns from the Republic or an army from the Republic to save the Catholics in the North, and to tell the truth, we didn't have an army then."

"Exit civil rights, enter IRA."

"Right. By ordering a search for guns that weren't there, the government in London saw to it that the guns appeared, and then once more there were gunmen in the streets. The Brits continued to do everything wrong. There was a power-sharing thing, Catholics and Prots working together on town councils and the like, even a Prot lord mayor in Derry. No decisions made unless both groups agreed. It was working very well indeed, too well for men like Ian Paisley, of whom you've doubtless heard." He cocked an eye over at me over his Guinness.

"I've heard of him."

"So there was a strike by the Protestant unions and demonstrations by Paisley's folk and hints that the British army in the North would mutiny if it was ordered to support power-sharing—that's an old game the Brits have played in Ireland before—and Harold Wilson, that fine liberal left-wing socialist, backed down. It's been the gunmen ever since."

"So what has all this to do with Clare Keenan, also known as Ciara Kelly?"

"Well, now, I'm not saying it has anything to do with her." He knocked the rest of his ashes out of his pipe and filled it once again. "Most of the civil rights kids gave it up. They left Ulster for England or the United States or even for the South. A few of them, like the wee lass—Bernadette— stayed and got themselves into a radical fringe group, Marxist mostly, if you take what they say seriously, and you probably shouldn't. By that time they'd been reading Frantz Fanon and Regis Debray—himself a fairly respectable part of Mr. Mitterrand's government in France now— and were convinced that violence would succeed where nonviolence had failed. Bernadette herself now talks a strange mixture of Marxism and Irish nationalism and violent revolution. Sure, after what they did to her and her husband and her kids, you can hardly blame her."

"And?"

"Well, a few of them set up their own little terrorist groups, alternatives to the Provos, who didn't much like them. Sure, your Provos went to Communion every Sunday. But at first they weren't all that much worried about your atheist Marxists, not so long as they were blowing up bridges and power stations and not blowing up Provos. Well," he lit the pipe, "one thing led to another, and some of these young people, without all of them hardly realizing it, began to blow up people instead of bridges and power stations and ammunition dumps. And not just British soldiers, but pubs full of Protestants. Well, for the most part they were more reckless than the Provos, and, one way or another, they got themselves caught or got killed in skirmishes with the Provos, who decided that they wanted no part of godless communism in their revolution, if you take my meaning?"

"More or less."

"Sure, a few of the youngsters were half daft by then—if they weren't half daft to begin with. They thought that when they were let out of prison finally, they had to have themselves a wee bit of revenge on their friends who didn't go to prison, if you follow me."

I followed him all right. Clare had returned from the Congo an angry, wounded idealist and, in defiance of her parents, went to school at Queens in Belfast, precisely so she could join the civil rights movement. Still hurting from her brutalization and angry at brutes wherever they were, she had drifted into one of the radical fringe groups of the IRA. My Ciara a terrorist killer?

"Are you telling me that the Irish government and the Special Branch can't find these men and can't protect people from them?"

"Ah, well," he puffed fiercely on the pipe, "sure we find some of them, and we've done a reasonably good job of protecting the ones that need protection. Not that certain other governments haven't helped us, mind you. But there's a couple of lads, one in particular, that are powerful elusive. Imagine a handsome young fellow with some medical training, call him Rory McLafferty if you like, an actor, a comedian, a charmer, great mind and a brilliant speaker, probably a bit of a psychopath all along but not so's you'd notice it at first. Then he goes to prison and, sure, the screws—that's what they call the prison guards—don't like him at all and they make his life miserable. He goes around the bend altogether and swears he'll have revenge on everyone who betrayed him. Finally he escapes from prison, slips into the world underground, goes to Libya and Syria and Iran and God knows where else, and comes back to finish off his enemies and continue the work he'd begun. Only finishing off the enemies is what really matters, even if it means blowing up a sailboat in Chicago with the wrong people in it."

"He didn't do that," I said. "The other governments aren't keeping you informed."

"Is that so?" he asked, now giving up completely on the pipe. "What do you mean by that?"

So I told him about the shoot-out in the Karwick Plaza a little over a week ago.

"Aye," he nodded sadly, "trust the intelligence agencies, first of all, to overreact, and then not to keep one another informed."

"So you people, or your friends, lifted Ciara out of Chicago for the wrong reason?"

"Don't blame me, Mr. Ryan," he said sadly. "I only found out about it afterward. But you take my point now, do you not? Your man Rory McLafferty is a genius and a madman. He's given the slip to police forces in five or six countries. You don't want to have anything to do with him at all, at all."

"Why would he want to have anything to do with me?"

The Garda's eyes widened. "Wasn't I after telling you that? Well, perhaps I was being too Irish and thus too indirect. You see, he seems to think that you will lead him to Clare Keenan."

"What?" I suddenly felt very cold. I could see where the whole conversation was pointing. Right at me.

And Jean.

"The IRA Provos are not the only ones who have friends in the United States and here in Dublin. Even a psychopath like Rory is thought to be the savior of Ireland by some people. His American friends sent him your name—never mind how we know, because I don't even know how we know. I suspect, if you push me, that the Provos, who would like to be rid of him, are feeding information to some of our fellas in hopes that we will do to him what they'd like to do."

"I see," I said, feeling a deep anger rise up within me. "And his Dublin friends have told him that I've showed up here asking questions. And your American friends have made the same reports to you?"

"He wants Clare Keenan and he thinks you're the man

to find her for him, if you don't already know where she is. And he suspects the latter. He'll stop at nothing, sir; that's why we beg you to take your daughter and go home to America."

Sage advice. But not the sort to which Finn MacCool listens.

"I'll kill him, Jaymo Finnegan. I'll kill him if he doesn't leave Ciara alone. I've killed men before for harming a woman I loved, and I'm quite capable of doing it again."

It was not the Brendan Ryan I've known all my life who spoke those words, but a stranger, perhaps a devil, who had taken possession of my soul during the wild spring ritual dance, an ancient Celtic berserker, perhaps even the great Finn MacCool himself.

Detective Superintendent Finnegan looked at me with the astonishment he might display at a visitor from the planet Uranus. "We have laws against murder in the Republic of Ireland," he stammered.

"It'll either be in self-defense," I said coldly, "or you'll never catch me."

"We can't allow you to risk your life, Mr. Ryan," he said, jamming his pipe and tobacco into the pocket of his raincoat. He was a good cop like Mike Casey, and a smart one too. But he lacked the mixture of brilliance and bureaucratic disrespect that made Mike one of the finest cops in the world. Not his fault, God knows.

"If you want to protect my life, then you can forget about trying to make me give up my search for Ciara—or whatever her name is—and you can forget about trying to make me leave Ireland. And many thanks for providing me with lots of information I didn't have before."

"They said you were a reasonable man." He rose uncertainly.

"Or did they say I was a quiet man and a coward?"

"They didn't say you were a fool." He stood up, pulled his cap out of his pocket, and jammed it on his head. "For the love of God, Mr. Ryan, stay out of this."

"No, Detective Superintendent Finnegan, it is precisely for the love of God that I will not stay out of it."

What a pompous ass I was.

30

The Dublin-to-Galway train on the C.I.E. (the Irish National Railroad identified by the first letters of its Gaelic name) bounced with uncomfortable determination across the countryside, passing first through rain showers and then what British Isles weather forecasters call "sun showers." The temperature outside was certainly no more than fifty; it seemed even colder than that in the railroad car. Jean, wearing beige slacks and an Aran Island sweater, huddled within a Windbreaker but resolutely refused to complain.

"It looks like Wisconsin outside," she observed.

"The books say that the counties like Meath and Louth have some of the richest farms in Europe. It's only when you get to the Shannon River at Alone that you cross into the west of Ireland and begin to encounter poor farms and even poverty today. Those are the parts of Ireland where they raise potatoes and where people either starved or fled to America, especially in famine times in 1848 and '49. Then for the rest of the nineteenth century they were the wretched refuse of the earth who fled to America. Our people, the common folk, in other words . . ."

I could babble about the countryside now, but my craving for Ciara Kelly was stronger than ever.

"I think, Daddy," she sniggered wickedly, "if you look again at the map you'll see the town is called Athlone, not Alone. Just above it the Shannon widens into a broad lake called Lough Ree. When we finally find your friend Ciara or Clare or whatever we're going to call her, I'm going to come back, rent a houseboat on Lough Ree, and spend a week taking pictures of the Shannon and the countryside around it."

"Fine with me."

It was madness to permit Jeannie to join my search for Ciara Kelly (and Ciara Kelly she would always be to me). She came home from the *Irish Times* with pictures of Clare Keenan marching with Bernadette Devlin and civil rights demonstrations in Derry. I repeated almost verbatim my conversation with Detective Superintendent Jaymo Finnegan of the Special Branch. "I'm going out to Castlebar and to Westport," I told her firmly. "And you are going home to the United States, where you'll be safe."

Jean tilted her chin defiantly at me. "Just try to make me."

"These are very dangerous men, Jeannie. They could hurt you or even kill you."

"Only if I don't kill them first."

"It's not like the shoot-out at the Karwick Corral. This is a different situation. I don't want to have to worry about you."

"And I don't want to have to worry about you," she fired back at me, her eyes blazing. "I'm not going to let you do this by yourself. Aren't you the one who told me that I shouldn't try to do things by myself?"

"That's different."

"*B-u-l-lshit!*"

The argument went on, though it was obvious to me after the first few moments that eventually I would lose.

Jean decided that the best way to make our trip would be to take the train from the Connolly Station across the Liffey, along the old Royal Canal north of Phoenix Park near the great seminary at Maynooth and on to Galway City. We'd spend the night at the Railway Hotel in Galway (built over the railway terminal) and then drive to Ashford Castle in County Mayo. The next morning we would go on to Castlebar and perhaps even, she conceded, spend a night at Keenan's Keep on Clew Bay—though "I'd hardly expect, Daddy, that we're going to find any clues there."

Clues? For Jeannie it was a game, a great adventure, a romantic search for a woman with whom she was already partly identifying—and also partly resenting. In the adventure movies we Americans see on television, the good guys always win. Unfortunately, there is no guarantee of that in the real world.

"Besides, if your man Jaymo is following us, which I'm sure he is, it would be easier for him if we stay in the big hotels that everyone knows."

The charming, witty young taxi driver who brought us to the railway station, the kind of devil-may-care comic who reminds you of the actor who played Florie Knox in the PBS series *The Irish R.M.*, promised us that we would have a "grand time out in the west."

"Sure," he said, "till you get to the Shannon all you meet is West Brits. The real Irish are all in the west. Few of us enough left these days. You won't see our like again."

"An endangered species?" I asked, half joking.

"Ah, endangered beyond repair," the cabbie agreed. "But, sure, we've been saying that for three thousand years. So you should not expect us to disappear tomorrow."

So it was that we passed through Athlone, now properly pronounced, in the driving rain and lumbered on to Galway city, a strange, bewitching mixture of the ugly and the picturesque, part Gypsy sorceress, part Gaelic princess, and part Aer Lingus hostess on a fully booked flight. It was celebrating its five hundredth anniversary, perhaps with a sigh of relief that it had lasted so long and still enjoyed reasonably good prospects for the future.

The sun was indeed going down on Galway Bay, and the splendid blue sky slowly turning dark when we checked into the Great Southern Railway Hotel above the railway terminal, a nineteenth-century dowager, quite conscious that she had once been among the very best of her kind and striving to remain sufficiently renewed and rejuvenated to be the most impressive lady in town without spending too much money. The corridors had been freshly carpeted and painted, the rooms were reasonably clean and newly wall-papered, and the veneer on the furniture in the room was effectively resistant to scratch and stain. Moreover, thank goodness, the central heating seemed to work.

I went upstairs to the Claddagh Grill for a late afternoon Jameson's overlooking Galway Bay and the "Claddagh" area (it meant quay), where at one time there had been a community of densely packed thatched cottages inhabited by an impoverished people whose culture was alleged to be unique in all of Ireland. The Claddagh was urban-renewed out of existence just a few years before the threatened destruction of such an ecological/historical resource would have brought out hordes of angry demonstrators.

There was a swimming pool next to the grill. You could

indeed sit at tables around the pool and sip your "jar" with the pretense that you were in a tropical resort. Where else but in Ireland would they put in a glassed-in swimming pool on the fifth floor of a hotel that was a hundred and fifty years old in a city five hundred years old next to a bay that song had made perhaps the most famous bay in all the world?

Jean appeared in the grill wrapped in an enormous towel, discarded the towel, and very quickly dived into the pool attracting, as one might expect, considerable attention from the pre-dinner drinkers who did not always see a lithe young woman in a string bikini on the fifth floor of the Great Southern Railway Hotel.

"Ow!" she screamed as she broke the surface of the water, "it's *cold!*" She kept on swimming, however.

Spring in Ireland—bikini-clad Yank colleen's swimming in an enclosed pool over Galway Bay.

Soon Ciara and I would swim in the same pool.

That was an absurd thought. Still I swore to myself it would happen.

Jean had bid Liam farewell in Dublin, promising to let him know when she returned. She also called Chicago to make her peace with Tim. "I apologized for being a bitch and starting both the fights," she confided to me as our train left Dublin behind. "I told him that if he still wanted to be friends when I came back we could talk about it. He was very nice. Daddy, what do apologies do to men?"

I thought of Eileen Kane on the balcony at Grand Beach. "Aphrodisiac."

"You're terrible." She poked my arm lightly, a means of communication that I had come to interpret as meaning I was really rather cute but I said some of the damnedest things. Nonetheless, she seem pleased by my answer.

Jean was enjoying the first phases of our search, but I was not. The conflicting emotions that rumbled inside me were hard to name or define. I was eager to find Ciara and deeply worried about her, convinced now that the terror which I had experienced in Chicago, and which intermittently returned, was terror that was still ahead for her. The pain and degradation were yet to come. They threatened but they might be averted. As much as I wanted to find her and save her, I dreaded the impending feelings of doom and death that weighed heavily on me since we'd pulled out of the Connolly Station in Dublin. I was worried about Jean, who was so much fun to be with but far too young and innocent to be permitted such risks. And I was implacably determined to kill Rory McLafferty if he threatened to harm my woman.

I killed him often in my sleep that night. He resolutely refused to stay dead.

The next morning we rented another Renault and drove across the Corrib River by the salmon weir, and around the great ugly gray pile of stones that is the new cathedral (the bishop of which was supporting communist regimes in El Salvador and Nicaragua and refused to meet President Reagan when he came to Galway. I've never voted for a Republican in my life, but I couldn't help but wonder whether his lordship would support a communist government in County Galway too).

Jean drove carefully out of Galway on the Headford road to Cong, just inside County Mayo (where the film *The Quiet Man* was made), and to Ashford Castle, one of the world's great hotels, which has been described as the kind of castle that God would create if He had as much money as a Philadelphia millionaire.

The hotel is a mixture of fourteenth-century castle, seventeenth-century hunting lodge designed like a miniature French château, nineteenth-century country home for the Guinness family, and a twentieth-century addition that expanded it to twice its size. It now looks like a Disney World medieval castle—broad, neatly trimmed lawns, thick oak beams, deep carpet, red brocaded walls, wonderful paintings of the Irish countryside (and a few nudes of an Italian peasant girl, painted by an artist whom the Guinnesses must have liked), and great windows overlooking the northern end of Lough Corrib, sometimes glowing peacefully in the sunlight, sometimes frothing in the wind, sometimes shrouded in fog or beaten by heavily dancing raindrops. Since it was Ireland, all of these things could happen in the same day or even in the same hour.

"What's this beautiful place?" Jean peered closely at a painting of water and beach and sun and green hills. "I want to take pictures of it. Is there any place in the whole world more gorgeous?"

"Ciara and you would agree." I looked over her shoulder at the copper plaque on the frame. "It's the strand at Inch, down in County Kerry. She says she wants to die there because it's the closest place to Heaven in all the world."

"I hate the woman." Jean lingered at the canvas. "Absolutely hate her. I'll make common cause with her against you when we find her."

"Spoken like a true Irishwoman."

"What else?"

Jean wanted to check in and push on to Castlebar, a market town and the administrative center of County Mayo (and the site of the battle described so vividly in the novel *The Year of the French*), to begin our inquiries.

But I wanted time to work out more clearly my game plan: first of all the hospital administrators, then the newspaper, then the parish priest, then the pubs. The questions had to be thought through very carefully and then translated into the peculiar, indirect, answer a question with a question West-of-Ireland style. We wouldn't get a second chance. Moreover, it seemed to me that Jean and I ought to work separately, that she should find the pubs and other gathering places of young people in Castlebar and see if there were any memories in the new generation of Clare Keenan, perhaps even a relative who could tell us something about her. While I sat in my vast and elegant nineteenth-century room, whose furnishings would have deceived anyone but an antique specialist, and wrote out the questions and committed them to memory, Jean dashed down to the concrete breakwater, to hire a boat for an exploration of the northern end of Lough Corrib. I warned her to be careful, and she replied by telling me that Cong was the faerie capital of Ireland and the little people would protect her.

As it turned out, they did a poor job.

I watched her haggle with two old countrymen at the pier in front of the hotel and then bounce confidently into a small boat—little more than a canoe—with an outboard motor and chug out into the lake.

In the distance a rainstorm was gathering over the ocean and moving in our direction. I was tempted to rush down to the pier to call her back, but it was too late and I would embarrass her if I tried. At first the rain was light and the visibility unaffected.

As I turned to my work of planning our campaign, I noted a big speedboat sweep by the castle and curve away toward the far side of the lake. They were going pretty fast, I thought idly.

After I had finished the final draft of my questions, memorized them, torn them up and, with a nod to James Bond, flushed them down the toilet, I telephoned Mike Casey in Chicago. "I'll fly over," he said simply. "Collect Nick Curran and catch a plane tonight."

"Thanks much, Mike, but not yet. If I need help I'll yell."

"You need help now."

"Not yet. A small reconnaissance team before we send in the main force."

Mike was not convinced, but he finally agreed. "Call me every day at this time at this number here at the gallery. If a day goes by and we don't hear from you, the main force will move in."

"You should have been a general." I laughed as I hung up. Very clever strategy. A shame I hadn't thought of it first.

Then I did have an idea. I called Mike back, hoping that no one at the switchboard was listening. "Can you get me an Uzi?"

"What the hell is that? An Italian painter?"

"You know damn well what it is."

"Do you know how to work one of those?" Mike asked tersely.

"I won the marksmanship prize with the M16 in ROTC, and I used one in Vietnam. I'm told the Uzi is a lot simpler."

"Too damned many people with marksmanship prizes," Mike said uneasily. "You and that impish little redneck chick."

"I'm not asking for an Israeli machine pistol for

Cindasoo. Though when you bring the reserves, maybe you could bring her along."

"Main force, not reserves. All right, you want one with a silencer, I suppose?"

"Naturally."

"I can get it to you, as long as the Special Branch isn't inspecting the packages that are sent to you. I doubt that they're doing that yet. There'll be one waiting for you at Ashford Castle the day after tomorrow. They come in very neat little packages."

"And enough ammunition too."

"Enough for what? To fight off the whole Irish Republican Army?"

"Enough to hold off whoever needs to be held off until the main force arrives."

"Fair enough."

The Uzi automatic weapon was seen by most people for the first time when John Hinckley tried to assassinate President Reagan. If you remember the pictures on television of the incident, the Secret Service men reached inside their coats, pulled out what looked like a little boy's toy, opened the plastic folding stock, and held in their hands a weapon a little longer than an ordinary pistol but with no resemblance at all to the beloved tommy gun of Chicago crime films, or even the automatic weapons John Wayne fired so recklessly in the many different wars in which he fought. The Uzi didn't look like much of a weapon. Nonetheless, it was the best machine gun or machine pistol or automatic weapon (choose your own name) made anywhere in the world. Much better, even, than its closest rival, the Russian AK-47.

Perhaps I was out of practice. It had been eighteen years since I had fired my M16 for the last time. Maybe, if worse came to worst, the Uzi's excellence would compensate for my lack of practice.

Even now I wonder, quite literally, what possessed me to make the second phone call and ask for the weapon. It was the same hidden berserker inside me, I suppose, who decided to go into Dufficy's Irish Store after I had written Ciara Kelly out of my life, the inner demon that had sent me on this wild-goose chase to Ireland, the residual Irish lunatic who sent me into the jungle in search of Marie's bathing pond, the reckless Celtic lover whose lips had drawn sweet milk from Marie Tho's pliant nipples and whose body had ruthlessly overcome Ciara's sexual fears. Ridiculous dissociation. Mary Kate Murphy would scoff at it. It was Brendan Ryan, not Finn MacCool, who had done all those things, Brendan Ryan who had told Superintendent Jaymo that he would kill Rory McLafferty if necessary, a Brendan Ryan whose existence I had pretended to ignore for most of my life, and now a Brendan Ryan who had crossed his Rubicon, or his Shannon, in search of an Israeli machine pistol.

I looked out the turreted window of my room. Torrents of rain were slashing into Ashford Castle. Lough Corrib had disappeared. The berth on the pier below me where Jean's little boat had been moored was empty.

I raced down the stairs and, hatless and coatless, dashed to the pier. Two old Irish countrymen in gray suits, gumshoe boots, and caps stood in the shelter of the boathouse, thoughtfully puffing on their pipes, like mourners in front of a funeral home.

"Did my daughter come back?" I shouted above the wind.

"Ah, sure, was she the wee lass in the Aran jersey?"

What a time to be answering questions with other questions. "Where the hell is she?"

"Wasn't I only after saying," said the other one, "maybe we ought to half think about taking the launch out to search for her?"

"That's the launch?" I pointed at a decrepit blue and white wooden boat that was at least a century older than the internal combustion engine.

"Ah, what else would it be but the launch?" said the first of the boat tenders.

"Are you coming with me or am I going to drive it myself?"

I jumped off the pier into the boat, which rocked in uneasy protest, shoved the hood back off the motor in the middle of the craft, pulled out what I supposed to be the choke, and turned over the key. The motor chugged reluctantly and refused to start. I jammed in the choke and tried again.

With great unhappiness and infinite weariness the old six-cylinder Chrysler marine engine, which certainly had existed longer than I had, spurted into life.

"Sure," said one of the old fellows, as he awkwardly climbed down next to me, "isn't that the first time the old gal has started so quickly?"

We putt-putted slowly into the whitecaps, small by Lake Michigan standards, probably only a foot or a foot and a half, but dangerous for a shallow little fishing boat like Jean's. "Which way should I go?" I demanded.

"Well, wasn't the lass saying now that she wanted to take a picture of the island down the lake where St. Patrick's navigator is buried? Isn't that Inchagoill?"

"Which way is that?" I had to shout because the wind was howling fiercely and the rain was pounding like a hundred drumsticks on the roof of the tiny cabin.

"It wouldn't be a mistake, would it," said the younger of the two boatkeepers, a man around seventy, I should guess, "to head straight south to Inchagoill Island? It's over in that direction." He pointed vaguely to the right with his pipe, which he then quickly replaced in his mouth. It was the closest to a declarative sentence I had heard from either of them. Dear God in Heaven, please let Jeannie be alive, please, please, please.

Ten or fifteen minutes later, after fighting our way through rain that was sometimes so thick we could barely see the prow of the boat (and the windshield wiper in the front of the cabin didn't work), the downpour eased, the clouds lifted, and the mists swept away temporarily. "Ah, sure," the young fella pointed with his pipe, "wouldn't that be something floating in the water over there?"

With tight throat and sinking heart, I turned the boat toward the floating object. It looked like the prow of a fishing boat. "Isn't that the Star of the Sea?" the older fella asked, gesturing with his pipe. "And hasn't someone cut it in half?"

"Doesn't it look like your man drove a launch right through the middle?"

With Jeannie in it.

RITE OF SPRING • 319

31

"Could the wee lass swim?" The old fella (about seventy-five) touched my arm respectfully as I slumped over the wheel of the boat, paralyzed by fear. "Might she have made it to the shore of the island?"

Gently he eased me away from the wheel and steered us toward the shore, throttling back to slow speed. "You wouldn't want to hit some of the rocks, would you now?"

We chugged around the island, maybe half a mile square of trees, thick underbrush, and rocky shoreline. On the far side he turned off the motor and we drifted toward a wooden plank, nailed perilously to a piling a couple of yards out into the lake. The plank was covered with three or four inches of water. The young fella tried three times to loop the boat's rope around the piling. Finally on the fourth attempt he succeeded, and the boat drifted against the plank. "You get out first, sir," said the old fella. "Aren't we a bit slower than you?"

I slipped on the plank, lost my balance, teetered towards the lake, and then steadied myself against the boat.

"Careful now," said the young fella, unnecessarily.

I stepped off the plank onto the slippery rocks of the shore and saw a patch of brown fabric, perhaps ten yards farther down the shore. Ignoring the two old men, I slipped and stumbled and finally fell towards the dead tree hanging out over the water on which the fabric was caught.

Jeannie's jumpsuit, torn almost in two. I slumped down on the rock, buried my head in my hands. I should have listened to Jaymo. Now Jeannie was dead, a victim of my own brash stupidity. The rain started again, the mist closed in, the wind howled through the trees, a banshee mourning for the dead, and I sat there mostly oblivious to the elements, grieving for my lost child. Dear God in Heaven, forgive me.

"Sure," said one of the old men standing behind me,

"she might have kicked it off to swim to shore. It wouldn't hurt to look around the island for her, would it now?"

No, it certainly wouldn't hurt.

So we searched the island, which was once the site, they told me, of a monastery founded by St. Patrick, later a nest of pirates, and still later a fishing village, now uninhabited " 'cause, sure, there's no way to earn a living on a place like this, is there?"

The two old men would only slow me down on a search of the shore, and I didn't want to risk their lives by keeping them out in the rain much longer. I told them to wait for me in the boat and that I would explore the shoreline myself. They protested, none too convincingly, and shuffled back to the boat.

There was no discernible trail along the shoreline, so I slipped on the rocks and plowed through the mud and beat my way through the underbrush, paying no attention to my chattering teeth or shivering body, or to the rain that now assaulted me through my drenched clothes. I suppose it took an hour before I circled around the little island and came back to the boat. No sign of Jean. I must not despair. There had to be something else we could do.

"The lass was a clever one, was she not?" said the young fella, meditatively puffing his pipe.

"She's pretty smart," I admitted.

I slumped against the bow of the boat as it nudged against the shore and realized, for the first time, that I was panting with exhaustion.

"Would she not have known about the cathedral? And might she not have gone there to stay out of the rain? Sure, there's not much of a roof on it, but it's better than nothing, now, isn't it?"

Hope released another supply of adrenaline into my veins. "Where's the cathedral?"

"Isn't it down the path there now?" He waved his hands at what seemed to me to be a solid mass of trees and underbrush. I plunged into it and stumbled toward the center of the island. The path was a barely distinguishable gap in the underbrush, probably created for the occasional tourist who came to the island to visit the tomb of St.

Patrick's alleged navigator (why St. Patrick would have needed a navigator apparently was a question that did not arise).

I missed the cathedral entirely on my first attempt and ended up on the far side of the island. Wrong path.

I thought, irrelevantly, that I should have brought a raincoat, and turned back into the forest. I felt like I was dashing back into one of the circles of Dante's purgatory, a soggy, slippery prison, smelling of damp vegetation, in which I was condemned to run, soaking wet and haunted by guilt, with aching chest and exhausted legs, till the final judgment day.

I worked my way back along the trail with more care; my guilt-ridden panic would be of no help to Jean if she were still alive. Perhaps a third of the way across the island, I found the fork that I had, in my pell-mell rush, missed the first time. I sloshed for perhaps fifty yards in muck and slime, and emerged in a small clearing, in the center of which was a tiny ruin of a very old church, even less cathedral-like than Glendalough. No psychic vibes here, fortunately.

I was wrong. Ciara Kelly. Ciara Kelly. Ciara Kelly.

Pain, fear, humiliation, terror. Carrying my child. My child threatened with destruction.

I shook off the psychic feelings as best I could. There was a real child whose life was in jeopardy.

"Jeannie! Jeannie!" I shouted, as I blundered awkwardly into the ruin, stumbling over the rocks to the entrance and crashing into one of the walls.

"Daddy, where's your raincoat?"

She was hunched down under the bit of roof that remained of the church, a soggy, crumpled little-girl doll wearing blue underwear with a white stripe, the ridiculous analogue of men's underwear which, for some crazy reason, women were now wearing, too.

I swept the soggy doll into my arms.

"You should have gone back for your raincoat," she insisted, hugging me fiercely. "You might get pneumonia."

"That'll be two of us."

"But I'm not *old!*" she giggled.

A very tough young woman, this daughter I was still getting to know. I offered to carry her back down the trail to the boat, but she insisted she was capable of walking by herself. "I wouldn't give those bastards the satisfaction."

"What bastards?"

"It was a big speedboat. They came out of the mists, saw me, turned around, and deliberately cut the boat in half."

"It wasn't an accident?"

"No way. I think they came back to run over me too, but I stayed deep underwater as long as I could. God, Daddy, it was *cold*! When I came up finally, the mists were so thick they couldn't see me, but I heard them buzzing around looking so I guessed which way the island was and swam here. I thought it would take forever. Then I remembered this church and figured soaking wet or not, it was better to be out of the rain than in it. I know how you feel, Daddy. I want to kill those bastards too."

Tomorrow I would tell her about Grace O'Malley, the pirate who once ruled in these lands. Maybe there was O'Malley blood in us.

By the time we'd returned to the boat and the two cheering old men, whose names, Jean whispered to me impatiently, were Seamus and Dermot, the storm had swept through. Cheerful white clouds were racing across the clean windswept sky, and Lough Corrib, smelling of fresh spring life, seemed to be merrily laughing with the four of us as we wrapped a huge blanket, found in the locker in the cabin of the boat (which blanket probably had not been cleaned since before the Easter rising of 1916), around my shivering but laughing daughter and helped her on the boat.

Her adventure seemed to have neither frightened nor daunted her. (She peeled off the underwear beneath the blanket—"We wear them, Daddy, because they feel sexy as hell.") In fact, her reactions seemed merely to be anger and determination to get even. Both emotions were enhanced— like a fire on which gasoline has been thrown—when we passed Grace O'Malley's Hen's Castle and Seamus, the old fella, told us the story.

Grace's husband, Donal O'Flaherty, had various nick-

names such as "the Battler" and "the Cock" because he was
an ill-tempered, contentious, difficult man ("Though, sure,
he didn't dare give herself any guff, not at all, at all").
"Well, he had a great terrible feud with the Joyces, and
themselves no better than they had to be, who lived in the
mountains south of here. One day the Joyces caught him
hunting in the mountains and killed him. They always
wanted this castle, called it Cock's Castle, they did, after
himself, and so, with him out of the way, they swept down
on it with a whoop and a holler, figuring that no woman in
the world could keep the Joyces away from a castle that
they wanted. Well, they reckoned without herself. Beat the
livin Bejesus out of them, she did, and ever after it's been
called the Hen's Castle, and mind ya, lass, that was a compliment."

Jean's eyes were shining brightly. "And then what happened?"

So by the time we'd got back to Ashford Castle, we'd
heard many of the Grace O'Malley legends, how she'd divorced her second husband, Iron Dick Burke, a year and a
day after the marriage, once she'd taken over his castle,
but, sure, after she got rid of the poor man, she discovered
that she loved him, so she took him back, and didn't they
have themselves a son who became the first Lord Mayo and
keep the O'Malleys going here in the county for another
couple of hundred years. About her being a better sailor
than Sir Francis Drake, about her ruling the whole of the
West of Ireland coast from her stronghold on Clare Island
in Clew Bay. Sure, she really wasn't a pirate at all, at all,
she just charged a heavy tax on them ships that wanted to
go through her part of the ocean. Mind ya, they all paid.
About how the English were afraid to fight her and made
peace with her, about the English governor who tried to put
her son in prison, and didn't herself go all the way to Queen
Elizabeth and get her son and all their rights and proper-
ties back? Whatever you say about Queen Bess, and she was
no better than she had to be either, she knew a real lady
when she saw one.

"Are all those stories true, Daddy?" Jean whispered as
we walked across the lobby of Ashford Castle as inconspicu-

ously as you can when you are soaking wet and one of you is wearing a battered old blanket that trails across the floor behind you.

"They are indeed, Jean. She was one of the greatest women of her time or, indeed, of any time. Women didn't run clans in Ireland in those days. But Grace O'Malley did, according to the historians, because the men who were her followers admired and respected and liked her. She was also supposed to be gorgeous, but then, of course, aren't all Irish women?"

Jean ignored my compliment, her shining brown eyes far, far away, doubtless on Lough Corrib or on Clew Bay when Granuaile's swift, maneuverable galleys swept forth to do battle for her family and her clan and her freedom.

Later that night I was in Jean's room. She was curled up in bed, shrouded in towels, a terry cloth robe, and blankets, and sipping Jameson's, to which she was rapidly becoming as addicted as her father. "I'm still furious, Daddy," she said through clenched teeth. "They're evil, crazy men. I'm not going to let them push me around."

"It's not the sixteenth century and you're not Granuaile O'Malley, kid." I was sipping my own Jameson's.

Before she could answer, the phone rang. I had a reasonably good idea who it was. "Good evening, Superintendent Finnegan. A bit late, aren't you?"

Silence. And then: "Have you learned your lesson? Are you going home now?"

"Are you suggesting, Superintendent, that I should leave Ireland because the Gardai are incapable of protecting tourists on a boat in Lough Corrib?"

"That was a bloody stupid trick, going out on that lake."

"If Granuaile O'Malley was in the Hen's Castle, no one would get away with what happened this afternoon. Lough Corrib seems to have been safer in her day than it is now."

"Your man is unpredictable. He probably started out with the intention of frightening the wee lass and through her, you. Then he saw a chance to kill and changed his mind."

"A chance offered him by the Irish police."

"We can't be frigging everywhere," Jaymo Finnegan shouted. "We're only human and we're busy now trying to provide protection for your frigging president."

"I didn't vote for him, Superintendent," I said curtly. "My daughter and I will assume, from now on, that the Gardai are not able to protect us, and we'll take proper measures to protect ourselves. Good evening, Superintendent."

"Gee," my daughter said admiringly, "I bet you could play on Granuaile O'Malley's team too."

"He's not a bad man." I picked up my Jameson's tumbler. "He can't afford to let anything happen to us, so he's going to watch even more closely, after what happened today. And he does have some legitimate excuse. The 'Great Communicator' is on tour."

"Did you see the woman from Cong on television the other night? No, of course you didn't. You were home in the hotel, and Liam and I were in a pub. Anyway, RTE—that's the Irish television—asked her what she thought about the president coming to Ireland and stopping at Ashford Castle. 'Ah, well,' she says, 'I suppose it's all right, but he's only an old politician. It'd be much different if it was J.R. or Sue Ellen!' "

We both laughed and thus dismissed Rory McLafferty and his psychopathic schemes.

For Jeannie, there was an excuse. She was young, she was a romantic, she'd never experienced real danger before. For me there was no excuse at all. Yet, that day at Ashford Castle was the turning point. I had ordered an automatic weapon from Mike Casey, had rescued my daughter from a muddy, rain-drenched little island on Lough Corrib in the land of Grace O'Malley. I had warned Jeannie that it wasn't the sixteenth century but somehow, I had begun to think of myself as a pre-Christian Irish chieftain, and an invulnerable one at that. Whoever the demon was that lurked within Brendan Ryan—and he called himself Brendan Ryan, too, when he didn't think of himself as Finn MacCool—took over that day. The quiet man who didn't like competitive sports, who almost never argued with his friends, who avoided conflict whenever possible, who al-

326 • ANDREW M. GREELEY

ways offered the most cautious and conservative advice to his clients, that Brendan Ryan, who knew he was very vulnerable indeed, went into eclipse.

Granuaile O'Malley's husband Donal O'Flaherty was called Donal-on-Chogaidh, Donal of the Battles. Fair enough. Now I was Brendan-on-Chogaidh. My enemies had taken my woman and threatened my daughter. I would show them no mercy. I did not give voice to any of this foolishness, I didn't even think it explicitly. I didn't have to. The lust-crazed Celtic berserker within me was convinced of his invulnerability. It was not necessary to think at all except about ways of destroying the enemy. What had started as a search for Ciara Kelly had now become a game that was an end unto itself.

We would learn only too soon, both Jean and I, that we were by no means invulnerable.

32

We were still feeling invulnerable and mindlessly exhilarated the next day as we pushed ahead in our search for Ciara. We sang Irish and Irish American tunes, Clancy Brothers variety, on our ride from Cong to Castlebar. My pitch was better than my daughter's, but I lacked her forthright confidence that she knew all the lyrics of a song, even if that meant she had to make them up.

The thick morning fog had blown away when we arrived at Castlebar, singing of "Bold Fenian Men." Jean may have had in mind the men of 1848. I was thinking of Finn MacCool's band of followers.

Castlebar, as the name indicates, was Norman in its origin. Now, however, it was a curious mixture of typical Irish village, with attractively painted storefronts and narrow sidewalks, and Wisconsin resort town with supermarkets, filling stations, and bustling crowds. If this is what the market center of County Mayo was like during a recession, I thought, what must it be like when the country is prosperous?

On the outskirts of Cong I told Jean about the film *The*

Quiet Man, which had been made just outside the town, and explained how in the original short story the protagonist was not a big fellow like John Wayne but a little man who even looked like a coward. Who could believe that John Wayne was a coward?

"Maybe I'm prejudiced in favor of little men," I concluded, watching in the sideview mirror to see if a blue VW hatchback with Dublin license plates, which seemed out of place on the main street of Cong, was following us.

"You're not little." Jean pushed the car around a lorry. "If you are then so am I. And I'm not. So that's that. Right?"

"Right." I could not see the blue car. Perhaps it was following but at a safe distance. Where else would we be going but Castlebar?

After we arrived in the town, Jean and I split up, she with a camera over her shoulder, since the photographer's role would give her an excuse to talk to young people her own age. Eight hours later I dragged myself wearily into the lounge bar of the Breaffy House, tired and frustrated. I had learned absolutely nothing.

Yes, indeed, they had told me at St. Mary's Hospital that Dr. Keenan had been the most distinguished surgeon in the whole of County Mayo and one of the best in Ireland in the 1960s. He and his wife had been dead for some time now, however. The children? There was a surgeon in Liverpool, and the other married to a surgeon in Los Angeles. Another daughter? Clare? Oh, yes, she was the one that went to Africa, wasn't she? No, they knew nothing about her at the hospital. Nurse's training? Well, yes, that might be true, but we have no idea where.

The newspaper editor remembered the Congo incident, poor thing. Her father was a hard man, but she still would have been much better off if she'd gone to the university, wouldn't she now? Nursing school when she came back? That would be logical, wouldn't it? Bernadette Devlin and the civil rights? Young folk in Ulster? Not that I know of. She really never came back to County Mayo after what happened in the Congo. No, I haven't heard a word of her in ten to twelve years at least.

The parish priest of Castlebar was a retired professor of

classics from Maynooth. "Keenan? Keenan. Let me see. Well, there's lots of Keenans around here, you know. All a part of the clan from that castle. Haunted? Ah, go along with you, Mr. Ryan, you don't believe in haunted castles now, do you? Dr. Keenan . . . I've only been here five or six years so I can't recall any Dr. Keenan. Lived in Westport, you say? Well, sure, that's another parish altogether. Involved with the civil rights movement? No, I can't recall anyone by that name. Of course, it's a long way from Derry and Belfast to Maynooth, especially if you're a professor of the classics. Assaulted in the Congo? Sure, that was long before my time. Not at all, Mr. Ryan. Glad to be of help. Sorry I couldn't be of more help."

Certain that Jaymo Finnegan's men were trailing us, I also suspected that they might have been ahead of us. The owner of the pub nearest St. Mary's Hospital admitted that "now and then a few doctors stopped by for the occasional pint" but could not recall a Dr. Keenan. "A surgeon, you say? Ah, well, they're the worst drinkers of all. I wouldn't want one of them cutting me open with a knife but, no, if Dr. Keenan took the occasional drink, he never took it here."

There were still several hours before I was due to rendezvous with Jean, so I drove down to Westport, a curious fading relic of the nineteenth century with just enough picturesque Anglo-Irish elegance to suggest that whoever was responsible for historical preservation in Ireland should rush in quickly. The bartender in the lounge bar at the hotel was of no help, neither was the parish priest, who was also a new man, though he did permit me to glance at the funeral records and see that Ciara's parents had indeed been dead for almost ten years, dying only a few months apart. And sure enough, there was her own name, Clare Fiona Keenan, born August 29, 1950. So she was not quite thirty-four. Ah, to be so young that you could give away three or four months!

There was still plenty of time and the weather was still lovely, so I drove south through the Murrisk, which was Grace O'Malley's stronghold, and into County Galway, the country of her bitter enemies, the Joyces. On the road to Letterfrack and Clifden, the heart of the barren, rocky, but somehow hauntingly lovely Connemara peninsula, I stopped at Kylemore Lake, on whose smooth waters stood stately and serene Kylemore Abbey, where Ciara had gone to school, according to the article in the *Irish Times*. The young nun who spoke with me was wearing a brief veil and a modified "airplane cabin attendant" religious habit that was popular in the United States fifteen years ago. She was very polite, very cultivated—Dublin haute bourgeoisie, I guessed—underneath the modern veneer, very much a strict S'ter of the Old School.

"Yes, of course, I knew Clare Keenan. We were classmates." (Had Jaymo's crowd not anticipated me here at Kylemore?) "What happened to her in the Congo was a terrible tragedy. We were so puritanical in Ireland in those days, it was almost impossible for a woman who had been through that kind of an ordeal to obtain any help. But her father was a doctor. He should have known better. Thank goodness women are finally obtaining their full rights in Ireland."

A stern young nun perhaps, but a feminist too. I didn't want to suggest that the problem wasn't so much women's rights as Victorian prudery enforced by Catholic obscurantism.

No, she had not seen Clare since they graduated. She'd heard that she went to nursing school in Derry. Civil rights movement? There was a rumor to that effect. S'ter was studying in Rome at the time. In recent years, nothing at all. No, wait, someone, yes, a classmate, told me several years ago that she'd seen Clare in London at the theater . . . or perhaps at a concert. In any event, she was teaching at an English university, not Oxford or Cambridge, I'm sure, but seemed quite happy. The woman felt that Clare had left most of her problems behind her."

"The Congo you mean?"

"The Congo and her parents. Dr. Keenan was a very rigid man. I'm sure Clare went to the Congo in the first place to escape from him . . . One summer, when we were still in school, perhaps fourteen or fifteen years old, my family urged me to invite her to spend several weeks of her summer holiday at our house on Achill Island. That's not too far from her home at Westport, you know. Her mother, who was a pleasant woman but not, ah, very strong, agreed. Dr. Keenan promptly refused permission. It was only when my father talked to him and assured him that we would be closely supervised that he acquiesced, I must say, reluctantly and with bad grace."

"I see."

"But she was such a lovely young woman." S'ter mellowed for a moment and smiled pleasantly. "Not only beautiful—though she was surely that—but intelligent and witty and very thoughtful of others." She sighed. "She had so much possibility. . . ."

"So many of us do, Sister." I rose and the nun rose with me, both with our own memories of failures that seemed senseless and unnecessary. And why did I have to pick women whose fathers were hotshot surgeons?

"I wonder if I have described her adequately?" We stood at the door of the abbey which was reflected perfectly in the calm waters of the lake. The serenity of the setting hinted at the wisdom of the ages. No matter what happened to Ciara and me, a nun would be standing here gazing at the waters, knowing all the answers that really mattered, a hundred, a thousand years hence. "She was what we would call today 'charismatic,' the natural leader of the rest of the class in serious work as well as in mischief. We all adored her. She was so good that I have often thought she should have been a nun instead of I. We all knew about her father, of course. He was a great County Mayo character of the old school, always worried about impressing Protestants, but she didn't seem to let him bother her—'Old Doctor,' as she called him, was usually dismissed with good-natured laughter. Is it fair to assume, Mr. Ryan, that you know her reasonably well?"

"Reasonably well, Sister."

"Is she all right?" the nun asked cautiously.

"I think she's going to be," I replied with equal caution.

"I suppose," S'ter sighed, "it was a question of the wrong time and the wrong place."

We shook hands cordially. "Until now."

For the first time I had spoken to someone who knew the same Ciara I knew. Sister Fiona had poured gasoline on the smoldering embers of my love.

Perhaps Ciara had told me her father was a lawyer because she knew I would be skeptical about another surgeon's daughter.

My own daughter was waiting for me impatiently in the lounge bar of the hotel with her now customary glass of whiskey and an open notebook. Her face was shining, her eyes glowing—Sherlock Holmes waiting for Dr. Watson. Or perhaps Cordelia Gray waiting for Adam Dalgliesh.

"It's Black Bushmills, Daddy." She pointed at the glass of whiskey. "I thought I'd try it to see how it compares with Jameson's. It's very good, tastes like cognac. I don't think Uncle Blackie would mind, even if it is Protestant whiskey. Did you have a productive day?"

"No. I see that you did."

"Right." Eager to begin, she flipped open her notebook and then paused. "She's some chick, Daddy. I suppose I'll have to hate her for a while because she'll be taking you away from me and because obviously she's not good enough for you—no one would be." She grinned mischievously. "But after a while, I'm sure I'll identify with her. Then you'll be in real trouble."

It was beyond my capacity to imagine at that moment a family made up of Ciara and Jean and me. Such a family life, perhaps with a house in Beverly, a cottage somewhere near the Ryan compound in Grand Beach, would exist in the world of ordinary reality. I was now living in the mythic world of the west of Ireland, a world peopled by such characters as Iron Dick Burke and Donal "the Battler" O'Flaherty and Rory McLafferty.

"I was certainly very much impressed by her, Jean," I said, hiding behind the formal reply.

"Okay. She did her nurse's training at the Royal Victoria Hospital in Belfast. Rory McLafferty was a medical student, a Dublin Catholic, as gifted as your man Jaymo said he is. They became caught up in the civil rights movement. Then Rory broke with Bernadette on the issue of violence. His group was never large, fifteen or twenty at the most. They weren't as careful or as professional or as well-disciplined as the Provos, who, by the way, were not sorry to see him caught by the Brits."

"By the Brits?"

"You better believe it. So they blew up bridges and power stations and munitions dumps and such like, and Rory McLafferty became a legend. In those days things were so bad for the Catholics in the North that anybody who hurt the Brits was a hero. Then he began believing his own legends, or so my friends tell me, and he turned to murder. One night after a football game, his group blew up a bus filled with Protestant fans. They boarded another bus and gunned down nineteen football players. Clare, or Ciara, had had enough. They were supposed to be an organization in which everybody agreed on everything, and he hadn't told her about the football massacre. . . . Incidentally, Daddy, they were supposed to be lovers." She poised her pencil over the notebook and avoided my eyes. "Does that bother you?"

"Sure it does." I nodded my gratitude to the waitress who brought me my Bushmills, Black Label. It was indeed "very good." I would report it to Blackie, who probably knew all about it. "But it doesn't make any difference."

"Right." She put the pencil back on the notebook. "Anyway, she said she was quitting. He said 'You can't quit.' She said 'Just watch me.' He said 'All right, you can quit, but only after we blow up this music hall filled with Prots. Once that's done, once you've got your hands bloody, then I'll let you go.' So she marched off to the British army and told them about the music hall plot. The Brits caught the whole lot of them, killed half a dozen, and put the rest behind bars."

"So she was an informer?"

"Yeah." Jeannie flipped the page of her notebook. "I guess that's something pretty bad here in Ireland. Wasn't there a movie about that once?"

"Nineteen thirty-five. Victor McLaglen."

"Who? Never mind. It doesn't matter. The kids I talked to think she was a heroine. They're not into violence around here anymore. It's like they wish Ulster could be towed out into the Atlantic somewhere near Iceland and sunk. They don't like the Brits very much, but they don't like the Provos either. The Provos, by the way, have nothing against Clare—they think she did them a favor, putting him out of circulation. The Brits wanted to give her money and a new life. She said to hell with you and went off on her own to the University of Sussex in England, where she got herself a degree in French literature, then stayed on the faculty as a reader, which is kind of like an associate professor. She was there six or seven years, until Rory escaped from prison and blew up the house in which she was living. Clare wasn't there and nobody else was killed. Then the Brits and the Special Branch and the CIA 'lifted' her."

"Lifted?"

"My friends tell me," Jean flipped another page, "that both the Brits and the Gardai are afraid that if they can't protect their informants, especially an informant that most people admire, like Clare, there won't be any more informants."

"How long ago did the house in England blow up?"

"About a year and a half ago." Jean closed her notebook and replaced it in her purse. "Nobody knows what happened to her. Maybe she was someplace else before she came to Chicago."

"And as soon as they heard about the explosion on my boat, they lifted her again."

"Poor dear woman." Jean shook her head sadly. "Anyway, I don't know where all of this gets us except that we now have most of the details. Oh, one more thing." She opened the notebook again. "I don't know how much this is worth, but one of my friends, she thought she saw her at a little B&B out on Achill Island a couple of summers ago, like maybe she'd come back to Ireland for a week or two, just to see what it was like."

Achill Island again. "How did you manage to collect all this information?"

"Oh, hanging around pubs, talking to the young people." She shrugged indifferently, taking the keys from my hand. "I told them I went to school at Stanford with a cousin of hers named Emily. I suppose Superintendent Finnegan didn't expect I'd be asking questions."

"He knows now that you were asking them." I considered ordering another Bushmills and decided against it. "And so does the other side."

"He's a bad man, Daddy, a very bad man, and we're going to have to swat him like a mosquito."

I was so carried along by the mythological demons I had created for myself that I didn't disagree. Yes, of course, Jean and I, a college sophomore and a tax lawyer, were going to swat a dangerous but brilliant IRA psychopath.

"You drive, Daddy." Jean tossed off the keys to the car, which was parked down the street from the hotel. "I had a drink while I was waiting for you. I think I'll curl up and nap."

And so she did, looking very sweet and innocent in a plaid skirt and light brown sweater, folded up like a little girl in the seat to my left. It was only a brief nap. She awoke about fifteen minutes out of Castlebar, stretched gracefully, straightened up, and began immediately to talk. "I'm afraid I don't have a good picture of her. She sounds like she's brave and tough, but also rebellious, discontented, something of a radical—the kind of woman who would become involved in kooky movements with psychopathic leaders."

Ah, the changing times. Stanford women wrinkling their noses at the word "movement."

"I suppose she does."

"On the other hand," she pursed her lips thoughtfully, "you describe her as sweet and funny and smart and, well, kinda cool."

"Can't she be both kinds of person?" I kept my eyes very carefully focused on the big lorry in front of us.

"I suppose." A long and thoughtful pause. "But only if she's done a lot of growing up."

"I see your point, Jeannie. Yes, I think she has done a lot of growing up."

The quest had changed: no longer *was* there a Ciara Kelly, but *who* was she?

Jeannie sighed. She'd learned the art very quickly. Her sigh sounded even more like a serious asthma attack than that of the nun at Kylemore Abbey.

"I don't know about you, Daddy." She sounded as though she were in deep, philosophical thought. "All kinds of women go ape over you, and you don't seem to be able to enjoy it."

"For example?" I tried to laugh.

"Well, for example, Grandma Ryan, Mom—poor Mom,

she just didn't know how to do it—Emily's mother, Aunt Eileen, Aunt Catherine, even Caitlin and Cindasoo."

"Cindasoo? I don't even know her!"

"She sure 'nuff glowed," Jean imitated her friend, "when you were talking to her after Mass at Aunt Catherine's. Got right flustered, she did."

"Aren't you leaving somebody out?"

"You mean Ciara?"

"No, I mean my daughter."

"I hadn't forgotten about her," Jean chuckled. "She can be such a little geek that she almost doesn't count."

"I think she counts. Anyway, what's your point?"

"You don't seem to know what to do with that love. Sometimes I don't even think you notice it. If this chick is what you say she is, you'd better be able to cope with her love or you'll be in a real lot of trouble."

"I can cope with her," I said firmly.

Another West of Ireland sigh. "It sounds to me like a hell of a roller-coaster ride, Daddy." She curled up again and, having delivered her warning, went briskly back to sleep. But not before she murmured her parting thrust: "Here in Ireland you act like you would be able to tame even Grace O'Malley. I don't know what happens when you go home to Chicago."

For the first time in the trip I was able to make explicit to myself the feeling about Jean that I'd first experienced in Dublin: I was watching a girl very quickly become a woman.

Keenan's Keep or Castle, choose your own title, was barely visible when we arrived. The fog was so thick that one could see only a few yards of water of Clew Bay. With the fog came the strong, salty smell of the Atlantic, more powerful yet cleaner than the sea smell in Dublin, suggesting a purifying detergent that would scour anything it touched.

The castle was a dark, somber, great gray-stoned pile watching us grimly as we drove up the neatly landscaped drive. "Wow!" Jeannie opened her eyes. "It's a night when Grace O'Malley would be out in her galleys."

"Or laying in wait for us in that hotel."

"That isn't a hotel." Jeannie shook her head. "That's a haunted castle. This is your idea, Daddy, not mine."

The gray, threatening sky, the stern and aloof mien of Keenan's Castle, did not have the slightest psychic impact on me. If the ghost of Constance Keenan was indeed present in that ancient pile of stone, she was keeping to herself.

Inside, however, the castle was as pleasant and friendly as it had been hostile on the outside. A warm fire was crackling cheerfully in a big fireplace "to take a bit of the chill off the air." The big overstuffed chairs and sofas, maroon in color, deep blue fabric on the walls, high oak beams, cheerful waiters circulating among the guests, clearing away the remnants of high tea and serving the first before-supper drinks. It was as though it were saying, "Look, I'm no Ashford Castle, but I can be warm and reassuring and clean. And don't believe any of the stories about ghosts. Patently, I'm too nice a place to harbor ghosts."

The rooms were small, as befits a medieval castle, but comfortable, dry, and clean. No trace of psychic clamminess.

Jean and I said we would meet in the lobby for a glass of sherry—"in honor of the good Jocelyn"—and then supper. She was waiting for me when I arrived, in an Irish hand-crocheted light tan dress, which clung to her firm young figure in a way that would have twisted the heart of a man of any age.

"Nice dress." I kissed her cheek. "It would drive Timmy or Liam out of his mind."

"That's what it's supposed to do," she said pointedly. "It kind of replaces my jumpsuit."

Was it only yesterday that I'd found her shivering in a deserted little chapel?

"Whatever an old daddy's opinion is worth, it's a decided improvement."

"Uh huh."

Then I saw that she was looking at a picture of a painting of a beautiful woman that hung on the wall in the lobby, the same painting I had seen in Dufficy's Irish Store.

"She's the ghost that haunts this place, isn't she?" Jean asked thoughtfully. "Funny, there's not a word about it in any of the brochures."

"Maybe they think that would frighten clients away."

"I suppose," her sigh had become a ritual, "there aren't enough tourists who go in for psychic kicks." She grinned sideways at me. "Does she look like Ciara, Daddy?"

I considered the tragic Constance Keenan carefully. Somehow, the resemblance didn't seem as strong as it had in the Irish store on Michigan Avenue. Or perhaps I'd forgotten how the real Ciara looked. "Not as pretty, not nearly as pretty."

Same taunting gray eyes, however; taunting, yet somehow also thoughtful.

"Like wow!" Jean said thoughtfully. "Some dish, huh?"

"I thought of an answer to the question you asked me in the car." I told her what the nun had said at the entrance to Kylemore Abbey.

"Uh huh." Jean studied my face carefully. "Look, Daddy, I'm sure we'll get along. Maybe she is good enough for you." She turned briskly away from the painting. "Let's have that sherry and supper. I'm starved."

"Done."

The sherry was delightfully delicate, the leg of lamb was perfectly cooked, the bottle of Bordeaux the best wine I'd had in Ireland. I returned to my room after a coffee and an Irish Cream in the lobby, safely out of sight of Constance Keenan's picture in much too mellow and relaxed a mood to seriously expect spooks. Then I remembered Mike Casey.

"Where the hell have you been?" he asked brusquely as he picked up the phone in the Reilly Gallery. "I was about to mobilize the main force."

"Drinking the best Bordeaux in Ireland," I confessed.

"The shipment will be at Ashford Castle by noon tomorrow. Be careful with it."

"I'm always careful, Michael."

"It must have been awfully good Bordeaux," he grunted. "Any developments?"

"We're finding more pieces of the puzzle," I said guardedly. "What's new on your end?"

"Some bad news, I'm afraid. John King Sullivan died last night. Apparently the tumors were worse than anyone realized. His wife is too sick to attend the funeral."

"God help us all!"

"He'd better! Or, as my wife would say, She'd better.
. . . There's no chance that Patricia Sullivan will ever stand
trial. Rich Daley has announced that the state's attorney's
office considers the case closed. Even that idiot Sam Norton
has given up."

"It's a strange world, Mike."

"You've noticed. Anyway, Annie sends her love. Be
careful."

The conversation sufficiently depressed me that I now
thought I was ready for Constance Keenan. I went to sleep
perfectly prepared to encounter her.

And woke up the next morning, sunlight streaming
through my tiny window. No psychic manifestations at all.

But one idea, a hint, perhaps, from Connie, or more
likely from my own unconscious putting a few things
together—a hunch, a stab in the dark.

"When fathers are later than teenage daughters," Jean
glanced mischievously at her watch as I joined her at the
breakfast table, "it's a bad sign."

"Senility."

"Back to Ashford Castle?" She buttered a thick slab of
brown bread and poured raspberry jam on it.

"Eventually—another stop to make first."

"Oh?" She delicately bit into the bread, licking the jam
off her lips with her tongue.

"A place called Achill Island." Her bread and jam
looked so tasty that I prepared a slice for myself.

"A little ghost tell you?"

"Oh, c'mon now, Jeannie, no sensible, well-educated
person believes in ghosts." We laughed together and departed for Achill Island.

The weather was extraordinarily friendly, the nicest
day since we'd been in Ireland. What better day to meet the
woman you love? And what better place than in the County
Mayo, whence your ancestors escaped, it would seem, in
the nick of time?

Small wonder one is required to add "God help us!"
Even on a gorgeous day County Mayo is a land of rocks:
rocks strewn in the fields, rocks piled neatly on fences,

rocks forming bridges, and even rocks fashioned into tiny houses—in the last case, whitewashed, the old cottage attached to a newer stucco cottage and an occasional new home. In Ireland it is bad luck not to preserve at least one wall of the old home.

County Mayo, between Westport and Newport and the corner of Clew Bay toward Achill Island, is desolate and unproductive. There are almost as many abandoned old cottages as there are those from whose chimney a faint trace of smoke curls across the blue sky. At the time of the famine in 1849, this was the most densely populated section of Europe, land good for potato farming and very little else. The abandoned houses, however, do not date from famine days—the pathetic little hovels of those who died or migrated during the famine have been long since cleared away. These huts, without roofs, and often missing walls, belonged to the immigrants who left during the lesser famines at the end of the nineteenth century, when the families of most of the American Irish departed. Yet the land is green and the houses are white, and the harsh hills and rocks are somehow wildly beautiful, as though you have come upon a set for a film about Ireland. Then you realize that they shoot films in Ireland only on days when it's not raining—unless it's a film about a man on the run, like Victor McLaglen's *The Informer* or James Mason's *Odd Man Out*.

If the sun lasts until you get to Achill Island, you're in for an incredible treat. As soon as you've crossed the somewhat dubious bridge separating Achill Island from the mainland, you enter another world. For a moment you think you've left Ireland behind and have been transported to Sorrento—wide beaches, gentle breakers, dramatically sloping hills, pink, blue, and green cottages as well as white. Only the well-groomed cattle, the shaggy dogs, countrymen and -women in their gray suits and black skirts remind you that you're still in Ireland.

"Oh, boy," Jean exclaimed enthusiastically. "Why hasn't anybody done a photo book on this place?"

"Probably 'cause days like this happen here only once every fifty years."

I sensed, felt, intuited—call it what you want—that Ciara was near and that I had to find her before it was too late. Where to look for her? How to find her? Who were the lurking enemies? We stopped at a pub across the road from the beach, perhaps a mile onto the island, and ordered a pint of Guinness each and a cheese sandwich. "Isn't it a glorious day, now?" Jean asked the pub man.

" 'Tis," the man admitted, "but sure we'll be paying for it with bad weather. That's always the way. Nothing good happens but you don't have to pay for it with bad."

"A quiet time here on the island?" I asked, trying to sound casual.

"Ah, now." The man shook his head dismally. "Sure, how could it be a quiet time with all them Gardai around? Aren't they a pain in the arse now?"

"Have a Garda station here, do you?" I slipped into the routine, which I had learned very quickly, of matching question with question.

"Station is it? Isn't the nearest constable across the way in Newport? Sure doesn't he have nothing more than a bicycle to get over here?"

I sighed, hoping it sounded authentic and intending it to be a request for more information.

The man took my meaning. "Still, I wonder why all them fellas be hanging around, particularly the men from the Special Branch."

"The Special Branch is it?" Jeannie said, peering at the man over the top of her Guinness.

"Can't you be smelling the Branch fellas a mile away? And themselves all hanging around that pink cottage miles down the road, just beyond Joe Tim's house? Fucking piss artists."

I would have leaped out of the booth at once, but Jeannie kept the man in conversation for a few more minutes. Then we walked casually to our car, which she backed to the road from the pub and roared down the highway at eighty miles an hour. We almost smashed into Superintendent James Finnegan's Volvo.

"I might have known you'd be here." The superintendent emerged from the rear of the car and regarded us susciously. "I suppose the lass is your daughter; sure she looks enough like you."

I attempted an introduction, which Jean, who did not seem to like Jaymo a bit, ignored. "Superintendent of the Special Branch or not, Superintendent Finnegan, you're driving on the wrong side of the road. In my country, even cops, even gumshoe cops, have to keep the law."

The superintendent turned beet red, perhaps because he was trying to suppress a laugh. "You're not in your country, young woman. And you've got no business to be on this road."

"I realize your civil liberties are more primitive than ours, Superintendent," I joined the argument, "but I doubt that even in Ireland you can keep us from driving down the road."

"This is all irrelevant," Finnegan replied wearily. "She's not here, she's gone, she's flown the coop altogether."

"Who?" I asked.

"Who do you think? Your woman, Clare Keenan or Ciara Kelly or whatever she's calling herself. We had her in a safe house here, herself insisting that it was only Achill Island that was good enough for her. A nice quiet place and agents to protect her. Then she ups and decides she's finished with our protection and she'd rather face your man McLafferty by herself. So she vanishes without a trace. You're late, Mr. Brendan Ryan. You're twelve hours late."

"She was here then?"

The four uniformed Gardai who were in the car with the superintendent closed in around him, not quite sure whether they ought to be protecting him from us.

"Oh, yes, she was here. I don't suppose there's any point in asking how you knew?"

"It was obvious." I tried not to sound too much like Sherlock Holmes. "Achill Island was a place she loved. She came here on vacations with her school friends. She came back here at least one summer and probably several summers when she was in school in England after McLafferty was put in prison. Then you and your friends send her to the States, panic when she tells you about the explosion on my boat, and pull her out of Chicago. She reads the papers and finds out that I'm still alive, then later on that I was the target, not her. She's furious at you and your buddies and insists on returning to Ireland. She's sick of running. All right, you folks say, Ireland it'll be, but we can't risk our informers being blown up so you tell us where you want to go. Then she says Achill Island. Where else?"

No room for Constance Keenan's ghost or my own intuition. All perfectly reasonable and all made up on the spur of the moment.

"Impressive," Finnegan admitted grudgingly, as he removed his pipe and tobacco from his pocket.

"Elementary," Jean observed with a perfectly straight face.

"And I suppose," he puffed desperately on his pipe, shielding the lighter from the wind that swept up from the beach and along our road on its way to the top of the mountain that was the center and the core of Achill Island, "I suppose you can explain to me, too, why she's flown the coop."

"That's easy," Jean said contemptuously. "She's tired of the mistakes that you gumshoes make. She realizes that if she relies on you, she'll have to run for the rest of her life and may still not get away from Rory McWhatever his name is. She figures she has a better chance of facing him alone. She's a very tough woman, Superintendent Finnegan. She's survived a lot. Now she figures she can survive a one-on-one with him."

I suppose I would have thought of that explanation eventually. Jeannie's quickness made me wonder if she shouldn't enroll in the police academy instead of Stanford University.

"That's about it," Jaymo sighed, despite his pleasure with himself that he'd managed to ignite the tobacco in his pipe. "It's like she signed her own death warrant. She won't have a chance against that lunatic."

"Maybe she'd rather be dead than live this way." Jeannie dug a stone from the roadside with a dainty foot. "You and your colleagues have not been exactly brilliant in protecting her."

"With us she had a chance," he insisted, waving the hovering Gardai away. "Now she doesn't have a chance at all. I don't suppose your Sherlock Holmes deductions tell you where she's gone?"

"You're going to keep searching?"

"That's me orders." The pipe went out, and with obvious disgust, he knocked the ashes into the wind. "Some very important people in Dublin and Washington insist that we do everything we can to keep her alive."

"Maybe she knows that." I removed the ignition keys from the pocket of Jean's jacket. "Maybe she assumes that out in the open and unguarded she'll be bait for McLafferty. He'll go after her, then you can go after him."

"Pretty reckless," Jaymo said disapprovingly. "Ah, sure, she always has been a reckless woman. I don't suppose I can persuade you to go back to New York?"

"Hardly, Superintendent. And by the way, it's Chicago."

"Aye, so 'tis." He paused respectfully. "So you two are determined to remain here and become bait yourselves?"

"We're not defining ourselves as bait, Superintendent," I said tersely. "C'mon, Jeannie, let's get out of here."

"You sure looked like bait on Lough Corrib."

"I'll drive, Daddy." Jean snatched the keys from my hand. "You think."

She started the car, turned it around, and pointed us back down towards the beach of Achill Island and the mainland. Sometime, I vowed to myself, Ciara and I would return.

"Where to?" Jean asked.

"Back to Ashford Castle, at least for the first stop."

"And then?"

"Tomorrow is Sunday, isn't it? You lose track of the days of the week over here. Let's spend Sunday thinking about it, and then take off for somewhere else."

I was not altogether sure that Jean would approve of the "shipment" that was waiting for me at Ashford Castle. There was no reason to tell her about it.

Clouds and rain returned in midafternoon, by the time we'd gone through Cong and turned off at the gray stone gate of the castle. The same battered blue Volkswagen hatchback that had been parked at the head of the street leading to the castle when we'd left was still there. Obviously it hadn't been following us.

Jean said that she needed a nap before supper, and I said that I probably did, too, though I knew very well there were too many emotions churning inside me. Ciara was trying a desperate, perhaps self-destructive gamble. Yet I could understand why she was doing it. She didn't know yet that we were in Ireland. If she'd only waited another twenty-four hours, we might have found her on Achill. We might have stumbled into her in a pub or a grocery and let her know that she was not alone.

On the other hand, she might have thought that I would be no more help than the Irish police.

There was no reason to think that I would be. Yet I was convinced that we would find her and save her from Rory McLafferty. When you're a mythological Irish hero, any other outcome is impossible. There's no fool like a fool in love. Especially when he thinks he's Finn MacCool.

Such were my thoughts as I opened the compact, carefully wrapped package that was waiting on the coffee table in my room, a surprisingly light, almost fragile package.

Inside were five smaller packages, neatly arranged and covered with plastic bubbles. Two of them were elements of the Uzi, one a long thin silencer and the other the weapon itself, with the plastic butt neatly folded back against the stock. In another wrapper were fifteen compact magazine clips for the weapon (a couple of hundred rounds). The fourth package contained a sturdy plastic strap and a light-weight vest, marked "U.S. Government Surplus," with a number of pockets—the Secret Service's holster for presidential bodyguards. Finally, in the last and smallest package, I found a .22 caliber pistol, cleaned, polished, and well oiled, which looked like a twin to the one with which Cindasoo had shot a bumbling Mafia hit man.

Why the extra gun? I wondered. For emergencies, probably. Only twenty rounds of ammunition neatly wrapped in brown paper. Obviously Mike didn't think the emergencies would require much use of the small pistol. Well, I wouldn't argue with his experience.

I hid the .22 under a stack of dirty shirts in my flight bag, and put four ammo clips and the silencer in one pocket of the holster vest and the Uzi in another compartment. Then I donned my jacket and trench coat. If I put my hands in the pockets of my coat and hunched over a bit, the coat looked no more bulky on me than if I were carrying a small camera and a pocketful of film cartridges. The weapon was a bit of a weight around my arm, but not nearly as heavy as an M1 or an M16.

I strolled out of Ashford Castle and walked casually across the green lawn, by the old Protestant church (St. Mary's), past the monastery ruins that were at the entrance (including one monastic cell that had been built out over the river so the monk could fish while he prayed), along the wall of the new concrete Catholic church, and into the town of Cong, a tiny, picturesque little village (with a "Quiet Man" pub), apparently undaunted by the presence of the last remnants of the faeries, the Tuatha Dé Danann, who are believed to lurk in the deep limestone caves underneath and outside the village.

At the miniature crossroads—Castlebar in one direction, Headford and Galway in the other—with its little fifteenth-century stone cross, I glanced down the main street and noted that the blue VW hatchback with the Dublin license plate was still parked in front of the tobacco shop. I ducked into a side street and avoided the car.

About forty yards down the banks of the Corrib River, I came to the "rising of the waters." Lough Corrib and Lough Mask several miles to the north are connected by an underground river, which centuries ago had carved its path through the porous limestone of this area of Mayo. In the nineteenth century the British built a canal between the two lakes so that the waterway would be navigable to the very head of Lough Mask. Construction provided jobs for many natives who otherwise might have perished in the famine.

Unfortunately for the British engineers, however, the ground was too porous to hold the canal, and save when Lough Mask is in flood, the waters sink through the rock back to the original underground path shortly after they leave Lough Mask and then bubble once more to the surface just above Lough Corrib. Another and more plausible story is that by the time the canal was finished, the railroad had been built and the engineers decided there was no reason to seal up the limestone. Twenty-five yards or so beyond the "rising of the waters," I climbed down the bank of the dry canal and found a few yards farther up a clump of bushes that provided me with a perfect screen. The rhododendron bushes on either side of the ditch, now wet and glistening from the rain, formed a cathedral-like arch to protect my experimentation. I listened carefully for a couple of minutes. The only sound I heard was that of an occasional bee who had emerged from his shelter to ascertain whether the rain had really stopped and whether it was dry enough to return to his busy work in the rhododendrons.

I removed the two parts of the Uzi from my pocket and slipped them together easily. It was an enormous improvement over the M16, light, simple, easy to assemble and disassemble. I aimed it, moved it slowly, then quickly in my hands, an unbelievably well-balanced and responsive weapon. How easy it had become to kill other human beings.

The Uzi, named after Major Uziel Gal of the Israeli army, who developed it, looks like a slightly elongated revolver when its folding butt is not extended. Loaded with a twenty-five-round magazine (in the pistol grip), it weighs eight pounds. When the butt is unextended, it is seventeen inches long. It fires its nine-millimeter parabellum bullets at the rate of six hundred fifty rounds per minute, which means you can empty a magazine in four seconds. It is meant to be fired in bursts during quick, short combat situations. It runs out of ammo too quickly to be used in sustained combat. But modern warfare rarely requires sustained combat. In the long run everyone is too dead.

They don't, in other words, ride around the fort all night long.

On the left side of the pistol grip is a change lever. Push the lever to "E," the forward position, and the weapon will fire automatically—till you take your finger off the trigger. Set it at the middle position, marked "D," and it will fire a single shot each time you squeeze the trigger. Move it to the rear, marked "S," and the weapon is on safety: it will not fire, no matter how hard you press the trigger and squeeze the grip safety. Deadly for the target and safe for the one who holds it, the Uzi does not fire accidentally if you drop it.

I slipped the ammunition clip into the magazine chamber, attached the silencer, which looked like a slightly elongated cigar, to the muzzle, set the weapon for a single shot, pulled the cocking bolt to the rear, squeezed the grip safety, and fired cautiously at a bush ten yards away.

At first I thought there was something wrong with the weapon and that it had not fired. Then I smelled the bitter, acrid aroma of exploding ammunition and saw a branch fall off the bush. Astonishing! Almost no recoil. The Israeli gunsmiths were geniuses.

Very, very carefully I adjusted the weapon for automatic fire, squeezed the trigger lightly, and then released it. The weapon made a light *thump thump thump* sound and half the bush collapsed, as though someone had sliced through it with a giant scythe. The empty shells, exiting out of the right side of the weapon by "blowback," lined the ground at my feet.

I put the safety back on and unloaded the magazine. Good heavens! I had fired off twelve rounds without realizing it. If the bush had been a human being, he would have been torn to shreds.

I carefully collected the empty shells and leaned against the canal bank, dismayed and faintly sick. This little toy gun in my hands, no bigger and not much heavier than a machine-gun water pistol with which I had played as a little boy (much against my mother's wishes since she did not believe that little boys should play with guns— despite her use of them during the war), was a devastatingly dangerous killing machine. I was not sure I wanted to have any part of it. Certainly I could not carry the thing around casually underneath my jacket.

Then I thought of Ciara and the terror that seemed to be a psychic aura around her. So I stayed there, close to the bank of the disappearing canal, and practiced with the astonishing little weapon for another half hour. Perhaps I wouldn't win a marksmanship medal with it, and perhaps I wasn't as sharp with it as I was with the M16 eighteen years ago, but if it was necessary to fire the Uzi to protect Jean or Ciara or my child, whom Ciara carried, then I could fire the weapon with terrible effectiveness.

I wondered what some countryman might think on Sunday morning if he happened to be walking above the "rising of the waters" and saw all the decapitated bushes and perhaps even discovered some of the spent bullets. Later I carefully deposited the ejected shells in a refuse can behind a public house on the main street of Cong.

Glumly I disassembled the weapon when my practice session was over, and most of the bushes in my part of the canal had been trimmed to half their size, and tramped back to the castle.

I stopped at the gift shop on the grounds of the castle and purchased an attaché case made from Donegal tweed, a perfect container for the components of the weapon and its ammunition.

I stored the case in the bottom drawer of my dresser and covered it with my Windbreaker. It seemed to me most unlikely that an Ashford Castle maid would open a guest's briefcase.

It was four o'clock in the afternoon. Perhaps I ought to nap for an hour or two before supper. My automatic weapons practice had exhausted me.

I took off my shirt and trousers and was about to pull the spread back from my bed when the phone rang. "Brendan Ryan? Ah, who else would it be now?" said a familiar womanly voice. "No need to say who I am, is there?"

"Where are you?"

"Room three-fourteen of the Railway Hotel in Galway city. I'll be waiting for you. Sure, you're a desperate man, aren't you now?"

The line clicked dead. The search was over.

I threw on my clothes, grabbed my trench coat from the closet in case the rain should return, and hurried out of my room. Halfway down the green-carpeted corridor I paused, thought for a moment, and then decided that Mike

Casey was a far more experienced detective than I was.

I returned to my room, removed the .22 caliber pistol from my flight bag, and slipped it into the trench coat pocket.

33

The forty-mile drive from Ashford Castle to Galway city required almost two anxious hours—hours of uncertainty, anticipation, and increasing sexual desire. Although it was Saturday afternoon, the roads were filled with lorries and autos streaming into Galway for Saturday night. (What do you do on Saturday night in a five-hundred-year-old city from which Grace O'Malley was excluded because she was "a bit too wild for them"?) The rain fell more heavily, the roads turned slick and dangerous, and the Irish drivers were only marginally more patient than American drivers—and on two-lane highways at that.

Finally I circled the new cathedral (as ugly as it had been a few days before), crossed the Corrib River, and crawled through the heart of the city. I drove around the main square, where there is a memorial to John F. Kennedy, God be good to him, and searched for a parking spot in front of the Great Southern Railway Hotel.

There was no vacant spot, so I circumnavigated the square again, a task that took ten minutes. In the slow movement around the corners, I noticed a dark blue VW hatchback that looked like the one from Cong a few yards behind me. It followed me around a second time. Either one of Jaymo's people or the other side.

I was pretty sure that Jaymo's men were skilled enough at ordinary police work not to be so easily found out.

The second time around, an Alfa pulled out of a slot across the street from the hotel and I pulled in. I caught the VW's license number as it went by.

Same car.

I was glad I'd brought Mickey's .22.

He parked around the corner, facing the square. I piled out of my car and stalled for a few moments, awkwardly putting on my raincoat. The tail was a few years younger than me, short, thin, dark, with a bushy mustache and a long, lean nose. He wore a brown cap and an old-fashioned black rain slicker. Central casting's choice for an Irish gunman.

Or an Irish bachelor farmer in town for a night.

I walked quickly across the rain-soaked cobblestone street and into the lobby of the hotel, my hand firmly on the .22.

Nothing happened. I shook the rain out of my coat and off my beret and watched the tail out of the corner of my eye. He was ambling with apparent leisure toward the hotel.

Perhaps all he wanted was a drink in the lounge.

I ducked into the cranky and obsolete elevator and rode up to Ciara's floor. No point in announcing myself, especially since I didn't know what name she might have used to register.

I knocked lightly on the door.

"Yes?" No mistake about the voice.

" 'Tis the man from Jerome's," I said, feeling slightly ridiculous about the perhaps needless code.

"Brendan?" A whisper from the other side of the door.

"Who else would it be, woman?"

The door opened a tiny crack. A wary gray eye considered me briefly. The door closed again so the chain could be removed. It then opened a slightly larger crack through which a man could slip if he was slender and quick. My hand still in the pocket with the .22, I glided through the door, which shut behind me almost instantly.

The woman was not Ciara. She had short blonde hair and thick glasses; she was heavily made up and wore a somewhat tawdry maroon dress, which was a size too small and whose neckline plunged too far. A whore making a trick?

Not with those gray eyes and not with the intensity of that embrace. A clever disguise. My Ciara is good at everything.

My long-frustrated sexual hunger exploded. So did hers. Our bodies, accustomed to and comfortable with one another, took charge.

Our love was not the sensitive, tender affection we had known the last time together in her anonymous room in the Chestnut Place. It was angry, demonic, violent love, our bodies yelling their protest against so long a separation. I stripped her quickly; dress, bra, panties were pulled away in a few glorious seconds. Then I covered her with savage kisses, assaulting her adored body with demanding affection. Finally I buried my head in the sweet-smelling darkness between her thighs, a mysterious forest where I would remain for an eternity of pleasure. The woman was mine, all mine.

Ciara's response was as violent as my attack. For a few minutes of wild passion and headlong, heedless pleasure, we existed only for each other.

In the dank little room with its musty smell and the sound of a combo somewhere in the hotel playing early Beatles, I knew that she was indeed my Holy Grail, my life, my purpose, my destiny. I might live without her, but it wouldn't be much of a life. God put me in the world for Ciara Kelly.

I must have dozed. Then I woke with a start to see her wonderful face close to mine, twisted in sadness and pain, like an Irish pietà. She looked, for the first time, not younger than thirty-three going on thirty-four, but much older, ten years at least. She was thinner than she had been. Too thin. Small wonder.

"How much have you figured out?" she asked sadly.

"Where did you do your university work?"

"Brendan, you're a desperate man." She kissed me. "Sussex. French literature." She pointed to a French novel on the minute bedstand. "Modern. I was a reader on the faculty too. Like one of your associate professors."

"You were good at what you did then?"

"They thought so."

"Should I call you Ciara or Clare?"

"Oh, Ciara, please. That's who I am to you." Tears, the first of them, in her anguished gray eyes. They were quickly dismissed.

"And you did therapy there?"

"Five years of analysis. Do you think it worked?" A faintly crooked grin.

I patted her superb ass. "You had to have a lot of guts to go through it and pull your life together. It must not have been easy."

"It wasn't. Sometimes . . . ah, damn it all." Horror-stricken face. "I'm terrible sorry about the bad word, Brendan. . . . Stop laughing at me. . . . Anyway, sometimes I think that maybe I'm a better person for it all. Then other times I tell myself that I've always been a mess and always will be."

"The first opinion gets my vote. Your nunnish class-mate at Kylemore wouldn't agree that you were a mess as a girl either."

Her eyes lit up, and she enthused about dear old Fiona. I had to recount, word for word, the story of my conversation by the waters of the still lake.

"What else don't you know?" She was somber again; Fiona was good for only so much escape.

"Rory McLafferty?"

"A grand man in those days, Brendan; kind and thoughtful and full of fun and jokes and laughter. We sailed a lot on Lough Neagh; you know how much I like sailing. My father never approved of a girl doing it, so I learned in secret when he was at the hospital. Rory was a grand sailor, and he took me out as often as he could. It was never seri-ous, like everything was with Father; always a good time and if you made a mistake you weren't lectured. I loved ev-ery second of my time with him, particularly when we were sailing. And it was like sex didn't exist beyond a hug and a kiss and a slap on the rear and a laugh at the end of the day.

"I suppose if I knew what I do now, I would have seen some psychopathic streaks. But I was lonely and scared and traumatized, and he was good to me and made no de-mands. I was in my first year of nursing and he in his sec-ond year at medical school, himself from Derry and an en-thusiastic disciple of Bernadette Devlin. I needed a cause to believe and a man to replace my father. The cause was good and the man seemed to be good too."

"You were lovers?"

"In a manner of speaking. He . . . he didn't seem to be much interested in sex. We went to bed now and then, more because he was being good to me, I think. . . . He was terrible good to me in those days; I suppose he loved me. As best he could love anyone. There weren't any others till you, Brendan." She stroked my face gently. "After therapy was over I tried a couple of times and lost my nerve. I would have lost it with you, too, darling, if you'd have let me."

"He turned gradually to violence in response to the Brits?"

She nodded. "You have to remember the times, Brendan. Purifying violence. Wretched of the earth, that sort of stuff. We read bits of Marx and quoted Marcuse and Fanon and Lenin and Trotsky, not understanding any of them much but enjoying it all and thinking we were the hinge of history. The Provos didn't read a thing. They knew what they wanted and what had to be done."

"Let me put the latch back on the door." I remembered the man with the long nose and the cap.

"Glory be," she said, "how dumb of me!"

"You had other things to do." I climbed back under the twisted and sweat-soaked sheet, making sure that the pocket of my trench coat with the .22 in it was but an instant's reach away. "So you felt that you should begin to imitate the Provos?"

"Not to say imitate, if you take my meaning. We had a love/hate thing going with them. We hated their ideological naiveté and admired the simplicity of their dedication. Idjits that we were, we didn't realize that it was the same thing. Anyway, we took to blowing up power-line terminals and railroad tracks and even one ammo dump. All harmless as far as affecting anything, but a lot of fun for us. I'll never forget how excited I was the first night we did the power terminal. It wasn't as good as sex with you, but it was an enormous emotional release. At last I was affecting reality, I told myself."

"Poor Ciara."

"Poor, dumb Ciara. Well, Rory was becoming wilder, though so gradually you wouldn't notice it unless you looked back over the months. He was a great actor and performer. Dominated the theatricals for the hospital staff. Terrorism was like a theatrical, a stage on which to act, a play to be performed, a leading role for him in which he was the perfect hero—Robin Hood, the Count of Monte Cristo, and Billy the Kid all combined. He'd scare the daylights out of us with the tricks he'd do on his own—violation of group discipline, he'd say, if any of the rest of us did it. He'd disappear and then show up a few days later with a trunkload of plastics or a couple of crates of Russian guns."

"AK-47s?" She nodded. "Where did he find them?"

"Your man Qaddafi, I suppose. Even then he was part of the shadow world, though the rest of us were too dumb to know about that world. He loved it, every second of it. He dropped out of medical school right before graduation because he said he wanted to be a doctor only in an Ireland that was free, united, and socialist."

"The rhetoric and the violence pushed him over the line?"

"We don't know much about psychopaths." She drew my head to her breasts, pillows in which it delighted. "Maybe he was already over the line. Maybe he would have gone over it anyhow, no matter what. But we were in the Falls when the Brits smashed the heads of Catholic women who complained because their poor wee homes were torn apart. We treated the lacerations and the concussions. We ministered to the wounded and the dying in Derry on Bloody Sunday, when the paras gunned down a crowd of peaceful marchers—I was there, Brendan." The memory of that distant event made her transiently an angry revolutionary again. "I'd seen terrible things before, as you well know. This was worse. It was not drunken savages. It was not nervous draftees losing their cool, like your National Guard at Kent State. It was calm, careful murder by disciplined professional troops. It would have pushed someone stronger than Rory around the bend."

"So people became the target?"

"Aye, the soccer buses. We had a great terrible row at the meeting of our council—which was all of us, no more than a baker's dozen of kids with enough firepower to hold off half the RUC for an hour or so. We were into participative democracy in those days; all of us had to agree. If there was not a unanimous decision, we didn't do it. Mind you, the discussion was about the principle of the thing. The soccer buses didn't come up. The issue was killing people— guilty people, as he called them."

"Guilty of being Protestant soccer players."

"Sure." She sighed heavily. "He had that in mind from the beginning. Anyway, a few of us voted against it, and that was that. He laughed it off, as charming when he lost an argument as when he won it. Some of the others told me how glad they were that I fought him."

"You were the leader of the opposition?"

"I was that, I guess. Even in those days, stupid, sick little idjit I was, I knew that killing people was wrong. So he and six others did it anyway. Four men and three women with guns killed over twenty people. Nice little toys," she said bitterly, "your AK-47s."

"Not mine," I said dryly. "They were fired at me too."

"Sure, Brendan, I'm sorry." She grabbed my arm apologetically. "It hurts even to tell this again. We had a meeting afterward. They strutted around like they'd won the All Ireland championship. They were the leading edge of the Irish people. The only morality that should be heeded was the morality of the successful revolution. Morality out of the mouth of a gun. Vote taking was bourgeois revisionism. Those of us who did not want to go along were enemies of the people. We were free to leave, but we would be treated as enemies."

"Lenin would have understood."

"Most of them quit. They were afraid of Rory and Seamus Cagney and Deirdre Mullens, but they were afraid of the Brits and the RUC too. I stayed."

"You did?"

She shook her head in agreement. "Rory made love to me after they killed the soccer players. It was spectacular. The first time I had any idea what fucking could be like. The last time till you, darling." A brief glow of gratitude and happy remembrance. "I was a dumb idjit, but not so dumb as to not know what he was and what would happen next. I had to stop it."

"You felt responsible for the soccer players?"

"Not really," she said slowly. "I believed Rory that there'd be no killing. But I would be responsible if he killed anyone else. The others could walk away with a nervous look over their shoulders and a pretense at a clear conscience. I didn't want to wake up some morning in my dorm at the hospital and hear that he'd killed hundreds. If that happened I was to blame as much as he."

Of such stern principles, I thought, are heroines made. Screwed-up little idjit that Clare Keenan was in those days, she was still made of the stuff of heroines. The kids Jean had talked to in Castlebar were right.

"Then?"

"My poor Brendan." She rubbed my cheek against a breast. "Such terrible pillow talk for you to have to be hearing. . . . Then I went down to Trinity Medical School in Dublin for a three-day course in trauma treatment—God knows I had enough firsthand experience—and took me a walk over to Dublin Castle and asked to see someone from the Special Branch. Your man Jaymo Finnegan was a sergeant then. He believed me. He put me in touch with a Brit in Belfast."

Now I understood the haggard affection I saw occasionally in his eyes when he spoke of her.

"You felt guilty about dealing with the Brits?"

"I hated their man in Belfast, one of your goddamned university graduates, like I would become later, so superior to the wee wild woman from County Mayo. And himself the grandson of Irish immigrants at that. Well, to bring an end to it, I found out about the music hall plans and tipped off the Brits. They bungled it and didn't raid our basement before we left. The plan, you see, was to set off the bombs and then gun down the people that were escaping . . . a dramatic liturgical gesture, Rory called it. Sure, he was madder than the hatter by then. The Brits were supposed to capture us as we crept out into the night and drove off in our cars to the hall. They disconnected the bombs all right, but there was a firefight when we pulled up in the car park next to the hall."

"Maybe the Brits wanted to kill most of you."

"I've thought of that often. Sure, they wouldn't have minded getting rid of me then. It was only when I survived that they began to worry about protecting an informer. It was a quick fight. In three or four minutes, everyone was dead but Seamus and Rory and me. They wanted to try them. I was useless.

" 'Get rid of the cunt,' someone said. A constable had his revolver pointed at my head before the inspector stopped him."

"The Congo again."

"I was used to it by then." She shrugged indifferently. "Blood and corpses were part of my life. Anyway, there were a couple of hundred people alive the next morning who would have been dead if I hadn't turned informer. Most of them Prots at that."

"So the word spread around that you were an informer and the English got you out of Ireland."

"It was a disgrace then. Still is mostly. The Provos were delighted of course, because they didn't want competition from idjits. I've never felt guilty. I did what I had to do, and I don't care what people think. Well, the governments in Dublin and London were convinced that I was a heroine, so they wanted to keep me alive. They manufactured a new identity for me and sent me off to Sussex. I wouldn't take any of their money. My parents had died, and I used the little bit of legacy they left me to stay alive in the first years in school and pay for a good private psychiatrist. You know the rest."

"No, I really don't. It's a story of heroism that tops the others. I'll have to hear it someday soon."

"No, Brendan, my darling," she said sadly. "You and your fierce little daughter must return to America. It's not your fight. You'll be in the way. I don't want you to be hurt. You're innocent, like the people in the music hall."

"You come with us. We can do better than those stupid Irish cops. I have some friends. . . ."

She pulled away from me. "They're good cops, Brendan. You don't understand how fiendishly clever Rory is. And how much money the Libyans have given him. He has bought his own gunmen, though none of them is as crazy for revenge as he and Seamus Cagney."

"Did Jaymo tell you what really happened to the *Brigid*?" I demanded fiercely, pulling her back to my arms.

"He did indeed. They overreacted. It doesn't matter. Rory would have caught up with me anyhow. I have to face him myself. It's between the two of us anyway. Maybe if he comes out in the open to hunt me down now that I'm alone, the Special Branch will get him before he gets me. I want you and the lass out of the line of fire. I have enough on my conscience."

"That's crazy," I shouted.

"Hush, darling." She touched my lips.

"How many men does he have? You'll be outnumbered."

"At the end it will be only the two of us, and maybe Seamus, who is big but dumb, too dumb to make any difference."

So, not a short man with a cap.

"It's your martyr complex, woman. Your shrink in Sussex would tell you that."

She considered thoughtfully. "Sure, maybe it is. Maybe if I rid the world of poor Rory, I'll have expiated everything."

"Expiated what? Bravery? Enthusiasm? Love? Or hate and some incestuous feelings toward your father?"

Oh dear God in Heaven, why didn't You keep my big mouth shut?

Ciara, however, was not offended. "You're terrible clever, Brendan Ryan. Maybe it is neurotic. Or maybe I still have to finish what I started ten years ago. He'll kill hundreds more if I let him."

"What are your chances of winning this soggy Irish version of *High Noon*?"

She laughed happily. "Ah, my little king, you're wonderful. Irish *High Noon* indeed."

"That doesn't answer my question."

"One in twenty . . . and don't argue. It's better dying than living with the threat of his vengeance haunting me for the rest of my life. If I win, I'll phone you. We can talk then about us."

I begged, I pleaded, I argued, I reasoned. She was a woman with an obsession. She had lived too long the life of a fugitive. She was in no position to think clearly about the subject. She had no real friends at Sussex. I would bring her back to an environment where there would be more friends than she would know what to do with (ah, my Ciara, how you would capture Grand Beach). We would protect her and love her. She would no longer be a fugitive. The spooks from Dublin, Washington, and London would have to deal with us. Cardinal Cronin's sister-in-law was a United States senator, on the Intelligence subcommittee. No more overreactions.

"You're a powerful debater," she said dubiously; but she was not totally unconvinced.

I ran for daylight. She was a mature and sophisticated woman, the girl that her classmates at Kylemore had adored, now at the fulfillment of a long and extraordinarily painful maturing process. The strain of running from Sussex and running again from Chicago had caused some old emotional wounds to be opened. She had dealt with the renewed pain very well. But now the pressures were so great that she had made an unwise decision. It was not too late to unmake it. All she needed to do was permit her intelligence to reassert itself.

"Maybe you're right, darling man." She laid her head on my shoulder. "I'm so tired from trying to think everything out that I don't know what I'm doing. Maybe I wanted to hear you say all these things."

If Mary Kate Ryan Murphy had been available, she would have told me that I had awarded myself victory too easily, that Ciara had a demonic need to seek a Götterdämmerung with Rory McLafferty. Looking back on the argument, I often wonder whether maybe Ciara was right. It may have been that she would be free from his lurking menace only when she herself obliterated it.

Anyway, I was convinced that I had saved her from disaster, one more victory for the Irish mythological hero, the Finn MacCool of the south side of Chicago.

So, to seal my triumph, I began to kiss her breasts, at first slowly, almost casually, then with a need so fierce that it frightened both of us.

"Oh, Brendan," she cried.

"Sorry." I stopped.

"I didn't say you had to stop." She gulped. "Sure, Ireland makes you one of them ravishing Irish mythical heroes."

"Like Finn MacCool?"

"For instance. Go ahead. I always wondered what it would be like to be ravished by Finn MacCool."

Our fantasies meshed. I don't know whether the result terrified Ciara. Her cries were indecipherable. It terrified me, however. I was indeed capable of becoming a wild pagan king. I discovered that there were many wonderfully violent things you could do with a woman and neither hurt nor degrade her. The rite of spring became more manic and more ecstatic.

We made love two more times, as desperately and wildly as when I first came into the room. I was once more triumphant, my child was safe and growing in her womb.

"Sure," she murmured contentedly, "you're not bad at all, at all as Finn MacCool."

Exhausted (really exhausted; I'm not as young as your man Finn MacCool in his prime, and the ravishing of women takes a lot out of you as the years go by), I fell asleep, confident that there was nothing more to worry about.

When I awoke she was gone. No message. Indeed, no sign of anyone besides me ever being in the room.

Damn stupid, stubborn Irishwoman, I thought, substituting willpower for intelligence. Off to the Congo again, asking to be a martyr.

Furious at her and at myself and grimly determined to find her and shake her back into her senses, I left the room, rode down the elevator, and stalked out of the hotel. The man in the cap was waiting in the lobby. He had fallen asleep. I studied his lean face carefully as I went by him. I would know him if I saw him again.

The ride back to Ashford was much quicker. The rain had turned into soft mist, and the roads were uncrowded. I was in my room shortly after midnight. I checked the Uzi. Safe and sound where I had left it. I was still outraged at Ciara's stupidity.

I asked the switchboard to ring Jean. I owed her an apology and an explanation.

There was no answer.

Jean was gone too.

five
THE STRAND AT INCH

34

*I*n the 4:00 A.M. sunlight pouring through the window, Detective Superintendent Jaymo Finnegan and I stood in Jean's room amid the confusion and disarray that mark the rooms of most late adolescent young women.

"You'd be thinking that this is the way her room usually is?" he asked, unlit pipe clenched between his teeth.

"Do you have teenage daughters, Superintendent?"

"I take your point . . . So we can assume that her abductors are responsible for none of it. She was taken without a struggle. Probably put out by an injection or a whiff of something strong."

"If she were awake, she wouldn't have left quietly."

Several Gardai, some in uniform, some not, were bustling about the room taking pictures and dusting for fingerprints. Useless activity, but it kept them busy.

"Aye, I suppose not." He sighed profoundly. "It would require only two people. One to hold her and the other to stick the hypodermic in her. Bundle her up in the blanket that's apparently missing, carry her down the back steps, and put her into a car."

"While your drugged constable slept soundly."

He puffed on the empty pipe. "We'll probably find that the maid who brought him the coffee doesn't work here."

"That's hardly an excuse."

"And he'll be able to identify her, when we show him the picture, as one of the people we know is working for McLafferty."

"Much good that will do."

Jaymo sighed again and eyed me curiously. He could not understand my reaction. Nor was I about to tell him that while I was furious about the kidnapping of Jean, I was completely convinced, with the certainty of a simple addition, that I would recover her and punish those who had frightened and perhaps hurt her. I was worried about Jean, guilty, remorseful, ashamed of my stupidity. Anger and the implacable certainty of vengeance were stronger than my other emotions. Was I not invulnerable? Even Ciara thought I was another Finn MacCool.

Looking back on such idiocy, I marvel that I could have so deceived myself. Jet lag, the turbulence of the last few weeks of my life, dead bodies lying at my feet, sleep deprivation, the excitement of the chase, a few lucky guesses, and some spectacular sex had made me feel that I was an actor in a mythological saga, the good Titan in conflict with a bad Titan. The dizzying speed of spring's sacrificial dance had driven me further round the bend than McLafferty.

Was not the Special Branch officer leaning innocently against the dresser in which my Uzi was waiting for the opportunity to dispose of my enemies?

"We have roadblocks set up all over the west of Ireland," the superintendent said tentatively.

"What does he want?"

"With a shitehawk like your man McLafferty," he waved his pipe in a gesture of bafflement and frustration, his language losing its diplomatic veneer, "you can never tell. He might snatch the lass for one reason and then change his mind and use her for another purpose, like he changed his mind when he rammed her boat out on Lough Corrib. With your ordinary international terrorist, do you see, there are fairly predictable patterns of behavior. We know in general how they behave, what they want, how they'll react, even where they're likely to hide. European police forces are ahead of them now. McLafferty?" He made a wry face. "He thinks he's an Irish Carlos. But Carlos, while he's a psychopath, is not an Irish psychopath, he's not a complete loony besides."

"So?"

"Your man Rory wants attention, he wants to perform, he wants a chance for the absurd dramatic gesture. That makes him more dangerous and harder to hunt down."

"And means that Jean is in greater danger?"

"Maybe. Maybe not. It all depends what kind of insane idea is in his head. Phases of the moon are more useful for predicting what he will do than any of our psychological profiles."

I inspected pictures of McLafferty and his crowd. Seamus Cagney, the only survivor of his original band, was a big, blond, overweight linebacker type. "Loves the women, especially when they don't want it," Jaymo remarked dryly.

Maeve Conroy. Thick, stolid, hair tightly bound behind a square, malevolent face. Glowing eyes that reminded me of pictures of Doc Holliday when he was in the final stages of TB. "She's the killer of the crowd, the professional. Enjoys watching bodies come apart."

Dick McBeen. Tall, skinny, bookish, with thick glasses. "Blows things up and operates radios and such like."

Conor Murtaugh. A little man with a big mustache. "Smuggles weapons, currency, and drugs. Runs errands. Enjoys torture." My friend in the blue hatchback.

Kevin O'Malley. Young fellow, handsome black Irishman with thick hair hanging over his brow. "Not too bright. Up from the streets of Derry. A marvel with the automatic weapons, if you take my meaning."

"Ireland knows how to produce terrorist kooks," I observed.

"Aye. We've had enough practice."

I should have told him that Conor Murtaugh had shadowed me to Galway. I should have told him that Ciara had been in the Railway Hotel. But Jaymo Finnegan and his constables and sergeants and inspectors were now at most useful auxiliaries. I would handle this matter myself. They would provide me with occasional information and assistance.

I did not even need Mike Casey and the "main force" from Chicago. Mike had sent me my weapons. That was enough. One Ryan was a match for half a dozen Irish gangsters. More than a match.

I would kill the lot of them and be done with this nonsense. The berserker was a Celtic innovation, wasn't it? Like the urban terrorist?

"What do you want me to do?" I asked tonelessly.

"Well," he studied me carefully, "we'll be doing all we can. Maybe, if you don't mind, you could wait in your room. Sure, your man Rory will be getting in touch with you when it suits him. We might make it easier for him to find you."

"Fine. I presume you'll monitor the calls."

"I wouldn't count on that, however. He doesn't make dumb mistakes. Rory is not as efficient as those Italian"—he pronounced it "Eyetalian"—"kids with their training in sociology. He blunders along and gets away with it because of recklessness and cunning, doesn't like to be held down to a routine or a detailed plan."

"Crazy but not stupid?"

"Aye. Here are some pictures of him in his various disguises."

The top picture was of a good-looking young man with curly hair, a thin sharp face, and an engaging smile. A big fellow whose broad shoulders and thick arms suggested athletic skill. He looked like an actor who plays minor parts in movies about Ireland—a drinking companion of John Wayne in the pub, perhaps—and whose name is on the tip of your tongue but you can't quite remember it.

Yet there was something not quite right about his face. All the parts were distinguished enough, but the fit seemed wrong, and there was a hint of exhaustion, of a man living on the edge, of a mountain climber, perhaps, who has been pushed beyond the limits of his resources.

Worst of all were his eyes. There was laughter in them,

but cold, hard laughter of the sort you would hear from a prankster specializing in cruel practical jokes.

Finn MacCool or not, I shivered. Poor Jean was at the mercy of a monster. I would save her. But in the meantime she would be terrified.

It was hard to believe that he was the same person in the other pictures—a devout old priest, a bluff seaman, a stoop-shouldered countryman, a bleary-eyed taxi driver.

The man who had driven us to the station in Dublin.

I told Jaymo.

"You see the problem. He's the very devil himself for creating disguises."

"That's fine when he's traveling alone." I handed the pictures back to a nameless inspector who seemed to lurk always at Jaymo's left elbow. "This crowd of his should be a little less easy to hide."

Again Jaymo Finnegan considered me thoughtfully. "Aye. 'Tis true. And he doesn't know yet that we are aware of whom he's hired."

"Your friends the Provos being helpful?"

"Let's say that there's lots of people in a position to know who hope that we get Rory so they won't have to do it later down the road. By the way, if you don't mind my asking, what kind of sleeping dress does the young lady wear?"

"A long T-shirt on this trip, green trimmed with gold. Notre Dame letters on the front in gold. The number fourteen on the back, also in gold."

"Patriotic," he sniffed. "I wish I could be more reassuring, Mr. Ryan. To tell the truth, Rory McLafferty is a very scary man."

"I understand."

A man who endangers my women and my children, born and unborn. A man with a very short life expectancy. We know how crazy he is. He doesn't know how crazy I am.

I waited in my room for several hours, calm, patient, and, as I fancied myself, deadly.

The phone rang. "Brendan Ryan."

"I imagine you'd be knowing who I am." An exuberantly cheerful voice.

I must be cautious. Neither panic-stricken nor threatening. Let him think of me as self-contained and straight-forward.

"Indeed."

"Sure, I suppose that fucking shite Jaymo Finnegan is somewhere listening. Top of the morning to you, Jaymo. I hope you'd be after giving me credit for not telling your man Ryan to stay away from the Garda. Always thought that was a foolish instruction."

"What have you done with her, McLafferty?" I said tersely, figuring that in this round I would set him up with his lines.

"To the pretty wee girl, is it? Nothing at all, at all. Ah, sure, we wouldn't hurt her for the world. You'll have her back in a day or two, if you do what you're told."

"What am I to do?"

"At the moment, nothing at all. Go back to Dublin and wait there till you get further instructions. Jaymo and his friends will be searching for us. Sure, they might be lucky and find us. And the lass might be lucky and not be killed when they do, but if I were in your position, Mr. Ryan, I'd be hoping that they weren't lucky, if you understand my meaning?"

"I understand."

"Aren't you going to ask for proof that we have her?" He sounded a bit petulant.

"All right, prove to me that you have her."

"Well, now, if I was a proper father, I wouldn't let a daughter of mine sleep in one of them green and gold T-shirt things, even if it does have 'Notre Dame' on it. Them things rip real easy, you know."

"Oh? And how do I know she's still alive?"

"That's better now." He sounded cheerful again. "Well, for example, let's listen to the T-shirt ripping . . ."

An anguished cry of a woman in terrible pain. He had done more than tear her clothes.

"You understand, Mr. Ryan?" He laughed softly. "We have her, and at the minute she's still alive. Would you like to say a word to Daddy, love?"

"Please, Daddy, please do whatever they tell you. I'm all alone with these monsters. They'll hurt me, they'll kill me. Please, Daddy, I'm alone with them. Help me . . ." Her voice was cut short by another terrible shriek.

"I asked you if you understand, Mr. Ryan?" Pleasant but mildly impatient.

"I understand."

"Good enough then. You go to Dublin and wait for my next message. If I were you I wouldn't leave the hotel for too long."

"I won't."

"Good man," he said approvingly. "Now, as for you, Jaymo, I'm sure you'll be trying to trace this call. It won't do you any good at all, at all. But you might as well have a go at it anyhow. It'll make you feel that you're not useless altogether. And you'll keep this out of the papers, won't you? I don't want the American Marines coming in here like they did in Lebanon." He chuckled. "Not yet anyway."

"I'm sure we'll keep it out of the papers."

"Good man. Well, don't be impatient, Mr. Ryan. I'll be in touch. Good day to you."

"Good day."

When Jaymo Finnegan burst into my room a few moments later, I was sitting by the window gazing calmly at Lough Corrib.

"You understand now what we're dealing with?"

"Oh, yes."

"He's going to want to trade the lass for Clare."

"I assumed as much. Why the delay?"

Jaymo slumped in the chair across from me. "To make you frantic with worry."

"Oh."

"He doesn't seem to have done that yet." He removed his pipe and put it back in his pocket. Doesn't the man ever take off his raincoat?

"I'm worried, Superintendent," I said coolly. "Very worried. I see no point in becoming frantic."

"Well, now . . ." His big brown eyebrows shot up. " 'Twould be a bit better if you sounded frantic the next time you talk to him. Otherwise he might turn skittish on us. Your man Rory doesn't like anyone spoiling his game."

"Yes. I understand that," I said softly. "Next time I will sound properly frantic."

"He's a quare one." He shook his head dejectedly. "None of your continental terrorists would have let the lass speak to you on the phone. They'd use a tape recording to make sure there were no hints given of where she was. None of that technological stuff for him."

"He probably thought she was too frightened."

"Still, it's a risk. But then our friend Rory likes the risks."

"Yes, that's clear."

"There were no hints, were there?" he asked hopefully.

"She didn't have enough time. He didn't take much of a risk. Tell me, Jaymo, does he have sympathizers who assist him?"

"There are people in Ireland who think he's a grand man for killing Prots and Brits. They say, turn Rory loose in London and he'll kill a few thousand Brits before they get him. That's the only way to drive the Brits out of Ireland." He shuddered. "There's some method in it, Brendan. If I were a Provo I'd think the same way. Murder gets easier the more often you do it. So, yes, there are people who will help him, just as there were Yanks who protected the crazies that kidnapped the poor Hearst kid."

"Many?"

"No. But enough to provide him with some cover. And they're not your typical Provo sympathizer, either. That makes it harder for us."

"I see. Well, I suppose I'd better pack and return to Dublin."

"If it's all the same to you," he stood up, "I'd like you to drive back with us. Sure, it's a long ride in the rain."

I laughed softly. "Delighted, Jaymo. I don't like driving on your Irish highways in the rain."

I packed my things and Jean's, finding some amusement in the thought that my arsenal would ride back to Dublin in the boot, as the Irish call the trunk of a car, of a detective superintendent of the Special Branch.

Mike Casey. I had called him yesterday to thank him for the delivery of his package and assured him that matters were progressing. It was too early to call him today.

Should I tell him about Jean? No, not yet. Not till it was clear that I needed the main force. Finn didn't call for the Fenians till the last minute, nor Robin for the Merry Men, nor Lancelot for the Round Table. So far, I was sure I could take care of the situation by myself. I wouldn't mention the kidnapping when I phoned him from Dublin.

The blue hatchback was no longer at the entrance to Ashford Castle. Conor Murtaugh, was it? Conor, your life expectancy isn't very great.

We drove through the Sunday afternoon rain from Cong to Dublin in silence. I was removed from the world, as immune to the passage of time as I was to terror. I would save Jean, and Ciara too.

"Would you mind if I ask a question?" Jaymo Finnegan, who had carefully refrained from lighting his pipe in the car, asked cautiously as we drove through Phoenix Park, inside the city limits of Dublin.

"By all means."

"Did you see much action in the war?"

"Some."

I wasn't going to admit that my combat experience had lasted no more than two hours.

"I see."

"Why do you ask?"

"Well," he hesitated, "begging your pardon if I'm being offensive, but you are a very cool man—as though you have had a lot of combat."

"Not that much, Jaymo. Pretty concentrated while it lasted. I'm calm because I'm confident."

"In us?" he asked dubiously as the car turned into what I guessed was the usual traffic jam on O'Connell Street.

"In myself."

"I see." He really didn't. "What will you do?" He shifted uneasily next to me in the backseat of the Volvo.

"I told you already, Superintendent. I'm going to kill the fucking piss artists."

Which wasn't exactly what I had said before but I was picking up the linguistic habits of the natives.

The woman constable who was driving the car and the silent aide-de-camp inspector who sat next to her both gasped.

"All of them?" Jaymo asked incredulously.

"Why not?"

"You're a fucking idjit," he said, not without some admiration.

I'm sure they all thought that I was more daft than Rory McLafferty.

"By the way, after I drop these bags with the hall porter at the Shelbourne, would you drive me back to the procathedral? I want to attend the five-thirty Mass."

"What if McLafferty calls?" He turned to look at me like I was a raving lunatic.

"Then he'll call again, I imagine. I'm a Catholic, and Catholics go to Mass on Sunday."

I pictured with considerable satisfaction the conversation they would have when they delivered me to the procathedral.

There was room for me in the Shelbourne. I returned to the Garda car. "All right. Now to the procathedral."

At Mass I prayed with fervor and intensity for Jean and Ciara that their hope would endure until I could free the one and find the other.

I prayed for myself too. With serene confidence that God would grant me victory. My cause was just, after all, wasn't it?

I walked back to the Shelbourne in the rain, enjoying Dublin in the mists and the smell of the sea on an early Sunday evening. The next week, I thought, would be very interesting.

I had already made one intolerable blunder, which I would not comprehend for several days.

Even Finn MacCool made an occasional mistake.

35

Monday morning I walked down Grafton Street from the Shelbourne to the Bank of Ireland in Grattan's beautiful old Georgian parliament building, across the street from Trinity College, stopping in Bewley's for tea and scones. I had picked out a number of men hanging around the lobby of the hotel who might have been Jaymo's tails. None of them came into Bewley's after me, but a young brown-haired woman, in a neatly belted dark brown raincoat, who looked like she might be a novice in a traditional religious order on a forbidden day off, did drift into the coffee shop. Hadn't I seen her in the Shelbourne too?

So, Jaymo.

I drank my two cups of tea, ate my hot scones, and returned to the chill mists. At the Bank of Ireland I demanded to see an assistant director and presented my letter of credit. The young man, who spoke like Ciara when she was affecting her Trinity College accent, glanced through his file of cables, came upon my recommendation from Continental Illinois, and agreed with a broad smile to cash my check for five thousand Irish punts (pounds to you who have never been there).

"The Continental is still open?" I asked lightly.

"Oh, yes, sir. We feel that the Fed will go first."

"Too bad they can't guarantee the Cubs."

"Yes, sir, it is," he agreed politely.

She never did go to Trinity, I thought as I left the bank; she did her graduate work in England. The woman is tricky. She is also splendid for ravishing, and there'll be more of that when I find her.

The brown-coated novice continued to trail far behind me when I left the bank and strolled across the Liffey, which smelled badly of fish, and into a shoe store on O'Connell Street. I purchased a pair of Adidas jogging shoes and a set of large galoshes of the sort that I had seen on the countrymen in County Galway.

In the next shop I obtained for myself a medium-size canvas duffel bag, which was wrapped up in a small package.

Then I walked leisurely back down the crowded streets in the heart of Dublin to my hotel. The young woman dropped out of sight at the corner of Dawson Street and Stephen's Green.

It would be reported to Superintendent Finnegan that the Yank drank tea at Bewley's, visited the Bank of Ireland, and made small purchases in two shops on O'Connell

Street. He would check with the bank, lift a thick eyebrow at my five thousand punts, assume that I was planning on jogging to stay in condition, and instruct the constable to continue to watch me.

From a public phone in the lobby, I made a couple of calls to auto dealers and finally found the one I wanted on the road back to Galway.

Then I settled in my room with a book of Seamus Heaney's poetry to wait for the call from Rory McLafferty, which I did not expect that day anyway.

The next morning I scanned the lobby briefly after I had purchased my *Irish Times*. The woman constable was in a corner eating a roll and drinking a cup of coffee. I rode up to my room in the dubious cage elevator, which seemed to be required for atmosphere in all Irish hotels, grabbed my raincoat, and ducked down the stairs, out the back door of the Shelbourne, and into busy pedestrian traffic on Merrion Street. I hailed a taxi and told the driver I wanted to go to the Gresham Hotel on O'Connell Street.

A few doors down from the Gresham and around a corner on a side street, I found a secondhand clothing store, where, after more time spent on negotiating and estimating sizes than I wanted to risk, I purchased gray trousers and jacket, two shirts that would never be white again, a worn sweater vest, a rubberized rain slicker, and a battered gray cap. The jacket was a size too large for me, leaving enough room for a vest containing an Israeli machine gun.

"It's a trifle roomy, sir," said the young clerk.

"Aye," I agreed impassively.

I found a taxi at the stand down the street from the Gresham and fretted impatiently on the slow ride across the Liffey to Merrion Street. The back door of the hotel was locked, but I slipped in with a man who looked like he might be in charge of elevator repairs.

"Not working again?" I asked when he glanced dubiously at me.

"Sure, it doesn't work half the time. And the other half it's fixing not to work."

I rushed up the stairs, dumped my bundles on my bed, checked with the switchboard to see if there had been any calls for me, and then strolled with elaborate casualness back down to the lobby. My novice friend was still there, reading the *Irish Times*. Actually, with her coat off, she looked more like a postulant.

Back in my room, I packed my purchases into the canvas duffel bag, along with slacks, a sweater, shoes, and some underwear for Jean, and settled back with a copy of Maeve Binchy's *Light a Penny Candle*. Before I began to read I played over again in my mind the scenario for the conversation I planned with McLafferty. I was certain that after that conversation I would be ready to move.

No reason for that certainty other than my blind arrogance.

Late that afternoon, the hall porter called my room to say that there was a package for me in the lobby. I asked him to send a bellman up with it.

"Did you see who delivered this?" I gave the young, red-haired bellman two punts and accepted the small, oblong box, which was wrapped rather sloppily in wrinkled brown paper.

"Let me see, sir." He frowned thoughtfully. "Was it a little man in a black cap?"

"With a big mustache and a short nose?"

"Long nose, I'd say."

Conor Murtaugh. Bad risk. What if Jaymo had enough constables to watch the front of the hotel and follow the blue hatchback?

Perhaps Rory McLafferty knew that the Special Branch didn't have enough personnel to do that. Still, what if they made an exception in this case? The poor fool must have thought he was invulnerable.

After the bellman left, I opened the package and called the number that Jaymo had given me.

"Hello."

"Ryan. I have a VHS tape here. Probably from McLafferty. Can you play it for me?"

"We'll be right over."

It was the same team that had drove in from Cong—the silent inspector, the sergeant who drove the car, and the blonde woman constable. Gallantry had triumphed over feminism: the inspector rather than the constable was carrying the VCR.

He plugged it in, and I inserted the tape. We settled back in our chairs and waited for the latest entertainment from your man Rory.

Entertainment it was, of the most vicious type imaginable.

A shaky picture of a wall panel, which did not look like a room in a house. The cameraman did not know how to use his equipment.

What kind of a room was it? First clue that Finn MacCool, mythical hero and invulnerable detective, missed.

The camera zoomed back, revealing Jean tied to a chair, hands behind her back. Her green sleep shirt had been torn on one side, revealing half of her body. She looked frightened and pathetic, but her little chin was still tilted defiantly.

"She a pretty wee thing, isn't she, Brendan Ryan?" McLafferty's voice in the background. "It'd be a shame to have to disfigure her, wouldn't it now. Sure, so far we haven't hurt her much at all. Have you ever seen your daughter naked, Brendan?" A hand pulled away her torn shirt. "Lovely, isn't it? Does it give you incestuous thoughts? Ah, well, fathers and daughters are often that way. It can't be helped, can it?"

"Stop them, Daddy." Jean was hysterical. "They hurt me all the time. I'm alone. There's no one to protect me."

"The poor girl is all alone." McLafferty giggled insanely. "Isn't that a pity, Daddy? Sure, she hasn't been hurt much at all, at all. Yet. No one has even raped her yet, though there's them here that wants to."

"I'm alone, Daddy," she sobbed.

"Alone is it?" McLafferty pretended to be offended. "That's not the way to talk about your Uncle Rory, who is protecting you from all the bad men here."

"Daddy. . . ." A heartrending cry.

McLafferty chuckled as the camera jerked to her face, showing an expression of abject horror.

"I'm a patient man, Brendan Ryan," McLafferty said

soothingly, as the camera zoomed back to show us Jean, slumped, perhaps unconscious, in her chair. Again a shot of the strange wood paneling, painted dark brown, in the background. "But there's a limit to my patience. You'll be hearing from me soon."

The picture ended abruptly. White electronic snow on a black background.

"Bloody bastards." Jaymo turned off the switch savagely. The young woman constable was weeping softly. The inspector, his fist clenched, was staring out the window at the fog-shrouded green.

"They're trying to frighten you, sir." Jaymo turned to me. "The lass is still alive. They've hurt her, but nothing too terrible yet. We'll find them, never fear."

"Of course, Superintendent. Of course."

I swore to myself that they would all die slowly and horribly. I didn't tell Jaymo who had delivered the package. Nor did I ask what clues, if any, they had. Soon my own plans would unfold.

"We'll take it back to the castle and analyze it." Jaymo motioned his inspector to pack up the video player.

"I'd like to see it again, if you don't mind."

The woman constable stared at me in disbelief. The poor wee man was way round the bend. Nonetheless, they played it again. A vague, as yet unfocused idea about the brown wall teased at my brain. I knew more than I was yet able to articulate. It would come. Soon.

Looking back now, I realize that I was a stupid fool to have missed it. I was too busy with the appearance of my new role as mythical berserker to see the obvious.

Jaymo and his crew left with many promises that they'd have Jean back to me "safe and sound" in short order. I hardly listened to them.

I sat there for hours, blankly watching darkness settle over the misty green. The streetlights glowing dimly beneath my window and across the street suggested Sherlock Holmes in a dangerous neighborhood in Soho.

I would kill them all, slowly, so that they would suffer terribly.

I drew the canvas attaché case from my closet and tenderly cleaned and polished the components of the Uzi. I fitted the components together carefully and squeezed the trigger to make sure that the weapon was in operating order. Then I checked, as an afterthought, Mike Casey's .22.

Finally I fell asleep and dreamed of bodies being torn apart.

McLafferty called at ten the following morning. His connection was poor, and the strong wind that was rattling my windowpanes made it even harder to hear him.

"Are we ready to do business now, Mr. Ryan?"

"I'll give you anything you want," I sobbed. "But don't hurt her anymore. Please don't hurt her."

"Ah, that's a sensible man now." He sounded pleased that my icy calm had been replaced by the reaction for which his script called. "I have nothing against the poor child and don't want to have to hurt her anymore. But there's some things, however tragic, that must be done in a nation's fight for freedom. I'm sure a Yank understands that."

Freedom ideology. I supposed he still thought he believed it some of the time.

"I'll give you all the money you want." I permitted myself to sound like I was crying. "Just give her back to me."

" 'Tis not money I want." He chuckled. "Sure, someone with more than you gives me all I need. I want something else."

Suddenly I understood where Jean was. I'd been a stupid fool. Folk heroes, however, do not permit such self-criticism to last long.

"Anything, anything." I tried desperately to concentrate on the scenario. The rest could wait. My heart, however, was thumping with eagerness for battle.

"Even Clare Keenan?"

"My God, McLafferty, I don't have her."

"Ah, sure, but you know where she is, don't you now?"

"Only that she's out there waiting to kill you."

"What?" He was astonished. "Kill me?"

"I saw her at the Railway Hotel in Galway." I stumbled as though I were in a rush to tell him everything. "She left when I was asleep. She knows you're after her. She's going to kill you when you catch up with her."

I bit my tongue to keep from telling him that his dumb friend Con Murtaugh had fallen asleep in the lobby of the hotel.

"She's against killing," he said dubiously.

"God in Heaven, Rory. You understand women. You know what they're like. A man pushes them around and pushes them around and they don't fight back. Then, one day, without any warning, they explode. A woman like that is as dangerous as a she-tiger."

"Aye," he said thoughtfully, accepting my implied flattery of his understanding of women. "That's true for a fact . . . but where is she?"

"How would I know? If she had told me, do you think I wouldn't have tipped off the Garda? Do you think I want her out there, ticking like a bomb?"

"Aye," he said again, pondering the reasonableness of my answer.

"You know her better than I do. Your guess as to where she's waiting for you would be better than mine."

I hoped I wasn't increasing the dangers for Ciara. At any rate, I would save her the same way I would now save Jean.

There was a moment of silence while Rory thought about it.

"Tell you what, Brendan, my friend; we'll work out a little compromise. We'll keep the lass while I have a look around. If I find Clare, we'll give the lass back to you. While I'm searching, we won't do anything serious to hurt her, just a bit now and then to keep up the morale of my people. If I don't find Clare, well, I'll be back in touch with you."

"Please don't hurt Jeannie," I screamed.

The phone line clicked dead, but not before he had a chance to savor my horror.

I waited a few minutes to make sure I was in full possession of myself and my plans. Then I put on my London Fog and slipped Mike's .22 into the pocket. I checked my jacket to make sure the wallet with the five thousand punts was there. Then I picked up the canvas duffel bag with my countryman's clothes and the tweed attaché case with the Uzi and opened the door to my room a crack. I looked in both directions down the corridor. No one in sight. I dashed to the stairwell and hurried down the stairs and out into the foggy alley behind the hotel. I thanked a gracious Heaven for the fog.

I boarded a taxi at the stand in Merrion Street and gave the driver the address of the place I had called on the Navan road, above Phoenix Park. He complained about the weather and the state of the economy for the whole trip. Nonetheless I tipped him generously and entered the used-car display room with a stern warning to myself that prolonged negotiations were essential if I did not want to stir up suspicions.

The negotiations were even more prolonged than I had anticipated. The car I wanted, a woebegone Morris Minor, would cost perhaps twelve hundred punts. But, sure, sir, you would not want to travel Ireland in a pile of junk, now would you?

I convinced them that I was an anthropologist from a university and it was a requirement of my work that I drive a moribund car. The salesman, who was tricky enough to be a law school dean, warned me that I could not export the car, "much as I doubt that you want to, sir, if you don't mind me saying so."

I could keep the license plates on the car while the registration was changed. Lucky accident. Finn MacCool, being a product of another age, with no understanding of modern law, had not thought of registration plates. I was covered, I assured him, by my American insurance policy. The Garda, he said, might want to see some proof of that in case of necessity but, "sure, you won't be getting into any accidents with this car, will you now, sir? It can't go fast enough to cause any trouble, can it?"

With some difficulty I got the Morris started, noticed that the roof leaked, and found a petrol station (see, I was learning the language) where, at the price of listening to doubtful comments about the car from the attendant, I had the gas tank filled. I continued west through Maynooth, where the seminary and the old castle of the Kildares

(Silken Thomas and his bunch) were hidden in fog, and on towards Mullingar.

I pulled off on a side road in the country and, protected by the fog, changed into my countryman's clothes, pulling the galoshes firmly up over my Adidas running shoes. I stuffed my own clothes into the duffel bag with the clothes I'd brought for Jean and transferred Mike's .22 to the pocket of my rain slicker.

I now looked something like an Irish countryman. If I remembered to walk slowly, speak very little, and nod my head like I understood everything, I might be able to pass for a few hours—which was all I would need.

I stopped in a hardware store in Mullingar and purchased three milk cans for the backseat of the Morris. The store owner talked to me knowingly about the problems of the dairy industry and about the "super levy"—whatever that was—and the present state of the Common Market.

I nodded and mumbled "aye" and "true enough" several times, and seemed to get away with it. Nonetheless I stopped at a tobacco store and bought a tin of pipe tobacco, two old pipes, a worn leather bag, and a lighter. I hadn't smoked a pipe since college. To be an authentic Irish countryman, you need not smoke a pipe, only suck on it.

Thus arrayed I left Mullingar, bound back to the West of Ireland and my confrontation with Rory McLafferty. He would, I was confident, be dead by nightfall.

36

I sat in the corner of the shabby pub which smelled like the men's room in a broken-down railroad station, drinking my pint of Guinness as slowly as I could. Guinness, they said, was good for you. I thought it tasted even darker than it looked and longed for my Jameson's. But a countryman does not drink Jameson's in the local. Paddy's maybe, but I didn't think I was that kind of countryman. Anyway, I'd as soon drink gasoline from my Morris Minor.

I was in the town of Athlone, where I would have been Sunday night if I had listened carefully to Jean's signal that she was "alone." She was somewhere above Athlone on Lough Ree on a boat—the brown wood in the picture screamed "boat" if you knew what you were looking for.

It was possible that McLafferty and his thugs were moving the boat down the Shannon, but unlikely. There were too many locks where someone might be suspicious. Lough Ree—a lake formed by a widening of the Shannon—provided plenty of room and was filled with boats. Nothing to arouse suspicion if you kept your distance from the others.

Which boat of the scores on the lake? I circled the lake as soon as I arrived in my burping and swaying Morris, looking for a dark blue VW hatchback parked between the road and the piers and marinas that lined the shore, particularly on the east shore of the lake. I could not find it.

I then scouted the town of Athlone, pausing a few moments on the bridge over the Shannon to watch that fabled water goddess (Sionna in Irish) rush under the bridge towards her Atlantic destination far away, while thick, angry sheets of rain flailed against her. I thought of Ciara, wondered where she was, hoped that I had not increased her peril, and then walked back to my invalid car.

It would not do to wander through Athlone asking questions. My countryman's disguise would not last five minutes if I did that. Moreover, if Rory had chosen to hide here, it meant that he had friends and allies, perhaps sharp enough to wonder even about a new silver-haired countryman.

It was probable that he had chosen a slip or a pier or a marina on the east shore of the lake, on the Dublin side of the Shannon bridge. While there were more boats on that side, there was less likelihood that new boaters would be noticed. On a weekend the lake would swarm with people. But today was Wednesday.

So I decided to sit quietly in the public bar at the foot of the gravel road leading up the east side of the lake. The fish on the walls, the boat models, and its name—The Brass Anchor—suggested it was a place for boaters to pause for their pint or two. I knew what his crowd looked like, and they didn't know I knew. I would wait at the tiny, scratched, pockmarked table in the corner, with a bowed head that discouraged conversation, and sip stout for a couple of hours.

Perhaps one of his crowd would drop in. Maybe Con Murtaugh, returning from wherever he might have gone in the hatchback. If that didn't work, I'd have to prowl the side of the lake after dark, looking for a boat that showed lights.

While Finn MacCool does not have second thoughts, I considered again, just the same, my decision not to call in Jaymo and his troops from the Special Branch.

Doubtless they were skillful in dealing with the Provos; and they had read the confidential reports that Interpol had circulated about patterns of continental terrorist behavior. By Jaymo's own admission, however, Rory McLafferty was so mad that he didn't fit any of the profiles.

So, if they located him, they would do what all institutions do in time of crisis—not good things or wise things, but the things they do well. However much Jaymo would realize that the classic response might not work with Rory, he'd do what he would do with a Provo terrorist group because he had to do something.

They would try their Athlone informants for information, perhaps providing Rory with advance warning. Then, in the absence of information about which boat the terrorists were using, they would surround Athlone with roadblocks and close in on the lake, systematically searching every boat on the lake. When they finally found the one, whether by a tip-off or a search or luck—perhaps finding the blue hatchback for which I, too, was looking—they would surround it and inform Rory that he was finished. With helicopters whirling overhead, armored cars blocking escape, regular army troops with perhaps a tank or two poking around corners, the next step would be the formula for negotiating the release of hostages at which the police of the Western world had become very good.

Then, according to the scenario, Rory would first send Jean out and after some hesitation come out himself, hands on the top of his head. Another victory for the Special Branch.

It was at the end that the scenario lost its plausibility. I could not, no matter how hard I tried, picture Rory McLafferty docilely surrendering.

It was at least as plausible that he would cut Jean up into little pieces and then blow himself and his gang sky high.

Alternatively, they might send in specially trained commandos with stun grenades, like the Israelis at Entebbe. Only this wasn't Entebbe, and the Irish commandos, however good, were not picked elite troops from the best army the modern world has ever known.

Anyway, Rory would doubtless know about them. Once he realized that he was surrounded, he would expect such an attack eventually and act quickly. No long negotiations for him. So the commandos would have to strike immediately, before the panoply of modern anti-terrorist forces was in place. That would be a political decision, made by someone much higher in the Irish power structure than Jaymo—his minister or perhaps even the taoiseach (prime minister) himself.

No way I would trust my daughter's life to a political process like that. Besides, I was Finn MacCool, wasn't I?

Moreover, Rory was daft enough to have mined the boat so that it would go up in fire and smoke should anyone attempt a surprise attack. I had thought of that possibility. Would the CO of the commandos think of it or believe it?

Thank you, Republic of Ireland, but no thank you.

At seven o'clock, however, finishing my third Guinness and noticing a strange look from the publican when I signaled for a fourth, I realized that I couldn't hang around much longer.

" 'Tis a wet evening." He put the dark, somber liquid in front of me.

" 'Tis."

"A cold night to be out on the road."

I sighed and knocked the ashes out of my pipe. "Ay."

"A man needs a few pints to keep him warm."

"True enough."

Apparently satisfied, he left me and went back to the bar. I dared not order another. Maybe I should leave now. From what I could hear of the soft conversation at the bar, the patrons didn't think much of the Dublin government. Provo supporters?

Not far enough west to expect it, but as Jaymo had said, Rory would have an offbeat group of friends.

I worked my way through the Guinness, spilling as much of it as I could. I gathered my rain slicker from the chair across from me. The Uzi components were in the pocket of the special vest under my huge, heavy jacket. Leave in another couple of minutes.

The pub was run-down, the floor slippery, the "Gents" a pigsty, the tankards dirty, the lights dim. The foul-smelling peat fire had turned the room into an oven. Underneath my thick wool coat I was sweating like it was August in Chicago.

The door opened, and Con Murtaugh slouched in. The men at the bar greeted him enthusiastically.

He asked a muffled question. The publican nodded in my direction. Con glanced my way and dismissed me with a quiet curse.

Fool.

As best I could tell from the snatches of conversation I heard, Con had "delivered" someone. Jean? Rory?

Should I stay or leave? Con's eyes nervously flicked in my direction again.

I'd better get out. He might remain a long time. I'd already overstayed my leave. It would seem less conspicuous if I departed now.

I put on my rain slicker, turned up the collar, pulled down my cap, shoved my smoking material into the same pocket as Mike's .22, and walked, I hope, at the country's appropriately slow pace toward the door.

"Night." I touched the tip of my cap at the door.

"Night," said the little knot of men at the bar. Con Murtaugh did not even look around. Which might have meant that he was very cool or that he wasn't worried about me anymore.

His blue hatchback was parked in front of the pub next

to the Morris. I choked my car to life and with considerable noise chugged down the road back towards Athlone. I parked it next to a hedge perhaps a hundred yards away and slogged back to the pub. I found a tree across the road, sloshed through a drainage ditch, and took up an observation post behind the tree. It was twilight, the long twilight which, I had discovered, was typical of rainy nights in Ireland in the spring. For a couple more hours I'd be able to see the edge of the lake well enough to spot a blue hatchback.

In the meantime I had no choice but to wait in the rain and discover that not only my cap but also my slicker was no longer rainproof. Everything was soggy, branches, leaves, grass, road, me. Ireland needed two things, Frank O'Connor had once remarked, to be left alone by foreigners and one hell of a big roof. Big and thick. Until then it would not dry out till a month after Judgment Day and then only if the final act is, as predicted, fire.

Con must have consumed only one pint. He reappeared at the doorway in a panel of bright light and a burst of laughter. What a crazy way to run a terrorist operation. Only a zany Irish psychopath would permit his personnel to wander around drinking with the natives.

Nonetheless, Jaymo and the Special Branch had not found them yet.

Con glanced up and down the road, a routine inspection, entered his hatchback, backed it up, and drove north on the gravel road away from Athlone.

I gave him five minutes head start and then hurried down the road to my Morris, which now resolutely refused to start. I cursed, I pleaded, I threatened. No use. The man at the petrol station had been right: "Sure, it deserves a daycent Christian burial."

I got out of the driver's seat, kicked the engine with disgust, as I would a mule, decided to try it once more, and turned over the ignition.

It worked.

I understand you now, my friend. You've the personality of a mule.

There was no hope of following the VW's taillights now. I would have to scan the side of the road.

I drove for some time, half an hour perhaps, down the slippery road at slow speed, peering anxiously in the slowly failing light for a dark blue car.

I was convinced that I had found it next to a small marina. I parked a quarter mile down the road, jammed four ammo clips for the Uzi into my slicker pocket, and walked as slowly as I could make myself back to the marina.

I heard loud and drunken voices on an ancient cabin cruiser at the far end of the marina. Huddling in the lee of what looked like a boat house, I assembled my weapon, affixing the silencer and unfolding the plastic butt, inserted a clip into the magazine, hid it under my slicker, and eased around the corner of the boat house.

The car was blue and a VW all right, but not a hatchback. I turned to rush down the road, remembered what happened to soldiers in Vietnam whose weapons jammed, and returned to the lee of the boat house to remove the clip, disassemble my Uzi, and replace it in the Secret Service vest that Mickey had thoughtfully provided. I hoped the weapon had not been soaked by its brief exposure to the rain.

Back in the car I restrained my impatience again and dried the weapon with a handful of rags. I then reassembled and loaded it and placed it next to me on the left-hand front seat of the car. It was now growing very dark, and I might need it quickly.

I continued down the road, almost to the north end of the lough, without finding the hatchback. I must have missed it. There was no way I could retrace the search in the failing light. How much longer could Jeannie survive the horrors of her imprisonment? Time was running out for all of us.

Then I saw it, hidden behind a clump of bushes near a solitary pier jutting out into the lake from a thick growth of reeds. At the end of the pier was what looked, in the near darkness, like an old wooden houseboat.

My mouth turned dry, my stomach tightened, my fingers dug into the wheel of the car as I forced myself to drive out of sight of the boat. I was back in Nam, waiting for the VC to materialize between the rows of rubber trees.

I disassembled the Uzi and hid it in my holster vest. I debated discarding the rain slicker. It made movement more awkward, but it helped to keep my weapons and ammunition moderately dry. I checked Mike's .22, pulled off my galoshes, and in my soft running shoes walked briskly and noiselessly back to the pier.

I slipped across the road, found an opening in a thick hedge, and, stooped over in a crouch, moved directly opposite the VW. The rich, raw smell of Ireland was thick in the damp air—equal parts, I surmised, of peat, manure, and rotting underbrush.

My Neanderthal hunting instinct—if that was what it was—took over again. They must have a lookout somewhere. On a cold, rainy night, where would he be?

In the car?

I prepared my weapon, released the safety, set it at single shot, and forced my way through the hedge. As quietly as I could, I sloshed through the drainage ditch toward the car.

Con Murtaugh was inside, smoking a cigarette. I altered my course so that I would come up from the rear of the car. I could not fire through the window because the noise might bring out the rest of them. Yet I could not stand in the rain for long or my weapon might become too wet to use.

I found a rock at the side of the road, no difficult task in Ireland, and threw it into the mass of reeds. It made a dull splashing sound as it hit the water.

Murtaugh, suddenly alert, sat up straight, looked quickly out the window, and hesitated, trying to make up his mind whether to investigate.

I threw another stone.

He opened the door and stepped out of the car, peering into the darkness toward the reeds. He shrugged his shoulders, reached inside for his cap, and sauntered toward the water's edge.

In my soft shoes, I followed carefully behind him, waiting till he was almost at the edge of the water. Then I stepped clumsily on a piece of wood and made a small sound.

"What the fuck . . . ?" Con turned toward me, saw me in a quick slow-motion frame, and began to reach for his jacket pocket.

I was perhaps five or six yards behind him. I fired twice at close range. *Thump, thump,* the sounds deadened almost completely by the silencer.

Con's voice disappeared, and so did his face.

I rushed forward to catch him so that he would not fall loudly into the water. I did not look at the remains of his face as I eased him to the ground. The end of Con Murtaugh's life was quicker in the event than in the telling. Modern violence is nightmare-fast—and leaves images that will linger for the rest of your life.

I felt no sense of vengeance accomplished. Indeed, I felt nothing at all. There was still work to be done.

I crept back to the car, planning my next move. There were still five armed thugs on the boat, four if Rory was somewhere else. Someone would have to come out eventually to replace Con. I closed the door of the car and hid in the bushes a few feet away. I had time.

I checked the magazine clip. Only two rounds expended. Twenty-three left—a few seconds of automatic fire. I put the safety catch back on.

As I waited, I remembered Ciara's diatribe about abuse of women. For most of our history men have tormented and abused other men's women as part of the routine strategy of war. It was taken for granted that they had the right to do so. How many times before in Ireland's history must it have happened? On the shores of this very lake. Women were pawns, bribes, hostages, tokens. Ron Crowley's philosophy pushed to its ultimate conclusion.

God be good to him. And teach him the truth.

A door opened on the houseboat. Laughter and light came briefly from the inside. A big man emerged, Seamus Cagney, perhaps.

He fiddled with the door as he closed it, perhaps resetting an alarm system. Or a trigger on an explosive device.

Then, singing something about "Bold Fenian Men," he weaved a dubious path down the narrow pier.

I moved the change lever on the left side of the pistol grip forward from "S" to "D" and waited.

"All right, Conor Murtaugh, you fucking little gombeen-man, it's my turn," he bellowed. "Leave some of the fucking booze in the bottle for me."

He bumped into the front of the car, hiccuped, and stumbled around to the door.

"Where the hell are you?" he demanded.

I gently squeezed the trigger three times. *Thump, thump, thump.* Cagney straightened up, hung for a minute as though suspended in space, and then sagged against the car, moaning softly as his life breath departed him. Since I would have to change the clip anyway, I flipped the weapon to automatic and touched the trigger.

The Uzi discharged its bullets with a whooshing gasp, a single sustained *thump*.

The remains of Seamus Cagney slid quietly to the ground, the back of his jacket a mat of fresh blood. I dragged him away from the car into the bushes.

The Uzi, I thought irrelevantly, was like the blowguns the Pygmies use—swift and silent death. So easy to kill.

Two down, four or perhaps three to go. I had to move quickly now.

The rain had dwindled to a light drizzle, the classic "soft night" of Irish tales. I put my weapon back on "S," picked up a rock from the driveway, wrapped it in a thick rag I had brought for such purposes, and walked quietly and carefully down the pier. No point in trying to hide now.

I stepped cautiously onto the boat. It swayed slightly under my weight, but no more than it would if it were pushed by an extra large wave. The name on its stern was *Mystamaid*. Not especially appropriate, I thought.

Blessing the Adidas company for their quiet shoes, I crept along the side of the big cabin.

Two men were talking.

"If your man isn't back by morning, I'm going to take her myself. Sure 'tis torture to have to look at a half-naked woman like that for four days and not be able to use her."

"He has his plans."

"Fuck his plans. I want her. And I want her first too. That'll be the most fun."

"It won't do."

"Who the fucking hell is going to stop me? You? Don't make me laugh."

The window on the side of the cabin was at the height of my chest and reasonably large for a boat. With infinite care I peeked through one corner of it.

Two men were sitting at a table playing cards, with an almost empty unlabeled bottle of whiskey between them. Great revolutionary leader you are, McLafferty.

McBeen and O'Malley by the looks of them. No Rory or Maeve Conroy. Where's Jean?

Then I saw her, trussed up in the same chair as in the videotape, her Notre Dame shirt in tatters, her mouth gagged with dirty cloth, her face contorted in anguish, her body slumped painfully against the ropes.

"Have you never screwed an American virgin, Dick me boy? Take it from me, there's nothing like it. You have to push them around a bit to get them ready, you know what I mean? But then they get in the spirit of the thing and it's all the way home."

There was at least one more room, possibly two more forward of the main cabin. Rory was not there. Maeve?

I had no choice. It had to be now.

I moved the change bolt forward to automatic, pulled the cocking bolt back, gripped the Uzi by its stock in my left hand, and brought the big, cloth-sheathed rock against the window. It shattered with a slight tinkle.

The two card players looked up, mildly annoyed by the unexpected sound. I brought my weapon to the hole in the window and emptied the magazine into them, sweeping it across the room at waist level and then back a little higher.

Bright red spots appeared on their bellies and their chests. One of them emitted a stifled cry, half scream, half sob. The other died quietly. The short one stumbled and fell forward with a thud. The tall one merely collapsed like a sprinter at the end of a race. The room filled with smoke. Blood poured out on the floor. Tangled pieces of human insides oozed out of their bodies.

A charnel house, I thought.

I pulled the gun out of the hole in the windowpane, ejected the spent clip, and grabbed in my pocket for another. My trembling fingers let it slip away.

I hadn't noticed that my fingers and every other part of my body were quaking.

Jean was shouting into her gag, eyes filled with horror. She was trying to warn me. Of what?

I gripped another ammo clip firmly, inserted it into the magazine, and then looked through the window.

The door of the main cabin next to Jean abruptly swung open, and a squat, solid woman in sweatshirt and jeans burst through it, an AK-47 waving wildly in her right hand. She looked around the wreck of the room in wild-eyed dismay and then focused on me at the window.

She pointed the AK-47 in my direction and fired.

37

The scene passed before my eyes in second-by-second frames. The bullets left the muzzle of the AK-47 with popping noises like a string of large and rapid firecrackers. Maeve Conroy's weapon was pointed above me at the wrong angle. She had fired too quickly, a fatal mistake for her. The bullets chopped through the wall above my head as if the wall were made of tissue paper.

I squeezed the trigger of my weapon and forgot to release it. The entire clip of ordnance, exploding with a soft *whoosh*, tore into her stomach. The first woman I'd killed. New kick.

The AK-47 fell from her hands. She grabbed at her dissolving gut, expressions of surprise, disbelief, anger, and then resignation moving rapidly across her face. She saw her blood and intestines pouring out onto the floor, gave up on life, and fell slowly forward, collapsing in front of Jean, who sobbed through her gag.

I closed my eyes briefly. Five killed in a quarter hour. Not exactly Hiroshima, but a massacre nonetheless. So quickly does the thin red line around civilization disappear. A bloody, violent rite of spring.

I look back now on those moments and try to recapture my reactions. Brendan Ryan, whose colleagues won't let him go into a law court for litigation because he is too gentle and uncompetitive, had become Finn MacCool the berserker. What did I feel? Physical reactions—the terrible stench of exploding ammunition, the muffled cries of the dead and dying, the slashing explosions of AK-47, the steady thumping of Major Uziel Gal's nearly noiseless machine pistol, the swaying of the *Mystamaid* as its walls were shredded by bullets, the quavering weakness of my own body, horror at the dead bodies and bits and pieces of bodies scattered around the dimly lighted cabin. No satisfaction, no sense of vengeful triumph, vague regret that Rory was not there and that Ciara was still in danger, joy, very mild and understated, that I had saved Jean. But mostly nothing at all. I was as emotionally empty as a psychopath.

A berserker perhaps, but not one of your really first-rate berserkers. Even as Finn MacCool, not really a winner.

All this is in retrospect. At the time itself I opened my eyes and shouted, "Rory?"

Jean shook her head negatively and shrugged her frail little shoulders.

"Is the door booby-trapped?"

A vigorous affirmative nod.

"The window?"

A negative shake.

Dumb question. If it had been, the *Mystamaid* would have already been blasted into the sky.

I knocked away the rest of the windowpane with the butt of my weapon and climbed into the cabin. I stepped over Maeve Conroy's disintegrated body and pulled the gag off Jean's mouth.

"Where's Rory?"

"He left this morning," she croaked. "Said he'd be gone for a day or two. Oh, Daddy . . ." I found a knife in a drawer near the small stove and quickly cut her ropes. Then I folded my child's tormented little body into my arms. She shivered as though she had hiked through miles of Arctic cold. Gradually, in the safe protection of my arms, the shivering slowed and stopped.

"Daddy, you look so funny in those old clothes."

Mr. Dangerfield is quite right. You get no respect. "We'd better get out of here." I released her and she instinctively pulled the remnants of her sleep shirt together. I found a sweatshirt with *Mystamaid* printed on it. Not one of theirs. Awkwardly, because her body was still stiff from being cramped in the chair, she pulled it over her head. She was indeed a wonderfully lovely young specimen of womanly humankind, a compact Celtic nymph, with nerves of the same tempered steel of which the finest swords are made.

"I'm all right, Daddy," she insisted. "Hurt and humiliated and frightened and angry as hell. But I'm all right. Don't worry about me. . . . Aren't you going to take the money?"

"Money?"

"Sure. The money the Libyans gave him. It's locked up in that cabinet. He'll have a hard time without it."

There was no reason to leave the money for Rory if he should return before Jaymo Finnegan and the seventh cavalry arrived. I took an ax from its mounting on the wall and chopped through the door of the locked cabinet. The cheap veneered wood splintered easily. I pulled out of the rubble a thin attaché case, handcrafted in elegant Florentine leather. Either Rory or his patrons had expensive tastes. I flipped open the cover.

Inside were neatly wrapped packages of hundred-punt notes, it looked like a hundred in each package. Nine of the packages were unbroken, almost a hundred thousand Irish pounds. The Libyan colonel was notoriously generous to his favorites.

Rory McLafferty could kill a lot of people with this kind of money.

I snapped the lid down on the leather case and gave it to Jean, quickly disassembled my Uzi and stuffed it into my holster vest, and climbed out the empty window. Then I lifted her out onto the deck of the *Mystamaid* and helped her step from the boat to the pier. She wavered dangerously, her muscles still cramped and uncertain. I tightened my grip on her arm.

"I'm all right, Daddy," she insisted.

"Who said you weren't?"

It was now the middle of the brief spring night and dark as the inside of a cave. The soft mist had been replaced by fog. The pier was slippery and uncertain. We tottered off it and onto the soggy shore. "I'll carry you," I said.

"I can walk," she argued.

"Not a hundred yards on a gravel road with bare feet."

"All right," she conceded reluctantly.

I scooped her up, briefcase and all. She did not seem a heavy burden to Finn MacCool. What was the name of his daughter anyway?

"First time since you were a baby," I said as we lumbered through the darkness. "You were a little lighter then. Not much though."

She giggled. "I'm all right, Daddy."

"That's three times, kid. I believe you."

"They wanted to rape me," she continued. "Rory wouldn't let them. He said I would keep till the proper time. He's a strange, scary man. He gets his kicks out of humiliating and tormenting people. I bet he couldn't get it up the ordinary way. . . ."

Such candid talk from my little girl.

"Poor Ciara. Have we found her yet, Daddy? We can't let him hurt her."

"Not yet."

Maybe I've helped him to search for her. Please God I have not.

"I knew you'd come," Jean babbled on. "I knew you'd understand what I meant by 'alone.' I didn't realize that you'd come all by yourself. That was very brave, Daddy. Kind of like a man in Louis L'Amour's westerns. A quiet man, quiet and deadly. Except I never knew you were deadly."

"John Wayne's film about Ireland was called *The Quiet Man.*"

"You're not like John Wayne at all. Just quiet and terrifying. I'll be a good little girl from now on." Another giggle. She was on the edge of hysteria and fighting it every inch of the way.

"Like, totally awesome, would you say?"

"Well, not totally . . . what a funny little car."

I looked funny and so did my Rocinante. No respect at all.

In the backseat of the Morris, Jean pulled on the clothes I'd brought her. "At least I don't look totally like a *Penthouse* centerfold anymore."

"Too pretty for *Penthouse*."

"Daddy," she said reprovingly as she jumped into the front seat with me. "Anyway," serious again, "I'm all right now."

I was prepared to believe it.

"They can hurt your body and humiliate it and violate it, but they can't get at you unless you let them."

True enough, in the short run. And as the prisoners in Korea and Vietnam had proved, true enough in the long run, too, if you were a person of exceptional stamina and courage. Perhaps Jean was indeed cut from that cloth. A tough little girl. No, not that anymore. A tough young woman.

I drove through the night toward Mullingar instead of returning through Athlone. I was not ready to risk another encounter with the publican at The Brass Anchor.

The first phone kiosk at which I stopped had no phone at all. In the second the phone didn't work. Finally we found one on the outskirts of Mullingar that accepted the emergency number Jaymo had given me.

"Hel-*lo*."

Frantically I shoved coins into the slot.

"Hel-*lo*." Louder and more upset. I had broken into his sleep.

"Push the A button, Daddy."

"Push the fucking A button," Jaymo shouted.

Ireland's favorite word. For want of the fucking A button, the war was lost.

"Brendan Ryan here, Superintendent. You folks could improve your phone system. Socialism doesn't work, you know. Sell it off to a private company."

"I'll take it up with the taoiseach."

"On the road on the east side of Lough Ree, almost at the north end, there is a boat called the *Mystamaid*. There was some shooting there tonight. A few bodies, two outside the boat, three on it. Rory is not one of them, unfortunately. You might find some clues. And, if I were you, I'd take a good, hard look at the publican in the Brass Anchor at the bottom of the road. Got it?"

"What . . . ?"

"Any news about Ciara?"

"No. What are you telling me . . . ?"

"One other thing. The boat is booby-trapped. The door to the cabin, anyway. Be careful."

"How do you know . . . ?"

"Good-bye, Superintendent. See you in the morning."

Jean babbled for the rest of the trip through the night and the fog to Dublin.

"I suppose," she said as we crossed the Liffey, ". . . hey, Daddy, your driving is not all that bad, considering."

"Quiet, deadly, and a not bad driver, considering. You suppose what?"

"Oh, I suppose that when we get home, I'll have to spend a few sessions with Aunt Mary Kate talking about all of this."

"It might not be a bad idea. I must say, though, you're a very tough young woman."

"Thank you, Daddy." She brushed my cheek with her lips. "I think I am too. It's the opposite that's the problem."

Jaymo and his usual crew were waiting in the empty lobby of the Shelbourne for us.

"Thank God the lass is all right," he said with some conviction as we walked in.

"No thanks to the Garda, Superintendent," Jean snapped at him. "My daddy had to do it all."

"Easy, kid. They're good cops, doing the best they can. They didn't create Rory McLafferty. If anyone did, it was the Brits and the RUC in the North."

"Well . . . all right, I'm sorry, Superintendent. Anyway, I brought a present for you."

There was no negotiation over what we would do with the money. Jean had made up her mind.

He opened the leather case. His crowd gathered around and peered in.

"Jaysus!" said the woman constable.

"Almost a hundred thousand punts," Jaymo said softly. "Dermot," to his assistant, the silent inspector, "make out a receipt for this."

"It belongs to either Libya or the Republic," I said. "Not to us."

"Aye." Jaymo winked. "The receipt is to make sure that no one can think any of us were tempted."

We checked Jean into the hotel, and I went with her to the room. "Do you want me to stay with you tonight, miss?" asked the woman constable.

Jean considered. "That would be wonderful, Constable Toole. Like, totally wonderful."

"Two Irishwomen together is a bad thing," Jaymo remarked philosophically as we walked back down the stairs to the lobby. "A bad thing altogether."

"Too true."

"That was quite a mess out there. The Gardai from Athlone said that it was like a slaughterhouse."

"Really?"

"Aye, they did. Your man with the machine pistol didn't take any halfway measures; butchered them into little pieces, he did."

"Nine-millimeter parabellum bullets."

"Might have been a little bit overanxious," Jaymo stared out at the green, "or a little bit out of practice."

"A fucking shitehawk," I murmured, experimenting with my newly learned Irish vocabulary.

"Your Gardai from Athlone were glad we warned them about the booby trap. The pension fund would be hard put to have supported all the widows."

"Indeed."

"It's the lot of them. Seamus Cagney won't haunt Miss Keenan anymore."

"Only McLafferty."

"Aye. We'll find him too." A long silence at the foot of the steps, next to the shuttered gift shop, while he lit his pipe. "By the way, the Gardai in Athlone say that your man with the gun must have had some experience with automatic weapons, like, for instance, one of your American M16s."

"Oh?"

"It's true." He considered me with both eyebrows lifted and keen brown eyes probing at my face and mind. "Mind you, it saved the Republic a lot of trouble."

"IRA factional violence."

"I imagine that's what the papers will say," he agreed. "The ting is," he puffed contentedly on his pipe, "the ting is that we're not sure where the automatic weapon is. This is a peaceful country, Brendan. A peaceful country."

"Sure, I wouldn't argue that at all. You can't have people wandering around with automatic weapons. Like that AK-47, which I understand was on the boat and which, I presume, was responsible for the killing."

"I suppose so. We could do ballistics tests to be certain. But then that would cost the Republic money that might well be spent on other matters, wouldn't it now?"

"You'd know that better than I."

"Indeed. Well, we'll be seeing you tomorrow, Brendan. Sleep well."

"Thanks, Jaymo. I'm sure I will."

After he left, but with several uniformed Gardai scattered about the lobby and the corridors, I went back to my "funny" Morris Minor—which I was now determined would be retired with honor at Grand Beach when we went home—removed the duffel bag with my "funny" clothes, and carried the cloth bag with the Uzi to my room while Jaymo's guards watched in total innocence.

I cleaned and oiled the weapon while I rewarded myself with two stiff shots of Jameson's. When this was over I would certainly cut down on my contribution to the distillery's income.

It was not the kingly hall to which a mythic hero is supposed to return after a victory, that he might hear the bards sing his exploits. But the market on mythic heroes is down these days, so my down-at-the-heels room at the Shelbourne would have to do. Anyway, I needed sleep, not a celebration. It would not require a third shot of Jameson's.

I went to bed and slept, if not as well as Jaymo had wished me, at least deeply. My dreams were about disintegrating human bodies.

Jean, pale but composed, told me at lunch that we were

being taken to supper at one of the musical pubs by her friend Liam and that she was going to phone Tim Murphy as soon as it was late enough to place a call to America.

"Not missing a base."

"No way," she agreed brightly. "Touch 'em all."

Jaymo called that afternoon to say mysteriously that they had "one or two important leads" on Rory and that I could stop worrying about Miss Keenan. "In a day or two it will all be over."

"Will it now?"

I realized then that the body which was being dismembered by automatic weapon fire in my dream was often Ciara's. So happy was I to have my daughter back, alive and apparently well, that I had almost forgotten my woman. Finn would never do that.

Dear God, bring her back to me. Please.

That evening in the lobby, before Liam showed up, Jean whispered that Timmy had been "like, totally sweet."

At supper and while we sang Irish songs, she was gentle and affectionate with Liam. My daughter, convinced that she could be tough when she had to be, was practicing tenderness.

I wondered from whom she had inherited or from whose example she had learned such a systematic approach to emotions and behavior. You'd think her father was an estate planner.

The next morning, Jaymo woke me with an early phone call.

"We have your man McLafferty trapped in a farmhouse near Athlone. The minister wonders if you and the lass would like to fly down there in a helicopter to watch us take him."

38

The Irish government's approach to a surrounded terrorist was pretty much what I had imagined it would be. Reality after a time imitates TV clips.

The farmhouse and the thick hedge around it were iso-
lated from the rest of the world by a circle of armored vehicles ("made right here in Ireland," the minister told me
proudly) and Garda cars. Three helicopters circled overhead. Down the road a couple of light tanks were poised,
their guns doubtless trained on the shabby white house. Behind the armored vehicles and police cars were Garda and
army troops equipped with gas masks, flak jackets, and
huge armored shields. A couple of hundred guns were
aimed at the farmhouse, and a score of tear gas grenade
launchers pointed hopefully at the dark gray sky. Behind
one of the armored cars, a dozen or so very tough men in
fatigue uniforms lolled with elaborate casualness. The stun
commandos, no doubt.

Why should the Irish do it any differently from anyone
else? Why send a lone berserker in with an Uzi? Finn
MacCool is obsolete.

All for one terrorist and his woman. Not Ciara, Jaymo
assured me repeatedly.

"I notice that your elite squad uses Israeli automatic
weapons, Mr. Minister."

Jaymo rolled his eyes.

"Irish weapons, actually, Mr. Ryan. We manufacture
them here in small quantities on license. They are the best
automatic weapons in the world. Much better than the
AK-47."

"So I'm told." I winked at Jaymo. "Ireland and Israel
. . . that's a combination that's hard to beat."

"True enough," said the minister.

He was a youngish man with glasses, a baby face, and
carefully crafted graying hair. A clone of Chicago's alderman Eddie Burke. I would not want him as an enemy.

We had flown down in an Irish army Sikorsky, itself a
clone of the ones that had rescued my men in Vietnam:
Jaymo and his Inspector Broderick (I finally learned
Dermot's last name from Jean), the minister, the commissioner of the Garda, Constable Toole and Jean (who were
now thick as thieves, a development that Jaymo tolerated
in part because he approved of close protection of Jean and
in part because, like any Irishman faced with a conspiracy

between two women against all the men in the world, he had no choice), and myself.

We sped rapidly just under a glowering gray sky above the endlessly changing green fields of Ireland. Jean, her Nikon operational again, squealed in delight at the photographic possibilities. Above the clacking roar of the rotor blames, the minister urged on me the need for continued American investment in Irish industrial development.

There are no free lunches and no free rides.

We were watching from a knoll, perhaps a quarter mile away from the farmhouse. One did not risk public officials and important potential supporters of the industrial development of the Republic by permitting them to be in range of a chance terrorist shot.

Jean had slung her camera to one side and was watching the white thatched roof of the house with a very expensive pair of binoculars. When had she bought those?

The commissioner and a uniformed Garda commander seemed to be in charge of the operation. Jaymo and the Special Branch were assigned the role of watching in the background, out of the limelight. If he minded, he did not show it.

The commissioner raised his eyebrow to the minister. The minister nodded. The commissioner raised a gloved hand to the commander. The latter turned to his walkie-talkie and gave an order. The usual soft mist was filling the air.

A determined voice—Big Brother is watching—split the peaceful rural silence. "We know you're in there, Rory. We don't want to kill you. You have three minutes to come out of there with your accomplice. Hands on your heads. We have enough weapons around you to destroy you. A hundred and eighty seconds. We are counting from this moment."

There was no motion inside the farmhouse. I glanced at my watch; fifty seconds gone already.

"Two minutes," said the disembodied voice, God warning us from the heavens.

Every person with a gun seemed to lean forward expectantly, waiting for the chance to dissolve the white

house in an avalanche of firepower. I watched the movement of my second digits.

"One minute, Rory. Fifty-nine seconds, fifty-eight."

A man and a woman emerged from the door of the
farmhouse, hands on their heads, and staggered uncertainly toward the first line of police pickets.

"It's not him," Jean snapped.

Much later in the day, before supper, Jean and I were
sipping sherry in the lobby of the Shelbourne as the remains of high tea were being cleaned away. We had sworn
off Jameson's—for the day, at any rate—and returned to
sherry. "A civilized drink," I was told, "in honor of the good
Jocelyn."

"Did you call her that?"

"After the first day. She asked me to."

There was no date with Liam tonight, though perhaps
there would be one with him tomorrow. There had been,
however, a phone call to Tim, who was described this time
as "nice" rather than "sweet." In addition, there was another boy named Cormac, who was a student at Trinity College medical school who had somehow entered the picture
with a suggestion for windsurfing on Dublin Bay. Jean was
having her own rite of spring.

She thought it was "kind of weird" that she had also
christened our Morris Minor Cormac. "Definitely a boy car,
Daddy." The Minor was no longer "funny" but "cute" and
"darling" and even "adorable." His retirement at Grand
Beach was a matter of absolute commitment.

I thought a lot about Grand Beach. Mike Casey had told
me when I made my call earlier that the next two days, Saturday and Sunday, he and Annie would be there, at Ned
Ryan's. "Ned can keep a secret better than anyone in the
world. Don't worry about calling."

"Are you and Annie going to buy a house up there?"

"There doesn't seem to be much choice, does there?"
He laughed.

"Keep an eye open for another one. Not too far from the
compound, but not too close. Something like Red Kane's lo-
cation."

"Large or small?"

A good question. "Kind of large."

Yes, I would buy the old family house on Glenwood Drive, which was supposed to be for sale, and a place at Grand Beach for my growing family. The conviction that Ciara was carrying my child was as implacable as ever.

Yet I was living in two worlds: one was the world of Brendan Ryan the estate planner, in which I knew with a sinking heart that I would never see her alive again. The other world was the half-light cosmos of Finn MacCool, who was confident that he would save Ciara Kelly and carry her back to Chicago and Grand Beach as his cherished prize. Unfortunately, the real Ciara, with whom I had made love in the Railway Hotel in Galway ages ago, existed in Brendan Ryan's world. The woman in the mythological cosmos had little more reality than did most mythological heroines; she was an object for the hero to pursue.

Perhaps my psychic propensities facilitated the movement back and forth between these two worlds. Perhaps I was slipping toward some kind of psychotic interlude as the result of exhaustion, restless sleep, emotional trauma, and fear. I will never understand it all, but I look back in astonishment and dismay at the man who calmly drank sherry with his daughter in the lounge of the Shelbourne that Friday evening as the sun once again turned the green across the street into an enchanted forest of gold (the clouds having inappropriately dispersed on our silent flight back from Athlone). He was serenely confident that he would find Ciara Kelly (though he didn't yet know how or where) and at the same time he despaired; Ciara was forever lost.

"Schizophrenic?" Mary Kate Murphy has scoffed when I have asked her about the phenomenon. "Maybe only Irish . . . besides, in their myths, if I am to believe my Joe, the women are not exactly passive objects to be pursued by the all-powerful hero."

In any event, that Friday afternoon I planned to carry Ciara back to Grand Beach and knew that I would never do so. Brendan Ryan, the conservative estate planner, did not tell his daughter that they were buying a house in Michigan.

"May I join you?"

Superintendent Finnegan had actually removed his raincoat, a sign, doubtless, of closer friendship. We made room for him and offered him a drink.

"Sherry is it? Well, I suppose it can't do me any harm."

"The Provos set you up?" I asked.

"We'll make the best out of it." He sighed profoundly. "Terry Lenihan is a nice prize, but I'm not sure we have enough on him to keep him in jail for long. We wouldn't have half bothered if we knew it was him. So that's why we were tipped off that it was McLafferty."

"Why did they want to betray him, Mr. Finnegan?" Jean asked respectfully. Even cops were the target of her campaign to be gentle.

"Who knows with them people? They have more doctrinal disagreements than a bunch of monastic theologians. I tried to warn the commissioner and the minister that it was a thin lead." Another, even more profound sigh. "Sure, they wanted a solemn high terrorist capture, Brendan, to impress you. I think you and the girl have frightened the minister half to death."

"Have we now?"

"They've decided over in Dublin Castle that you're not just a regular run-of-the-mill rich Yank tourist. Someone looked up your mother and father's war record, and that scared them even more. Now that your man has gone home to the White House and the nuns and the punks aren't demonstrating against him anymore, they're assigning every available man to the search for Rory McLafferty. I wanted to tell you that. We'll have him soon enough now. We're watching every harbor and airport, every train station and bus terminal. He won't be on the loose for long."

Once more doing what you do well, even if it is not much good in the search for a madman like Rory McLafferty.

"Why are they afraid of us, Mr. Finnegan? . . . I think you can just leave the decanter here, waiter."

"Thank you, lass . . . Well, they know at least the outline of what might have happened that night on the *Mystamaid*. They're not sure what you're going to do, but they know whatever it is, you're quite capable of doing it, Mr. Ryan. They only hope the Irish race survives."

He grinned like a lean, middle-aged leprechaun. It occurred to me that Jaymo Finnegan admired me.

"A berserker on the loose?"

He considered the cheerful color of his sherry and then looked at me thoughtfully. "Something of the sort."

Which was all I needed to hear. Great big fucking legendary hero.

Fuckin' idjit too.

Whom his colleagues would not permit inside a law court.

It was the next day after Mass that I knew where to look. I knew not because I had figured it out but because someone smarter than me suggested it.

I had called Mike and received the weather report from Grand Beach—sunny but cool. However, the lake, according to the kids, was warming up. Eileen and Catherine were doing well, considering. Only a few more weeks now for both of them. The word was that Tim and Jean were burning up the phone lines between Dublin and Chicago.

I didn't tell him about Liam, Cormac, and Brian (a new name, which was casually mentioned to me as though I were well aware of his existence).

Then Jean and I walked across the river to the procathedral, in which the Saturday afternoon Mass, like every Saturday afternoon Mass in the Catholic world, I suspect, was a folk Mass with guitars. There was, however, some very nice music for the Ordinary, as I would have called it, in Irish. By the late Sean O'Riada, who had rediscovered Irish language religious music, Jean told me.

As we walked back to the hotel, Jean was thoughtful, preoccupied. Worrying about how to balance her large supply of swains, I assumed.

"I bet I know where she is, Daddy," she said softly.

"What?"

"She figures she's going to die, right? Didn't you tell me in Ashford Castle that she said that the strand at Inch was the most beautiful place in the world and that she wanted to go to Heaven from there because she thought it would be the shortest route? Well, if she's as much a romantic as you are—and I figure she is probably even worse—then I bet she's somewhere around the strand at Inch."

Brendan Ryan said perhaps. I have to go somewhere. Why not Inch? And Finn MacCool knew that his woman was there. So he took over and sent Brendan Ryan into exile through the next couple of days.

For weal or woe.

Jean had a dinner date with Cormac (I think). I proposed that I have a sandwich in my room and ponder the implications of her insight—which I admitted made sense. When she came home, she should stop by and we could talk more about it.

"I won't be too late," she promised. "After a certain hour, these Irish boys begin to get the wrong idea."

"What hour is that?"

"It depends."

I knew enough not to ask any more.

It was not quite one o'clock when she knocked on the door.

"Nice date?"

"Better than yucky, but not awesome." She tossed her raincoat on my bed. "What gives?"

I had not noticed before the almost transparent qualities of her Irish knit dress. I almost suggested that she should wear a bra the next time she put on the dress. Then I realized that I would be playing the role of the father stereotype. Besides, she did look most appealing in the dress. Which is the way, I told the father stereotype, that young women ought to look.

"I drive down there tomorrow in Cormac and begin to search. You stay here. I'll call you regularly twice a day. You keep in touch with Uncle Mike for me." I explained to her about the daily call to Mike Casey, and also, for good measure, about his illegal weapons shipment. She was impressed. "If I'm more than an hour and a half late, you get through to Uncle Mike immediately and tell him to come at once with the rest of the Knights of the Round Table."

"I don't like it," she said bluntly.

"Two reasons: first of all, I need someone to keep the link open to America in case there's real trouble. It's dumb to risk your communications. Second, one person can move more quickly than two. It would have been impossible for me at Athlone unless I was by myself. An older man and a young woman traveling together are too obvious. It would be like sending up smoke signals telling Rory's friends—and he probably has some in County Kerry too; it's always been pro-Republican—that we're coming."

"And third, Constable Toole will keep me out of trouble here," she said skeptically.

"That's true, Jean. But if I thought I needed your help, I wouldn't hesitate to ask you to run the risks. You've suffered more than I have in this craziness. I think this way is more effective."

She nodded in agreement, not totally convinced—when is a woman with Irish genes ever totally convinced?—but sufficiently persuaded to go along with me.

So the next day, after fierce hugs and kisses, I bid her good-bye and loaded Cormac rather ostentatiously with my duffel and weapon bag. Let Jaymo know I was leaving. I wouldn't mind his flat feet trailing behind this time; and he wouldn't try to stop me now. I set out in the sturdy Morris, now perhaps savoring the prospect of his retirement in America, at a speed which at the best didn't quite make it to forty-five miles an hour, toward Limerick.

It was the hottest day of the year in Ireland—as high as eighty-three degrees Fahrenheit—and the road through Naas, Port Laoighise, and Nenagh to the ancient city of Limerick was jammed. The crush of traffic did not bother Finn MacCool. Nothing bothered him, the dummy.

Limerick, at the head of the Shannon estuary, was shrouded in a haze of thick humidity, making it look like a faerie city in a fantasy film, a kind of down-at-the-mouth Camelot. Somehow the humidity was more burdensome than in America. Maybe because there was always a lot of rain to be soaked up, or maybe because the Irish complained more about the heat than we Yanks would at the same temperature. Limerick was sometimes shabby and sometimes picturesque and all times jammed with bumper-to-bumper traffic.

I drove along the Shannon estuary, where the traffic was thinner, and into the ancient kingdom of Cairaighe, older by a thousand years than Limerick, older even, if you were to believe Kerry authors, than Ireland itself. I cut through the town of Listowel, which produces a big crew of writers every generation (sure, 'tis something in the water supply) and then on to Tralee, the rather uncolorful city of the colorful Rose Festival, and finally to Castlemaine between Tralee and Killarney, where I left the main road and headed out toward perhaps the loveliest part of Ireland— Dingle Bay and the strand at Inch, where both *Playboy of the Western World* and *Ryan's Daughter* were filmed.

The road to Inch, clinging to the edge of Dingle on the north side of the bay, was the most crowded of the day. It was after nine when I arrived at the Inch Hotel on the spine of the peninsula, looking out on the strand, the bay, and, shimmering in the distant haze on the other side of the bay, the brooding Macgillicuddy's Reeks, the highest mountains in Ireland.

The woman at the desk of the Inch Hotel couldn't find my reservation, even though Jean had phoned it from Dublin earlier in the day.

"Not to worry." She grinned cheerfully. "We'll find it if it's here. Sure, there were more Kerrymen soaking up sun hereabouts than any time since Adam and Eve. We'll never have another day like this for the rest of the century."

She found me a room finally; it was small and not particularly comfortable, though clean enough by Irish standards. I needed no Irish whiskey to sleep that night. The dreams, however, were about disintegrating bodies, as they would be for many nights to come.

The next morning, bright and clear with the haze swept away by a brisk wind from the Atlantic, I was the American anthropologist (with a neat cloth attaché case in the left front seat of his battered old Morris Minor and a bulge in the deep right-hand pocket of the black Windbreaker he was wearing), who was searching for the sister that he had promised to meet at an unspecified time in spring in the County Kerry. She was rather tall, blonde, "quite attractive," and wore thick glasses. Had the estate agent rented anything to her lately? She had a special fondness for the beach . . . uh, strand.

I struck pay dirt the first time. Ah, sure, I remember the woman well; she'd rented the wee cottage out at the very end of the strand, another twenty yards and she'd be in Glenbeigh, across the way. She said someone might be looking for her.

If it was that easy for me to find her, it would be equally easy for Rory McLafferty. Ciara Kelly was as crazy as the rest of them. Obviously she wanted to be found. Forward Light Brigade.

Dingle Bay is almost bisected at its upper end by a series of massive sandbars formed by centuries of waves and tide. Glenbeigh on the south side of the bay is the first, and behind it, longer and larger and forming Castlemaine Harbor, is Inch, a massive reef of sand four miles long and in places a mile thick. Its spine is a continuous ridge of dunes, covered with dune grass, flowering bushes, and occasional trees. The floor of the bay in front of the strand is little more than a continuation of it, a shallow shelf of sand on which the tide rises and recedes very rapidly.

"Sure, 'tis hard on boats," the woman in the hotel told me, "if anybody is crazy enough to try to bring one in except when it's dead calm."

In front of the dunes is one of the world's most perfect beaches—hundreds of yards (at low tide) of smooth, soft, clean sand. When the sun is out (and you always have to make that qualification when discussing Ireland), the mixture of long, smooth, white breakers, blue sky, popcorn clouds, wide beach, and green dunes, with the Reeks in the distance, is indeed one of the most beautiful sights in the world, the kind of place that demands a romantic adventure story with strong knights and beautiful women and wizards and witches and mythological animals.

I was assured by the helpful estate agent that I could drive down the beach to the cottage, as long as I did not get too close to the sand which had been made soggy by last night's tide. "Sure, you have no business riding on the dark brown sand. Otherwise you'll be all right."

Cormac, my only mythological beast, had his doubts about the sand and at first refused even to start. However, properly coaxed, like any Irish male, he did as he was bidden. Nonetheless, it took almost forty-five minutes to reach the end of the strand. As the agent had said, the little old thatched cottage could not be missed.

There was no sign of life around it. I parked underneath the dune, a hundred yards short of the cottage, assembled my Uzi, put Mike's weapon in the pocket of the Windbreaker I was wearing, and, following the tactics recommended in my ROTC course long years before, crept up through a gully to approach the cottage from the rear.

I pushed the change bolt on my Uzi from "S" to "E," rushed from the gully to the rear of the house, then around to the front, and kicked open the door.

The tiny, primitive little room was empty.

There were a few clothes, including the dress she had worn in Galway, and a stack of French novels.

And a large bloodstain on the unmade bed.

39

All that day and all the next day I searched. Cleverly, ruthlessly, systematically, like a man in the grip of a divinely inspired project.

I adopted disguises, stories, excuses, spinning out tales with the glib facility of the gombeen-man of the Western world. I looked for Ciara Kelly everywhere: In the charming city of Killarney, with its statue of the mythical Kathleen Ni Houlihan, the spirit of Ireland. In the restaurant at Glenbeigh. In the Purple Mountains behind Glenbeigh, where the countryside was as quiet as an empty cathedral. In broken-down country pubs near Castlemaine and Killorglin. In the Railway Hotel lounge in Killarney, in the Europa Hotel on the side of Killarney Lake, where Ger-

414 · *ANDREW M. GREELEY*

man was spoken more frequently than English. On the heights of Aghadoe, the ancient capital of the kingdom of Cairaighe, from which one looked down on the lakes and the town of Killarney as at a canvas of a Dutch painter, with lights and shadows racing each other across the scene. At Slea Head at the end of Dingle, where the now unoccupied Blasket Islands hovered in the distance, silently remonstrating with the world at their desertion. At the top of Connor Pass on the spine of Dingle, as the mountain sheep grazed untroubled by the fog below them, which concealed both Dingle Bay and Brandon Bay whence my namesake, the sainted navigator, is alleged to have sailed for Barbados. In Dingle town itself, on the long pier that jutted into the tight little harbor.

She had been seen everywhere and nowhere—an attractive woman with short blonde hair, how many of them wander the world? A charming man with curly brown hair and a glow in his eyes—and what else can you find in the West of Ireland?

Your sister? Your cousin? Your wife? Ah, sure, the Irish are a helpful people. Certainly, they would tell you they saw her. Maybe they had after all, and it would be a shame not to help the poor man.

It was only two days now before the solstice. The days were absurdly long and the nights hardly more than a token. Like their pagan ancestors, the Kerrymen and Kerrywomen stayed up late, reveling in the light, mostly sunlight, since the weather continued fine, against the days at the other end of the year that would be so short—storing it all up, a woman in a tobacco shop in Ventry, halfway between Dingle town and Slea Head, told me. So I searched, always under great pressure but never quite in panic, for almost twenty hours both days. On Monday night I slept no more than half an hour. I devoted the rest of the time to studying the map, oiling my weapons, pondering, analyzing, wondering, worrying.

I was pushing myself dangerously close to the breaking point. Brendan Ryan couldn't take much more stress without collapsing. Finn MacCool, however, had a limitless supply of adrenaline in his bloodstream.

I called Jean in the morning and evening of both days,

filling her in on the details, rambling on needlessly about my brilliant but fruitless ideas. She sounded worried about me, as well she might have been. Her father was living very close to the edge.

I did not have a chance after the adventure ended to ask where the Special Branch was. Probably Jaymo's troops were frantically pursuing me and marveling at how fast the wee daft man was running. Then, at the end, I quite unintentionally gave them the slip.

In our second phone call on Tuesday the nineteenth of June, Jean once again proved that she was Holmes and I was Watson. Yes, she had spoken to Uncle Mike. Something about that tone of voice triggered my highly keyed sensitivities. Probably, I decided, Mike had been in touch with Jaymo Finnegan. No harm in that.

"Daddy," she said slowly. "I may be making it all up, but I think that terrible man loved boats. He said something about separating yourself from land to do your work. And he did use a boat on Lough Ree. Do you think he may have a boat somewhere down there?"

Bingo! Ciara had said that he loved to sail on Lough Neagh, outside Belfast.

You see that I was already thinking of the finale as a confrontation between myself and McLafferty, without paying much attention to the implications of such a definition, especially the possibility, indeed the certainty, once you reflected on it, that he was thinking of the finale in the same fashion. Not one of your really bright berserkers either.

"That's a hell of an idea, kid. As always. I'll be back to you tomorrow with the results."

The old-timers in countryman's dress with the smell of fish about them, who hung around the long concrete pier at Dingle, told me that yes, indeed, a man who answered the description of my brother had chartered an aging cabin cruiser, the *Kerryman*, painted blue with red trim, on Sunday evening. "Sure, it's not much of a tub, if you know what I mean. You'd not get very far in it before the engine quits on you altogether. He said he wasn't going very far, just kind of anchoring out there in the bay."

I drove up the side of the hill behind Dingle town and,

with the binoculars I had borrowed from Jean, scanned the bay beyond the harbor mouth. About two miles along the shore in the direction of Inch, at a spot my ordnance map called "Bulls Head," lay the blue and red boat.

I became crafty and cunning, MacCool preparing for battle. I struggled out of my slacks and sports shirt and donned the black jeans and turtleneck I'd bought in Killarney, and my gray Adidas running shoes. Then the black Windbreaker over the Secret Service holster vest. (I did not, however, blacken my face, as commandos do in the late night films, but only because I had no black shoe polish.) I checked my weapons and ammunition, thought through again my plan of action, and drove the faithful Cormac back to the pier in Dingle town.

I avoided the fishermen who had been my previous informants and found someone who was willing to charter me an outboard fishing boat for the night, "Fifty punts for the night, and two hundred and fifty punts deposit, in case you lose it."

Why would I lose it?

Sure, there's bad weather coming up.

And you haven't got it insured against one of your clients piling it up?

Ah, sure, there's no point in taking chances, is there? Besides, if you run it up on Inch, it would break apart altogether. The storm could push you in one direction and the tide running out in the other. It would be no fun at all, at all.

I'll be back before midnight. All I want is a few hours of fishing on the bay. I hear it's good on these long spring days.

The fishing is grand all right, but it's the storm coming up about midnight that worries me. Well, two hundred punts deposit. I found out later that the boat had drifted ashore undamaged. I bet he reported it as an insurance loss anyway.

I donned the black baseball cap I'd also bought in Killarney, packed my cloth bag with the Uzi under the seat of the boat—it was a small dory with a twenty-five horsepower motor—and glided through the harbor and around a point called Beenbane. I dropped anchor fifty yards off-shore and went through the motions of fishing with the rented tackle that accompanied the boat—for twenty-five more punts. The gentle rise and fall of the bay was not abrupt enough to make me any more than slightly queasy. A storm might drive me to the side of the boat for a night of vomiting. But Finn MacCool does not get seasick.

The blue cruiser, a twenty-five-footer, was about a mile and a half away, gently floating at anchor on the flat waters of the bay. There was no sign of life on her.

Not once did I ask myself whether it was not all too easy.

Rather, I calculated the process of boarding the cruiser. Obviously I couldn't run up to it with the outboard, which wasn't very fast but was very loud, going full blast. I would have to use the oars, a skill at which I was without much experience, and try to slide up to the cruiser quietly. It would be difficult enough even if the bay remained calm. But it might not remain calm. The charter boat man had warned of a storm. Already there was a haze, ugly and threatening, moving in from the mouth of the bay.

The Atlantic Ocean was out there. I did not want to have to wrestle with it. I remembered the huge waves from *Ryan's Daughter*.

If the bay turned mean, I would have to fasten onto his anchor line, climb up the rope—I hadn't done that since Fort Benning—and catch him by surprise.

I turned on the motor again and steered, still close to the rocks of Dingle, into an inlet called Trabeg. Protected from motion sickness, I could hug the shore from the mouth of that inlet without being noticed until I was only a little more than two hundred yards from the cruiser. Maybe after dark, depending on the distracting sounds of the wind and the water, I could get even closer before I had to turn to the oars.

Slowly, like a teenager who is in no rush to go home because he knows he'll be in trouble when he gets there, night slipped down the bay from Killarney and Inch. With it came the wind, at first a fresh breeze, exhilarating against your face and then stiffer and more ominous. It was blowing at an angle, across the Dingle mountains and into the bay. If it should move around a couple of points, it would be coming right up the bay from the Atlantic.

The bay itself grew more restless and uncertain, as if it were pondering a temper tantrum and had not quite made up its mind.

I rigidly forced myself not to move out of the Trabeg inlet until it was dark. The haze above me had turned into clouds. The mountains behind me were dark and somber, perhaps watching my folly disapprovingly.

I spent some of that purgatorial time of waiting examining my Uzi once again, for the final time, I told myself. I assembled it without the silencer, which didn't seem to be necessary this time, and crammed ammunition clips in all my pockets. I took Mike Casey's .22 out of my right Windbreaker pocket so that I could fill that pocket, too, with ammo clips. I thought about it for a few seconds and decided I had more than enough ammunition to rout a platoon of terrorists and returned the little gun to its resting place.

I fastened the strap, which had come with the Uzi but which I had never used before, on the holders at both ends. Plastic, but high-quality plastic. Not likely to break. Trust the Israelis to do it right.

Finally, when it was dark, or dark enough, I started the outboard, not without considerable difficulty, and moved very slowly out of the inlet toward the cruiser, a dim smudge of black against a slightly less dark sky. At low speed the motor was relatively quiet. I finally turned it off and began to row awkwardly toward McLafferty's boat, fighting against my own ineptitude and the rising swells. And against the first touches of seasickness.

What did I expect to find on the cruiser?

McLafferty, certainly. Ciara? Most likely, though there had been no mention of anyone boarding with him or being carried on board. Ciara alive?

Viewing the affair from the wisdom of hindsight, there was no reasonable probability that she was still alive. Why would she be? Rory McLafferty wanted revenge. Now he had the opportunity to take it. Why should he delay? Yet he was there, almost certainly—it seemed to me then—and he must be destroyed before he hurt others. Why he would so obviously and patiently wait for me to find him was a question that simply did not arise.

Jean probably would have asked it if she were with me.

At the very outer limit of my own sanity, however, and confusing myself with an Irish mythic hero, I had at that point only one goal—to dispose permanently of Rory McLafferty.

I lost the cruiser several times, finding it again only when a swell brought me high enough to see the light in its cabin. So there was someone on it . . . fine.

Then I seemed to lose it permanently. And the land too. The swells were turning into waves, not the quick, choppy waves of Lake Michigan, but rollers, gentle still, but menacing. I thought perhaps I should give up and return to the inlet. I would be no use to anyone drowned or disastrously seasick in Dingle Bay. I had no idea now where the inlet was.

Then Dingle Bay did me a favor. It heaved me up on an especially high swell and showed me that I was only twenty yards from the bow of the *Kerryman* and even closer to its anchor line. The rest should be easy.

It was very difficult, however. I had no choice but to tie on to the cruiser's line—which meant that with the Uzi strapped around my neck, I would have to climb up the line, hand over hand. Capturing the line turned out to be immensely difficult, even though I was only a few yards away. I stabbed at the line with my boat hook time after time, but the dory had a mind of its own, the bay was becoming rougher by the moment, and the wind was now howling in my ears.

Not so loud, however, as to drown out the scream of a woman in a terrible agony of pain.

She was still alive.

I reached desperately for the anchor line, tilted the dory precariously toward the water, straightened up, and tumbled backward, lurching towards the far side of the boat with more than enough momentum to carry me over the side.

I fell to my knees with a thud. The boat swayed dangerously, and then righted itself. I felt another twinge of seasickness, much stronger this time. A swell lifted us again and dropped the boat literally on top of the line.

Another favor from Dingle Bay, for which much thanks.

I tied the dory line securely to the anchor line with one of my best yachtsman's knots and pulled the boat up the line till I was close to the cruiser. Only a few yards of hand-over-hand climbing. I hung the Uzi around my neck, making sure the change bolt was pulled all the way back on "S," zipped up my Windbreaker, stood on the front of the dory, and gripped the cruiser's line securely with both hands.

We were hit by a mighty swell, which heaved the dory above the cruiser, so high that I was looking down at the single light in its cabin. I was thrown out of the dory and hovered for a moment over the dark, cold waters of the bay.

Then the line snapped taut and my arms and shoulders were wrenched by a vicious jerk. Pain shot through my whole body. For a moment I thought my arms had been torn out of their sockets. The bay grabbed my feet and ankles and my legs up to my thighs, then released me. My agony was so great that I wanted to drop into the water and end all foolishness. Then I heard another scream from a woman. I clung to the line, my hands aching from pressure against its coarse fibers, and slowly, hand over hand, inched my way up the bow of the *Kerryman* and onto its forward deck.

The Uzi was still there. My bloodied fingers could still press its trigger. The cabin windows were heavily curtained, which was why I had not seen the light at first from the mouth of the inlet. I eased my way around the side and slipped, I hoped lightly, into the cockpit.

This was the moment of truth. I was tense, sore, exhausted. My mouth was dry and my stomach tight again. I loved every second of it; my battle instinct was aroused for fulfillment.

I took the Uzi off my neck, shoved the safety bolt all the way forward to automatic, took a final deep breath, and kicked savagely against the door between the cockpit and the cabin.

It swung open easily. I rushed into the cabin ready to squeeze the trigger.

"Ah, good evening to you, Brendan Ryan." Rory McLafferty was holding his scalpel at Ciara's throat, his other hand covering her mouth. "I've been expecting you. It took you long enough to find us. And, to tell you the truth, like the fucking shitehawk you are, you made a godawful racket coming on board."

40

He looked older than I had expected, thinner and more haggard. His handsome face was lined with deep ruts, his hair was dirty white; his kinky smile reminded me of that of a man in a Southern prison walking from his cell to the gas chamber for the amusement of TV viewers. His eyes glowed with fire, indeed, but with a fire about to be blown out by too much draft. Inside Rory McLafferty there was a lost soul seeking release. The charming medical student who had been so kind to a young woman who had been the victim of savage rape had long since died and was now trapped in the cruel prison of his own demented flair.

His zombie, however, held a knife at the thickest part of Ciara's carotid artery. As I looked into his wild eyes I saw myself, hunched over my PC XT, enthusiastically cheating the world with demented schemes. There was not that much difference between Brendan Ryan and Rory McLafferty. We both were isolates, we both played wicked games, we both loved the same woman. I was able to distinguish still between my games and reality. But I had not been trapped in the insanity of Ulster.

The cabin was tiny, like that of all small cabin cruisers, no more than ten feet long and less than five feet wide, and crowded—two bunks, a fixed table with the leaf down, some cabinets on the wall, a floor littered with gear. Ciara, most of her clothes torn away, was tied in one of the bunks, her left hand and right foot free. Her face was bruised and swollen, her lips caked with blood, her body marked with bruises and cuts and what looked like burns.

"Get away from her," I ordered.

"Ah, no," he said with a smirk, "I won't do that. Maybe your terrible fine gun, which killed all my troops, will kill me before I can cut her throat. Maybe; then again, maybe not. But, sure, you're not all that good with your wee Uzi. They said you butchered my troops. Suppose," he crowded close to her, almost using her as a shield, "that you butcher her as well as me this time?"

I hesitated. What indeed if I did miss?

"Kill him, Brendan." She yanked her mouth free. "He'll torture us to death."

"Quiet, woman." He deftly jabbed at her breast with the scalpel, causing a thin line of blood to appear. "And herself ambushing me, would you believe it, able to kill me and losing her nerve. Sure, she doesn't believe in killing. Wanted to give me a last chance for redemption. Can you imagine that, Brendan Ryan? Me redeemed?"

It was back in slow motion now. He was a babbler. I would wait patiently until he was far away from Ciara as he was likely to be, and then shoot. As unobtrusively as I could, I moved the change bolt back to single shot.

"I see you're hesitating. Well, that's a good thing. The longer a man hesitates, the less likely he is to do something dangerous, like butchering a woman he loves, isn't that true, Brendan Ryan?"

"You leave her alone and I'll let you go free," I said calmly.

"Ah, you're the cool one, now, aren't you?" The boat swayed dangerously. "Sure it's a right fine storm you brought with you, too, isn't it?" He chuckled drunkenly.

I slipped the change bolt back to the safety position. It could be flicked off again in an instant. I did not want a swell to cause me to pressure the trigger enough to fire.

"Fair trade," I said.

"You know," he observed in a friendly, conversational tone, "I believe you'd really keep your word. You are like all your other dull bourgeois capitalists. You don't understand the morality of a revolution at all, at all. . . . But we're talking about art, not fucking politics. I'm engaged in a work of art, don't you see?"

"Art?" Keep him talking and wait for the right second.

"Art, indeed." He adopted the tone of a senior surgeon instructing a new team of interns. "You'll note that the woman has been injured a bit, enough to hurt but no permanent damage, not yet, anyway. Note, too, by the way, how intelligently she is bound. One foot and one hand are free for resistance. The right hand is bound, needless to say. She can fight back, not effectively and at considerable expenditure of her energy resources, but it both amuses me and increases the foolish hope for rescue. Interesting concept, isn't it?"

Except that Ciara was left-handed. Had he forgotten that? Or had he never noticed?

"She knows in her head she will die a slow and horrible death. But human nature is such that our hope won't let us accept the obvious realities. Maybe it's not human nature." He waved the scalpel as though dismissing that point. "Maybe it's the capitalist system. For our purposes that doesn't matter, does it now? Anyway, the work of art is to slowly push back the frontier of hope so that it turns in the opposite direction. As I progress in my little exercise—with a professional doctor's skill, mind you—she'll continue to hope. After all, she'll say then, her wounds are not so bad that plastic surgery can't repair them. So, despite the obvious evidence, she'll hope that I'll stop. I'll encourage that hope, recall all the grand times we had together when we were kids. She'll know I'm lying, but she'll hope against hope that maybe I'm not.

"Then we'll progress a little further and she'll know that she'll be disfigured for life, an ugly and unwanted hag, but the urge to live is still strong, so she'll revise her hope again and, against all sound judgment, pray that I'll judge such a fate is a sufficient punishment for those who betray the people's cause." For a moment a tone of dedicated patriotism crept into his demented babble. "A traitor to the people of Ireland, Brendan Ryan."

I listened calmly, knowing that my silence would anger

him and make him less likely to stay dangerously close to Ciara.

"Well, to return to the issue, though I'm offended that you're not more interested, there'll come a time, postponed as long as possible, naturally, when the only hope is death. There is nothing left in the body to live for. All that remains, all that can ever remain, is pain—certain limbs permanently mangled, that sort of thing. She'll pray to God in His mercy that I've had enough revenge for the betrayed people of Ireland. She'll hope that I'll let her die. What more can she possibly suffer? You see what has happened, the direction of hope has been reversed." He giggled witlessly. "Isn't that a scientific breakthrough, a work of great art? The important question, on which we have little scientific data despite the interesting work the Germans did during the war, is how far a given person has to be pushed in pain before the hope turns towards death. And as for an ending of the work of art, well, I'm not quite sure what that will be. It makes the story more interesting doesn't it?"

"You're completely round the bend, McLafferty. A demented lunatic."

That made him angry, as it was supposed to. "Oh am I, Mr. Brendan Ryan who killed my command, stole my treasury, and destroyed my plan of battle? Well, why do you think it was so easy for you to find me? Why do you think that I have postponed everything but a mild beginning of my research on this slut? I'll tell you why." He laughed crazily. "I'll tell you why: you're part of the experiment. You're going to watch it every step of the way. And she's going to watch the same things being done to you." He was ranting incoherently now. I slipped the safety bolt to single shot. "It will be a double execution. Two war criminals at the same time."

Just as my finger touched the trigger, there was a violent lurch as the cruiser heeled over almost on its side. The Uzi jumped out of my hands, though not before I had activated the safety again. McLafferty and I crashed into each other. Desperately I brought the edge of my hand down on his wrist the way I'd seen Caitlin do at Grand

Beach. I didn't break anything, but the scalpel fell to the floor next to the bunk.

We threw ourselves together in desperate hand-to-hand combat, two jungle beasts fighting for their turf, shoving, kicking, kneeing, gouging. He was bigger than I but surprisingly weak. I was out of practice and lacked the fury of madness. I probably would have won if either of us had been able to do any damage to one another. However, we were tumbled around the cabin, crashing into the table and the bunks and the walls as the boat twisted and turned back and forth like a cork in a whirlpool.

As we struggled, I watched Ciara's free hand groping for the scalpel. It was only an inch or two away from her fingers.

I broke away from his grip, reached for the Uzi, felt it with my fingertips, and then careened across the room as the boat heeled in the opposite direction. My head smashed against the edge of the table. A current of savage pain cascaded through my body, tearing and twisting at my consciousness. I blanked out for what must have been no more than a couple of seconds. Then I was looking up at Rory McLafferty cradling my weapon lovingly in his hands.

"He who lives by the Zionist gun dies by it, Brendan Ryan. But you're not going to die yet, not for a long time."

Ciara clutched the scalpel tightly in her hand. He was too far away for her to reach him.

I struggled desperately to escape from the daze that imprisoned me like quicksand. There was something I could do, if only I could remember what it was.

"I'm going to kneecap you to begin with." He chortled wildly. "You won't be able to move. Then I'll shoot off your hands. I won't have to tie you up for the rest of the experiment, which I am hereby dedicating to the Republic of Ireland, one and indivisible!"

He pointed the weapon at my legs. At such close range he would chop them to pieces. I would fool him and bleed to death.

But what was it I was supposed to do?

He squeezed the trigger.

Nothing happened.

"Goddamn, fucking kike gun," he shouted, fiddling with the various mechanisms.

He found the firing safety on the rear of the grip and aimed again.

Again nothing happened. Vaguely I prayed that he would throw the gun away and jump on me.

"Ah, it's the wee bolt on the side, is it now?" He examined the pistol grip with idiotic interest. "The kikes are clever, aren't they? Sure, I reckon 'D' is for repeat."

He was wrong, but it did not matter. He took aim again. I waited for the searing pain in my legs.

A voice shouted at me, a woman's voice. "Mike's gun, you damn fool."

What gun?

The Uzi still would not work. "You forgot to cock it, you frigging idjit," he screamed at me as he pulled the firing bolt back.

I remembered the .22.

His face twisted with manic fury, he pointed the Uzi at me for the last time.

I fired Mike Casey's .22 through the jacket of my Windbreaker. Twice. Both bullets hit his shoulder and spun him away. The single shot from the Uzi exploded far above my head. He tried to point the gun in my direction.

I knew I should rush him, but my body was not following the orders coming down from my brain. I fired Mike's pistol again. It missed.

He ducked away from the shot as the blood soaked through his shirt, and toppled against the bunk on which Ciara was tied.

Without hesitation or a wasted movement, she slashed him neatly across the throat.

A geyser of blood erupted, spilling over his face and the front of his body. The Uzi slipped from his hand. "Cunt," he bubbled, as blood began to pour from his mouth.

"Oh, my God," Ciara was praying, "I'm heartily sorry for offending You because I dread the loss of Heaven and the pains of Hell but most of all because they offend You, my God, who are deserving of all my love . . ."

Rory McLafferty appeared to nod. He raised his hand

to his forehead and dropped it to his chest—what might have been the first half of a sign of the cross—before he fell forward and died. The lost soul was free.

Perhaps not lost at all. In accordance with Blackie Ryan's instructions, I put no limit on God's passionate love for each of us.

Who was the woman who screamed at me about Mike's gun? I don't know. It could not have been Ciara because she didn't know about the .22. It was, I think, a familiar voice, but I can't be sure. Sometimes I imagine that she sounded like Madonna, but that's perhaps the wish being the father of the thought. Maybe it was only a network of cells in my brain issuing a demand for survival.

Ciara had retched as the blood of her onetime lover and friend spilled over her body. Struggling across the swaying cabin, I picked up the scalpel from the floor, cut her bonds, and took her in my arms.

"I'm all right, Brendan." She leaned against me. "Some ice, a few patches, and some burn ointment, and I'll be as good as new."

Why do battered women have to assure me that they're all right?

"I love you, Ciara." I held her as tightly as my aching skull and disoriented brain would permit.

"You're a desperate man, Brendan Ryan," she sighed.

Then the boat heeled over again. This time it did not right itself. Instead, it spun drunkenly around and around.

"The anchor line has snapped," Ciara cried. "The poor idjit was too round the bend to use the right line."

41

I lay in a pool of blood under the rudder wheel of the cabin cruiser, vomiting desperately, not because of the blood-covered floorboard, nor because of the rictus of death, which made the remains of Rory McLafferty grin even more witlessly than he had in life, but because of violent seasickness.

Never was it written that Finn MacCool, mythic hero, was immune to motion sickness.

Above me, Ciara, wearing only torn panties, was trying desperately to start the engine and at the same time steer the tipsy craft away from the rocky shore of Dingle Bay.

I was too sick to note how beautiful she was, even bruised and burned and wounded. Now I tease my memory to recall that scene of the warrior woman taking command.

It merely makes me sick again.

We were rushing and spinning up the bay, pushed by the big rollers and pulled by the tide, which was now running in the opposite direction. The Atlantic was more powerful than the tide. We must, I thought, be plunging toward the strand at Inch. It would be rather humiliating to straggle in before God's judgment seat and vomit at the Deity's feet.

"He was totally off the wall, poor man. He would have killed me tonight. You came just in time."

I wonder even now. My arrogance and stupidity might, after all, not have made any difference.

"You don't owe me anything."

"Begging your pardon, bloody hell I don't. I should have listened to you in Galway. But no. Ciara Kelly, if you want to call her that, was going to do it all herself."

Before I was wiped out of action, I had tried desperately to fix the engine, a Chrysler marine eight-cylinder, probably older than Noah's ark. Not only could I not fix it, I couldn't even figure out why it didn't work.

The man on the pier at Dingle had said the old boat wouldn't go very far. It was going farther than he had anticipated, but hardly under its own power.

"Brendan, darling," Ciara called above the roar of the wind and the crashing of the waves. "I can see the white of the strand ahead of us. The boat will flounder and break up. We'll stand a better chance if we wait till the last minute and try to swim to shore."

"Swim in these waves?"

"We'll wear life preservers, you poor idjit. With some luck, we'll float up to the beach. Would you ever be able to get them out of the cabinet?"

"Just a minute." I was swept by another attack of nausea, vomited violently, and then between attacks staggered to the cabinet and pulled out two very ancient and decrepit-looking orange kapok life jackets.

"Don't look like much, do they? Take off your shoes and your trousers and your Windbreaker, they'll only pull you down."

"How cold is the water?"

"Warmer than Lake Michigan in May." She spun the wheel again. As if insulted, it spun her back, momentarily escaping her grip. "Bloody thing." She grabbed it and struggled with it fiercely.

Another wave of nausea. I regretted that I had eaten nothing in the last couple of days. There was little inside me for my stomach to reject.

"Put on your life jacket, Brendan," she commanded as though I were an unruly child. "Here, let me fasten it. Well, I've seen better, but I'll suppose these will have to do."

"Sorry," I mumbled, retching yet another time.

"Remember that there may be an undercurrent. When it tugs at your feet, kick them up and float with the top of the water, if you take my meaning?"

To this day, I don't know whether she laughed at that or not.

I had no sense of time. In what was both an eternity and seconds I heard a grinding crash. The boat seemed to put on its brakes and grind to a dead halt. Then it spun free and leaped violently to one side. I heard water rushing into the hull.

"I guess we've had it now. Come on, my little king, let's swim for the strand."

She guided me out the cabin door and into the cockpit, and helped me up on the gunwale. I vomited into the wind, which retaliated by slapping most of my meager contribution back into my face.

"Jump as far as you can, do you understand?"

I tried to nod.

"I love you, Brendan. I'll always love you!" She pushed me off the gunwale.

I did remember to leap far. Just as the frigid waters of Dingle Bay deprived me momentarily of my capacity to breathe, I saw her dive in after me.

A graceful dive. Ciara Kelly would not stumble awkwardly to God's judgment seat.

No way.

The cold waters of Dingle Bay are apparently a fine cure for motion sickness. At any rate, they so shatter you that you forget you're sick. As I was tossed around, pushed and pulled, tugged and beaten by the rollers and the contending currents, I tried to remember what I had read in a Dick Francis story about how long a human could survive in various temperatures of water. It didn't make much difference because I had no idea how cold Dingle Bay was. Not as bad as the Atlantic when the *Titanic* sunk. Low fifties maybe. Didn't bother some of the crazy Ryan kids at Grand Beach on Memorial Day. They didn't remain in the lake as long as I would stay in the bay, however.

I thrashed and flailed and tried to swim, but without much purpose or success. The white blob that was both the beach and the rollers breaking on it was near, but no nearer, it seemed, than when I had jumped into the water. I was, I suppose, still jarred by the blow on my head from the cabin table. The final act of our drama was obviously happening to someone else.

A couple of times I thought my feet touched bottom. Then I was tugged away. Undertow or ebbing tide? Didn't matter much.

Then I was very weary and very cold. It was all too absurd. What the hell was Brendan Ryan doing bobbing around in the waters of Dingle Bay? He was a quiet, competent, conservative tax lawyer. A loser, as his best friend had once said. Was that best friend still alive? Brendan couldn't quite remember. There were a lot of dead people lately.

Brendan Ryan quit. And Finn MacCool, returned to the many-colored lands in the West, was no longer there to help.

Someone did help, however. A hand grabbed the back of my life jacket. A voice accompanied the hand. "Don't quit now, you bloody idjit, we're almost there."

No ghostly voice that.

So Brendan Ryan, good Irishman that he was, did what his woman told him to do. He didn't quit after all. His feet felt sand again; the waters tore at him, but he pushed ahead up the sand and broke out of the tug of the bay. Correction. He didn't push, he was pushed.

Then an avalanche of water hit him from behind and knocked him to his knees. Someone was pulling him farther up the beach when a second avalanche clobbered him.

Then there was nothing at all. For a long time.

I woke up slowly and promptly vomited. I was now both sick and bitterly cold. The cold-turkey cure for motion sickness was no longer operative.

One improvement, however; I now had something to vomit—salt water. One deterioration to match. Not only did my stomach feel like a tight ball of pain, my lungs hurt like hell. So, in fact, did my head. And my jaw, where that deranged Irishman had hit me. Who was it? I couldn't remember, but it didn't matter. He was dead, quite dead.

But I was alive, demonstrably alive. I hurt, therefore I am. And, no matter how cold, no longer in the water. Heaven? Not likely. Purgatory? According to common conviction, the temperature problem should be in the opposite direction, shouldn't it?

There was Dante's position to consider.

I said to hell with it and ordered my eyes to open. At first they refused to comply. Then reluctantly they went along. To my surprise it was light. Dawn. More than dawn. Pushing sunrise.

Indisputably, I was on the Strand at Inch. Hence, logically it seemed, alive.

Ciara!

I sat up and, forgetting my aches and pains, looked around desperately. No Ciara. Dear God in Heaven, please, please!

Twenty yards down the beach, a body stretched out, facedown on the sand, life jacket torn away, looking terribly blue from the distance. Womanly rump covered with a shred of fabric.

I ran, crawled, lurched, threw myself to her side.

"Ciara!" She seemed frighteningly blue and cold.

An eye opened and considered me gravely. Then its companion. They quickly inspected the environment.

"Wasn't I after telling you," she mumbled through her injured lips, "that the Strand at Inch is the most beautiful place in the world altogether?"

I turned her over and cradled her in my arms, telling her, rather unimaginatively I fear, how much I loved her.

"I'm all right, Brendan," she said again. "Nothing wrong with me at all, at all, that some ice and a few butterfly bandages and a tad of burn ointment won't cure. Then maybe a bit of food."

The thought of food, the suggestion of it, made my stomach rumble again. It had the grace, however, to do nothing more.

"Why do women always have to tell me that they're all right?" I demanded in a choked voice that sounded like someone else's. What had I done to my throat?

"So you won't fret, idjit," she said sleepily.

We clung together, shivering, I thought, in unison with one another. Or at least in harmony.

"Brendan, darling, I'm cold." A bedmate asking for another blanket.

Her short, dirty blonde hair was pasted to her head. She was not bad as a blonde, but I wanted her black hair to be straining in the wind over the beach as a pennant of victory. That could wait.

"I'll see what I can do." I struggled to my feet.

"Be careful of the boat, it's breaking up."

It was, indeed, capsized, and ground and shattered not far down the beach. We would surely be dead if we had stayed with it. But the tide was ebbing, the storm had passed through, and the waves were diminishing. I splashed through the water. My God, was I in that last night?

Then I realized that if Ciara knew that the boat was on the beach, she had been conscious before I was. She had dragged me up on the beach. Saved my life. We were even.

In a burst locker, I found two old navy blue blankets which were still reasonably dry. Rory McLafferty was still there, battered now to a shapeless pulp. So was my Uzi, caught between Rory and a smashed wall. Take it with me for a memento?

No, Cormac would suffice. The Uzi represented death. In his own cantankerous and gallant way, Cormac represented life. Maybe Ireland too. Have to think about that.

I took another blanket for good measure. Inside it, dusty and old, was a quarter-full bottle of Jameson's Twelve Year Special Reserve—itself now nearly twenty years old.

I drank a great, powerful gulp and felt warm again.

Holy Grail indeed.

I wrapped one blanket around Ciara, who cooed, "Darling man."

"I found this, a gift from God, I think."

She accepted my dusty grail, blinked at it in astonishment, and then pressed it to her bloodstained lips.

"The Lord takes away and the Lord gives," she said with a chuckle as she gave the bottle back to me. "Don't drink it all, you idjit."

We passed the bottle back and forth till it was empty. The world felt considerably more pleasant.

The two of us together, mostly naked, on the Strand at Inch, battered, sore, sick, and slightly tipsy. We had come home, even if our promised lovemaking would not occur, today anyway.

Today? The last day of spring. Our rite of spring, Ciara's and mine, was over. Summer was still ahead. At Grand Beach it didn't really begin officially, according to the Ryans, until July 4. We'd be there in time.

"It's all over, Ciara."

She sighed. "Yes, it's all over. I wonder if I'll ever believe it." She sat up. "Come on, little king, let's walk till we find help. The woman needs some decent clothes, and we have to do something about that terrible lump on your head."

So we struggled to our feet and, shrouded in musty blankets, painfully limped along the strand toward the road to Castlemaine. I brought the Special Reserve bottle along. You shouldn't litter the strand. The bottle would spend the rest of its life in the museum, along with Cormac, the museum at our house in Grand Beach.

That reminded me of a detail to be resolved.

"Come home with me, Ciara Kelly." The words emerged spontaneously, without any thought or planning.

Pain, grief, resignation swept across her face. My heart sank. She was about to tell me that it could never be.

Then, blessedly, as she changed her mind, mischief in her wondrous gray eyes. "You want me to go home with you, do you now?"

"Would you be pregnant by any chance?" I asked stupidly.

"Well, not so you'd notice it, anyway." Her lips parted in a painful smile. "That shouldn't be hard to correct, if you've a mind to."

At a distance down the strand there were people hurrying toward us. Two tall men, one thin, one broad. Mike and Nick. The main force. The Knights of the Round Table. And between them a stubby little man. The monsignor himself. Merlin in residence. I'd need a priest in a day or two. Behind them the whirling blue lights of Garda cars.

I raised my hand in a weak wave.

A small figure emerged from the Knights, a princess in Aran sweater and brown jeans, and ran desperately toward us. At the last instant Jean made a remarkably wise and gracious decision.

She embraced Ciara first.

The blanket fell off Ciara's shoulders. The two women clung to one another, crying for joy as only women can do, especially if they are Irish. My daughter winked at me above my woman's naked shoulder. They would, as she had promised, make common cause against me. I would be outnumbered four to one.

Then I understood. My Neanderthal kink had not deceived me. In the future Ciara Kelly would give me other children. In our rite of spring she had given me back my daughter.

NOTE

The statistics on the prevalence and incidence of psychic phenomena are based on national sample research continuing at NORC under the direction of my colleague William McCready and myself. The descriptions of the experiences are drawn from interviews with those who have had them. Thus the reader may rest assured that the information contained about such phenomena in this story is accurate. Brendan Ryan is part of that three or four percent of the population, men and women perfectly normal in every other respect, for whom these phenomena are a routine part of life.

One critic of an earlier novel in which a character had similar experiences complained about "violations of the order of nature"; obviously he is the kind of man for whom some phenomena cannot happen as a matter of dogmatic a priori principle. As Blackie Ryan says, such a man would have voted against Galileo. I have no need either as a scholar or as a priest to postulate any explanation other than a natural one for psychic experiences. I am content with the position taken by Blackie—they occur too frequently to be dismissed as impossible, save by dogmatists masquerading as scientists. Perhaps Blackie is correct: psychic experiences are the result of mostly useless vestiges of communication aptitudes that were selected in the evolutionary process before we had developed the physical capabilities for elaborate speech.

Some readers may observe that the Strand at Inch was the locale for the climax of my first novel, *The Magic Cup*. The similarity is not accidental. This story of spring, like the story of the earlier book, is a retelling of the old Irish version of the quest for the Holy Grail, a story which, in its primordial form as a liturgical cycle, was also part of a spring ritual. In the ancient story, the quest is for a cup and a woman who represent a divine power that operates not so much by creating and ordering, but, long before Alfred North Whitehead, by inviting, calling, alluring, enticing. Slavic music and Celtic story.

Like all quest stories (indeed like stories in many other genres, western, adventure, spy—in which latter this tale participates to some extent), my story contains considerable violence, which will doubtless lead to complaint from those who want no violence in fiction. There is less of it in the story than there is in life, and less than in shoot-'em-up westerns. Those who like adventure stories without danger and violence are perfectly free to pass my story by and search for something more to their tastes. Try the *Odyssey* or the *Aeneid* or the *Morte d'Arthur*. Or *King Lear*. Or the Book of Judges.

Both my stories about a quest for a sacred vessel which is also a magic princess more closely parallel the ancient liturgical cycle than does the Arthurian grail legend, which has had such a decisive and in my judgment negative impact on Western culture. Compare, for example, the wisdom of Blackie Ryan (Colum of Iona in *The Magic Cup*) to the wisdom of Merlin, his counterpart. The latter tells us that we must always seek for and never find our Ciara Kelly. The former asserts that each of us can and must find her, and that indeed she is searching for us as part of God's tricky game plan for a more beautiful cosmos.

Catholic Christians, at any rate, simply cannot accept the life-denying, flesh-denying theme of the tale of Merlin, Lancelot (poor, dear man), and that crowd. Not at all, at all.

—AMG
First Day of Summer 1983
Tucson, Chicago, and Grand Beach

THOMAS
PAINE
GREAT WRITER OF THE REVOLUTION

SPECIAL LIVES IN HISTORY THAT BECOME

Signature LIVES

THOMAS

PAINE

GREAT WRITER OF THE REVOLUTION

by Michael Burgan

Content Adviser: Julie Richter, Ph.D.,
Independent Scholar and Consultant,
Colonial Williamsburg Foundation

Reading Adviser: Rosemary G. Palmer, Ph.D.,
Department of Literacy, College of Education,
Boise State University

COMPASS POINT BOOKS MINNEAPOLIS, MINNESOTA

Compass Point Books
3109 West 50th Street, #115
Minneapolis, MN 55410

Visit Compass Point Books on the Internet at *www.compasspointbooks.com*
or e-mail your request to *custserv@compasspointbooks.com*

Managing Editor: Catherine Neitge
Lead Designer: Jaime Martens
Photo Researcher: Marcie C. Spence
Cartographer: XNR Productions, Inc.
Educational Consultant: Diane Smolinski

Art Director: Keith Griffin
Production Director: Keith McCormick
Creative Director: Terri Foley

Library of Congress Cataloging-in-Publication Data
Burgan, Michael.
 Thomas Paine / by Michael Burgan.
   p. cm. — (Signature lives)
 Includes bibliographical references and index.
 ISBN 0-7565-0830-4 (hardcover)
 1. Paine, Thomas, 1737-1809—Juvenile literature. 2. Political scientists—
United States—Biography—Juvenile literature. 3. Revolutionaries—United
States—Biography—Juvenile literature. 4. United States—History—
Revolution, 1775-1783—Juvenile literature. I. Title. II. Series.
 JC178.V5B87 2005
 320.51'092—dc22   2004018744

REVOLUTIONARY WAR ERA

The American Revolution created heroes—and traitors—who shaped the birth of a new nation: the United States of America. "Taxation without representation" was a serious problem for the American colonies during the late 1700s. Great Britain imposed harsh taxes and didn't give the colonists a voice in their own government. The colonists rebelled and declared their independence from Britain—the war was on.

Table of Contents

1 THE POWER OF WORDS

৵৽৹৹

In the late summer of 1776, fiery writer Thomas Paine and other American soldiers worriedly watched British warships unload their cargo. From his camp in northern New Jersey, Paine had a clear view of the troops and supplies coming ashore on New York's Staten Island. He also saw some of his fellow soldiers, struck with fear, desert their posts and head for home. He knew his fellow patriots needed encouragment and inspiration.

Paine was one of thousands of Americans ready to fight the British. Just a few months before, Great Britain's 13 colonies had declared their independence and renamed themselves the United States of America. Paine had played a part in that historic declaration. His pamphlet *Common Sense* had

Thomas Paine fought the British with weapons on the battlefield and with his mighty pen.

attacked the policies of King George III. Americans could never be truly free and enjoy all their rights, Paine wrote, until they were independent. Paine's words encouraged many Americans to accept the idea of independence.

On the battlefield, however, the Americans struggled to win their freedom. By the end of September, Paine was stationed just outside of New York City. He talked with generals of the Continental Army and saw the fighting firsthand. From time to time, he said, he heard "the whistling of a cannon ball." When he finally returned to his home in Philadelphia after a long walk along dirt roads, Paine did what he did best. With pen in hand, he wrote about what he had learned, in clear and colorful language.

A 1776 French engraving shows the burning of New York City by the British.

Paine knew that the American soldiers were not as disciplined as the British. He had watched his fellow soldiers retreat as the British fought their way through New York. He also knew many of the Americans were volunteers eager to return home as soon as possible. But without enough loyal soldiers, General George Washington—the Continental Army's commander in chief—had no hope of defeating the enemy.

Paine hoped to end what he called the "fears and falsehoods" that gripped Pennsylvania and New Jersey. Filled with anger for the British and love for the Americans, he wrote some of the most famous lines of the American Revolution: "These are the times that try men's souls."

Paine complained about the "summer soldier and sunshine patriot" who only supported the battle for independence when the American cause went well. But the war for independence would be lost if people did not help during the difficult winter ahead. Paine said the soldiers who stayed to fight for Washington

The American colonial military was greatly outnumbered by the British during the Revolutionary War. Great Britain had the largest navy in the world and a huge army. At the start of the war, the American colonies had no army and no navy. On June 14, 1775, the Second Continental Congress established the Continental Army. George Washington was named commander in chief and chose not to be paid for his services. The American navy was established on October 13, 1775.

Thomas Paine's
American Crisis I
is considered his
most eloquent
pamphlet.

The *American* CRISIS.

NUMBER I.

By the Author of COMMON SENSE.

THESE are the times that try men's fouls : The fummer foldier and the funfhine patriot will, in this crifis, fhrink from the fervice of his country ; but he that ftands it NOW, deferves the love and thanks of man and woman. Tyranny, like hell, is not eafily conquered ; yet we have this confolation with us, that the harder the conflict, the more glorious the triumph. What we obtain too cheap, we efteem too lightly :---'Tis dearnefs only that gives every thing its value. Heaven knows how to fet a proper price upon its goods; and it would be ftrange, indeed, if fo celeftial an article as FREEDOM fhould not be highly rated. Britain, with an army to enforce her tyranny, has declared, that fhe has a right (*not only to* TAX, but) " to " BIND *us in* ALL CASES WHATSOEVER," and if being *bound in that manner* is not flavery, then is there not fuch a thing as flavery upon earth. Even the expreffion is impious, for fo unlimited a power can belong only to GOD.

WHETHER the Independence of the Continent was declared too foon, or delayed too long, I will not now enter into as an argument ; my own fimple opinion is, that had it been eight months earlier, it would have been much better. We did not make a proper ufe of laft winter, neither could we, while we were in a dependent ftate. However, the fault, if it were one, was all our own ; we have none to blame but ourfelves*. But no great deal is loft yet ; all that Howe has been doing for this month paft is rather a ravage than a conqueft, which the fpirit of the Jerfies a year ago would have quickly repulfed, and which time and a little refolution will foon recover.

I have as little fuperftition in me as any man living, but

my

---

* "The prefent winter" (meaning the laft) " is worth an " age if rightly employed, but if loft, or neglected, the whole " Continent will partake of the evil ; and there is no punifh- " ment that man does not deferve, be he who, or what, or " where he will, that may be the means of facrificing a feafon " fo precious and ufeful."   COMMON SENSE.

---

wanted just one thing—"that the country would turn out and help them to drive the enemy back."

Paine called his pamphlet *The American Crisis.*

It first appeared in Philadelphia on December 19, 1776. General Washington soon read it to his men, to boost their spirits as they prepared for another battle. Commanders throughout the army also read it to their troops, and printers along the Atlantic Coast sold thousands of copies to civilians. The effect of Paine's pamphlet was powerful. James Cheetham, a newspaper publisher of the day, said after Paine wrote *The American Crisis*, "hope [replaced] despair, cheerfulness [replaced] gloom."

In many of his writings, Paine expressed what many others felt. He made people think about their rights and the possibility of forming a new country and creating a new government.

Paine's life was filled with personal success and much sorrow. He was one of the most famous men of his era, yet he died poor and with few friends. Thomas Paine remains one of the most important writers in the modern world, yet he is sometimes one of the forgotten heroes of the American Revolution.

2 ENGLISH UPBRINGING

❦

Thomas Paine was born in the farming village of Thetford, Norfolk, England, on January 29, 1737. Thomas's father was Joseph Pain. (Thomas Paine later changed the spelling of his family name.) Joseph made corsets, which are tight undergarments that many 18th-century women wore under their dresses to make them look slimmer. He also farmed. Thomas's mother was Frances Cocke, the daughter of a local lawyer. Joseph Pain was considered a poor but honest man, who had an interest in local politics.

When Thomas was approaching his second birthday, his parents had a second child, Elizabeth. She died shortly after she was born, and Thomas remained an only child after this. His mother later admitted that she spoiled her son.

A statue of Thomas Paine stands in Thetford, England, about 70 miles (112 kilometers) northeast of London.

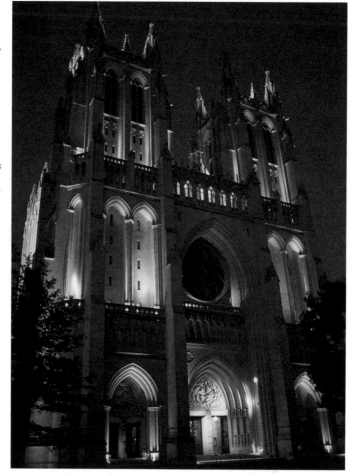

Washington National Cathedral in Washington, D.C., is an Episcopal church, and part of the Anglican Communion to which Thomas Paine belonged. Construction on the church began in 1907 but plans were envisioned in 1791 when the District of Columbia was designed.

Religion was an important part of daily life for many people in the 1700s, both in England and its colonies. Thomas grew up influenced by two religions, which would play an important part in his later writings. Thomas's mother belonged to the Anglican Church, which in the United States today is known as the Episcopal Church. The head of the

Anglican Church in Great Britain is the king or queen, and the government collected taxes to support the church. Anglicans follow many of the teachings of the Roman Catholic Church, which had once been the official religion of England. They also believed the clergy played an important role in their church.

Thomas was baptized as an Anglican and later was confirmed, making him a full member of the church. Yet later in life, Thomas remembered thinking as a boy that Christian religions were "a strange affair." He did not understand why God would kill his own son. He thought God could have found a less cruel way to help humans than to have Jesus die on the cross.

Thomas's father belonged to the Society of Friends. Its members are commonly called Quakers. In 18th-century England, the Quakers and members of other small, non-Anglican churches were called Dissenters. This meant they did not share the same ideas as the Anglicans. Dissenters also

> *The Society of Friends was founded in the 1650s by George Fox of England. The name Quakers came from the church's enemies, who said the Friends' bodies quaked during their religious meetings. Fox and his followers believed that everyone had an "inner light" within them that came from God. Through prayer, Quakers could discover this spirit and know God's will. Everyone could have a direct relationship with God, and so everyone was equal. Unlike the Anglicans or other Protestants of the time, the Quakers let women lead their meetings. Quakers also opposed violence and believed in living simple lives.*

rejected most of the teachings of the Catholic Church.

From time to time, Thomas's father took him to the weekly Quaker meetings, and Thomas learned more about the faith directly from his father. As an adult, he was impressed with the Quakers' belief in educating the young and helping the poor. Still, he never formally joined any church, although he believed everyone should be allowed to freely practice any religion, or none at all, if they chose.

When he was 6 years old, Thomas attended the local grammar school, just a short walk from his home. At the time, many English children did not attend schools, and about half of all adults could not sign their own names. Thomas was lucky to live in a town that provided free schooling for local boys (but not girls). Although the school was free, the Pains had to pay for Thomas's school supplies. He later wrote that his parents "distressed themselves" paying for them and for extra classes that met on Tuesday, Thursday, and Saturday afternoons

At the school, each day started with Anglican prayers. The students were divided into two groups.

> *On his own as a young student, Thomas Paine read such great English writers as William Shakespeare and John Milton. Shakespeare is considered the greatest English playwright of all time. Milton was a poet, but he also wrote about politics, including a strong defense of free speech.*

One studied the classics—ancient books written in Latin. Thomas was in a second group, which focused on reading and writing in English and studying math and science.

Thomas showed an early interest in writing. At 8, he wrote his first recorded poem, which described the death of his pet crow.

> *Here lies the body of John Crow,*
> *Who once was high but now is low;*
> *Ye brother Crows take warning all,*
> *For as you rise, so must you fall.*

When Thomas was 13, his parents took him out of the Thetford grammar school so he could become

Young boys in England and the American colonies worked as apprentices to learn skills.

an apprentice for his father and make corsets. At this time, many young boys in Great Britain and its American colonies became apprentices. They worked for a master for seven years so they could learn a skill. The master provided food, clothing, housing, and some education in reading, writing, and math. Masters usually controlled their apprentices' lives and could be harsh. Thomas was lucky that he could learn his trade from his father and not from a stranger.

At age 19, Thomas Paine ended his apprenticeship. His father's corset-making business seemed to be struggling, and Paine decided he wanted to do something else with his life. Paine later said he was "raw and adventurous" as a teenager. He was a short young man with brown hair. His dark eyes, one friend later wrote "were full, brilliant ... and piercing."

In 1756, Paine went to London and signed on with a privateer—a privately owned ship that had government permission to attack ships from enemy nations. At the time, Great Britain was at war with France. The two powerful nations fought over their colonies in North America in the French and Indian

In North America, the French and English fought for control of the fur trade, for the possession of land between the Appalachian Mountains and the Mississippi River, and each other's claims to fishing grounds off the coast of Newfoundland. The French and Indian War resulted in Britain's gaining almost all of France's territory in North America.

A navy ship lies off the English coast in 1757. The British used navy ships and privateers in the war against France.

War (1754–1763), a part of a larger European conflict called the Seven Years' War (1756–1763).

The ship Paine signed on with was the *Terrible*,

The French defeated the British at the Battle of Hastenbeck in Germany in 1757. The fighting that had started in North America spread around the world and was called the Seven Years' War.

and its captain had the gruesome name of William Death. Before Paine could go to sea, however, his father came to London and asked him not to go. Paine agreed, and the decision was a good one. In late 1756, the French captured the *Terrible* in waters off the coast of England, and more than 150 sailors died in the battle.

Safe in London, Paine found work as a corset maker, but soon he was ready to try another sea voyage. He signed on with the privateer *King of Prussia*, which sailed from London in January 1757. Thanks to his training as a corset maker, Paine was comfortable working with his hands and could easily handle all sorts of tools.

After six months at sea in the Atlantic Ocean and the English Channel, the *King of Prussia* returned to England. For his services, Paine probably received about 30 pounds, more money than he had ever earned before. Today, that sum would be worth about $5,000. With his pockets bulging with cash, Paine returned to London.

City life in the British capital was different from village life in Thetford. London was one of the world's largest cities, with more than 650,000 people. Thetford was a small town with several thousand people, most of whom were British born. London's residents included a variety of Europeans as well as some North Americans. London was a center of art, politics, and education, and Paine met a variety of people. He pursued his interest in science by reading books and attending lectures by noted scientists. He probably also learned about politics—at a time when some British thinkers were beginning to challenge old ideas.

Before the 18th century, aristocrats dominated European society. England, however, also elected lawmakers who served in a branch of Parliament called the House of Commons. By the middle 18th century, when Paine lived, some people believed those

The House of Commons was the lower house of Parliament. The House of Lords was the upper house. Its members were the aristocrats of society.

lawmakers should have more power in government than the aristocrats or the king. The members of the Commons represented the interest of the majority of people—and the common people, not those with money and power, were considered to be the true creators of government and society.

People in England known as Whigs called for reforms that would give the average citizen even more influence over the government. For example, at the time, only men who owned property could vote, and most of these people lived in the countryside. The Whigs wanted to give the cities more representatives in Parliament and to let people who did not own property vote.

These changes would create a true republic—a government in which elected representatives debated issues and made laws, and did what voters wanted them to do. This idea was sometimes called republicanism, and the form of government was called a democratic republic. ॐ

About 2,500 years ago, the people of Athens, Greece, created a government in which all the male citizens met to make major decisions for their city. Each man voted on the major issues. This form of government was called a democracy. Around the same time, in the sixth century B.C., the city of Rome developed a republic. The city was too large to have every citizen vote on every issue. Instead, voters elected people to represent them to create laws and set policies. The republicans of Paine's day borrowed ideas from the ancient Greeks and Romans as they created modern democratic republican governments.

3   NEW CAREERS

❧❀❧

Thomas Paine did not stay in London long. The money he had earned on the privateer ship ran out, so in 1759 he started his own corset business in the town of Sandwich, about 85 miles (136 kilometers) from London. Thomas married Mary Lambert, a local maid, and they moved to the nearby town of Margate.

In 1760, Mary and her baby died during childbirth. Paine never wrote or said much about this painful loss. The next year, he gave up the corset business and returned to his boyhood home of Thetford, where he studied for a new career as an exciseman.

Excisemen collected taxes for the British government. An excise was a tax placed on certain goods sold within Great Britain, such as alcohol, coffee, salt, soap, tea, and tobacco. In his job, Paine visited

Benjamin Franklin (standing), who represented the interests of the American colonists before the British lords in London, would play an important role in Thomas Paine's life.

merchants to see how much they sold of a particular product and collected excise taxes from them. He also kept an eye out for people who tried to avoid the tax by smuggling.

During his life, Thomas Paine lived in England, Pennsylvania, New York, New Jersey, and France.

Paine began his new job in 1764. The work was steady, but Paine had to pay for the horse he rode to collect taxes, and after his expenses, he did not have much to live on. He also had to face the hostility

of people who did not like to pay taxes and so did not welcome a visit from the exciseman.

Within a year Paine was out of work again. He was accused of stamping and lost his job in August 1765. When excisemen did not visit the merchants as they claimed in their written reports, this offense was called stamping. One historian suggests that Paine may have been fired because he did not want to speak out against a supervisor who was breaking the law. If Paine had betrayed his boss, he would have lost his job. By not betraying him, Paine took responsibility for the stamping—and lost his job.

Paine once again made corsets to survive, settling in the small town of Diss. The town sat on a lake, and one observer at the time wrote that Diss "stinks exceedingly" from dead fish. In 1766, Paine asked for his old job back. The government agreed, though he had to wait for a new excise position to open. For a while, Paine had little money, until he managed to find a job as a teacher in London.

The school stood in a busy neighborhood filled with theaters and bars. It was run by Methodists and offered free classes to poor children. The Methodists were former Anglicans who broke away from the Church of England. They believed in helping the poor and said everyone was equal in God's eyes.

For a time, Paine studied Methodist beliefs. With his teaching job, he saw the importance of education for poor children. He also continued to educate himself, once again attending lectures and reading on his own. He later wrote, "I have seldom passed five minutes of my life … in which I did not acquire some knowledge."

In 1768, Paine started his next tax-collecting job in the town of Lewes. The town had many Dissenter churches and a strong republican influence in its local government. A group called the Society of Twelve controlled the town's politics. It tried to prevent area aristocrats from running the town. The Society of Twelve chose men to run for local political offices and collected some local taxes.

Paine soon took part in the group's meetings. He had a chance to see local government in action. He also belonged to a club that debated current political issues. Years later, another club member wrote that Paine had a strong "depth of political knowledge."

While living in Lewes, Paine married Elizabeth Ollive in 1771. About 10 years younger than Paine, she was the daughter of his landlords. Paine said he married her for practical reasons, not for love. He needed someone to look after his daily needs, such as cooking his meals and washing his clothes. Thomas and Elizabeth separated in 1774 and never lived together again. A legal document noted that Paine "promis[ed] to claim no part of whatever goods she might gain in the future." For the rest of his life, Paine devoted himself to politics and writing and did not remarry.

During his six years in Lewes, Paine published his first writings. He wrote several pieces for his club, including a poem that made fun of three local judges. The judges wanted to punish a man who had not voted for their candidate for Parliament. "They took revenge," Paine said, "on his dog, which they caused to be hanged for [chasing] a hare." Paine thought the judges were "ridiculous" for using their power this way.

Thomas Paine published his first major work while serving as an exciseman.

Paine's first major writing appeared in 1772. A group of excisemen asked Paine to write a pamphlet asking the British government to raise their salary. He called his work *The Case of the Officers of Excise.* Paine said that the low pay and harsh conditions led some excisemen to become corrupt. Many excisemen accepted bribes from merchants to reduce the amount of tax the merchants owed. But they were not at heart bad men. "Poverty and opportunity," he wrote, "corrupt many an honest man." Paine received compliments for his writing, but Parliament ignored the call for a pay raise.

After publishing his pamphlet, Paine traveled to London to push the case before Parliament. While he was there, a small shop that he ran with Elizabeth before they separated began to suffer. In 1774, Paine auctioned all his goods to earn money. While he was in London, he met Benjamin Franklin, one of the most famous Americans of the day. Franklin had spent years in London representing the interests of Pennsylvania and several other colonies. With Paine, he discussed both science and politics.

The London bridge in the mid-1700s

Benjamin Franklin, one of the leading citizens of Philadelphia, was known as an inventor and scientist.

His scientific work made Franklin a respected thinker in Europe. By the time he met Paine, Franklin was a leading American patriot with definite ideas about colonial government.

In September 1774, when Paine decided to start a new life in North America, Franklin helped him. He wrote letters of recommendation for Paine to give to William, his son, and to Richard Bache, his son-in-law who was a merchant in Philadelphia. In the letter, Franklin called Paine "an ingenious worthy young man." But Franklin had no idea that Thomas Paine would play a major role in the battle for American independence that was soon to come. ❧

Benjamin Franklin was born in Boston in 1706. He became a printer and writer while working on his brother James's newspaper. In 1723, Franklin moved to Philadelphia and later started his own printing business. His most famous work was Poor Richard's Almanack. *Franklin filled the yearly book with wise and witty sayings about human nature.*

4 THE ROAD TO COMMON SENSE

❧

Thomas Paine once wrote that he read about the North American colony of Virginia when he was a child. "My [desire] from that day of seeing the western side of the Atlantic [Ocean] never left me." With the letters from Benjamin Franklin in his pocket, Paine was confident that he would find plenty of help from Richard Bache and other important Americans. But first Paine had to survive the harrowing trip across the ocean.

Rough seas made Paine seasick, and then he caught ship's fever, an illness that often struck passengers on 18th-century sailing ships. Although Paine rode in first class, conditions on the ship were still crowded and dirty. Paine suffered from headaches and a fever, and had trouble sleeping. When he

A tax commissioner is strung up on a pole while another is about to be tarred and feathered in a Stamp Act protest.

reached Philadelphia, Pennsylvania, on November 30, 1774, he was extremely weak and spent many days in bed. By January 1775, he was finally strong enough to explore his surroundings and begin to look for work.

Philadelphia in 1775 was the largest and wealthiest city in British North America. Its 25,000 residents included Germans, free and enslaved African-Americans, and people from all parts of Great Britain. Philadelphia had been founded by English Quakers, and it welcomed people of many faiths. The city was a colonial business center and major port. Ships carried crops grown in Pennsylvania, New Jersey, and Delaware to other colonies and to England. The city's streets also bustled with activity, as merchants sold imported goods and craftsmen made the tools needed for colonial life.

Philadelphia was also becoming an important political center for all the American colonies, and it was the site of the First Continental Congress. In September 1774, delegates from every colony except Georgia had met to discuss recent problems with Great Britain. The roots of these problems went back to 1764, when Parliament tried to introduce new taxes in the colonies.

Under a law called the Sugar Act, the British placed duties on certain goods, such as coffee, lumber, and sugar. The next year, in 1765, Parliament passed the Stamp Act, which required the colonists to pay a tax on all printed documents and newspapers. Each document had to carry a royal stamp to show the tax had been paid.

Some began to question these new taxes. They believed the taxes violated the British constitution. Under the British constitution, patriots claimed, the government could not place a tax on the people without their consent. This approval came through the representatives elected to Parliament by voters. But the colonists did not have any representatives there. They believed the new tax laws were an example of "taxation without representation," and so were viewed as illegal.

The tea destroyed in the 1773 Boston Tea Party was worth about $1 million in today's currency.

In the late fall of 1773, three British ships loaded with tea sat in Boston Harbor. Local patriots did not want to pay a duty on the tea, and they asked the governor to let the ships sail back to Great Britain. He refused. Rather than let the tea come ashore, the patriots organized the Boston Tea Party. On December 16, a group of men disguised as Mohawk Indians boarded the ships. Working silently, they dumped 342 chests of tea into the water. The protest led to the new British policies that put the American colonies and Great Britain on the path to war.

Violent protests in 1765 convinced Parliament not to enforce the Stamp Act. But the British lawmakers declared that they had the right to tax the colonies even though the colonists did not have representation.

In 1773, another tax, this time on tea, led to a protest in Boston, Massachusetts. After the Boston Tea Party, Great Britain shut down Boston Harbor, named a British general as governor, and limited the power of local governments. Those actions, which were called the Coercive Acts in Britain and the Intolerable Acts in the colonies, led to the First Continental Congress. Patriots in every colony saw the new British policies in Massachusetts as a threat to all Americans' rights as British citizens.

Hostilities toward Britain were nearing their peak when Thomas Paine reached Philadelphia. He took a job at a new publication, the *Pennsylvania Magazine*, which covered a wide range of topics, from science to business to foreign news. Paine soon had the chance to express his opinions on political issues.

Since writers of the day often did not sign their names, historians are not sure of all the articles Paine wrote for the magazine. But historians do agree he wrote at least 17 articles. Most of Paine's writings reflected his opinions on political and social issues, such as slavery and Great Britain's harsh policies in India.

The owner of the *Pennsylvania Magazine* did not want the magazine to stir up arguments. But after April 19, 1775, Paine began to write forceful words against the British. On that date, British troops and local militia clashed in the Massachusetts towns of Lexington and Concord, marking the beginning of

The first shots of the war were fired on April 19, 1775, on Lexington Green.

the American Revolutionary War. Within months, Paine wrote that America had been "set on fire about my ears, [and] it was time to stir." He believed that "the Almighty [God] will finally separate America from Britain." Paine did not like violence, but he believed that defending liberty was worth the fight.

In the first months of the war, the American forces had some military success. They captured New York's Fort Ticonderoga from the British, along with cannons and weapons.

But as the fighting went on, many Americans still hoped to end the war and improve relations with the British. These loyalists thought being a part of the British Empire had many benefits. The British had a powerful navy that could protect American shipping. Trade with Great Britain helped colonial farmers and merchants. And despite the recent problems, Americans still enjoyed more political freedom than most people in the world. Americans also felt a strong tie to the British because of their shared language and history. Not even all of the patriot leaders wanted the colonies to declare their independence from Great Britain.

One of the leaders who did favor independence was Benjamin Franklin. Like many colonists, Franklin once considered himself a loyal British citizen. But by the summer of 1775 he believed the American colonies had to win their freedom. He wrote a declaration of independence and gave it to the Second Continental Congress. The congress had delegates from all the colonies who discussed ways to protest Great Britain's policies and whether they should declare independence. The very idea of independence, wrote one congressional delegate, "revolted" most members of the congress.

Benjamin Rush was active in the Sons of Liberty, an anti-British political group.

By the fall of 1775, Paine had met Benjamin Rush, a young doctor in Philadelphia who shared his views on many political issues and also was a friend of Benjamin Franklin. Rush believed the American colonies needed to be independent from Great Britain.

Still, when Rush learned Paine was preparing to write a pamphlet on the war and the colonies' future, he cautioned Paine not to say much about independence or republicanism. The doctor knew that many average citizens and members of the congress did not want independence. Paine, however, ignored Rush's advice as he sat down to write one of the most powerful political statements ever.

Benjamin Rush was born in Pennsylvania in 1745. He studied medicine in Philadelphia and Scotland and then settled in Philadelphia. Rush represented Pennsylvania at the Second Continental Congress and signed the Declaration of Independence. He also served for a time as the chief doctor of the Continental Army and taught medicine. After the American Revolution, he focused on correcting social problems. Rush opposed the drinking of alcohol, worked for better treatment of prisoners and the mentally ill, and led an organization that opposed slavery.

Paine wrote through the fall of 1775, drawing on notes he had written over several years. At times, he read parts of it to Rush, then made changes. Paine gave a copy to Samuel Adams, one of the leading patriots in Boston. Adams was well known for powerful writings on liberty and protecting the colonists' rights. Benjamin Franklin also reviewed the pamphlet and gave Paine some suggestions for improving it. Paine wanted to call the document *Plain Truth*. Rush came up with the title the world knows today: *Common Sense.*

Paine wrote that "the cause of America is in great part the cause of all mankind." The British, Paine argued, were trying to destroy the colonists' natural rights. These included the right to live peacefully and freely, as long as a person's actions did not harm anyone else, and the right to own property. Governments existed to protect life, liberty, and property, and the power to rule came from the people.

King George III considered those who believed in independence for the colonies as rebels and traitors.

Paine rejected the idea of "divine right," where God chose kings and queens to hold power over their subjects. In general, Paine believed that kings and queens should never rule. They claimed power over other people, saying their subjects were less important than they were. But when humans first appeared on Earth, Paine argued, they were all equal. Splitting people into two separate groups—subjects and kings—was a "distinction for

43

which no truly natural or religious reason can be assigned."

Paine wrote that the American colonies did not benefit from being part of the British Empire. British

Thomas Paine's name did not appear on the title page of Common Sense.

COMMON SENSE;

ADDRESSED TO THE

INHABITANTS

O F

A M E R I C A,

On the following interesting

S U B J E C T S.

I. Of the Origin and Design of Government in general, with concise Remarks on the English Constitution.

II. Of Monarchy and Hereditary Succession.

III. Thoughts on the present State of American Affairs.

IV. Of the present Ability of America, with some miscellaneous Reflections.

Man knows no Master save creating HEAVEN,
Or those whom choice and common good ordain.

THOMSON.

PHILADELPHIA:

Printed, and Sold, by R. BELL, in Third-Street.

MDCCLXXVI.

trade and military policies helped the British, not the colonists. Because of the war, the colonists could never have good relations again with Great Britain, and they should not want to be ruled by a king again.

Declaring independence, Paine believed, could also bring an end to the war. At the time, the rest of the world still saw the American colonists as British subjects rebelling against their king. By declaring independence, the rest of the world would see America as a separate country. Foreign nations would then be more likely to help the colonists and treat them as equals. And over time, Paine wrote, "nothing but independence ... can keep the peace of the continent."

Paine wrote in a simple, direct style that most people of the day could understand. He talked about ideas from the Bible—the one book that almost every colonist knew. Paine also appealed to his readers' emotions and used forceful language. At one point, he called George III a "royal brute," words that could have gotten him arrested.

At first, Paine found no one in Philadelphia to publish *Common Sense* because of its bold language and ideas. When the pamphlet finally appeared in print, Paine's name did not appear on it.

Some people guessed the author of *Common Sense* was Benjamin Franklin, or perhaps Samuel

Adams or John Adams. But by late February 1776, people in Philadelphia knew Paine was the author of this powerful pamphlet. By then, Paine had published a third edition of *Common Sense.* Copies of it were printed in German so that the large number of German immigrants in the colonies could read it. A French version appeared in Quebec, Canada, and by the summer, Europeans also had seen *Common Sense.*

Common Sense stunned people across North America and Europe. Although people had written many of the same ideas before, no writer had combined so many important ideas on society and politics in such a clear, forceful way. At the time, a successful pamphlet might sell 2,000 or 3,000 copies, but Paine's work sold about 150,000 copies, with new editions printed in all the major cities.

This pamphlet was read aloud to people unable to read. A British writer noted that when these people heard Paine's words, they believed in independence, "though perhaps the hour before [they] were most violent against the least idea of independence." George Washington

Selling 150,000 copies of one pamphlet in 1776 would be like a modern author selling 15 million copies of one book. Paine, however, did not become rich after writing Common Sense *or any of his other works. He often gave the money he made to charity. Paine used his profits from* Common Sense *to buy mittens for American soldiers.*

was then serving as the commander of the Continental Army, the colonists' main fighting force. He wrote, "I find that *Common Sense* is working a powerful change in the minds of men."

Historians have tried to explain why Paine's work was so popular and powerful. Part of it was his timing. The Revolutionary War was spreading as the British began attacking colonists outside of Massachusetts, and more people had direct contact with the violence. Paine also dared to write what others might only think or discuss with their closest friends. Colonists realized that other people longed for liberty and independence just as they did.

A portrait of John Adams by famous painter John Trumbull

In 1805, John Adams, a leading patriot who wanted independence and later became the second president of the United States, wrote, "I know not whether any man in the world has had more influence on its inhabitants or affairs for the last 30 years than Tom Paine."

A British cartoon printed during the Revolutionary War shows England trying to control the colonies. The American in dark pants is most likely Tom Paine, who is presenting his backside to his native land.

Not everyone welcomed *Common Sense*, however. Some members of the congress still did not wish to declare independence. Loyalists challenged Paine's ideas in letters to newspapers. An English visitor traveling through Virginia called *Common Sense* "one of the vilest things that was ever published to the world." As these attacks on *Common Sense* increased, Paine wrote articles to defend himself and his ideas. He claimed that one letter attacking him was filled with "absurdity, confusion … and the most notorious and willful falsehoods."

Paine's writings played a significant role in Pennsylvania in 1776. The law-making branch of the state's government, the Assembly, was filled with loyalists who did not favor independence. Wealthy landowners and businessmen controlled it, and they resisted creating a true republican government in Pennsylvania. The working people of Philadelphia and farmers far from the city felt their interests were not heard in the Assembly. Paine and other patriots in Pennsylvania worked with those people to elect Whigs to the Assembly.

These newly elected members of the Assembly favored independence. They also wrote a new constitution for Pennsylvania. For the first time, all free men had a right to vote, and the western part of the colony where many farmers lived received more power in the government than it had ever had before.

Another important event took place in Philadelphia in 1776. On July 2, the Second Continental Congress finally voted for independence. Two days later, the lawmakers approved a final version of the Declaration of Independence, written for the most part by Thomas Jefferson of Virginia. All the Americans had to do now was defeat the British on the battlefield.

Chapter

5 AT WAR

⁓⋇⋇⁓

Once the decision was made to fight for independence from England, Paine joined the war effort as a soldier. He first served as an infantryman with a group of Pennsylvania volunteers that marched to New Jersey. By this time, the main British force was gathering in New York. Paine's unit did not see any action in New Jersey, and Paine moved on to New York, where he served under General Nathanael Greene.

In November 1776, the British defeated General Greene and his troops in New York at Fort Washington, and the Americans retreated into New Jersey. The Continental Army did not have enough men, and many of General George Washington's soldiers would be going home by the end of the year, their tour of duty over. Washington's troops were also

On the night of December 25, 1776, Hessian soldiers— German mercenaries hired to fight for Great Britain—celebrated the Christmas holiday. At the same time, General George Washington began a sneak attack on the Hessians' camp in Trenton, New Jersey. The Americans crossed the Delaware River in a snowstorm, then surprised the Hessians before they could reach their weapons. Washington followed this victory with another one a week later in Princeton, New Jersey. These successes boosted American confidence at a key time during the Revolution.

unskilled and sometimes lacked supplies. The British victory in New York weakened the Americans' desire to keep fighting.

Paine returned to Philadelphia and soon wrote his first version of _The American Crisis_. He called on both soldiers and civilians to have faith that the Americans would win. During the war, Paine wrote 12 more articles with the same name, one for each colony, adding a Roman numeral after the title to distinguish them. He also added three more _Crisis_ pamphlets, which were not numbered.

A week after _The American Crisis I_ was published, George Washington had it read to his troops, just prior to launching a surprise attack against the British in Trenton, New Jersey. The Americans won the battle, which gave them an important victory. Paine, like other patriots, welcomed this good news. They knew, however, that more fighting was still to come.

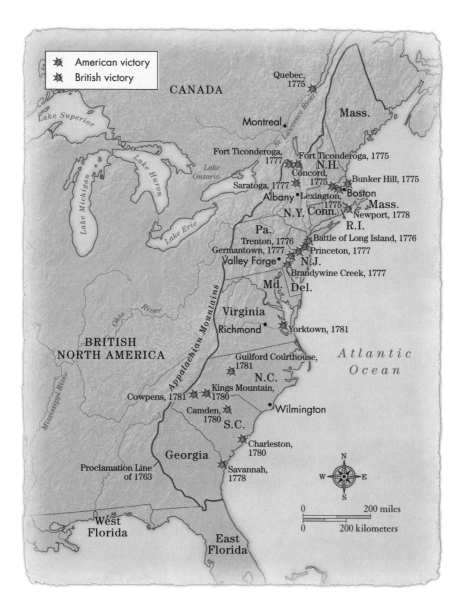

Map Legend:
- American victory
- British victory

CANADA

Lake Superior

Lake Michigan

Lake Huron

Lake Ontario

Lake Erie

St. Lawrence River

Quebec, 1775

Montreal

Mass.

Fort Ticonderoga, 1777

Fort Ticonderoga, 1775

N.H.

Concord, 1775

Bunker Hill, 1775

Saratoga, 1777

Albany • Lexington, 1775

Boston

N.Y. Conn.

Mass.

Newport, 1778

R.I.

Pa.

Trenton, 1776

Battle of Long Island, 1776

Germantown, 1777

Princeton, 1777

Valley Forge •

N.J.

Brandywine Creek, 1777

Md. Del.

Ohio River

Appalachian Mountains

Virginia

Richmond •

Yorktown, 1781

BRITISH
NORTH AMERICA

Guilford Courthouse, 1781

Atlantic Ocean

N.C.

Kings Mountain, 1780

Cowpens, 1781

Camden, 1780

• Wilmington

Mississippi River

S.C.

Charleston, 1780

Georgia

Savannah, 1778

Proclamation Line of 1763

W ⊕ E
N
S

0   200 miles
0   200 kilometers

West Florida

East Florida

Early in 1777, Paine worked with Pennsylvania
Whigs who supported the state's new constitution.
Then in April, the congress chose Paine to serve

Major battles of the Revolution were fought throughout the colonies.

*Americans
Benjamin
Franklin, Silas
Deane, and
Arthur Lee
appeared before
King Louis XVI
in 1778 to seek
French support
for the war effort.*

as secretary of the Committee for Foreign Affairs. The committee's main goal was to secure aid from France and Spain to help with the war effort. John Adams suggested Paine for the job. Although Adams did not agree with all of Paine's ideas, Adams knew Paine was poor and needed work, and

his writing skills would be useful. Paine's main job as secretary was to record the committee's actions and write letters to American diplomats, including Benjamin Franklin.

Late that summer, British troops neared Philadelphia. In his fourth *American Crisis*, Paine urged the city's residents to show "manly resistance" if the enemy entered the city. But the British captured Philadelphia, the American capital, and members of the congress fled to Lancaster, Pennsylvania. Thousands of Philadelphia residents also sought safer ground. Paine had hoped to organize a small army to fight the British in the streets, but few patriots remained in the city. In late September, Paine finally left Philadelphia and headed to New Jersey.

In December 1777, Washington's army camped outside Philadelphia at Valley Forge. With food and clothing often scarce, the American soldiers struggled to survive through the winter.

> *General George Washington and his troops camped at Valley Forge, Pennsylvania, during the cold winter of 1777–1778. Many of the 12,000 American men and boys often went barefoot. Food was sometimes scarce, and disease spread through the camp. On December 23, 1777, Washington wrote: "We have this day no less than 2,873 men in camp unfit for duty because they are barefooted and otherwise naked." An estimated 2,500 soldiers died at the camp. The name Valley Forge has come to represent the American colonists' deep longing for independence, no matter the cost.*

Paine spent some time at the camp before heading to York, Pennsylvania, where the congress briefly met.

By the summer of 1778, the British pulled out of Philadelphia, realizing that taking the city had not helped their war effort. As the British headed back to their old base in New York City, Paine and the lawmakers returned to Philadelphia.

Paine continued to write letters, articles, and poems, always showing his hatred for King George III and his faith in republican government. Some American officials were also criticized in his writings. One was Silas Deane, an American diplomat in France.

Because of the letters and reports he saw on his job, Paine distrusted Deane. Paine believed the diplomat had received some supplies for free from the king of France, then told the congress he needed money to pay for them. Paine accused Deane of lying, which angered those

> _Silas Deane was a successful businessman before the war. He served in the First and Second Continental Congresses. Early in 1776, he became the first American diplomat sent to France to seek aid for the Revolution. Most people considered him a loyal patriot, but Deane hoped to make a fortune during the war through secret business dealings. He was also a good friend of an American who worked for the British as a spy, although Deane did not realize this at the time. By 1781, Deane believed independence was not good for America. He lived in Europe for several years, then died in 1789 while waiting to sail to Canada._

members of the congress who supported Deane.

Some lawmakers who had never liked Paine wanted to fire him as secretary of the foreign affairs committee. Instead, in January 1779, Paine resigned. In a letter to the committee members he wrote, "I came into office an honest man, I go out with the same character."

Again without a job, Paine struggled to earn

Thomas Paine served as secretary of the Committee for Foreign Affairs for nearly two years.

money. He also faced insults because of his role in the Deane affair. Once while walking down the street, Paine was pushed into a gutter, and local writers called him names. Still, the patriots of Philadelphia considered him an ally, and in November 1779, they chose him to serve as clerk of the Pennsylvania Assembly. In that job, Paine helped write a law that would gradually end slavery in the state. He had long believed that slavery was wrong and that it did not belong in a country concerned with its freedom and independence.

The British captured Charleston, South Carolina, in May 1780.

By 1779, the major battles of the Revolutionary War moved to the southern colonies, as the Americans and British battled in Georgia, the Carolinas, and Virginia. In May 1780, the British won a key victory when they captured Charleston, South Carolina, a major seaport.

About this time, Paine came up with a bold plan. He wanted to return to England to stir up a rebellion against King George III. Some members of Parliament were already trying to limit the king's power. Paine thought he could pen articles to promote republicanism and call for peace with the Americans. Several of Paine's friends, however, feared for his safety and told him to drop the idea. Paine agreed, but he soon found another reason to return to Europe.

Late in 1780, the congress chose John Laurens of South Carolina to go to France and seek more aid. Like Paine, Laurens had served in the Continental Army, and he asked Paine to accompany him to France as his personal secretary. They left for Paris in February 1781. Paine was already well known in France because of *Common Sense* and his other writings. Before starting his official duties, Paine traveled to the French city of Nantes, where the residents greeted him as a hero.

Once in Paris, Paine spent most of his time with other Americans living in the city. In his role as sec-

The French fleet controls Chesapeake Bay as the British surrender to the Americans at Yorktown, Virginia.

retary, he recorded what was said in meetings with French officials. He could not take part in any discussions, however, since he spoke very little French. He relied on a translator to communicate with his hosts. By the spring, Paine and Laurens returned to North America, bringing with them money and supplies for the Continental Army from their French allies.

As Paine's ship landed in Boston, General Washington and his troops were headed to Virginia for a major attack on the British. The decisive battle came in October 1781. British General Lord Cornwallis had stationed his troops in Yorktown, Virginia, overlooking the York River, which flowed into Chesapeake Bay. French naval ships took control of the bay, preventing a British escape to the open sea. Then, French and American ground forces closed in on the British camp. Cornwallis was forced to surrender, rather than risk the lives of thousands of British soldiers.

Americans celebrated the victory, and within months Great Britain began peace talks. The war was almost over, and the Americans had won their independence. Paine was glad for the Americans, but personally he felt lost. He had almost no money and no decent job. He also knew many people still disliked him because of the Deane affair and his strong republican beliefs.

Paine's situation soon began to improve. In 1782, Washington and others arranged for Paine to work for the new government. His main job was to convince the states to give money to the congress and help boost the new national government's powers. Paine also received money from France for his past writings attacking the British.

Then, in 1784, the state of New York gave him a large farm in New Rochelle that had once belonged to a loyalist. The farm was a reward for his writings,

General George Washington made a triumphal entry into New York City in November 1783.

which, New York lawmakers said, "inspired the citizens of this state ... and have ultimately contributed to the freedom ... and independence of the United States."

During this time, Paine wrote his last *American Crisis*. It appeared on the eighth anniversary of the Battles of Lexington and Concord. Paine wrote that the "greatest and completest revolution the world ever knew is gloriously and happily accomplished."

In November 1783, he spent time with General Washington in New Jersey. One Sunday, before heading to church, Paine dropped off his coat at a friend's house. Later, he found out the friend's servant had run off with the coat. Washington then gave Paine a coat, and for years after, Paine proudly told people that the coat had once belonged to the great American general.

From New Jersey, Paine traveled with Washington to New York, and he rode on horseback next to Washington during a victory parade through New York City. Paine already sensed, however, that the United States might not be his permanent home. He had often considered himself a "citizen of the world." Still, he would "always feel an honest pride at the part I have taken and acted" in the Revolution. ❧

Chapter

6 BACK TO EUROPE

❧⌘❧

For the next several years, Paine spent most of his time in Philadelphia and at a cottage he had bought in New Jersey, while renting out his New York land to a local farmer. Paine preferred to be close to a large city, with its many activities and educated people.

He enjoyed spending time with his friend David Rittenhouse, a Philadelphia scientist. The two men sometimes conducted experiments together and admired new inventions, such as the steamboat. Paine had always enjoyed science and working with his hands, and the experiments let him pursue both interests.

Throughout his life, Paine paid more attention to ideas than to practical, everyday concerns. He was sloppy and absent-minded, and he relied on house-keepers to take care of him. His appearance didn't

Thomas Paine was caught up in the French Revolution, depicted here in a detail from Jean-Pierre Houel's painting, Storming the Bastille.

During the mid-1780s, Thomas Paine developed a passion for iron bridges. At the time, most bridges were made of wood or stone. After reading about bridge building, Paine and an assistant designed an iron bridge. Paine wanted to build one across the Schuylkill River in Philadelphia. For more than a year, he built models and tried to get money to construct a full-sized bridge. Pennsylvania's lawmakers, however, did not support the plan.

concern him. On his 1781 trip to France, he did not bathe regularly, and a man traveling with him finally insisted that Paine "stew for an hour, in a hot bath." Paine agreed only after the man gave him a stack of newspapers to read while he sat in the tub.

Most people who met Paine thought he was self-centered. Paine knew he was a talented writer and was not afraid to tell others about his own skills. He loved to talk about himself and felt he deserved rewards for his talents and efforts to improve the world. Yet Paine disliked powerful people who used their power to hurt others, and he always spoke out against leaders who hurt the interests of the poor and working people.

In 1787, Paine sailed for France and England. He spent several months in France, often talking with Thomas Jefferson, who was working there as a U.S. diplomat. The two had only met briefly before, but over time they became good friends. During Paine's time in France, Jefferson introduced him to French officials. He asked Paine to carry letters for him when he headed to England.

Paine went back to his birthplace of Thetford for the first time in many years. He spent time with his mother and arranged for her to receive an annual payment from money he made in the United States. Paine's father had died the previous fall.

Through 1788, Paine worked to build an iron bridge in England. The project eventually failed, and he once again turned to politics. He paid close attention to events in France, where another revolution was brewing. Many French citizens demanded that King Louis XVI give them a greater role in government and a written constitution to protect their rights. Louis XVI was willing to give up some control, which upset France's aristocrats and Roman Catholic priests, who also held political power.

Thomas Paine

Adding to the king's problems was France's struggling economy. The French government spent more than it received in taxes, and many people could not afford to pay the taxes the government tried to collect. By 1789, France was

The Estates-General met in 1789 for the first time in 175 years.

ready for radical change, and Paine was curious to see what would happen.

In May 1789, France held its first meeting of the Estates-General since 1614. The Estates-General was an assembly that France's kings called during times of crisis. The three separate estates, or groups, that comprised it were the aristocrats, the priests, and the common people.

The commoners, average French people who lacked political rights or wealth, were sometimes called the Third Estate. King Louis XVI tried to address the concerns of the Third Estate, without upsetting the aristocrats and the church. The common people, however, did not think the king was acting quickly enough to address their concerns, and the members of the Third Estate soon formed the National Assembly.

Although Paine opposed King George III before the American Revolution, he believed Louis XVI as king was making a real effort to help his people. He also knew that the French government had played a key role during the American Revolution, sending money, troops, and supplies. Paine thought the French king could peacefully turn his nation into a republic.

Early in 1790, he wrote to George Washington that Louis XVI and the National Assembly were setting a "happy example" for the rest of Europe to follow. What no one anticipated, however, was that reform in France would soon turn into a bloody revolution and the country would not become a republic at this time.

Paine spent time in Paris during 1789 and 1790, seeing for himself the changes taking place in

King Louis XVI was married to the beautiful Marie Antoinette of Austria. Her extravagant spending and foreign status made her very unpopular in France. As a young queen, she lavished money on friends and paid no attention to France's fiscal crisis. Once, when an official told Marie Antoinette the Parisians were angry because "they have no bread," she was said to have replied, "Then let them eat cake." Marie Antoinette was tried for treason, and died on the guillotine on October 16, 1793.

69

France. He watched a crowd attack the Bastille, a large prison in Paris, seeking to capture gunpowder stored there. The people freed the seven prisoners inside. Paine was also in Paris about the time the National Assembly took lands owned by the Roman Catholic Church and sold them to raise money.

Paine's Rights of Man *was written in response to Edmund Burke's criticism of the revolution in France.*

RIGHTS OF MAN:

BEING AN

ANSWER to Mr. BURKE's ATTACK

ON THE

FRENCH REVOLUTION.

B Y

THOMAS PAINE,

SECRETARY FOR FOREIGN AFFAIRS TO CONGRESS IN THE AMERICAN WAR, AND
AUTHOR OF THE WORK INTITLED *COMMON SENSE.*

LONDON:
PRINTED FOR J. JOHNSON, St PAUL's CHURCH-YARD.
MDCCXCI.

During his stays in France, Paine took notes on the developing revolution. He also expressed his support for the changes taking place in a letter to a British lawmaker and personal friend, Edmund Burke. Unlike Paine, Burke detested the revolution that was ending the old French monarchy. In November 1790, Burke published a pamphlet called *Reflections on the Revolution in France*. He criticized the changes occurring in France, since they went beyond anything allowed by the French constitution. In the book, Burke correctly predicted that the French Revolution would become violent.

Paine disagreed with Burke, and their opposing views on the French Revolution ended their friendship. Burke's pamphlet led Paine to write a two-part response, *Rights of Man*. Like *Common Sense*, it attacked kings and promoted natural rights, such as the freedom of people to freely join together and create a government. "Individuals

Edmund Burke (1729–1797) was born in Dublin, Ireland. He trained for the law before becoming a writer and entering government service. Before the American Revolution, Burke was one of the leading lawmakers who opposed Great Britain's policies in the colonies. He hoped the colonists and the British could avoid a war. In general, he disliked violence as a way to solve political problems, which explains his strong feelings against the French Revolution. He thought society needed kings and that people should respect the social and political systems created by those who came before them.

themselves," he wrote, "each in his own personal and sovereign right, entered into a compact with each other to produce a government, and this is the only mode in which governments have a right to arise."

Paine's book also called for government programs to aid the elderly, the poor, and retired soldiers. In monarchies, he believed, too much tax money was spent to support the rulers. Paine said that giving money to the poor would end their current suffering and enable their children to go to school. He claimed that "ignorance will be banished from the rising generations, and the number of poor will … become less, because their abilities, by the aid of education, will be greater." The kind of government programs that Paine proposed did not exist when he suggested them, but they are now in place all over the world.

Paine published the first part of *Rights of Man* in February 1791. The first printer he hired refused to publish it. Paine found another printer, and the pamphlet was sold cheaply so almost everyone could afford it. The second part appeared a year later, and both were translated into numerous languages. *Rights of Man* eventually became Paine's most popular book. During his lifetime, the work sold more than 1 million copies in Great Britain alone.

Paine's ideas on government upset Burke and

A political cartoon of his time shows Thomas Paine appealing to the English to overthrow their monarchy and organize a republic.

political leaders in Great Britain. After the first part of *Rights of Man* appeared, the British government began to attack Paine and his writings. Advisers to the king paid a government official to write a biography of Paine that argued he was a poor writer who had failed in every job he had undertaken, as well as in his personal relationships.

After Paine published the second half of *Rights of Man*, the British government banned any "wicked and seditious writings" that would threaten the government's ability to rule. Paine's book was clearly the target of this ban. Finally, British leaders came after Paine himself, ordering that he stand trial for his writings. The government delayed the trial until December 1792, but it continued to attack him in print and encouraged others to speak out against him.

In September 1792, Paine left England for France. As he left, an angry mob shouted threats at him. A local newspaper reported that Paine "trembled every joint" in his body as the crowd taunted him. He was still in France when his trial took place in England. Paine's lawyer argued that freedom of

King Louis XVI of France, his wife, Marie Antoinette, and three of their four children

the press gave Paine the right to express his ideas about the French Revolution and the British government. The jury, however, disagreed and found Paine guilty. Booksellers could no longer sell *Rights of Man*, and Paine risked arrest if he returned to England.

France, however, welcomed Paine as a hero. Even before he left England, the French government had made him a French citizen, and the people of Calais, France, elected him to represent them in the new National Assembly. When he arrived in Calais, he told the people that "his life should be devoted to their cause." Paine soon left for Paris, and at each stop along the way he was greeted warmly.

France was about to enter a chaotic period. Although a new constitution limited his power, Louis XVI played a role in the government. Still, some French people wanted him removed.

In August 1792, a crowd had stormed the palace where Louis XVI and his family lived. The king was arrested, and the people called for a constitution that would create a true republican government.

Thomas Paine was not the only one connected to the American Revolution who was honored by the French. In 1792, the National Assembly made U.S. President George Washington, Secretary of the Treasury Alexander Hamilton, and future president James Madison honorary citizens. None of these American leaders, however, supported the French Revolution as much as Paine did, and Hamilton actively opposed it.

In the weeks that followed, violence broke out in Paris when supporters of the revolution massacred people who had been arrested for opposing the new government.

In general, Paine welcomed the effort to create a French Republic. He attended the convention that helped write a new constitution for France. The French rebels were roughly split into two groups, the Jacobins and the Girondins. The Jacobins favored using violence and ignoring the constitution, when necessary, to protect the gains of the revolution. The Girondins, the larger group, had more moderate views and preferred to follow the law. Paine was friendly with members of the Girondins.

The Girondins and the Jacobins disagreed on a key issue: whether King Louis XVI should be put to death for his actions before and during the revolution. The Jacobins thought Louis XVI should face trial and be executed. Paine and the leading Girondins supported the trial, but they opposed killing the king. Paine wrote to a friend that the government should show "some compassion … when it decides his punishment." Paine believed the king's execution would upset Americans, especially since so many already opposed the violence that had broken out in France.

Paine, as an elected official, took part in the voting that decided King Louis's future. He believed that Louis XVI should be sent to jail while France

King Louis XVI was beheaded at the Place de la Revolution in Paris on January 21, 1793. His wife, Marie Antoinette, followed him to the guillotine in October.

fought Austria and Prussia, which opposed the revolution. The French could then exile the king after the war. A number of lawmakers agreed with Paine, but not enough to save Louis XVI. He was beheaded on the guillotine on January 21, 1793. ✑

7 A HATED MAN

❧

The execution of King Louis XVI and the growing power of the Jacobins worried Paine. He wrote to Thomas Jefferson in April 1793 that "the prospect of a general freedom is now much shortened." By this time, France was at war with England. Paine could not return to England, and the war made it risky to sail to the United States, so he remained in France. He moved to the countryside, where he lived simply and often met with visitors from England and the United States. For the most part, he did not play an active role in politics.

By June, however, he briefly returned to Paris, where he saw the Jacobins threatening to arrest the Girondins. A leading Jacobin warned Paine not to get involved, or he might be labeled an "enemy of

Prisoners await their death march to the guillotine in the Luxembourg Prison in Paris.

the revolution." Returning to the country, Paine became depressed and began to drink heavily. It saddened him to see that French rebels had turned against each other.

By the end of the summer, the Jacobins firmly controlled the French government. Some of the Jacobins became suspicious of Paine because he did not support them and because he was English—even though most people now considered him American. The French leaders also worried that Paine might write pamphlets attacking them and their actions. They were afraid that Paine's opinions might influence Americans to stop trading with France.

The English version of The Age of Reason *was published while Paine was in jail.*

In December, the French government arrested Paine and put him in jail in Paris. Paine worried that he might be executed, but the French merely wanted to keep him out of sight and unable to publish books. Before his arrest, however, Paine had finished *The Age of Reason.* An early French edition had appeared in the fall, and early in 1794, while Paine sat in jail in France, a longer English version was published.

The Age of Reason was a controversial publication that reflected Paine's interests in science and religion. Like many educated British and Americans of his day, Paine believed in God. Yet he also believed that people had to consider the laws of science when considering the Bible or other religious teachings. Based on his knowledge of science, Paine believed that the Bible was mostly filled with myths, not true events.

In *The Age of Reason*, Paine attacked organized religions, priests, and ministers. He believed Christianity and other faiths limited the freedom of people to think for themselves. "My own mind is my own church," he wrote. Paine believed people had to create their own religious beliefs, following the laws of nature. Too many people, he thought, claimed to follow a religion because other people expected them to do so, not because they truly believed a church's teachings. Paine called this "mental lying" that

> *Thomas Paine's religious ideas came from an informal religion called deism. Deists believed that God existed and created the universe, but did not continue to play a role in human affairs. Instead, God created natural laws that humans discovered through their reason and then followed. The deists did not have a formal church, although some attended Christian churches and accepted some Christian beliefs. Some of the leaders of the American Revolution were deists or accepted deist ideas, including Thomas Jefferson and Ethan Allen. With The Age of Reason, Paine became the most important deist thinker in the United States.*

created "moral mischief."

As in *Common Sense*, Paine did not express many new ideas in *The Age of Reason*. Some scientists and other educated people had been writing and saying similar things for decades. But as always, Paine wrote in a simple, direct style that anyone could understand. That worried both religious and political leaders in Great Britain and the United States.

Religious leaders feared people would stop attending churches and ignore the Bible. Readers of Paine's book might also stop giving money to their local churches. Political leaders worried that people who challenged traditional religious beliefs might also question their political leaders and demand changes.

The Age of Reason quickly became a best seller. Once again, British officials tried to prevent their citizens from reading Paine's book. In the United States, critics said that Paine was ignorant and immoral for attacking the Bible and churches. Even people who did not have strong religious beliefs thought that Paine's ideas were dangerous. They thought that organized churches helped keep order in society. Yet Paine did not want to destroy those churches. In *The Age of Reason* he wrote, "Let every man follow, as he has a right to do, the religion and worship he prefers."

The success of *The Age of Reason* continued while Paine sat in jail. At first, he was able to send

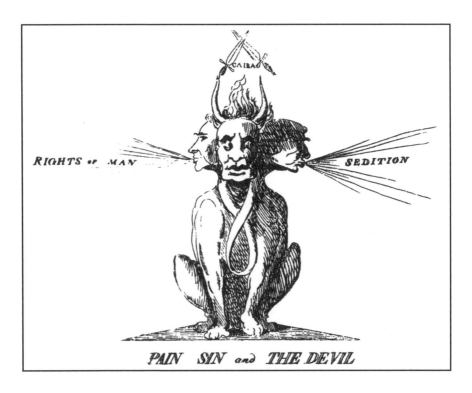

RIGHTS of MAN .... SEDITION

PAIN SIN and THE DEVIL

and receive letters and see visitors. Soon, however, the French restricted Paine's freedom. He later wrote, "I neither saw, nor heard from, anybody for six months."

Outside the jail, the French Revolution grew increasingly violent. The Jacobin leader, Maximilien Robespierre, was now in control, and he executed anyone who opposed his plans. Paine watched with horror as the French prisoners around him were taken to be executed.

The strain of seeing this and prison life in general made Paine sick. For several weeks, he had a

A contemporary English political cartoon suggests a conspiracy between the devil, Thomas Paine, and Joseph Priestly, a British scientist and minister. Priestly moved to Pennsylvania and in 1796 helped found the oldest Unitarian church in the United States.

A list of people to be executed by the guillotine was posted during the French Revolution. Thousands of people died during the revolution's bloody Reign of Terror from June 1793 until July 1794.

LISTE

DES

GUILLOTINÉS

SUR la place de la Révolution, et au ci-devant Carouzel

1. LOUIS·DAVID Collenot, dit d'Angremont, ci-devant secrétaire de l'administration de la garde nationale à la maison - commune, commandant en chef la bande assassine, convaincu de conspiration.

2. La Porte, ci-devant intendant de la liste-civile, convaincu de conspiration.

3. Durosoi, homme-de-lettres, et ci-devant rédacteur de la *Gazette de Paris*, et d'une autre feuille intitulée *Le Royalisme*, convaincu de conspiration.

4. Jean Julien, ci-devant charretier à Vaugirard, convaincu de conspiration

5. Jacques-Joseph-Antoine-Léger Backman, natif du canton de Glaris, âgé de 59 ans, militaire depuis son jeune âge, demeurant à Paris, rue Verte, fauxbourg St-Honoré, ci-devant major-gééral des ci-devant gardes-suisses, convaincu de conspiration.

6. Nicolas Roussel, natif de Ville-Rosoi, département de la Moselle, âgé de 49 ans, ci-devant employé dans la régie générale, convaincu de conspiration

7. Jeanne-Catherine Leclerc, âgée de 50 ans, cuisinière, convaincue de conspiration.

8. Anne-Hyacinthe Beaujour, ci-devant colonel du 3è. régiment d'infanterie commandé par Dumouriez,

A 2

Fac-similé de la liste des guillotinés vendue dans les rues sous la Terreur.

fever. Only the care he received from three Belgian prisoners kept him alive. During this time, Paine and his cellmates were ordered to be executed. A mark was made on their cell door, telling the guards to take them away the next day. The guards, however, never saw the mark, and Paine and his cellmates escaped death.

In July 1794, Robespierre's enemies forced him from power and killed him. Robespierre had been the one who ordered Paine's arrest. With Robespierre gone, Paine tried to regain his freedom. He sent a message to French officials asking that he be released. French friends also tried to get Paine out of jail. Finally, in November, Paine was freed, and he moved in with James Monroe, the U.S. ambassador to France and future president of the United States.

After his release, Paine once again took an active interest in French politics, and he also found time to write his last major work, *Agrarian Justice*. The pamphlet expanded on some of his ideas in *Rights of Man*. Poverty, Paine argued, was first created after individuals began buying and owning land, instead of communities sharing the land they lived on and farmed. The development of

When Thomas Paine was arrested, the U.S. ambassador in France was Gouverneur Morris. He disliked Paine and his politics and did not actively try to win his freedom. Paine argued that he was a U.S. citizen and that Morris should do more to help him. Morris believed that Paine had given up his citizenship when he served in the French National Assembly. In August 1794, James Monroe replaced Morris as the U.S. ambassador. Monroe helped Paine, and wrote to him: "By being with us through the revolution, you are of our country, as absolutely as if you had been born there."

A bust of Paine sits atop the Thomas Paine Monument in New Rochelle, New York.

private property, Paine said, made some people wealthier and some poorer, compared to the "natural state" of sharing the land.

Paine suggested taxing the wealthy who owned land to create government programs that would help support the poor. Paine did not want to abolish private property or limit a person's freedom to make money. He did think, however, that since land once belonged to all humans, people who made money from land had a duty to help the poor.

For the next several years, Paine kept a strong interest in the French Revolution and France's foreign relations. He disliked the U.S. government at the time because it did not openly support the French. Paine upset some Americans in 1796, when he wrote a letter to President George Washington that questioned his military skills during the American Revolution.

Paine's feelings against the U.S. government grew when John Adams served as president. At one point, France and the United States argued over the rights of American ships at sea, and the two nations fought several sea battles. Paine suggested the French should invade America's seaports.

By 1797, France's generals were slowly taking over the government, as the country battled its European neighbors. The most important general was Napoleon Bonaparte. At first, Paine did not mind that dictators ruled France to prevent a return to monarchy. But when Bonaparte took complete control of the government in 1799, Paine dropped out of politics and lived quietly. 🐦

Riots
treasons
Plots
conspiracies
civil war
Burk

RIGHTS
of
MAN

PRICE
PRIEST
TOW

8 A LONELY END

Chapter

ecxno

Despite speaking out against the U.S. government, Paine still wished to return to the United States. Over the years, Paine had written many letters to Thomas Jefferson. After Jefferson was elected president in 1800, he wrote Paine that he planned to send a warship to bring Paine back to the United States. The letter soon appeared in a newspaper that opposed both Paine and Jefferson.

By this time, Paine was unpopular among some Americans. His ideas seemed too radical, and he had publicly attacked George Washington, the country's beloved first president. *The Age of Reason* had also upset many Americans who held traditional views on religion. One newspaper called Paine a "loathsome reptile." He was also called an alcoholic and an atheist.

The Federalists despised Thomas Paine. He wrote that they were "witless dogs."

The split between the
Federalists and the
Anti-Federalists began
at the 1787 Constitutional
Convention. James
Madison, a leading
Federalist who is
called the Father of
the Constitution, urged
the establishment of a
government with
national authority.
Madison and the other
Federalists did not
think the Constitution
had to spell out the
protection of certain
rights. The Anti-
Federalists disagreed
and demanded a bill of
rights. Thomas Jefferson
helped convince Madison
to change his mind and
accept the bill of rights.

The Federalists led the attacks on Paine. The Federalists were a political party that developed during the 1790s. In general, they supported a strong central government and wanted to develop new businesses in the United States. They backed Great Britain and opposed the French Revolution.

Jefferson and his supporters belonged to the Republican Party, later called the Democratic-Republican Party. They favored good relations with France and supported the interests of the country's farmers. The Jeffersonians also believed state governments should have more power than the national government.

Paine finally reached the United States in the fall of 1802 on a private ship, not the warship promised by Jefferson. Paine still had some supporters, who remembered his important work during the American Revolution. The Federalists, however, continued to insult him in their newspapers and in person. In Washington, D.C., customers in two

A Federalist cartoon, "Mad Tom in a Rage," attacked the administration of Thomas Jefferson in 1801. Historians differ as to whether Mad Tom is meant to be Jefferson or Thomas Paine.

taverns said they would leave if the owners let Paine enter. To get a room at an inn, Paine had to use a fake name.

After taking all sorts of abuse, Paine, as always, could not keep silent. He wrote a public letter that called the Federalists "witless dogs" who thought government only existed so the leaders could make themselves rich. In other letters, Paine attacked George Washington and John Adams, both Federalists. Paine's writings upset many Federalists, and some Republicans worried that voters would turn against their party because of Paine's writings. At times, even Jefferson kept his distance from Paine.

Today's Democratic Party traces its roots to Thomas Jefferson and his followers in the Democratic-Republican Party. The modern Republican Party was founded in 1854.

Through 1803, Paine traveled and met old friends. Some of these people, such as Benjamin Rush, ignored him because they disliked his later writings. In most stops, however, strangers came out to meet the famous writer and discuss politics with him. By the end of the year, Paine had visited his farm in New Rochelle, New York, and then moved on to New York City. In 1804, he wrote a series of articles on organized religion and the Bible, which again upset some Americans.

During this time, Paine sold some land on his farm to pay debts. Since his days in France, Paine had borrowed heavily from his friends. Yet in his home, he lived simply. Visitors noticed that he owned few items and generally lived like a hermit. He split his time between his farm and friends' houses. Paine had always relied on other people to help him with cooking, cleaning, and caring for his home. Now, as he approached 70 years old, Paine needed more help than before.

Despite his age and weakening health, Paine continued to write about U.S. politics and foreign affairs. He also hoped Jefferson would send him as a diplomat to France, but the president refused. By

A portrait of Thomas Jefferson by famous American painter Gilbert Stuart

Thomas Paine's body was buried on his farm in New Rochelle. In 1819, the radical English journalist William Cobbett dug up Paine's bones and took them to England. Cobbett had once disliked Paine, but he came to share many of Paine's ideas and considered him a hero. Cobbett wanted to rebury the bones in England and create a monument to honor Paine. He never built the monument, and Paine's bones were still in a box when Cobbett died in 1835. No one knows what happened to the bones afterward.

the spring of 1806, Paine was depressed. He began drinking large amounts of alcohol and completely ignoring his appearance. When his friend William Carver discovered him, Paine was wearing torn, dirty clothes. Carver took Paine to his home in New York City.

In New York, Paine enjoyed drinking with the working men of the city, but his love of alcohol and lazy ways upset Carver and his family. After a few months, they asked Paine to leave their home. Paine also continued to upset those who disliked his political ideas. A local official denied him the right to vote, saying Paine was not a U.S. citizen.

Paine's personal problems continued to grow. His health weakened, and he often lacked money to pay rent. He did not want to sell his farm, but he did not want to live in the countryside. So he remained a poor man in New York City.

Several times, he wrote to the U.S. Congress for money. He wanted to be paid for his work during the

American Revolution. In one letter, Paine noted his "many years of generous services." He suggested that if Congress did not pay him, he would move to another country, where he would receive better treatment. Congress rejected his request.

Paine spent his last year in a rented room just outside of New York City. As his health failed, he wrote his will. He said, "I have lived an honest and useful life to mankind; my time has been spent in doing good." Paine died June 8, 1809. He was 72 years old.

A portrait of Thomas Paine by English-born American painter John Wesley Jarvis

Many Americans of his time did not consider Paine a great hero of the American Revolution. One historian noted that during Paine's life he had known most of the important political leaders in France, Great Britain, and the United States. But "not one of them, publicly praised him after his death."

Today, however, Paine is remembered as a great hero. His words influenced people around the world during his lifetime, and they are still read today. ⌘

PAINE'S LIFE

1737

Thomas Paine is born on January 29 in Thetford, England

1750

Begins his apprenticeship as a corset maker

1756

For about eight months, Paine works as a sailor

1755

1738

Englishman John Wesley and his brother Charles found the Methodist church

1749

German writer Johann Wolfgang Goethe is born

1756-1763

The Seven Years' War is fought; Britain defeats France

WORLD EVENTS

1764

Starts a new job, as an exciseman

1772

The Case of the Officers of Excise, Paine's first pamphlet, is published

1774

Sails for North America after earlier meeting Benjamin Franklin in London

1770

1768

British explorer Captain James Cook leaves England for a three-year exploration of the Pacific

1774

King Louis XV of France dies and his grandson, Louis XVI is crowned

PAINE'S LIFE

1787
Returning to England, Paine begins a project to build an iron bridge

1776
In January, Paine publishes *Common Sense;* in December, he publishes the first of a series of articles called *The American Crisis;* the last one appears in 1783

1777
Takes a job with the congress, which lasts until 1779

1785

1776
Scottish economist Adam Smith publishes *The Wealth of Nations,* heralding the beginning of modern economics

1783
Joseph Michel and Jacques Étienne Montgolfier become the first human beings to fly with their invention of the hot air balloon

1786
The British government announces plans to make Australia a penal colony

WORLD EVENTS

1791

Part one of *Rights of Man*, Paine's defense of the French Revolution, is published; the second part appears the next year

RIGHTS OF MAN:

BEING AN

ANSWER TO Mr. BURKE's ATTACK

ON THE

FRENCH REVOLUTION.

BY

THOMAS PAINE,

SECRETARY FOR FOREIGN AFFAIRS TO CONGRESS IN THE
AMERICAN WAR, AND
AUTHOR OF THE WORK INTITLED COMMON SENSE.

LONDON:
PRINTED FOR J. JOHNSON, St PAUL's CHURCH-YARD.
MDCCXCI.

1789

Visits France after the start of the French Revolution

1792

Chosen to help write a new constitution for France

1790

1788

The *Times* newspaper in London is founded

1791

Austrian composer Wolfgang Amadeus Mozart dies

PAINE'S LIFE

1793

In December, Paine is arrested as an enemy of France; he barely avoids execution and is freed the next year

1794

Part one of *The Age of Reason* is published; the second part appears in 1796

1796

Publishes his last major work, *Agrarian Justice*

1793

Poland is divided between Russia and Prussia.

1795

J. F. Blumenbach writes his book *The Human Species* thus laying the foundation of anthropology

WORLD EVENTS

1802

Returns to the United States, where he is now widely disliked for his ideas on religion and his support of the French Revolution

1809

Dies on June 8, 1809, in New York City

1805

1801

Ultraviolet radiation is discovered

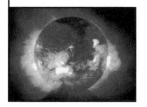

1805

General anesthesia is first used in surgery

1809

Louis Braille of France, inventor of a writing system for the blind, is born

DATE OF BIRTH: January 12, 1737

NICKNAME: Tom

BIRTHPLACE: Thetford, England

FATHER: Joseph Pain (1708-1786)

MOTHER: Frances Cocke Pain (?1696-?)

EDUCATION: Thetford Grammar School; apprenticeship as a corset maker

SPOUSES: Mary Lambert (?-1760) Elizabeth Ollive (?-?)

CHILDREN: Only child died at birth in 1760

DATE OF DEATH: June 8, 1809

PLACE OF BURIAL: New Rochelle, New York (bones later removed and taken to England where they were lost)

In the Library

Bohannon, Lisa Frederiksen. *The American Revolution.* Minneapolis: Lerner, 2004.

Davis, Kate. *Thomas Paine.* San Diego: Blackbirch Press, 2003.

Fish, Bruce, and Becky Durost Fish. *Thomas Paine: Political Writer.* Philadelphia: Chelsea House Publishers, 2000.

Kaye, Harvey J. *Thomas Paine: Firebrand of the Revolution.* New York: Oxford University Press, 2000.

McCarthy, Pat. *Thomas Paine: Revolutionary Patriot and Writer.* Berkeley Heights, N.J.: Enslow Publishers, 2001.

Meltzer, Milton. *Tom Paine: Voice of Revolution.* New York: Franklin Watts, 1996.

Ross, Stewart. *The French Revolution.* Austin, Texas: Raintree Steck-Vaughn, 2003.

On the Web

For more information on *Thomas Paine,*
use FactHound to track down Web sites
related to this book.

1. Go to *www.facthound.com*
2. Type in a search word related to this
book or this book ID: 0756508304
3. Click on the *Fetch It* button.

FactHound will find the best
Web sites for you.

Historic Sites

Thomas Paine National Historical
Association
983 North Ave.
New Rochelle, NY 10804
914/633-1776
To see documents relating to Paine's life
and a monument honoring him

Independence National Historical Park
143 S. Third St.
Philadelphia, PA 19106
215/597-2458
To visit the building where the Declaration of
Independence was signed

agrarian
related to farming

atheist
someone who does not believe in God

Constitution
the document that describes the basic laws and
principles by which the United States is governed

dictators
rulers who take power during a crisis and ignore
certain laws

diplomat
a person who represents his or her government in
a foreign nation

guillotine
a machine that chopped off a person's head when
a blade is dropped between two posts; it became
the symbol of the French Revolution

Hessians
people from the Hesse region of Germany

mercenaries
soldiers hired to serve in the army of a
foreign country

militia
an army made up of private citizens, not
full-time soldiers

posterity
all future generations

radical
extreme or beyond what most people think
is correct

seditious
to take part in resisting lawful authority

Chapter 1

Page 10, line 11: David Freeman Hawke. *Paine.* New York: Harper & Row, 1974, p. 59.

Page 11, line 22: Gordon S. Wood, ed. *Common Sense and Other Writings.* New York: The Modern Library, 2003, p. 83.

Page 12, line 1: Thomas Paine. *Collected Writings.* New York: Library of America, 1995, pp. 85-86.

Page 13, line 9: *Paine*, p. 61.

Chapter 2

Page 17, line 14: John Keane. *Tom Paine: A Political Life.* New York: Grove Press. 1995, p. 24.

Page 18, line 24: Ibid., p. 26.

Page 19, line 8: Ibid., p. 25.

Page 20, line 14: Ibid., p. 32.

Page 20, line 17: *Paine*, p. 14.

Chapter 3

Page 29, line 16: *Tom Paine: A Political Life*, p. 59.

Page 30, line 3: Ibid., p. 61.

Page 30, line 17: Ibid., p. 69.

Page 30, line 25: *Paine*, p. 20.

Page 31, line 11: David Powell. *Tom Paine, the Greatest Exile.* New York: St. Martin's Press, 1985, p. 266.

Page 31, line 25: *Tom Paine: A Political Life*, p. 74.

Page 33, line 15: Ibid., p. 84.

Chapter 4

Page 35, line 3: *Collected Writings*, p. 132.

Page 40, line 2: *Tom Paine: A Political Life*, p. 101.

Page 40, line 4: *Paine*, p. 38.

Page 43, line 9: *Common Sense and Other Writings*, p. 11.

Page 45, line 14: Ibid., p. 28.

Page 46, line 25: Ibid., p. 4.

Page 47, line 5: Henry Steele Commager, with Richard B. Morris, eds. *The Spirit of 'Seventy-Six.* New York: Harper & Row, 1967, p. 283.

Page 47, line 25: Claeys, Gregory. *Thomas Paine: Social and Political Thought.* Boston: Unwin Hyman, 1989, p. 1.

Page 48, line 6: *Tom Paine: A Political Life*, p. 123.

Page 48, line 10: *Collected Writings*, p. 60.

Chapter 5

Page 55, line 11: *Collected Writings*, p. 149.

Page 55, sidebar: John C. Fitzpatrick, ed. *The Writings of George Washington from the Original Manuscript Sources, 1745-1799.* Vol. 10 in the American Memory Collection of the Library of Congress. James Madison Center. http://www.jmu.edu/madison/center/main_pages/madison_archives/ constit_confed/congress/valleyforge.htm#65

Page 57, line 5: *Tom Paine, the Greatest Exile*, p. 115.

Page 62, line 1: *Tom Paine: A Political Life*, p. 251.

Page 63, line 1: *Collected Writings*, p. 348.

Page 63, line 17: Ibid., p. 354.

Chapter 6

Page 66, line 4: *Tom Paine: A Political Life*, p. 211.

Page 71, line 28: Philip Foner, ed. *The Life and Major Writings of Thomas Paine.* New York: Carol Publishing Groups, 1993, p. 278.

Page 72, line 12: Ibid., p. 425.

Page 74, line 10: *Tom Paine: A Political Life*, p. 344.

Page 75, line 17: *Paine*, p. 256.

Page 76, line 22: Ibid., p. 271.

Chapter 7

Page 79, line 3: *Tom Paine: A Political Life*, p. 373.

Page 81, line 28: *The Life and Major Writings of Thomas Paine*, p. 464.

Page 82, line 24: Ibid., p. 512.

Page 83, line 3: *Tom Paine: A Political Life*, p. 407.

Chapter 8

Page 89, line 14: *Tom Paine: A Political Life*, p. 456.

Page 91, line 6: *Paine*, p. 357.

Page 95, line 2: *Tom Paine: A Political Life*, p. 530.

Page 95, line 22: Ibid., p. 401.

Blanco, Richard L. *The American Revolution, 1775-1783: An Encyclopedia. Vol. I-II.* New York: Garland, 1993.

Claeys, Gregory. *Thomas Paine: Social and Political Thought.* Boston: Unwin Hyman, 1989.

Commager, Henry Steele, and Richard B. Morris, eds. *The Spirit of 'Seventy-Six.* New York: Harper & Row, 1967.

Faragher, John Mack, ed. *The Encyclopedia of Colonial and Revolutionary America.* New York: Da Capo Press, 1996.

Fitzpatrick, John C., ed. *The Writings of George Washington from the Original Manuscript Sources, 1745-1799.* Vol. 10 in the American Memory Collection of the Library of Congress.

Fleming, Thomas. *Liberty!: The American Revolution.* New York: Viking, 1997.

Foner, Eric. *Tom Paine and Revolutionary America.* New York: Oxford University Press, 1976.

Foner, Philip, ed. *The Life and Major Writings of Thomas Paine.* New York: Carol Publishing Group, 1993.

Hawke, David Freeman. *Paine.* New York: Harper & Row, 1974.

Keane, John. *Tom Paine: A Political Life.* New York: Grove Press, 1995.

Liell, Scott. *46 Pages: Thomas Paine, Common Sense, and the Turning Point to Independence.* Philadelphia: Running Press, 2003.

Paine, Thomas. *Collected Writings.* New York: Library of America, 1995.

Powell, David. *Tom Paine, the Greatest Exile.* New York: St. Martin's Press, 1985.

Roberts, J. M. *The French Revolution.* Oxford: Oxford University Press, 1978.

Schmittroth, Linda, and Barbara Bigelow. *American Revolution Almanac.* Detroit: UXL, 2000.

Schmittroth, Linda, and Barbara Bigelow. *American Revolution Biographies. Vol. I-II.* Detroit: UXL, 2000.

Wood, Gordon S., ed. *Common Sense and Other Writings.* New York: The Modern Library, 2003.

Michael Burgan is a freelance writer of books for children and adults. A history graduate of the University of Connecticut, he has written more than 60 fiction and nonfiction children's books for various publishers. For adult audiences, he has written news articles, essays, and plays. Michael Burgan is a recipient of an Educational Press Association of America award and belongs to the Society of Children's Book Writers and Illustrators.

Image Credits